Acclaim for the novels of Patrick Lynch

Figure of 8

"Creepy. . . . Lynch has a talent for suspense tinged with horror and this fast-paced ride appeals."
—*Publishers Weekly*

"A relentless, clock-stopping psychothriller about a neurotic Ukrainian figure-skating champion trying to make it in Hollywood, her marginally psychotic bodyguard, and the insidious stalker who guards a secret that could shatter her career . . . breathless, gory, thoroughly enjoyable."—*Kirkus Reviews*

"Keeps the reader's attention from start to finish. . . . A gold medal tale."—Harriet Klausner

The Policy

"Engaging and cerebral . . . builds a sense of unease and anxiety that is ultimately effective."
—*Chicago Tribune*

"A top-notch thriller. . . . The wintry Rhode Island setting is cut like a Cranston accent, while cold corporate games, masquerading as camaraderie, cast an icy menace throughout the proceedings."—*Publishers Weekly*

"Nonstop and ultra-speed. . . . The excitement continues long after the last page is completed."
—*Midwest Book Review*

"Fascinating and believably menacing."—*Kirkus Reviews*

"A labyrinth of terror . . . a tale of suspense that blends medical technology with science, greed, and, eventually, murder."—*Abilene Reporter-News*

continued on next page . . .

ALSO BY PATRICK LYNCH

The Policy
Omega
Carriers

FIGURE OF 8

PATRICK LYNCH

A SIGNET BOOK

SIGNET
Published by New American Library, a division of
Penguin Putnam Inc., 375 Hudson Street,
New York, New York 10014, U.S.A.
Penguin Books Ltd, 27 Wrights Lane,
London W8 5TZ, England
Penguin Books Australia Ltd,
Ringwood, Victoria, Australia
Penguin Books Canada Ltd, 10 Alcorn Avenue,
Toronto, Ontario, Canada M4V 3B2
Penguin Books (N.Z.) Ltd, 182–190 Wairau Road,
Auckland 10, New Zealand

Penguin Books Ltd, Registered Offices:
Harmondsworth, Middlesex, England

Published by Signet, an imprint of New American Library, a division of
Penguin Putnam Inc. Previously published in a Dutton edition.

First Signet Printing, December 2000
10 9 8 7 6 5 4 3 2 1

 REGISTERED TRADEMARK—MARCA REGISTRADA

Printed in the United States of America

PUBLISHER'S NOTE
This is a work of fiction. Names, characters, places, and incidents either are the
products of the author's imagination or are used fictitiously, and any resem-
blance to actual persons, living or dead, events, or locales is entirely coincidental.

For Sylvie and Sarah

ACKNOWLEDGMENTS

I would like to thank the following for their generous help with the factual background to this story:

Detective Paul A. Wright of the Los Angeles Police Department's Threat Management Unit (TMU), Lt. John C. Lane, Jr. (ret.), TMU founder and head of The Omega Group, and Dr. Park Dietz of the Threat Assessment Group, Inc., for sharing their unique knowledge and expertise in the field of celebrity stalking, the people who do it, and their victims; Dr. Pedro M. Ortiz-Colom, Deputy Medical Examiner, Department of Coroner, Los Angeles County, for guiding me through the forensic science detail; sports personality manager Marvin Demoff and Julia Chasman of Addis Wechsler for their insights into the world of celebrity management; Eric Young, director of Post Production Services at Walt Disney Pictures and Television, his colleague Mary Redmond, and director Alex Abramowicz for taking me through the technical and logistical aspects of making commercials; and, finally, Dr. Helena Scott and Dr. Rupert Negus for their help with the medical elements.

Los Angeles
November 24, 1993

Stacey came out of the bathroom late Tuesday night, the Gillette dripping foam in her left hand, and a blank, faraway look on her face. Where the black smudge of her sex had been there was now a neat V shading into darkness. She said it was going to simplify things. She said it was going to make it clean. That was how it started.

By three o'clock Wednesday morning they'd stripped the carpet out of her bedroom and washed the floor with Clorox. It was crazy. There was no way the room would ever be sterile, and anyway the procedure didn't require it. It was just nerves. It was the weight of events bearing down.

They stripped her bed, throwing the satin pillows, the cuddly toys, and the Scorpio duvet cover into a carton that went into the garage with the camper. They jacked the foot of the bed up on house bricks which they wrapped in polyethylene. He even thought about washing the walls, but Stacey drew the line at touching her posters.

"He has to be watching," she said, pointing a finger at the face on the ceiling. "I want him to see this."

She was on the bed now in what the doctors called the supported knee-chest position. There was an armchair on either side of the foot of the bed to support her feet, pushing her thighs up against her abdomen so that her vulva was completely exposed. Her Zodiac T-shirt had rucked up a little, showing the pale, veiny underside of her breasts. She took a long shuddering pull at the fat joint she'd rolled, tapped the glowing end on the ashtray, and said something he couldn't make out. She was getting stoned, floating off on the diazepam and the Jimi Hendrix coming through from the living room.

He would have preferred to have her under completely. He had gone to a lot of trouble and expense acquiring the nebulizer and the tanks for the administration of the halothane, but here again she had put her foot down. She was nervous about having him anesthetize her. After all, it wasn't as if he was qualified, and people died under anesthetic. But she knew better than to question his medical competence openly, so she had said she just wanted to "be there." She wanted to feel it "happening to her." He'd explained about the danger of contractions, about the damage one spasm could do, but it hadn't made any difference. She'd said she wasn't going to do it any other way, so he might as well play along. In the end they'd had a couple of dry runs using oral diazepam and Stacey's favorite grass. There had been no contractions.

"You okay?" he said.

Her head with its crown of short spiky hair rolled over and she tried to focus on him.

"I am *bhanda*," she said, and she let out a crazy laugh.

"Banda?"

"The vessel, the pot, the dish." The smile vanished from her face. "*His* dish."

She was getting into her Hindu bullshit now, normally a sign of *extreme* relaxation. He took the joint from between her fingers and carried it from the room, then came back in with the sterile towels, which he draped over her legs. He opened the black leather bag that was on the floor at the foot of the bed and took out a steel instrument that looked like a bird's beak.

"I'm inserting the speculum," he said.

But she was no longer listening anyway, her eyes riveted on the actor's face that smiled down from the ceiling, her lips moving in a barely voiced mantra. He smeared a little sterile saline on the steel beak and pushed it into her. She held her breath for a second, relaxed. He turned the screw, opening the two halves of the beak, establishing a clear passage through to the cervix.

"S'cold," she said, her words coming from far away.

"Only at first."

He dabbed around the opening with cotton wool soaked in saline solution. When he was satisfied that everything was ready, he stood up.

"I'm turning out the lights."

"*Bhaga,*" she said sleepily. "Womb, vagina, good fortune, happiness, ex-cel-lence."

First blackness. Then slowly, as his eyes adjusted, a subdued, purple glow suffusing the room. The purple was Stacey's idea. She had draped a scarf over a reading lamp.

"I'm going into the bathroom," he said. "I want you to relax."

Jimi Hendrix switched into "All Along the Watchtower."

The bathroom was the pre-op. He'd read how there was less bacteria on a toilet seat than on the average kitchen sink, and had figured that with all the tile this was the one space he could get really clean. The shower curtain had gone in with the cuddly toys. He'd Cloroxed everything else, and then wiped the surfaces with an alcohol-soaked cloth.

He kept a hand over his eyes as he switched off the light, then stood there taking deep breaths, aware of the rising tension in his neck and shoulders. It was always going to be hard, he knew that. They were crossing a line. It was a life they were dealing with. There were going to be powerful emotions. He worried that he'd overdone the Benzedrine. If he got the shakes at the wrong moment it could be disastrous. He closed his eyes, told himself that it was a straightforward procedure. Nurses did it in some clinics, not even doctors. All he had to do was cross 4.9 centimeters of darkness to bring the tip of the catheter to the waiting wall of blood.

He placed a surgical mask over his nose and mouth. He checked his eyes in the mirror.

"It's easy," he said. "It's the easiest thing you ever did."

Taking a deep breath, he removed the caps from the dishes.

Five minutes later he walked out of the bathroom, holding the syringe with the flexible catheter attached.

"I want to get down from here," Stacey said. "Get me down from here."

Out of her head, but still a pain in the ass. With her legs up like that, she looked like a Thanksgiving turkey.

"It won't take long."

"*No.*" She looked up at him and he could see that she'd been crying. "I don't want to *do* this."

She slumped back, her doubled-up legs swaying—too far gone to even roll over.

"Are you crazy?" he said. "We agreed about this, Stacey."

"I don't want to."

"We can't wait. It's now or never, you know that."

Her shoulders were shaking, but she didn't say anything.

He kneeled at the foot of the bed. The steel speculum looked like part of her. It made him think of the metal tag in the ear of a cow.

"I'm inserting the catheter," he said. "You're going to feel this, but it's important you keep very still."

She didn't answer. She was slowly shaking her head from side to side.

According to the gynecologist, her uterine cavity was just under five centimeters long and slightly anteverted. In the dry runs they'd had no trouble with obstructions. He advanced the catheter to the cervix, then very gently entered the narrow neck, using the speculum as his reference point against the markings on the Teflon sleeve. It was vital that the tip of the sleeve stay outside the uterine cavity, away from the lush volutions of the fragile endometrium.

"Baby baby baby baby."

He kept his head down. She wasn't talking to him anyway, was probably unaware he was even there. He felt sorry for her. Then he frowned, forcing himself to focus on the syringe in his hands. The flexible inner catheter entered the rigid sleeve, and he was in the uterus, flying blind, going by feel. He had to cross the dark, all the way over until he reached the fundus, the area at the top of the uterus between the entrance of the fallopian tubes. He blinked the perspiration from his eyes, watching the flexible catheter disappear into the sleeve millimeter by millimeter. He got a flash of the child growing, its tiny heart pumping. Its eyes. Was it a boy or a girl?

His hands were shaking. Why did it matter, the sex? It wasn't a person. It was an idea, a dream.

"Get a grip."

"Wha—?"

Her head rolled to one side.

And then he was there: maybe not five millimeters from the fundus, but as near as he dared go. He shut his eyes.

"I think it's done."

Then he was aware of the music again. Stacey was crying softly. He gently withdrew the catheter and looked at the tip. Only now did he realize that he had left the lights off during the whole procedure. He had to go back into the bathroom to check the catheter, to see that everything was all right.

Stacey worked herself up on her elbows.

"You have to stay lying down."

"Is it going to be okay?" she said, her voice sleepy from the drugs.

He touched the steel beak where it was still fixed between her legs.

"Trust me," he said.

I

Sexual
Morphology
Female

1

Brentwood. A winding street off Mandeville Canyon Road. Detective Larry Hagmaier looked through thickly growing cactus towards the main building. Three floors rising through bougainvillea and palms. A plantation house was what it looked like most. Fluted columns supported a deck that ran all the way round the second floor.

"The help says we can't turn off the sprinklers."

Hagmaier turned to see Matt Kronin heft a chunky-thighed leg up onto the mound of freshly disturbed earth. He mopped his face with a handkerchief.

"They're on a timer," he said. "Should cut out anytime now."

They both looked down at the black garbage bag they had used to cover the hole.

"So what's the deal?" said Hagmaier.

Kronin jerked his thumb at the pool house and Hagmaier followed him inside.

It took a second for their eyes to adjust. Then they were looking at teak sun loungers, a fancy brushed-steel barbecue on fat rubber wheels, a big beach umbrella in one corner, Rollerblades. There was a smell of damp plaster and chlorine, and on one wall the paint was coming away in thick curls. Kronin snapped a piece off and crumbled it to dust between finger and thumb.

"Mrs. Cusak's got a problem with the pumping system. She's losing water into the soil. The contractors didn't put in a proper damp course, so she gets this."

"Nice."

"The contractors came out yesterday afternoon, dug around a little. Then sometime last night—this is what the help thinks—sometime in the night the dog got in from the next house. Dug around some more."

"She heard it?"

"Says she thought she heard it. Next door's been having trouble with people trying to get pictures of Mrs. Cusak. So he got a dog. A Doberman."

"People?"

"Yeah, like paparazzi, you know."

"I didn't know she was still news."

"I don't think she is. But she just got divorced from Douglas Gorman."

"Oh yeah, right. Guess she got the house then, huh?"

Back outside a smell of cooking bacon drifted across from the next property, and Hagmaier realized how hungry he was. He looked around for the responding officer, thinking maybe they could get him to go look for donuts, a Danish, whatever, but the guy was nowhere to be seen—probably trying to get a peek at Cusak's bedroom. The lab techs would be arriving any minute along with Serratosa's people from the coroner's office. Maybe they would bring something.

"So it was the help called in the complaint?" he said abstractedly.

"Right, Mrs. Dominguez. Just after seven. Mrs. Cusak went out early. An interview or some such."

"She okay?"

"Who?"

"Dominguez."

"A little shook-up."

The sprinklers stopped.

Hagmaier stepped down into the hole, careful not to disturb the earth too much. He removed the garbage bag and stared down at the hank of dry-looking hair still attached to what was left of the scalp.

The house. The room with its smell, with the continuous faint seething sound like rain on tar paper. The TV on a pile of textbooks so that he can see it from the bed.

"Remember this?" says the woman's voice.

Ellen Cusak climbing onto the podium at the world championships to receive her gold medal.

"And this?"

The screen fills with Ellen Cusak—suspended in midair, coming down off a slo-mo triple lutz, overrotating, hitting the ice *hard,* her mouth stretching open, her knees buckling. She picks herself up. Then she is crying, holding her face in her hands as she glides off the ice.

The talk show lady is back. Big glasses. Big hair. Rhoda something.

"On that fateful night in 1993 Ellen Cusak fell from grace. Walking out of the rink, she walked out of the lives of her millions of adoring fans. It was the end of one of skating's shortest but most dazzling chapters. Well . . ." She smiles, looking away from camera, looking at someone else on the set. ". . . now she's back. Here to talk to us about love, life, and her return to the rink is Ellen Cusak. Ellen, it's great to see you."

The face. Radiant. Studio lights give her white-blond hair a hard sheen. She lost a little weight, looks like she might even be below the 118 pounds she used to compete at. *Yelena.*

"Dry soil here. Basically desert," said Serratosa, dragging dirt away from the blackish, mummified head. "Body fluids rapidly absorbed, so you get a . . ."

He paused for a moment and pointed at something. The police photographer came forward and shot close-ups with the macro. When he was finished, Serratosa, using his pen, dragged a pair of glasses out of the dirt. He looked up at Hagmaier.

"Lady's spectacles."

"Hers?"

"Yes, I think so." He pointed at the side of the head. Dry skin peaked in a little flap where the ear had been. Above the flap a shadowy line ran horizontally towards the empty orbit of what was once the left eye. "And this mark suggests that she was wearing them—that they were on her as the flesh was mummifying. Probably the dog disturbed them. There will be residual material on the frame if I'm right."

"You think this is a woman?" said Kronin.

"The skull looks effeminate, and there's the hair. This is"—he rubbed the dry reddish hair between his rubber insulated fingers—"dyed, I think. Not conclusive of course. We'll know for sure when we examine the pelvis."

"If there is a pelvis," said Kronin.

Serratosa looked up at Kronin and shaded his eyes with his left hand. The deputy medical examiner was a small, dark-complexioned man who smiled a lot. He smiled now, showing Kronin coffee-stained teeth.

"Good point, Detective."

Still smiling, Serratosa went back to the remains. The partially mummified skeleton was exposed down to the collarbone now. Scraps of skin, drum-taut, like fine brown leather.

"What's that around her neck?" said Hagmaier. "Is that a scarf?"

"I would guess what's left of her sweater. Roll-neck. Blue. Wool." He pushed gloved fingers into the dirt in back of the skull and came up with a nylon label.

"Gap," he said. "You could run a check on when Gap introduced this line. It might help date the time of her disappearance."

"Any guesses on that, Doctor?"

"From the appearance of the bones, I'm thinking three years maybe, but we'll know more later."

Hagmaier turned to look at Kronin.

"How long's the house been here, Matt?"

Kronin shrugged, made a note of the question.

"It's a George Stanford Brown. Doug Gorman had it built in '96, I think it was."

They all looked for the source of the comment, found the responding officer, shifting his weight from foot to foot, his eyes darting back and forth, obviously having the time of his life.

"How the hell do you know that?" said Hagmaier.

The officer shrugged.

"Magazines," he said.

Hagmaier shook his head and went back to watching Serratosa, who was digging again, talking all the time in a low voice. The crackle of police radios and, in the distance, a barking dog made it difficult to hear.

"And she's wearing a . . . I think this is Gore-Tex. She's wearing a ski jacket of some kind. So for the time being let's say she disappeared in the colder months. Not last winter, but maybe the winter before last."

Hagmaier frowned.

"Dressed kind of warm for these parts, Doc. Even for winter."

"Maybe." Serratosa sounded unconvinced. "My wife gets kind of cold in the winter months. At night anyway."

"Could be she wasn't killed here," said Kronin. "Could have been killed somewhere colder. Maybe in the mountains."

"Yeah, right." Hagmaier shot a look at his partner. "Kill her in a remote location and then bring the body somewhere you can count on witnesses." He turned back to Serratosa. "What do you think killed her, Doc?"

Serratosa frowned. He didn't like being rushed.

"I see no . . ." He pulled at the dirt more boldly now. The left shoulder appeared. A rent in the red jacket gave a clear view of the left clavicle and the top of the rib cage. "I see no ligature, no wounds to the head. I mean—listen, it could be this lady was hit by a car—was dumped here. She's in a—I would say an unusual position. Kind of upright. Maybe there was a hole here and whoever killed her just dropped her in. If we can just get a look at the hands we might . . ."

He paused for a moment, said something to himself in Spanish. Hagmaier leaned forward, his feet slipping a little, sending loose soil down into the hole.

"What is it, Doc?"

Rhoda wants all the bad news first. First Ellen's father's death and then the divorce. First the career and then the abandoned career. When she gets to the marriage, she starts to shake her head, straining at empathy.

She wants to know when Ellen first realized the marriage was in trouble.

"I know it must be hard to talk about," she says.

Ellen grips the armrests of her blue velvet throne.

"It was . . . I mean, pretty early on it was clear that Doug and I didn't, um, *connect* on certain issues. Didn't see eye-to-eye."

"Your career, Ellen, is that what you mean?"

"No, not that. After the Worlds in '93—"

"After your fall?"

"That's right. After that I decided I didn't want to skate anymore anyway. And it seemed like the best thing to do for the marriage. But . . . there were other issues."

Rhoda leans forward, head on one side, voice hushed.

"Was it . . . was it the other women?"

For a second it looks like Ellen is going to answer, but she presses her mouth into a line, shaking her head. This is blood in the water to the producer. The camera jumps up close.

"I'm sorry. I . . . I guess I'm not ready to talk about all that just yet."

Rhoda's face gets a pinched look. Then she gets a signal of some kind through her earpiece and moves on.

"So here you are, twenty-seven years old, a divorcée." She waits a second, hoping for a reaction, but Ellen just stares. "It must seem like a long way from that podium."

"I was different then," says Ellen eventually. "Kind of on the cusp of everything."

"Did it happen too fast?" says Rhoda, already nodding.

"Sometimes I think that. But then again, I don't know if you can, like, slow it down. Fame, I mean."

"Overnight success, rags to riches."

"That's just the way it is." Ellen shrugs. "It's like a jump. You can spend months working on it, but nothing prepares you for the real thing, with the lights, the music, the crowd. Suddenly you're airborne, spinning at a million miles an hour."

"And sometimes . . . you fall," says Rhoda with maximum gravitas.

Ellen shrugs again.

"Yes. I fell."

"But you got back up."

This is something Rhoda looks happy about. Ellen smiles too. Her perfect smile. Her famous smile—worth a million a year in endorsements when she was still nailing those triple-triple combinations.

"The kids had a lot to do with that," she says.

"You're talking about the kids at the Franck Institute?"

"That's right."

"Tell us a little about that."

"Well, the Franck runs a program for kids with learning difficulties: a music and movement program that I've been helping with. I see the pleasure these kids get when we take them on the ice, and . . . it's been good for me. It's given me a way back into skating seriously."

Rhoda nods, fascinated, delighted.

"And the next step?"

"The *Nutcracker* tour. I'm playing Clara. It should be fun."

"I understand it's actually a pretty punishing schedule."

"It sure is." She glances straight at the camera. "We're doing twenty cities in November alone. One-night shows mostly. But I'm looking forward to it. The promoters have put a great team together. There'll be Todd, Brian, Nicole. I'll be skating with friends."

"And competition?" says Rhoda. "Can we expect a

comeback there too? Are you going to follow in the footsteps of Elaine Zayak?"

"I don't think so."

Rhoda laughs.

"You're not saying you're too old."

"Hey, at twenty-seven I *am* getting a little old," she says.

"Seriously?"

"Well, yes. To jump those triples you really have to be under a hundred pounds. Once you start . . ."

"Developing?"

"Right, filling out—you're really up against it. I mean, you're up against the other girls, the judges, *and* gravity. It's the hardest thing for a young skater and we all go through it. You become a woman and your jumping goes to hell."

"You sound like you would have rather stayed that little girl."

The faintest flicker of emotion in Ellen's blue eyes.

"No," she says. "No, being a woman is okay."

Serratosa came up out of the hole, looking gaunt and tired. He removed a handkerchief from his pocket and dabbed at his forehead. Behind him the camera flashed despite the bright sunlight.

"So not a road traffic accident," he said. "A homicide. I'm thinking a blitz attack. Defensive injuries to the left hand—we'll get the bones under the microscope and be able to tell you about the murder weapon, but I'm thinking a knife. Something big. Small bones in the left hand are split—splayed apart, like in a—like with a crucifixion. She's trying to fend him off and he's banging away with the knife. I'm thinking a carving knife maybe. Then . . . similar markings on the thorax. Multiple markings, all on the left side of the rib cage. The sternum shows signs of multiple trauma and two ribs are broken"—he touched a gloved finger to his chest showing them what he meant—"over the heart."

Kronin looked towards the house.

"You, er . . . you *sure* this is a man we're talking about, Doc?"

Serratosa looked back down at the body.

"I'd say a man—probably a strong man. And right-handed."

"Probably," Kronin repeated.

"Right. And he really wanted her dead, like he wanted to dig her heart out, and then"—Serratosa raised his hands in a little whaddya-know gesture—"he dresses her in clean clothes."

"Dresses her?"

Serratosa turned to consider Hagmaier's puzzled face.

"Yes. From what I can tell, there is no blood on the clothing, and the clothing—it's worn through and ripped here and there, but from insect activity, I think. I think whoever did this, afterwards, he put clothes on her. So maybe she was naked when he killed her. That would seem to me the most . . . the most likely."

Hagmaier thought about it for a second, and then shook his head.

"Yeah, but why put the glasses on her, Doc?"

2

Tuesday, July 27

Where Karen Bonner's eye had been there was nothing now but ashes. Pete Golding drew the lighted cigarette slowly down her cheek, cocked his head on one side, considering where to go next, then buried it in the middle of her top lip, just beneath her perfect, surgically enhanced soap-star nose. The paper blackened, blistered, punctured.

"I know how it is, Raymond." He made a circle with the cigarette, enlarging the little glowing O. "You write a nice letter. Just to say how you love her show. Telling her what she means to you. And what do you get back? A two-line letter initialed by some flunky. So you write again—I mean, if it wasn't for people like you, she wouldn't be up there, pulling in all those big bucks. She'd be *nobody,* right?"

Raymond Lubett, obese, forty-three, sat staring through thick lenses at the mutilated poster. It was hot in the kitchen. There was a stink of garbage and burnt fat.

"She . . . she *signed* that," he said, pointing feebly.

Golding took a drag at his cigarette, held the poster at

arm's length, admiring his work. Karen Bonner's face
was no longer a face. It was a theater mask: no eyes, no
mouth. He flicked a speck of ash from her cleavage.

"You write another letter and this time you don't get
a reply at all," he said. "Nothing. So you write again.
And again. And again. Every damned day, because
you're *entitled* to an answer, right? Just what the hell is
going on? And then some fuckin' lawyer tells you
you're harassing her. I mean, is that fair?"

Lubett swallowed. Golding wasn't tall especially, or
heavily built. He had clean-cut features, blue eyes, and
light brown hair. A regular guy, who looked younger
than his thirty-five years. But there was a fragility in his
stare, a kind of lost look that was unnerving because
you knew it didn't fit. You sensed that any moment he
might get upset. And then he wouldn't be responsible
for his actions.

"So you've gotta go up there, right? I mean, they don't
leave you any choice, do they? You've got to speak to her.
You've got to make her understand, right, Raymond?"

He was rolling up the poster now, face out, rolling it
tight into a hard tube. The sweat was running off Lubett's scalp, into his sideburns and his long straggling
ponytail.

"I just . . . I just . . ."

"You just wanted to clear things up. She's got all that
money and all those flunkies filling her head with bullshit. They've got her thinking she's too good for a regular
guy. But at the end of the day"—Golding turned, pointing at Lubett so that the rolled-up poster brushed the end
of his nose—"she's a woman and you're a man. All she
needs is a little reminding about *where she stands.*"

"I never wanted to . . ." Lubett struggled to catch his
breath. "I could never hurt her. I—"

"Shut up, Raymond."

Golding turned back to the range and switched on the gas.

"Say, how do you light this thing?"

"You still got that guy working for you, Tom? You know the one: Goldberg, Gold . . . something."

Tom Reynolds, founder and head of Alpha Global Protection looked up from the pile of letters on his desk and then quickly looked down again.

"Pete Golding, sure. He's on the payroll. One of our private investigators. But I don't think we're—"

"The way he nailed that son of a bitch—the Maddy Olsen thing?—that was really something. I think maybe we could use that guy. I think maybe a little direct action's exactly what we need here."

Reynolds held up a hand. Lenny Mayot was an old acquaintance and potentially a useful one. A small man of forty-three, bald on top with a face that seemed almost angelic when smiling and pugnacious the rest of the time, he'd started out as a criminal lawyer, defending drunk driving and minor assault cases. But all that was behind him. Today he managed the careers of about a dozen celebrities, including one up-and-coming news anchorman, a TV chef, and a clutch of retired athletes, including the skater Ellen Cusak. It wasn't the most dazzling portfolio in town by a long way, but Lenny was always hustling and networking and everyone knew his name. He was the kind of contact Alpha needed to cultivate, because celebrities were its business—celebrities and the unwelcome attention they attracted from obsessive fans, and worse. The only trouble with Lenny Mayot was once he got hold of an idea he just wouldn't let go.

"I mean, these guys are sick, okay," he said. "I can accept that. I can even feel sorry for them. But you've got to be *really* crazy not to understand a gun when it's pointed at you. You see what I'm saying? A gun pointing at you is my idea of a universal language."

Reynolds followed Mayot's gaze to a set of LAPD retirement memorabilia framed on the wall: a badge, a pair of gold-plated handcuffs, and a gleaming .38 revolver.

"Mr. Mayot, we don't really operate along—"

"A gun *and* a guy who knows how to use it. Like this Golding guy."

Reynolds bared his teeth in what he hoped was a smile.

"What I mean is, the Olsen case was a one-in-a-million. McGinley opened up with a shotgun, okay? Pete returned fire. It was self-defense, pure and simple. We aren't in business to shoot people."

Lenny held up his hands.

"I know, I know. All I'm saying is it's nice to know you will when you have to. I mean he saved her life, right? You can't argue with that."

"Of course not. I just don't want you to—"

"Must have been good for business, too, right? I mean that's what I *call* global protection."

For a moment Reynolds didn't know what to say. It was true, of course: the Olsen incident had been good for business. The company had been up and running just a month when Madeleine Olsen called. She'd hardly qualified as a celebrity—had done a couple of sitcom appearances and a solitary commercial for fruit juice— but they'd taken the case because it was the only one going. Ten weeks later Arthur McGinley, a man Olsen had first met two years earlier while working as a receptionist, had turned up outside her house in Pasadena

armed with a loaded Ithaca Mag-19 Roadblocker, a
Bren Ten .45-caliber automatic, and a hunting knife, in-
tending, according to the video diary he left behind, to
shoot her and then himself. What he had in mind for the
hunting knife was not clear. Fortunately for Olsen, Pete
Golding was outside the house at the time. McGinley
died seconds later with three bullets in his chest. The
shoot-out made the news coast to coast, and within days
Reynolds had found himself in the novel position of
having to turn down business. Thankfully, the fact that
Maddy Olsen had quit as a client of Alpha's sometime
before the incident had taken place was not reported,
nor were her reasons for doing so.

Since then Reynolds had been able to hire more people and move the operation to smart new offices in
Century City, overlooking Beverly Hills and the Avenue of the Stars. All the same, he had reservations.
Reynolds had gone into the private sector after twenty
years at the LAPD, where he'd helped set up the Threat
Management Unit, the first police unit of its kind to
focus on long-term threat and harassment cases. And in
all those years, most of them working Homicide, he'd
never once fired his gun in anger. Alpha was supposed
to provide analytical services, assess the level of risk,
advise on evasion and security. It was supposed to help
people avoid confrontation, not do the confronting for
them. And it was supposed to go *strictly* by the book.
There were times when he wondered if Golding understood all that.

"Well, anyhow," he said at last. "Pete's on a case right
now."

Rolled up tight, the poster took a while to catch.
Golding hummed to himself as he held it to the gas

burner, pulling it away every few seconds to see how it was going.

"You can't be too careful cooking with gas," he said. "Specially in a place like this. All this grease and shit everywhere. You should clean up once in a while. You sure don't wanna be burned to death, fat guy like you. I mean you'd burn like a fucking candle. It could take *days.*"

Lubett shot a glance at the door, wondered whether he could make it.

"Look, I didn't mean anything. I was angry, just like you said, I—"

"You got into Miss Bonner's building, Raymond. You bluffed your way in with a fake police ID." He reached into his jacket and pulled out the cheap imitation badge, holding it up like a piece of evidence. "I guess it was lucky for her she was out, right?"

"No, no. I wasn't going to touch her. I—"

"But you said you were going to have to teach her a lesson. We have that call on tape. You said you were going to—how did you put it?—give her *a taste of your pain.* What did you mean by that exactly?"

The poster was burning now. Golding turned, took a step closer, holding it out in front of him, still looking at it critically, being creative, seeing what suggested itself.

"Please!"

"Are we talking about the kind of pain you gave your wife? I mean your ex-wife?"

Orange flames licked the air a few inches from Lubett's face.

"She lied. She lied." His voice rose to an adolescent falsetto. "I never touched her."

"One time you broke her arm. Put her in the hospital. Was that what you had in mind for Karen?"

"She fell. I didn't mean it, I swear."

"Or are we talking about something more permanent?"

"No, no, I—"

A crack like a starting pistol, wood splintering. Lubett lurched backwards, legs flailing, hit the floor, lay there rasping and gargling, the chair in pieces beneath him. Golding threw his cigarette end into the sink and walked over.

"Now that was an accident waiting to happen," he said. "Fat guy, cheap furniture."

Lubett's forearms were doing a jerky dance around his torso and his face, trying to protect everything at once.

"I *know*," said Golding brightly. "You should go on a diet. Yeah. A charcoal diet. Soak up some of that shit inside you." He looked at the tube of paper in his hand, flipped it back and forth until the flames died. "Here, have some charcoal, Raymond."

And he pushed it in his mouth.

"It's always distressing to receive letters like this, of course," said Reynolds. "And I know how Mrs. Cusak must feel. But what you have to remember is that in most cases it's *designed* to distress. We can draw comfort from that."

"Comfort?" Lenny pointed at the letters. "The guy says he's gonna cut her face off, for Christ's sake. Cut her pretty face off and stick it in the deep freeze."

"Yes, I saw that. My point is that in cases like this the violence is usually *in* the letters, and only there. This guy wants to get to Mrs. Cusak for whatever reason; so he tries to frighten her. And that does it for him. If he really wanted to hurt her physically, he would be putting his efforts into that, not just writing letters."

Lenny frowned.

"So you're saying we have nothing at all to worry about?"

"Probably not."

"Probably?"

Reynolds sat back in his chair, balancing a ballpoint between his fingers.

"My colleague Dr. Romero's done some interesting studies on this. A lot depends on the nature of the relationship between the subject and the victim."

"Relationship?" Lenny held up his hands. "There *is* no relationship."

"Well," said Reynolds, nodding thoughtfully, "that's something we have to establish. You see, if there has been some face-to-face contact, something that might have seemed trivial at the time, that Mrs. Cusak might not remember—an argument over a parking space, a professional disagreement of some kind—then that makes our guy touchy, angry, insecure, all kinds of things, but probably not dangerous. If, on the other hand, the relationship is all in his mind, or doesn't exist at all, then we're talking genuine psychiatric problems: paranoia, schizophrenia, erotomania even."

Lenny pushed a finger inside his collar and worked a little sore patch next to his windpipe. Something about this conversation was making him uncomfortable. He felt the way hospitals made him feel: a sudden, unsettling proximity to a universe of suffering.

"Erotomania? Would that be better or worse?"

Reynolds smiled at the naïveté of the question.

"On balance, potentially, worse, I'd say. We're talking there about a delusional disorder. Someone who's imagined a relationship with Mrs. Cusak and is now angry or jealous that she hasn't responded. We'll have to examine these letters in more detail for signs of that. However, the statistics show that a clear majority of erotomanics are women, and their targets men. So I'd be surprised if we find many unequivocal markers for delusion. An obsessional disorder, on the other hand—that may be nearer the mark."

"Right, right. So, er . . ." Lenny glanced at his chunky diver's wristwatch. He had a lunch appointment in fifteen minutes. ". . . cutting to the chase here, Tom, are you saying we have a problem or we don't?"

Tom Reynolds took a moment to refocus on the question. He hated being rushed. At the Threat Management Unit he'd always been able to talk as long as he'd wanted to, because people knew he had knowledge and experience, and, more important, rank. In the private sector all people wanted was their problem to simply disappear, never mind the how or the what. It was something he still wasn't comfortable with—not least because when you were dealing with crazy people it wasn't always possible to deliver.

He cleared his throat.

"What I'm saying is that the letters by themselves aren't much to worry about. But there are certain types of obsessional disorder—the kind that may not come to the attention of the authorities or the medical profession—which may just possibly be involved here. We'll look into that just to be on the safe side, but the odds are your client is not in danger."

"Good. But you're gonna send someone over anyway, right?"

Reynolds nodded.

"No sense in taking chances."

"Right. See, what I want here, Tom, is the bases covered. I don't want Ellen losing any more sleep over this. I want her to feel that everything's been taken care of here. You have no idea how long it's taken me to draw her out of her shell. She's a *very* private person."

Reynolds nodded again.

"So I understand."

"No, you don't." Lenny smiled, shaking his head. "You couldn't. She's been out of the picture the last four years. Completely. Refused everything. Know why? Because of the intrusion. See my point?"

"Yes, I—"

"And now, just when she gets the divorce over with, just when I start getting her a little more exposure, finally when things start to happen again, they go dig up a . . . a . . . those *remains* behind her pool house. I mean, that's enough to freak anyone out."

"Yeah, I heard about that. It must have been quite a shock."

"Damn right. So, besides a little reassurance, what I want is to deal with this situation quickly and cleanly, if a situation is what it comes to."

"Right," said Reynolds, nodding, trying to follow. "A situation."

"If this guy . . . makes himself *known*. Becomes a genuine problem. I don't wanna drag Ellen into court for restraining orders and any of that stuff. She's had enough of courts, way too much. Too public, too messy. Very unhelpful. You catch my drift?"

"Yes, I think so, but sometimes—"

"So why don't you put your man Golding on to it? I can't think of anyone *I'd* find more reassuring, and if, by any remote chance, things turn nasty . . ."

Lenny finished the sentence with a shrug. Once again Reynolds found himself playing catch-up. That was the trouble dealing with personal managers and lawyers rather than the clients themselves: there were always agendas—agendas that subtly blurred his picture of what the client's best interests really were, but that had to be recognized and accommodated nevertheless. It was so much simpler when people spoke for themselves.

"Lenny, uh ... I *really* don't think Golding's your man for this. Strictly between ourselves"—he leaned across the desk, dropping his voice—"Pete has a little problem with commitment."

Lenny frowned, unconvinced.

"What are you saying? He's lazy?"

Reynolds pursed his lips.

"What I mean is, he can get a little *too* committed. Some people find him a little ... excessive."

Lubett was propped up against the fridge, still spitting flecks of charred paper from his mouth. His lips and chin were a mess of saliva and ash.

Golding reached into his back pocket and pulled out a single sheet of stiff white paper, folded in three.

"Now this here is a temporary restraining order signed by Judge Irving." He talked slowly as if explaining something to a child. He unfolded the paper and held it up a few inches from Lubett's bloodshot eyes. "It says you are not to call Miss Bonner. You are not to write to Miss Bonner. You are not to go within three hundred yards of Miss Bonner by order of the Superior Court, until the hearing next month. At which time we shall seek and obtain a permanent order to the same effect."

He folded the paper up again and reached for the V of Lubett's sweat-stained blue tennis shirt. Lubett flinched, his head bumping the fridge door.

"Now you can do what you like with this," said Golding. "You can burn it, you can flush it down the can, you can eat it. I don't care." He pinched a fold of the fabric between two fingers and carefully tucked the paper inside Lubett's shirt. "But if you *ever* bother Karen Bonner again, I'm gonna come back here, and next time I'm gonna be upset. You don't want that to happen, do you, Raymond?"

Lubett jerked his head from side to side.

"I don't—I don't want any trouble."

Golding stood up.

"I know you don't, Raymond." He wiped his hands on a handkerchief. "And you know what? Deep down, in her heart of hearts, I think Karen Bonner knows it too."

3

Golding came into the office carrying a takeout from China Joe's. He was on his way into the small open-plan section of the suite he shared with the other PIs, Denison and Ross, when a voice called him back.

"Mr. Reynolds wanted you to step in as soon as you arrived."

It was Andrea Craig, the office administrator, doing her turn behind the reception desk. Thirty-one years old, thin, with efficiently styled short brown hair and a pale complexion that she tended to disguise with heavy makeup, she was the only person in the place with a genuine corporate background. Golding had never really warmed to her.

"Well, I guess I'll step in then," he said, putting the takeout down beside the potted plant Andrea had recently bought for the reception area.

"You also had a call," she added. "I think it went through to your voice mail. From Jackie?"

Just the mention of the name was enough to set up a

wash of queasy emotion—love, guilt, loss. He hadn't
seen his sister for three days, not since Saturday night,
when they'd had dinner at her place. He hoped she was
okay.

Dr. Frank Romero was in with Reynolds when Golding knocked. Romero was Alpha's other founder, a
forensic psychiatrist who had specialized for most of his
career in stalking and obsessional behavior. A fellow of
the University of Southern California's Institute of Psy-
chiatry, Law, and Behavioral Science, he had worked as
a consultant on hundreds of cases for both private and
public organizations, including the Threat Management
Unit, where he and Tom Reynolds had met. The two
men made an unlikely but effective pair: Reynolds, tall,
somber, face weather-beaten, but hair neat, with a dress
sense that was pure G-man; Romero, below-average
height, stocky, always casually dressed—corduroys and
V-neck sweaters—but intense, a man who loved and val-
ued his work. It was Romero who got you believing you
needed help, and Reynolds who offered you the life-
line—at least, that was the way Golding saw it.

"Tom, Frank."

Golding remained in the doorway, hoping this wasn't
going to take long, wanting to get back to that message.
Romero, who was standing by the window reading
something, turned and acknowledged him with a nod.

"Serve the papers on Lubett?" said Reynolds.

"Sure, no sweat."

"How'd he take it?"

Golding shrugged.

"He took it."

Reynolds nodded to himself for a moment.

"He gonna comply?"

"You know Lubett. I don't think even *he* knows what he's going to do next."

"You didn't lean on him too hard, right? You didn't . . . do anything?"

Golding turned over his palms.

"I served the papers. I explained the position."

"Good, good. Okay." Reynolds did some more nodding, then gestured towards a chair. "Take a seat, Pete, we've got something for you."

Golding took a deep breath and sat down. Romero was still hovering behind him, reading whatever it was. It was late afternoon now, the low sun flamed on the glass and steel of the tower blocks opposite.

"Ever heard of Ellen Cusak?" Reynolds went on.

"Sure. Figure skater. World champion—what was it?—seven years ago?"

"Eight. Just got divorced."

"She just did that Ford commercial," said Romero.

Golding recalled a four-by-four sedan cutting high-speed curves across a frozen lake, intercut with two-hundred-pound Cougars wearing warpaint, burning up the ice, body-checking, slamming into each other—and in the middle of all the mayhem a figure skater sailing through the air. The slogan went something like: *What is power without grace?*

"Anyway," said Reynolds. "Seems she has an admirer."

He slid a fat plastic dossier across the desk. It contained a stack of about a dozen letters and envelopes on paper of different sizes and colors, most of them handwritten in ballpoint using block capitals, a couple of them typed on an electric typewriter. Before Golding could take one out, Romero handed him what he'd been reading.

"This is the latest," he said. "Came two days ago."

It was written on a sheet of pale blue paper, the kind people used for personal letters. The black ballpoint was scored into the surface, the obscene words double-under-lined. The edge of the paper was stained—coffee maybe or beer. As he read Golding felt himself grow cold.

"They started turning up about two months ago," said Reynolds. "She threw the first batch away. Since then she's been getting them once or twice a week."

"No approaches, no calls?"

"Not so far," said Romero. "But he's talked about it. The phrase *I'll be waiting* has cropped up three times in the last four letters. And the violence has become more graphic lately too."

"We're worried he might be psyching himself up for an approach," Reynolds added.

Golding flicked through the dossier.

"The Ice Man. That's kind of poetic."

"The Ice Man, Nemesis, Lover Boy. He likes to swap it around. But they're all from the same guy. He's basi-cally very repetitive."

Golding looked up at Romero.

"So, what kind of crazy is he?"

It was the sort of question Romero didn't like. He propped himself up against the window ledge and folded his arms.

"He has problems certainly. This is not the work of a balanced person. I certainly wouldn't rule out substance abuse, but clinically insane? It would be hard to draw that conclusion."

"So he's just pissed. Anyone know why?"

"The focus of his resentment seems to be her per-ceived wealth and status," said Romero. "Her supposed disregard for ordinary people. The sexual aggression stems from the same thing: an anger at her unavailability—although it's a fact that the letters only began *after* Mrs. Cusak's divorce."

"When she should have been available," said Golding, guessing. "So this guy asked for a date and got turned down."

"Apparently not," said Reynolds. "Mrs. Cusak has no idea at all who this person is. According to her manager, she's had no approaches of that kind."

"Her manager?"

Reynolds nodded significantly.

"Lenny Mayot. You'll meet him. 'Course it wouldn't do any harm to double-check. Just in case she's forgotten something."

"Sure," said Golding. "If I get a chance. Do I talk to her manager or her publicist?"

"You'll talk to her. You're going up to the house tomorrow, twelve o'clock noon. As a matter of fact, I don't think she runs to a publicist."

Golding pulled one of the envelopes from the file.

"Any idea where they're coming from?"

"According to the postmarks, mostly right here in L.A.," said Reynolds. "Santa Monica, Venice. He's a local boy, not much doubt about it."

"And he knows where she lives," Romero said. "Not that that's especially troubling. I understand the house has been featured in a number of magazines over the years. So it wouldn't take much effort to find it."

"Doug Gorman hired some celebrity architect," said Reynolds.

"Isn't that where they just dug up a body?" said Golding.

"Yeah, that's the place. But before you start making connections, it was in the ground well before Mrs. Cusak and her husband moved in. I checked downtown. It'd

been there for at least four years. Anyway, our client's
been going through a difficult time just lately, and . . .
well, just don't go scaring the hell out of her, okay?
Coming to us wasn't her idea, it was Lenny Mayot's."

"The manager."

"Right. Reassurance is the thing here. Nothing heavy.
Tell her what she has to do security-wise, set up the
monitoring, and tell her not to worry about anything."

Golding frowned, looked around at Romero to see
how he was reading this, but Romero was already on his
way out of the room.

"Maybe she should be worrying," Golding said. "We
don't know anything about this guy."

The door shut with a click.

Reynolds shook his head.

"The letters are unpleasant but they're nothing unusual. You heard what Frank said. The guy's just fooling
around, blowing off steam. He's not crazy enough to try
anything."

"And if he is?"

Reynolds reached across the desk and planted his
hand on the dossier as if he were about to take an oath
on it.

"I saw thousands of letters like this at the TMU, Pete.
And they mostly never amounted to anything. You
know how the bad ones are. They *want* something. They
want attention, a relationship, everything. This guy
doesn't even *ask* her to respond. He's just happy to
think he's scaring her." Reynolds held up his hand. "Just
read the letters, Pete. You'll see what I mean. They're
nasty but they're just talk. *That's* what I want you to
stress when you get up there. You with me?"

Golding shrugged.

"Whatever you say, Tom."

The phone rang and Reynolds picked up. Another manager, another anxious client. Business was booming. Golding was halfway out the door when Reynolds pointed to a copy of *Skating* magazine in his out tray.

"Here, you can read all about the great comeback," he said, and went on with his call.

Jackie's recorded voice sounded slow, the consonants slurred by fatigue or drink. Golding hoped it was just fatigue—Jackie did a six-till-six shift at a Howard Johnson—but recently she had started drinking again, so there was no way to be sure.

"Sorry to bother you at work, big brother, but I got me a problem with the heater again. The hot water comes through and I swear it's steaming. John says it's the thermostat. He won't be back till after midnight, and I thought maybe you could come by and give it a kick. Don't worry if you can't make it."

Golding replaced the receiver and looked down at his hands. His sister had come to L.A. three years ago from Chicago, where she had been living with a couple of nurses in a squalid brownstone. He was the one who suggested she come out west, making big claims for the beneficial effects of California sunshine. She had met John the week she arrived. John worked for AT&T. He was a nose-picking retard whose idea of a fun evening was to smoke a lot of grass and listen to his Eric Clapton albums. He didn't always sleep at home, and when Jackie thought she was going to be left on her own for the evening, she would call Golding up on any pretext to get him to go over there. This looked like one of those pretexts. Golding knew how it would be. They'd start off okay, but then he'd say something about John, and Jackie would fly off the handle, accuse him of resenting her relationship, accuse him of not caring, of never having cared.

The takeout had found its way to his desk and was sitting there on a plain white china plate. An oily sauce had spilled out through a tear in the now saturated paper bag. He pushed the plate aside and picked up the copy of *Skating*. It fell open at the article on Ellen Cusak.

Below the title—"The Return of a Skating Legend?"—were two pictures, column-height, on opposite sides of the spread. On the left Yelena Cusak, seventeen years old, holding the pose at the end of her medal-winning program at the Nationals—her first appearance at the competition—dressed in the famous dark blue tunic. On the right, Ellen Cusak, a decade later, drinking water from a plastic bottle, a spotlight behind her, taking direction from a bearded guy in a crane chair at the shooting of a commercial for Ford. Golding turned the page and found a third photograph, smaller than the others and older. *Cusak and her father Stepan during a training session at Lake Arrowhead, taken a few days before the Southwest Pacific Junior competition, where Ellen won her first title.* Stepan Cusak had thickly growing gray hair and wore a scarf that hid much of his face. Despite that, you could see that he was smiling as he crouched down to hear what his daughter was saying. According to the article, his sudden death from heart failure two years later marked the beginning of the end of Ellen's career in competition.

Golding finished reading the piece and tossed the magazine onto his desk. Unlike just about everyone else in his family, he'd never much cared for skating. All through the season his folks would try and tempt him onto the ice, bribing him with gleaming new skates, ice hockey gear, even trips to see the Chicago Blackhawks. But Golding had never taken to it. He hated the endless Midwestern winters, the cold unyielding ground, the vistas of white against which nothing could hide. He hated the cheery camaraderie of man against nature that colored people's words, the blankness, the space, above all, the silence. That was what he'd come to L.A. to get away from.

4

"**S**o what do we have?"

Hagmaier reached across for the case file on Serratosa's desk and flipped it open. At the top of the stack was a fingerprint card, a blank square in the top right-hand corner where the face should have been. Jane Doe no. 273.

"Arthur Gill managed to lift some clean prints from the left hand," said Serratosa.

"Great. He did a great job."

Serratosa nodded, but he could see Hagmaier was disappointed.

"Yeah, it's a tricky process. Disodium ethylenediamine tetracetic acid mixed up in a detergent solution. Arthur has his own recipe. Prints came up nice. Good enough for a positive ID."

Four good prints and a ragged smudge for the little finger, a ragged smudge like a brown candle flame. Hagmaier put the card back.

"Yeah, great if we had something to match it with."

The two men looked at each other for a moment.

What they actually had was blind alleys, barren paths stretching away to some point in the future when, maybe, some scumbag would tell him who did this as part of a plea. Because otherwise it was looking pretty bleak. Though fully clothed when buried, the corpse had been without a Social Security card or driver's license—without ID of any kind. Hagmaier's guess was that the killer had cleaned out the woman's pockets.

The frustrating thing was, despite the number of physical peculiarities that set her apart from the norm, so far there hadn't been the slightest echo from the databases that tracked America's host of the missing.

"So we're saying . . . ?"

Serratosa shrugged and put his hand on the case folder.

"Cranial and sexual morphology female—Caucasoid. Trotter-Gleser for white females estimated from femur and tibia gives us around sixty-eight inches. So let's say five eight, one hundred thirty pounds."

"And you think late twenties?"

"Skull suture suggests maybe twenty-eight, twenty-nine, give or take a few years."

Hagmaier knew all this from the autopsy report, but he wanted to hear it directly from Serratosa—to see if he could get something extra, something beyond the cold hard facts. Despite his cautious scientific air, Juan loved to speculate. It was something he was good at.

"What do you make of the fractures?" said Hagmaier after a long silence.

The fractures—all premortem apart from damage to the sternum and a couple of broken ribs—were a big issue, and Hagmaier could not put them out of his mind. They seemed to speak volumes about the kind of life this woman had led. They had shown up in the X rays Serratosa's people had taken in the hope of revealing medical procedures that could then lead to positive identification. At some time in her life, probably when she was a little girl, something or someone had broken her nose. Her left clavicle also showed traces of having been broken twice, probably at different times. The radius and ulna in her left arm was similarly marked. She was missing premolar and molar teeth on the right side of her mouth, and had been found with her dentures in place.

"Could be abuse," said Serratosa. "But it could be something else."

"Like a sport?"

"Sure. A sport. Muscle attachment areas are well developed, particularly in the legs. This lady could have been a runner."

"You don't break too many bones on the track, Doc."

Serratosa smiled his smile.

"No, maybe not. But this lady was an athlete of some kind. I would bet money on it. Who knows what—a surfer, a kickboxer maybe. She maybe did roadwork to build up her stamina."

"A kickboxer with a child?"

Parturition scars on the pelvis indicated a birth. Hagmaier hoped this meant that there was a significant other—out there somewhere. Someone they could eventually link to the body. If it was a stranger killing, the chances of closing the case were that much more remote.

Serratosa drew a hand across his eyes.

"Female kickboxers are still female," he said. "But if you want my—what I really think, I think this lady . . . I think maybe this lady was abused as a child. Sport came later."

Hagmaier frowned and looked at the prints on the card. Delicate fingers, delicate-patterned whorls. Raised and trembling as the knife chopped down. Too much suffering for one person—that was the thought that came into his head. He blinked and gave himself a little shake.

"So—"

For a moment he didn't know what to say.

"Who did it?" suggested Serratosa, smiling.

Hagmaier smiled too, realizing that Serratosa was probably right—this probably *was* the question he wanted to ask, however futile it might seem.

"*You're* the detective," said Serratosa after a moment.

Hagmaier felt a sudden urge for a cigarette, but Serratosa didn't allow smoking in his office. He forced himself to focus on the little dabs of information the woman's fingertips had left on the card.

"Someone who knew her," he said, almost to himself. "Guy kills her in a rage. He nearly cuts her in half with a—what was it your guy thinks?"

"A carving knife. Pointed. One sharp side. At least six inches long."

"Sticks her with this—with this big *knife* and then . . . then feels bad about it. He tries to make her look normal. Even puts her glasses back on again. Then he dresses her—dresses her up real warm: roll-neck sweater, ski jacket, like it's cold."

Serratosa nodded slowly.

"Since when does it get so cold around here?" he said.

"That's what Matt said. Thought maybe they were up in the mountains, but I don't buy it. Why come all the way down here?"

Serratosa locked his fingers together.

"Maybe he wrapped her up to contain the blood, didn't want it on his car. Maybe he just didn't want to see it anymore."

"Maybe," Hagmaier said. "Trouble is she wasn't *wrapped,* she was carefully and deliberately dressed."

Serratosa shrugged.

"Maybe he *plans* to bury her in the mountains. Wants her to be warm."

"I think that's maybe closer to it," Hagmaier said. "Who knows what was going through this guy's head? If it is a guy." He thought about it for a few seconds. "He has in mind to leave her in the mountains but only makes it to Brentwood. He's driving around with the corpse and he sees the empty lot, decides to get rid of her there and then."

"So he finds this hole . . ."

"And puts her in it."

Serratosa sucked his teeth—something he did when he was unhappy or unconvinced.

"He isn't worried about the corpse being found?" he said. "If this is a construction site, I mean. With all that digging going on?"

"Maybe he doesn't know. He just sees this lot—what might look like an abandoned lot."

"How about your canvas?" said Serratosa. "What did that reveal?"

Hagmaier made a face.

"It's ongoing. We drew a blank with the neighbors except for the guy next door, but he's a little paranoid, says there have been all kinds of suspicious types over the past few years—fans, people trying to get pictures of Doug and Ellen."

Serratosa scratched at his chin.

"How about the construction company?"

"The foundations were laid in October '96. Hanema Domus. Top-dollar firm working out of the valley. Hanema have pretty high turnover, especially with the on-site people. Couple of guys are still there, but they weren't much help. We're onto the carpenters, glaziers, electricians, but frankly I'm not very hopeful."

"And the previous owners?"

"Walter Thorn, partner in a law firm. Moved down to Orange County with his wife. Showed me pictures of the old house, a kind of Spanish villa. The guy was pissed at Doug Gorman for pulling it down, though frankly . . ."

Hagmaier's voice tailed off to nothing. He looked at Serratosa's wall planner and let out a big sigh.

"So what's next?" said Serratosa. They had come to the end of the road with what they knew.

For a moment Hagmaier stared blankly.

"We go public," he said eventually. "We have a guy working up a likeness based on—on what's left of the head. We get a picture we're happy with and then we flood the streets."

Serratosa said nothing. Then he decided to look on the bright side.

"Somebody must have known this lady," he said.

5

"**E**verybody knows her," said Lenny. "This Ford thing's put her right back on the map, and when *Nutcracker* starts to roll she'll be—"

Gil Knapp raised a hand.

"Come on, Lenny. How long's that commercial going to run? Three months, six?"

Lenny leaned back from the little round table and took a breath, forcing himself to draw the air deep into his trunk the way his yoga teacher was always telling him. He was sounding shrill, overeager—exactly the wrong way to be with Knapp, co-head of production at Knapp-Weinstein

"Okay, Gil." He looked around at the restaurant's tasteful gloom and took a sip of his drink. "Look," he said significantly, "I wasn't planning to talk about this."

Knapp lowered his weather-beaten head into his shoulders and gave Lenny a patient, leonine, okay-I'm-listening face.

"The thing is Ellen's doing a book with Barbara Christian."

Knapp stared. It was clear the name meant nothing to him.

"Barbara Christian. She's a journalist at *Variety*. Does these books for Argyle as a sideline. Softcover only, six dollars a pop, quantity discounts on bulk purchases, sold at checkouts in—you know those little stands you get in supermarkets with the horoscopes and the recipes?"

Knapp nodded.

"Celebrity biographies—film stars, athletes. Turns out she's crazy about skating, skates herself—just did a thing on Nicole Bobek. Big hit. Sold a ton of books."

"What's a ton?"

"Scads. Hundreds of thousands anyway."

Knapp shrugged, and gave his scotch a swirl.

"Lenny—this is books. Abe and me, we do video, we do TV."

"I'm *talking* about video, Gil. I'm talking about Ellen Cusak—her profile. Christian is very excited. She's already working on the first draft, and get this: Argyle plans to go to press before Christmas."

"Christmas?" Knapp frowned. "That's only five months away."

"*That's* the beauty of it, Gil. These books run to one-fifty, two hundred pages max, and Christian puts them together real quick. I wouldn't say this to her face, but it's journalism really—you know, with up-to-the-minute material, and nice photographs, but you publish it like a book." Lenny sipped his drink, swallowed. "And Ellen's life—well . . . not wishing to seem callous here, but what can I say?—it makes great reading."

Knapp raised his eyebrows and nodded.

"The kid's certainly been through the mill."

"Damn right. We start with her coming over to the States in '86, escaping the communists with her dad. She skates her way to a world championship title, skates her way into everybody's living room, and then"—Lenny raised his hands—"dad *dies*. Things fall apart on the ice. The marriage hits the skids and—" Seeing the look on Knapp's face, he decided to curtail the doom and gloom. "And now—the *comeback*," he said brightly.

Knapp finished his drink and looked away. Lenny eyed the older man's profile and gave a sharp involuntary nod. Knapp-Weinstein would be perfect for Ellen. The products they turned out were not of the highest quality, but Gil and Abe were hustlers. They knew how to make a dollar, and their salespeople were plugged into video wholesalers and supermarkets nationwide. If anyone could sell Ellen Cusak in the Midwest, these were the people.

"Now consider the timing, Gil. December fifteenth—the publication date Argyle's talking about—by that time Ellen Cusak will have been skating at venues around the country for approximately six weeks. Looking sensational, getting all those little girls on the edge of their seats, making all those moms wish they looked so good in a leotard."

Knapp was nodding again.

"Okay, now go forward a month," said Lenny, rolling his right hand—"January fifteenth. Too much *roast beef*, too much *dessert*. Mom's back in the supermarket looking for the lite coleslaw and what does she see?" He raised his hands and dabbed at the air with a corny up-there-in-lights gesture.

"The Ellen Cusak fitness video," said Knapp, sounding underwhelmed. "A Gil Knapp–Abe Weinstein production."

Lenny dropped his hands.

"It's a shame Abe couldn't make this meeting," said Knapp with a sigh. "I think he'd go for this."

"But what about you? What do you think, Gil?"

Knapp considered his empty glass for a moment.

"Well, actually a couple of words come to mind," he said. For the sake of accuracy, he counted them off on his finger and thumb. "Ice and Magic."

Lenny forced himself to nod, to give the appearance of a responsible adult chewing over a reasonable objection. *Ice Magic.* It was like a fucking albatross around his neck. Halfway through the '96 Champions on Ice tour, a tour for which Ellen had been paid $750,000, she had withdrawn complaining of pains in her knees. Ice Magic, the tour's promoters, had sought medical confirmation of the problem, and when none was forthcoming, had turned ugly. Every twist and turn of the acrimonious legal dispute that followed had been reported in the press. For a month it had seemed to Lenny that he couldn't pick up a tabloid without hearing either about the failing marriage or Ellen's problems with Ice Magic.

"I understand that, Gil, but what *you* have to understand is . . . well that's why this is a comeback. That's what Ellen is coming back *from*. And she's . . . the thing is, Ellen—she's *motivated* now. Maybe more than she ever was. You saw the Ford commercial. They had her jumping triples for days just so they could light it properly."

Knapp put his head on one side.

"Let me get this straight, Lenny—we're talking about, what, skating for fitness? That sort of thing?"

"No, no." Lenny shooed this away two-handed. "The normal thing. Aerobics, step, stretching, maybe intercut with bits of Ellen on ice. Maybe some nutritional stuff."

Knapp nodded some more.

"You know how these things work, Gil. Ellen Cusak is beautiful, a former world champion—a focus for people's aspirations. If she says this is the secret to looking the way she does, people will buy the tape."

"Could we film inside the house?"

Lenny sat up straight.

"I mean, if we're working the celebrity angle," said Knapp, coming forward, putting his elbows on the table, "I think the house might be a useful prop. People are pretty keen on Gorman too, remember. And with all this divorce shenanigans—well, I just think people might like to see what Ellen settled for."

"Christ, Gil. This is a fitness video, not a documentary." Lenny swept his hand over the tablecloth. Knapp nodded, but he was clearly unhappy. "Gil, the problem is . . ."

The problem was Ellen was a little sensitive about her privacy at the moment. What with the police digging up the garden and some maniac sending her threatening mail, she might not like a camera crew setting up lights in the greenhouse.

"What?" said Knapp. "What is the problem?"

Lenny shrugged.

"Well, you know, with all this—with this—"

"The corpse? The stiff they found in the garden? Is that what we're talking about?"

Lenny nodded.

Knapp smiled and sat back in his chair.

"Jeez, Lenny, I thought that was something you cooked up to keep the press interested."

6

Ellen Cusak sat waiting on a bench beside the Pickwick Rink in Burbank, watching the Tuesday night crowd doing leisurely circuits on the ice. There seemed to be more couples than usual, men and women skating with their arms around each other, some of them even attempting passes and spins, like slow-motion rock 'n' rollers. At half past eight the rink would be turned over to the skating club so that its young hopefuls could train. But until then it was open to all comers. Ellen watched the flushed, laughing faces and tried not to think about the meeting she'd had a few hours earlier with her accountant.

It was clear Martin Wardell, a tightly wrapped bean counter of the old school, considered her naive and irresponsible. He seemed to take it as a personal affront that during her divorce proceedings she had not gone after her ex-husband's future earnings with more determination, settling instead for the house in Brentwood plus a half share of the puny savings portfolio that had survived Doug's five-year spending spree and his disastrous forays into the restaurant business. With all the grimness of a sentencing judge, Wardell had laid out for her the "inescapable facts" of her financial situation. A $200,000 mortgage on the Brentwood property remained, and had to be serviced. Unless she was able to start earning regularly again, her position would rapidly worsen to a point where she would face repossession or worse. With a glance at the Mercedes convertible parked in his driveway, he had suggested she consider "certain lifestyle adjustments" unless and until the house was sold and her position "stabilized." Perhaps he had laid it on thick because he thought that as a pampered onetime celeb, she might have difficulty reconnecting to the real world. She might simply try to blot out all thought of her reduced circumstances with a credit card binge on Rodeo Drive or a few weeks' helicopter skiing in New Zealand.

What Mr. Wardell didn't know was that the house was already on the market. That was why she had wanted to get the pool fixed. The fact was, nobody was buying. The realtor had been apologetic. Normally he'd have fielded a score of serious inquiries by now. The house was beautiful. The market was in good shape. They'd advertised widely. But there was a problem: the recent "discovery" in her garden put people off. Everyone had heard about it. There'd been one offer, but it had been so far below the asking price he hadn't bothered to pass it on. "Right now that house is bad karma," he'd said, before advising her to take it off the market and try again in a year's time. It was either that or take a big hit on the price.

Wardell had softened a little bit when he heard this. He softened up even more when she told him she'd just spent three thousand dollars overhauling the Mercedes so that she could at least sell that. They'd gone through the options in detail, looking for where other economies could be made. He seemed impressed at what she had already done. He even advised her on the make of used car (he favored Japanese). But on one point he was adamant: the full-time housekeeper was a luxury she could no longer afford. A once-a-week cleaner was one thing, but a well-paid full-time employee was quite another.

Maria Dominguez had been with them for the past four years. Ellen had come to think of her as one of the family, and Maria's own children (she had three) had often come up to the house when they were too young to be left at school. If Ellen was there, she would play with them in the garden or sit with them while they watched TV. They called her "Tía Elena." She still remembered their birthdays with cards and presents. A childish scrawl of a thank-you letter from eight-year-old Teresa was pinned to the frame of the mirror on her dressing table.

She dreaded the thought of letting Maria go. The last thing she wanted was to be even more alone in the house, especially with all the weird things that had been happening recently. But if she really *could* make that comeback, if Lenny could keep the deals coming, then maybe she could keep Maria on. Selling the Mercedes would surely earn her a breathing space. In the autumn there would be the *Nutcracker* money—less than she used to get, but still helpful. And by the time that was over, maybe she could sell the house for a fair price, and Maria could work for the new owners.

Her thoughts were interrupted by a feedback screech from the PA system. There was a cough, then a female voice announced that it was half past eight and time to clear the ice. A minute later she saw Sam Ritt and one of the clubs trainers coming out of the locker room, followed by half a dozen juniors with their skates under their arms.

Ellen and Sam went back a long way. It was Sam who had helped her prepare for junior competition when she first came over from the Ukraine, and Sam who had allowed her to train for next to nothing. He had also been instrumental in getting her into the elite training center at Lake Arrowhead at the beginning of the nineties. She had lost touch with him during the five years of her marriage—just one of the many mistakes she'd made during that turbulent time—and it had been a complete and welcome surprise when he had gotten back in touch through Lenny. Thinking about it afterwards, she'd wondered if Lenny hadn't had something to do with the reunion, hadn't cooked it up as part of his plan to get her skating again.

The reason for Sam's call was hurrying towards Ellen right now with a smile on her twelve-year-old face. Tina Tucker was an exciting prospect: compact, feisty—so bouncy on the ice that Sam had immediately dubbed her Tigger. Like most girls of her age and ability, all Tigger really wanted to do was jump—breathtaking triples she tended to prepare with the explosive run-up of a long jumper. Style came a poor second. Sam had heard that Ellen was back on the ice and wondered if she would be interested in helping with the expressive aspects of Tina's dance. Since then Ellen had made four trips to the Pickwick Rink, trying to help introduce economy and grace into Tigger's movement on the ice. She found herself looking forward to each session almost more than anything else—not just because Tina was an eager pupil and a quick learner, but because she was fun to be with.

Almost before she could say hello, Tina took both her hands and led her towards the main entrance.

"My folks are here," she said breathlessly. "They're *dying* to meet you."

Ellen saw a middle-aged couple standing with their backs to the ice, trying to look like they were there for no reason in particular. Margaret Tucker was slim and handsome, with dark hair like her daughter's, but cut to a shortness that was almost too sensible. She was wearing a pastel blue matching jacket and skirt that looked as if they had just come from the dry cleaners. George Tucker was an affable-looking man with a full head of wavy gray hair and a deeply lined face. Ellen had heard from Sam Ritt about the sacrifices Tina's parents had made to give her the best possible chance. They were anything but rich, and the coaching, equipment, and private ice that Tina needed to develop her talent already cost thousands of dollars a year. Soon it would be tens of thousands: a serious investment with no certainty of a return. That was one reason why Ellen had agreed to help Tina for free. She knew only too well how hard such choices could be.

"I just can't tell you how excited we were when Tina told us you were going to be coaching her," Margaret Tucker said as soon as they were introduced. "We've always been huge fans of yours."

"Huge," said her husband.

"Always. Thank you *so much.*"

"Please," said Ellen, beginning to feel embarrassed, "I love working with Tina, I really do. She's got a very special talent."

"Do you *really* think so?" said Margaret.

George Tucker bounced proudly on the balls of his feet.

"Absolutely," Ellen said. "She's a natural. Do either of you skate?"

"We used to do a little pairs skating," said George. "Not anymore, though. Strictly amateur."

"So it's in her blood then," Ellen said.

"Well, I guess. Say, would you . . ." George shot his wife an uncertain glance. "We'd be so honored if you'd . . . well, come round for a drink sometime. Or . . . or dinner. I feel we owe—"

"Oh, *George.*" Mrs. Tucker placed a firm hand on her husband's forearm. "I think we're getting quite enough of Ellen Cusak's time as it is." She rolled her eyes at Ellen. "We can't expect her to trail all the way over to the fringes of Glendale just so you can brag to your pals in the office."

Ellen caught the crestfallen look on Tina's face.

"No, no really," she said. "I'd love to. I really would. Anytime."

"Well—well, that's great," said George.

"I've got private ice booked two weeks on Thursday," said Tina. "Ellen could come back with me."

Ninety minutes later Ellen was walking back across the floodlit parking lot. It had been a good session, and at the end of it Sam Ritt had come over and asked if she would be willing to help refine a couple of programs he had planned for the Southwest Pacific Junior Championships the following winter. She'd agreed, and then immediately found herself fielding questions from him on the state of her health, questions that took her right back to her teenage years. He asked her about her diet, about carbohydrate content, and then about how much sleep she was getting. It was then that the half-truths began. She told him that if anything she was getting too much sleep—getting up late most days and even dozing off in the afternoons. She *was* doing these things, of course, but only because her nights had recently been anything but restful.

It had started with the letters. She had stopped reading them a while ago. Lenny had insisted she put them to one side rather than throwing them in the trash—that way they would have a record. But whenever she saw the crude, brutal writing on the envelopes, it frightened her. And just knowing that someone was writing them, that another message of hate was probably on its way even as she lay down in the darkness, was enough to keep her awake. And now there were calls in the middle of the night. The first time whoever it was had hung up as soon as she'd answered. By morning she'd forgotten about it. But last night it had happened again, only this time he'd spoken: *I'm going to change your life, Yelena,* he'd said. That was all. She couldn't tell if it was the same guy who wrote the letters or not.

If she wasn't sleeping it was only natural.

And then there was the woman in the garden. It didn't help to know that she had probably been dumped there before the construction of the house. The fact was she had been out there all that time, slowly falling to pieces while the marriage went to hell. When she did eventually fall asleep, it was only to wake a couple of hours later, drenched with sweat, her heart pounding, certain that she had just been through the most horrible nightmare, but unable to remember anything about it; as if waking was the same as resurfacing, bursting through the surface of a lake, unable to look back down.

It was hot outside after the chill interior of the rink. Back in her car, Ellen turned on the air conditioning and watched the other cars slowly maneuvering around the lot, the moms and dads picking up their kids after the training session. Listening to the cheery greetings as passenger doors swung open, hearing the snatches of enthusiastic reports as the kids jumped in, she felt a sudden stab of loneliness. She liked Tina Tucker and her parents, she liked talking to Sam Ritt again, she liked being on the ice, working on technique, working on expression: she felt she was going back to something familiar, to a world she had once belonged to completely. But at the same time there were shadows, regrets, unresolved issues.

Out of nowhere she was remembering the first time she had gone onto the ice, how terrified she had been.

Freezing winter. Iron and stone.

Her father had taken her on the train from Kiev, a journey she still remembered as one of the most uncomfortable of her life. Only five years old, she had not understood that he had been fleeing their home. He hadn't wanted to be in their cramped apartment on her mother's birthday—the first since the cancer had taken her. They had stayed in a hotel on Franz Mehring Platz. Ellen could still remember the hard bed, the weak drizzle of forty-watt light, her father's immense sleeping form next to her, a view of smokestacks belching lignite into a sky the color of pewter.

He had taken her to the Grosser Müggelsee to see the ice.

They had walked out onto the frozen surface in silence. *Come, Yelena, come.*

She could still see his face as he ran from her, laughing, sliding wildly but keeping his feet nevertheless. Thinking about it now, she realized how odd it had been for him to behave that way. Her father had never been a risk taker, but something about that day had made him crazy, had changed him. She wondered if he had been drinking. There was always drink on his breath, a faint smell of spirits, but she wondered if he had drunk more than usual to kill the pain of that terrible birthday. She could see his flushed face now, the plume of breath shooting from his mouth as he capered and danced. She had tried to follow, but had slipped and fallen.

Come, Yelena. Head up. Bend your knees.

She tried to get up, but fell over again, and a third time. It hurt. She started crying. But her father wouldn't give in.

Yelena, come to me!

She struggled up again, the tears rolling down her cheeks. She was afraid of the ice and afraid of her father—afraid above all of disappointing him. Biting her lip, she pushed off again, reaching out for him. And then suddenly she could do it, she could skate. She ran hard at the flat whiteness and then jammed her little boots in a long skid. It had felt like flying through the air. The tears froze on her face.

They slipped and skidded further and further out.

When they eventually stopped to get their breath, they could no longer see the shore. They could not even see the tops of the trees. All around them was a uniform gray-white. It was impossible to distinguish the sky from the lake's frozen surface.

Look, Yelena. Look at the ice.

Her father was standing over her, towering over her, pointing downward. She looked down at where their feet had scuffed the thin layer of snow and saw blackness.

Ellen jumped as someone close by hit their horn. One of the kids waiting by the entrance came running over and climbed into a dark blue pickup. She shook herself and turned the ignition. Riverside Drive was busy with fast-moving traffic, and the cars were having to get in line to leave the parking lot. She found herself waiting behind the pickup, staring at the word TOYOTA in big white letters.

The darkness of the lake—with her now, sufficiently present to give her gooseflesh. Reaching out of the frigid depths, she had seen ribbons of weed, the twisted knuckle of a frozen branch. A memory of her mother had come to her in that moment—the way she had looked a week before her death. The cancer had eaten her muscle tissue until there was almost nothing left. Her hands were clenched across her chest, the fingers locked together against the pain. In the last few days her chin settled somehow so that her top teeth seemed prominent. Looking down through the ice, it had been as if Ellen had suddenly felt what death was, how numb, how dark. In panic she had grabbed her father's legs. The ice was just a skin, a skin on darkness.

Someone behind her leaned on their horn. The pickup in front of her was nosing its way into the middle of the road, trying to make a left. A Lexus braked and swerved, cutting around the front. Suddenly Ellen realized that a small group of people on the sidewalk were looking at her. She recognized one of the older kids from Sam Ritt's class.

"That's Ellen Cusak," he shouted, pointing for the benefit of what looked like his girlfriend. "Ex-world champion."

The girl leaned forward until her face was just a couple of feet from the car window. Ellen smiled, not noticing the camera. The flashgun went off in her face just as the driver behind her hit his horn again. With a screech of tires the Toyota completed its turn. Ellen swung out behind it. She didn't see the Buick until it was too late.

7

Jackie rented one of the ground-floor units of a brick building in Van Nuys, only three miles from his home. It was Golding who had found her the place; he had wanted her to be near enough so that they could see each other without too much trouble.

She opened the door in her housecoat. It looked like she'd been wearing it all day.

"Hey, sis."

He walked in, pecking her on the cheek as he went past, and put the groceries he was carrying on the dining table. Jackie pointed.

"What's this?"

"I just called in at Vons," said Golding. He draped his jacket over the back of a chair. "Thought you might need some stuff."

The brown paper bag was full of vegetables and fruit, things Jackie wouldn't normally touch. They had endless rows about the way she ate and the junk she put into her body. As a less confrontational alternative, he had taken to bringing stuff over from the supermarket, hoping that some of it would end up on a plate. Of course

Jackie knew what he was doing, but she generally let it go with just a significant look.

Her face was a little puffy tonight, her eyes red. He wondered if she had been crying. When they were kids, people had often mistaken them for twins, even though there was a year between them. They'd had the same sandy brown hair and blue eyes, but Jackie's features had been a softer, feminine version of his own. She had been beautiful. Since then, since adolescence, she had gained weight, losing control altogether in the past few years, blowing up to just under two hundred pounds, so that her fine features were lost, leaving just her beautiful eyes staring out at him from simpler, happier times.

"What time did you get back?" said Golding.

Jackie touched at her throat.

"I didn't go in," she said.

They went through to the kitchen, and Jackie pulled a couple of beers out of the refrigerator. There was a dirty glass on the table next to the ashtray where John kept his half-smoked roaches. Jackie told him how she had woken up feeling sick and had called in to the diner to say she wouldn't be making it. Golding shrugged and looked down at his Bud.

"How was your day?" Jackie said.

"Oh, you know, the usual. I served some papers on a guy. I'm going to go see Ellen Cusak tomorrow."

"The figure skater?"

"The very same."

He sipped his beer, trying to think of something to add, something light and inconsequential, but it just wouldn't come. He looked up at his sister's lovely eyes.

"So this heater . . ." he said.

She struggled up out of the chair and led him through to the closet where the hot-water heater was housed. They talked about the problem as Golding stared in at the white enamel tank, at the spaghetti of pipes with their regulating gauges.

Jackie was watching, waiting to see what he would do. She liked to see him do things. It was as if it reassured her to see him making sense of the world with his hands.

"Mom called," she said.

She was standing close behind him, so that he could hear her breathing through her open mouth, could smell the sweat in her clothes. He reached out and turned a small plastic knob, watching one of the gauges, hoping he was doing the right thing.

"She's out of the hospital," said Jackie. "It went well apparently."

His mother had suffered a bad fall, and had gone into the hospital to have a hip replacement. Golding knew about all this through Jackie. He hadn't spoken to his mother in ten years. He kept his eyes on the gauge. It didn't move even a little bit.

"She says she's going to keep the house. There's a woman next door who's going to come by to see if she needs anything."

The needle flickered and dropped a little.

"Don't you even care?" said Jackie.

He turned and looked at her face. Up close he could see the scribble of thread veins on her cheeks.

"Sure," he said. "Sure. I'm glad she's okay."

Jackie frowned. She looked like she was going to say something significant, something like he should call his mother, that they should try to get together, that they should try to break the ice. But she was too tired. Too tired or too down. She looked past him into the darkness. She asked if he thought it was going to be okay now.

8

There was still a scraping sound when she turned the wheel to the right. The fender on the driver's side had taken most of the impact, but there was damage to the door as well. She didn't even want to think what it would cost to get it fixed. The Buick had come off a lot better—it just had a cracked headlight and a broken radiator grille. The guys inside had been understanding. They were English, over in L.A. on business, and the Buick was a rental. Anyone could see that the accident was her fault, and that meant she would be paying the excess and taking the hike in her insurance premiums. Worse than that, she wouldn't be able to sell the Mercedes until the whole thing was sorted out.

She was back on the freeway when her portable phone rang.

"Ellen?"

It was Lenny. He immediately launched into an energetic monologue, saying how well the lunch had gone with Knapp-Weinstein.

"Do you think they really want to do it?"

"I can't say for sure. But they want to meet you. In my experience that's a very good sign."

"Great. When?"

"They suggested next Wednesday."

"Count me in."

"You're breaking up on me. Are you in the car?"

"Yeah, what's left of it. I managed to crash the Merc. I was down at the Pickwick arena."

"Shit! You okay?"

"Don't worry, I'm fine. It was just a bump."

Lenny talked about a couple of near misses he'd recently had. He was thinking of replacing his Lexus with something bigger, a sports utility vehicle maybe.

"So, how'd it go with this Tigger kid?" he said eventually.

"Good, she's great."

"Sam Ritt says she reminds him of you."

"She's nothing *like* me," said Ellen, more emphatically than she had meant to.

"Nothing like as good I guess, but—"

"I didn't mean that. She's very good. Really good. She just doesn't—she's completely fearless. For her the ice is just slippery white stuff."

There was a moment's silence.

"And big Sam?" said Lenny uncertainly. *Slippery white stuff?* She had confused them both.

"Same as ever. He asked me if I was eating properly."

"Good, good."

"Wanted to know if I was getting enough carbohydrates."

"Really? Well, that's good."

This was too many *good*s. Even for Lenny. Ellen decided to help him out.

"So—Lenny, what's the—?"

"Oh yeah, I forgot to mention." There was a rustling of papers. "I spoke to some friends of mine about your problem."

"What problem?"

"The *letters* guy. The Ice Man or whatever he calls himself."

Ellen shivered. She cut over to the right lane. She was two exits from her turnoff. She hadn't told Lenny yet about the late-night calls.

I'm going to change your life, Yelena.

"Lenny, we don't even know—"

"We don't know anything, I know. But anyway I spoke to some people who know what to do in these— in these cases, and they're sending a guy over to talk to you tomorrow."

"Jesus, Lenny."

"No big deal. We have the meeting with Barbara Christian, and then we bring in this guy."

She pressed the heel of her palm to her forehead. She had completely forgotten about Barbara Christian. She was coming over to discuss the sports biography. Where was her head?

"Lenny, I—"

"I know, honey, but I think you gotta bite the bullet on this one. And I'm telling you this guy's the best."

She looked across to the Santa Monica mountains— in the dying light a dark, brooding hump.

"Lenny, he spoke to me last night."

"Who did?"

"This person. Whoever's been writing the letters."

She heard a sharp intake of breath, followed by a bout of violent coughing.

"Jesus—Jesus *Christ*. What did—did he say any-thing?"

"He said he was going to change my life."

"Change your life? The freakin' psycho! Well, listen—honey—Ellen . . . Jesus, you didn't say anything back?"

"He hung up before I had a chance."

"Thank God." There was a moment of silence as Lenny collected his thoughts. "Honey, listen—rule number one. *Don't engage.* Ever. Okay? Rule number two: *Never forget rule number one.* If he calls again, don't say anything."

"Maybe I should just change my number."

"No good."

"What?"

"He'll just find the new one. If you got the right equipment you can stand out in the street and get the number. Reynolds, the guy I was talking to, he was explaining all about it. It's ingenious what these people can do."

This was the worst of it.

"But how? How can they?"

"How should I know? I'm not a stalker."

"So—?"

"So like I was saying, we get a professional to deal with it. I went down to this firm, Alpha Global. Reynolds runs it, an ex-cop, and this other guy, a shrink with diplomas up to the ceiling. These people *know* from nutcases, I'm telling you. And this guy they're sending, Pete Golding, he's the best they've got. He's the guy who shot the Maddy Olsen stalker."

Ellen had a vague recollection of a face, of a man trying to hide his face from the camera, shots of a body on the sidewalk, blood next to the head like a cartoon speech bubble. She shuddered.

"But, Lenny, aren't these guys incredibly expensive? There's no way I can afford to pay the kind of—"

"They're very reasonable, believe me. They checked out the letters for nothing. Plus I negotiated a special rate. It has to be worth it, just for the peace of mind. You can't be too careful in this town."

The electronic gate swings open and the big Kraut car noses into the driveway. His pulse quickens as he raises the binoculars, sees her perfect, snow-queen face in the glow of the dashboard. Her blond hair is tied back, the way she wears it when she's been on the ice. Something glistens on her mouth. Saliva, he thinks, or maybe lip gloss. She stops outside the garage doors. Another signal and the doors open. She drives inside, thinking she is safe.

Maria was in the kitchen chopping vegetables with the twelve-inch Kitchen King. On the stove the big chrome steamer jiggled and hissed. Now was the time to say something, Ellen knew that. It was kinder to tell her now, give her the chance to get a good job lined up elsewhere, than to wait until things got out of hand. Ellen smiled, struggling to hide how bad she felt.

"Taking a sauna, Maria?" she said, dumping her sports bag on a chair.

Maria smiled back through the steam and leaned forward to flip on the exhaust fan.

"It's good for my skin."

"There's nothing wrong with your skin," said Ellen. It was true. Maria, though short and a little on the heavy side, was pretty, with beautiful dark eyes.

"Because here I have the sauna," she said, waving the big knife at the cloud of steam.

Ellen reached into the refrigerator for a bottle of water.

"Maria, there's—"

"There were some calls while you were out," said Maria, significantly. "A Mr. Kit Walker left an interesting message."

Kit was a guy she'd met at a couple of parties. He was supposed to be an old friend of Doug's, but now he was circling her for a date. She hadn't really made up her mind about him.

"Oh, right. Thanks."

"Laura Mead also. A charity thing, she said."

"Laura, right."

"Plus Lenny," said Maria with a shrug, as if Lenny didn't count.

Ellen nodded, then took a sip from the cold bottle.

"The thing is, Maria—"

"And I *also* had a call."

"You did?" said Ellen, confused.

"From my little Teresita. It's her first communion this Sunday. She's so excited about it."

"Her first communion," Ellen said, feeling her resolve beginning to weaken. "That's . . . that's wonderful."

Maria turned to her, the big Kitchen King still in her hand.

"And she wanted me to tell you that you're invited. She said I was not to take no for an answer."

Ellen smiled and nodded.

"Of course," she said. "I wouldn't miss it for the world."

He moves swiftly through the trees, the dusty earth cushioning his steps. There is a light on in the kitchen: the housekeeper making supper. He sees her shadow move across the blinds. Approaching unseen through the deepening darkness, he feels the hum of the Benzedrine, and beneath it, like a deep tidal flow, a hard, euphoric vitality more powerful than any drug.

He stoops, crosses the road, then heads along the western side of the property. The smell of the spruce is heavy in the warm air. Halfway down he checks around him and ducks through dead foliage into the garden.

Despite the care and the time and the effort she had put into the house, Ellen wanted to be rid of it now. In every corner of every room there were memories that reminded her of the failure of her marriage. It had been too big even when Doug was there. For her at least, it was always meant to be a family house. Now it felt empty, hollow. The discovery of the body next to the pool house had made it all worse. The leak from the pool was fixed now, but she still hadn't gotten around to asking her once-a-week gardener to refill it.

She walked into the living room, zapped the stereo into life, and then went up to the second-floor landing, where she entered what had become her bedroom. Maria had laid clean towels on the bed with the light cotton bathrobe she used as a housecoat. She had moved out of the main bedroom three months earlier, when it had finally become clear that the divorce was going ahead. Nothing had ever been said to Maria about it. She had simply noted the change of arrangements and gone with the flow.

The room was simply furnished with a divan bed against the wall facing the window and an ornate late Victorian secretary upon which stood a babushka doll, the only memento from Kiev that her father had allowed her to bring. It had been touched and handled so much over the years that most of the enamel on the outside had worn away, and it was missing the innermost figure. The vibrant yellow walls of the room were broken up by a series of black abstract linocuts that Doug had picked out in consultation with the decorator. Ellen had always found them pretentious and oppressive, but had yet to get around to replacing them. As in all the other bedrooms, there were French doors leading directly onto the balcony that ran around the second floor.

She pulled the T-shirt and sports bra over her head and stood for a moment looking at herself in the small gilded mirror. In an unconscious gesture of effacement she covered her breasts with her hands, and focused on her face. She looked tired. Staring at herself, taking in the regular, clean features and the big green eyes, she was, as always, mildly puzzled by what she saw. When she had first started to be noticed on the ice, the press had referred to her as a melancholy Slavic beauty, a magical snow queen, and it had annoyed her intensely. She had always considered herself a cheerful, straightforward person with her back firmly turned to Russia and all its spiritual sentimentality. But looking at herself now, noticing faint dabs of shadow under her eyes, noticing the pallor that was beyond blondness, she could see that she was starting to look like the melancholy person the press so enjoyed talking about.

Then she did what she always did in these introspective bedroom moments—she went through to the bathroom and stepped on the scale. It was something she had done for as long as she could remember. In the bad old days when she was having problems with eating, it was something she might have done ten or twelve times a day. The needle flickered on 116 pounds.

Humming softly to herself, she turned on the shower and stepped under the stream of warm water.

He sees the lights go on in the bathroom and steps into the middle of the lawn, hoping to catch a glimpse of her through the narrow gap in the drapes. In a few moments steam begins to drift across the ceiling. He holds his breath, listening, picking out the faint hiss of water above the sound of the music. He nods slowly, understanding: now she will not be able to hear him.

He reaches into his pocket and takes out the pick gun, a solid black cylinder the size of a small flashlight. It cost him just under five hundred dollars but it opens most pin tumbler locks in a couple of seconds. He reaches the corner of the house, sees the open door.

Maria pushed the chopped carrots into the steamer and then put back the lid. Behind her cool air drifted in from the garden. She had switched off the fan. The noise annoyed her, and keeping the door open was the best way to clear the kitchen of steam and cooking smells. She turned from the stove, the heavy knife in her right hand.

Ellen came down the stairs, tying the robe around her. The music had stopped. She could hear the sound of the radio coming from the kitchen. Maria had pulled the drapes shut but there was a draft coming from somewhere. Cool air chilled her ankles. Next door's dog was barking again.

She walked over to the baby grand piano—another of Doug's "lifestyle" purchases—and stood looking at the photographs they had put up over the walnut drinks cabinet. When Doug had lived there, the wall had been virtually covered with pictures, mostly of Doug and other celebrities having a great time. He had taken his favorite snaps when he had moved out—pictures of him sharing a joke with Jonathan Demme, him pretending to strangle a studio head Ellen couldn't remember the name of, him eating seafood with Kiefer Sutherland—and Ellen had filled the gaps with pictures from her past: a pram in a smudgy Kiev street, a small dog on a blanket, formal black and whites of her mother and father, their carefully coifed heads tilted slightly within the frame. Looking at the picture of her mother, she had a sharp recollection of clasped hands, of pain, of a submerged branch twisted by the strength of ice.

"Maria?"

The sound of her voice, its smallness, made the house seem, if anything, emptier.

"Maria?"

She walked back into the hallway. She felt the draft again, heard saucepan lids rattling on the kitchen stove.

"Maria, are you . . . ?"

The kitchen was empty. Two of the burners were still on. One of the saucepans was boiling over.

"Maria?"

Something told her to look for the knife. Her gaze came to rest on the chopping board. It wasn't there.

"Maria, where are you?"

Cool air touched her face. She jerked around and saw the open door. It moved slightly in the breeze. Next door's dog was going crazy.

"Maria? Are you out here?"

She took another step. The air was cold on her throat. Cactus leaves speared the gloom behind the house. Her heart jumped as she saw the figure coming along the path. She jerked back from the threshold and pulled the door shut. A hand slammed against the glass, a hand holding a knife.

Ellen let out a shriek.

"Mrs. Cusak! Mrs. Cusak! Let me in."

Maria's face pressed against the glass.

It took Ellen a moment to take in what had happened. She fumbled for the catch and opened the door. Maria came into the kitchen pale-faced.

"My God, Maria, you scared the hell out of me."

Maria, wide-eyed and gasping for breath, pointed at her with the knife.

"You scare *me*. I thought the door close with the wind, and I'm locked out in the garden."

"What the hell were you doing out there?"

"Cutting parsley."

She showed the bunch of parsley in her left hand. The smell of the herb was pungent and sweet.

"With that damned knife?" said Ellen, beginning to laugh.

Then the phone was ringing. Still laughing, she snatched it up.

"Hello?"

Nothing. The barking dog. Her heart started to jolt before she'd had time to work out what was wrong.

"Hello? Who is this?"

Nothing.

"She's . . ."

A man's voice. *Him.*

"Look, you—" Ellen pressed her hand against her

mouth, remembering Lenny's rule. She could hear the dog barking clearly. It was confusing.

"She looks so pretty in that blue dress. Don't you think she looks pretty, Yelena?"

And then the line went dead.

9

A length of yellow crime scene tape was plainly visible from the terrace. Lenny watched it twist in the breeze, sheltering his eyes from the bright morning sun.

"Mrs. Cusak sends apologies," said Maria, handing him a cup of coffee. "She'll be down in just a minute."

"Right, yeah, thanks," said Lenny distractedly, still watching the tape and the tarpaulin behind it, wondering now if it was helpful or not it being there, asking himself if it didn't add a kind of macabre mystique to the Ellen Cusak story—as Gil Knapp had implied—and then worrying if macabre mystique was really where they wanted to go.

He took a sip of coffee, wondering how curious Barbara Christian was going to be about the discovery of the body. Was she going to ask about it? He hadn't considered the possibility before, but maybe her interest in doing the biography had been prompted by the story, at least in part. Of course, everyone knew that the property had been no more than a construction site when the corpse had been buried, that it had nothing to do with Ellen herself, but maybe Christian saw it as emblematic of something—of bad luck, a kind of curse. The idea made Lenny uncomfortable: Ellen as the victim of dark, unseen forces. It had its appeal certainly—its mystique—but Ellen herself would never go for it. Just getting her to talk candidly about her skating career was going to be tough enough, let alone her failed marriage.

He turned and went back into the house, shaking his head. It had always been a struggle with Ellen Cusak, and always would be. She was talented and charming and ready to work, but she just couldn't separate her private and public selves. She took everything too personally.

"Sorry, Lenny. I didn't know what to put on."

Ellen came into the room, smiling, tucking a pin into the back of her hair, holding another between her teeth. She had chosen a pair of dark pants and a loose silk shirt. She looked sensational.

"No problem, no problem." Lenny grinned broadly, taking in the general effect. He would have preferred something more feminine, a dress maybe, something floral, but there was no denying it—the dark burgundy silk made her blondness all the more striking, you would have to be blind not to see her star potential.

Ellen sat down on one side of the sofa opposite, tucking her legs up under her. She smiled back at him.

"So how are you feeling?" said Lenny. "It was great to hear about the coaching thing, by the way. How's that going?"

"Terrific." Ellen looked down at a big Lalique ring she was wearing, then gave a nod. "Tina is . . . I really think I can help. I mean I really think I can add something to her performance."

"Great." Lenny frowned. There was something on her mind, he could tell. "Working with kids. That's great, really great. Sometimes I wish I'd . . . you know, with my kids. But, hey, can you picture me on skates? Little bald guy like me? People'd think I was the puck."

He leaned back in the chair, laughing. It came naturally to him, making jokes at his own expense. It put people at their ease, usually.

" 'Course they're pretty much grown-up now, the kids. Sammy went skiing last spring with some college friends. Didn't much care for it, though, his mom says. I guess he takes after his old man. Anything under sixty-five degrees and I'm running for cover."

He looked at Ellen for a moment, the smile dying on his lips.

"Any decision from the video people?" she said.

Lenny shook his head.

"Not yet. Tell you the truth, I don't think Gil Knapp's the one we should be talking to. Abe Weinstein's the man. This is more his thing. That's why I fixed to go over to their offices next week. This time they'll *both* be there."

"Right." Ellen nodded. "That's good."

"Yuh. They're on La Cienega. Anyway . . ." —Lenny drew out the words. "It would be helpful if, er . . ."

"You want me to be there?"

"I think it might help. This is partly an image thing, Ellen. We can't run away from that. And it could *really* help us right now."

"No problem. I'll be there. You can count on it."

Lenny smiled.

"That's great, Ellen. They're gonna love you, I know. Now, let's talk about Barbara Christian. She's a very good writer. Still on her way up, but I'm hearing lots of good

things about her. Did you catch that piece of hers in the
New Yorker?" He lifted a hand from the armrest to prevent Ellen from answering, although she hadn't made a
sound. "Who cares? Who reads that thing anyway? More
to the point, her Nicole Bobek book just missed *The New
York Times* best-seller list. I think she's exactly who we
want for this thing. And she has integrity. Lots of it. We
can trust her not to . . . you know . . . to . . ."

Ellen was staring out into the garden, towards the pool
house, searching for something, it seemed like. For a moment there was silence. Then she turned back to him.

"To what?"

"Well, to, er . . . sensationalize. You know how it . . . *can
happen*. But I'm sure it won't happen with her. She's a
good writer. She knows how to make the most of what
she has—I mean, the facts. She doesn't need to make it
up." He nodded slowly, eyes narrowed, the shrewd manager. "I think the two of you'll hit it off, I really do."

He took a sip of coffee. He checked his watch again.
It was ten minutes after ten. The meeting was scheduled
for quarter past.

"Ellen. You are happy about the bio, right?"

She took a moment to answer.

"Yes, absolutely. I mean, I'd like to . . ."

Lenny eased forward in his chair, anxious to pick up
what she was about to say. But she didn't say anything.

"Ellen, honey, are you okay? You look like you've
seen a ghost."

She pressed a palm to her forehead.

"Sorry, Lenny. I'm just a bit . . ." She took a deep
breath. "He called again last night. The guy—the Ice
Man. I'm not sure . . . I'm not sure, but I think he was
outside the house."

"*What?*"

"When he called I could hear a dog barking in the background. It sounded weird. Like . . . like an echo."

"An echo? But if he was on the phone, how could he be—?"

"There was a dog outside. Mr. Glazer's dog, barking. Last night I realized . . ."

Lenny looked confused: "You heard the dog outside or on the phone?"

Ellen looked at him.

"Both."

It took a moment for Lenny to understand what she meant: the stalker was outside when he made the call, and the dog was barking at him. His head snapped around to the window.

"Jesus, Ellen, no wonder you couldn't sleep."

Ellen hunched her shoulders together, pushing her hands between her knees. She seemed to grow smaller, frailer. It looked like the big sofa was about to swallow her up. It struck Lenny that the whole house was like that now. It had been designed as a family house, but there was no family in it, just Ellen and a housekeeper.

"Still," he said. "You can't be sure, right? I mean, echoes . . . it could have been just the acoustics playing tricks on you."

"Maybe."

"What did, er . . . what did he say?"

"Something about a . . . a dress. It didn't make any sense."

"Well, that's good." Lenny pointed a finger at her. "That's good because the crazier they are the more harmless they are. I have that from an expert. Apparently most of these bozos can't even tie their own shoelaces in the real world."

Ellen didn't look reassured.

"The guy's probably delusional," Lenny went on. "You have to remember that. He may seem dangerous to you, but in reality he needs medication for a trip to the store."

"He got hold of my number, though. He found my unlisted number."

Lenny shook his head regretfully and brushed something off the arm of his tan sports coat.

"You know, Ellen, that isn't so hard. Not as hard as it should be anyhow. People trade in these things. Just check out the Internet. Jesus, you wouldn't believe what's on there." He held up his hands, changing tack. "In any case, you don't have to worry. Just leave it to the man from Alpha Global Protection. He'll take care of it, believe me."

"He'll be here at noon?"

"Right. My guess is you've heard the last of this lunatic already."

Ellen slid her legs off the sofa.

"We don't even know who he is."

"Oh, I think these guys'll find him," said Lenny, grinning knowingly. "They're professionals. And when they do . . . well, let's just say, they know how to make an impression."

"I just *loved* you on that breakfast show," said Barbara Christian, pointing at Ellen with four manicured fingers. "Very classy."

Ellen put down her orange juice, shaking her head in disbelief.

"I hated doing that show. And I really messed up, too. Let's be honest."

"You did not," Lenny protested.

"I did. They pretty much told me what they were going to ask beforehand, but when the time came I . . . I just didn't have the answers."

"You were spontaneous," said Lenny. "You were natural. It was great."

"Just great," echoed Christian, taking a sip of black coffee. "And the *camera* loved you. They just couldn't wait to come in close."

"That's just what I always say," said Lenny, shaking his head. "The camera loves her. She's a natural."

"I had to be up at five-thirty for that show," Ellen said. "I must've looked like death warmed over."

"You looked great," said Lenny. "Have you actually seen how you looked? Did you make yourself a tape?" Ellen shook her head. "Well, I did, and I'm gonna send you a copy. Then you can see for yourself."

Christian nodded reassuringly. She was about seven or eight years older than Ellen, with auburn hair that tumbled in curls to her shoulders. High cheekbones and big dark eyes gave her an appearance of guilelessness, even innocence.

"Seriously, Ellen," she said, dropping her voice to a gentle woman-to-woman level, "that interview was a good move. I'm sure you'll get more invitations on the back of it, provided you can keep the ball rolling."

"It's rolling," said Lenny immediately. "The Ford commercial's on all the time. I've heard the company's very happy. Then we've got *Nutcracker* for the fall and"—Lenny shot a glance at Ellen—"we're this close to a major video deal."

"Great," said Christian. "I certainly feel the time's right for a bio, don't you? I mean, quite apart from . . . all the stuff you've mentioned, Lenny, there's a lot of interest in Doug Gorman. And you've got insights on him, Ellen, that nobody else has, in the whole world. It's perfect."

Lenny felt suddenly warm. He knew they would have

to get around to the subject of Doug Gorman and the failed marriage, but so soon?

"Well, of course," he said before Ellen could respond, "five years of marriage, it's a part of the story, no doubt about it. Has to be. But we don't want this book to be about Doug Gorman. This is Ellen's story. We should—"

"Sure," said Christian. "And I want to go right back too. I always think the childhood is key." She put her head on one side and looked at Ellen with a thoughtful, dreamy expression on her face. "It must have been tough, leaving your home country at the age of—what was it?—fourteen. Leaving your family and your friends at that age. Terrible."

Ellen took a deep breath. Lenny could tell she was already uncomfortable.

"It was for the best," she said quietly, almost to herself. "My father . . ."

Christian waited for her to finish her sentence, and then, seeing that she wasn't going to, said: "Did he ask you if you wanted to leave?"

"Yes," said Ellen, a little too quickly. "Of course. It was for the best. I knew that."

"You must have been very close," said Christian. "He must have been all you had, for a long time."

Lenny fought the urge to change the subject. He never mentioned Ellen's father these days. His loss was a wound that would probably never completely heal. But he had to let Barbara Christian do a little probing. She had to go away thinking there was something intriguing about Ellen Cusak, or she wouldn't want to do the book.

Ellen looked down into her lap for a moment, and then up again.

"Yes," she said. "That's right."

Christian smiled, a patient, understanding smile that

Lenny knew masked frustration. If Ellen wasn't ready to talk about her marriage or her upbringing, the book would need to spend a lot of pages discussing the intricacies of the triple axel. Trying to keep the subject alive, he pointed to the wall above the drinks cabinet where a large cluster of framed photographs were hung together.

"Stepan Cusak's in most of those pictures," he said. "The one on the left? Handsome guy, huh? You can see where Ellen got her looks."

Immediately Christian put down her coffee and stood up to get a closer look.

"Yes, I can see. Was he the one who first taught you to skate, Ellen?"

"I wouldn't have skated at all if it wasn't for him," said Ellen. "I actually didn't like it at first. I was afraid."

"Of falling?"

"Of . . . the ice. It was . . . It's a hard thing to explain. I was just a child."

Christian smiled at her and turned back to the pictures. In one, a twenty-something Stepan Cusak, his hair short, slicked back, was accepting a prize from a clutch of burly-looking old men in heavy coats. In another, smaller picture, black-and-white like the other, but blurred where the other was sharp, he was standing in a park next to a slim blond woman who must have been Ellen's mother. A formal portrait of the pair hung directly beneath it.

"And this must be you as a child," she said. "How old were you—four, five?"

Ellen took a sip of juice.

"I don't have any pictures of me then," she said without looking up. "They were lost."

"Who is it, a niece?"

Ellen frowned over her glass.

"I don't have a niece."

Christian went on studying the picture: a young girl on skates smiling at the camera, late-evening sunlight, the photographer's shadow stretched out across the ice. It was different from the others: the colors clear and unfaded, the image sharp. It could have been taken that very day. The frame was different too; the others were all of dark wood, professionally mounted. This one was plastic, with a thin line of imitation gold paint around the edge, the kind they sold in drugstores. It wasn't hanging straight either, as if somebody had put it up in a hurry.

"She's so pretty," said Christian, "in that blue dress."

Ellen froze.

"So who is it?" Christian asked.

Ellen was on her feet, walking towards the picture on stiff legs.

"Ellen?"

It was hanging where another photograph had been, a photograph of her at Lake Arrowhead, at her first competition.

"Ellen, is something—?"

The glass shattered against the corner of the table. Christian leapt back.

"Jesus! What the—?"

"He's in the house. Lenny, he's *in the house.*"

Lenny was braced against the armrests of his chair.

"What? Ellen, what's . . . What are you talking about?" He tried to laugh, like nothing was really going on, like it was a piece of fun. "We'd better get that mopped up. Barbara, I hope you didn't—"

"Listen to me, that picture"—Ellen was still backing away from it, pointing, her foot crunching broken glass—"I've never seen it before. He *put* it there."

Lenny got up.

"Ellen, what are you . . . ?" He still had a crooked grin on his face. "The picture?"

"We have to—we have to call the police."

She was hyperventilating, almost hysterical. Lenny grabbed her by the arms.

"Hey, calm down, okay?"

She pulled herself free.

"He was outside last night. He must have found a way in."

And before he could say anything else she was gone. He could hear her calling Maria's name through the house.

When he turned around, Barbara Christian was looking at the photograph again.

"I, er . . ." He shook his head. "The truth is, Ellen's been having a little trouble lately. Since you're in the loop, you might as well know."

"Trouble?"

"Some crazy guy. Writes these sick letters, and now he's calling. Seems he got in here somehow."

Christian fixed him with her dark eyes.

"My, how awful," she said flatly. She looked back at the picture.

"Yeah, well, what can you say? It's the price of fame."

Christian nodded. With a finger she reached out and gently pushed at one corner of the frame so that it hung straight. "Kind of looks like her, though, doesn't it?"

10

Leaning against the trunk of the tree, he focused the binoculars on a gap in the foliage, got green blur then curved steps shading down into the blue of an empty pool—imagined Ellen Cusak doing laps—then panned right, hoping to get a look at the pool house where they'd found the girl. He picked out a coiled garden hose on a patch of grass, a sun lounger—no sign of any towel—and then just leaves. Leaves and flowers.

There weren't many places on this side of the hill that afforded a clear view of the house. The road was narrow, snaking back and forth as it climbed. Golding had gone all the way up and then down again, looking for a place to pull off. Only here, close to a hairpin bend that cut through a cluster of thirsty-looking pines, could he tuck the car away so that it didn't cause an obstruction. He had to pick his way through the prickly undergrowth for about twenty yards before the red tiles of the roof came into view.

Even in the shade it was way too hot. Golding had left his lightweight suit in the closet, thinking it was proba-

bly better to show up in something a little more professional. But now he was regretting it. The blue wool
snagged against his knees, and when he took off the
jacket he had sweat patches across his chest. He wiped
his eyelids on his shirtsleeve and raised the binoculars
again, this time taking in the side of the house. The shutters were closed, all except one on the second floor. He
could see the end of a bed, a carved wooden footboard,
a dressing gown or a dress draped across it. It looked
like a small room, too small for the master bedroom.
That would be at the back of the property, giving onto
the balcony and with a view of the garden.

Then something moved. There was someone in the
bedroom. He tightened the focus, held it, waited. A
slight figure in dark clothing was walking back and
forth. Then through the unsteady lenses he saw a young
woman's face. She was standing directly in the front of the
window, her palms pressed together. It took him a while
to realize that he was looking at Ellen Cusak. She looked
different from the magazine photos: smaller, paler. The
healthy glow of exercise, or maybe makeup, was missing. She looked like an ordinary person.

Where it gave onto Brooklake, the Cusak property
was protected by a chain-link fence, more or less completely smothered by thickly growing spruce. The gate—
horizontal bars welded to a steel frame—kept any casual
callers at the bottom of the drive, where there was a
buzzer in one of the granite posts. As soon as Golding
got out of the car, a dog started up next door. All around
him similar properties dozed behind magnolia and ficus.
He pressed the buzzer, looking for the video camera in
the bushes, but there was none. A woman's voice, slightly
distorted by the intercom, asked what he wanted.

Eventually the gate swung open and he drove on up the drive, parking next to a red Lexus that was in front of the garage doors.

The maid showed him through to a high-ceilinged sitting room. Left alone for a moment, he stood with his back next to the big French windows, enjoying the almost chilly air-conditioned atmosphere and checking out the room. Decorated in a mixture of modern and antique, it struck him as a little too clean, a little too tasteful. Except for a wall full of photographs over by the grand piano it lacked any sign of personal involvement or interest. It was the kind of room you'd pick out of *Architectural Digest*—the kind you'd have your decorator buy.

The maid returned with iced tea.

"Please make yourself comfortable," she said. "Someone will be down soon."

Golding smiled, sipped, and listened, hearing voices from somewhere upstairs now. A man's—low, remonstrating—and then a woman's—plaintive, monosyllabic. He took a seat, tugging the pants clear of his knees, and noticed a wet patch on the carpet—pieces of broken glass.

He was squatting down, picking little fragments out of the carpet, when a small, balding guy in a tan sports jacket entered the room.

"Lenny Mayot." He shot out a hand. "How're you doing?"

Golding could see something was wrong.

Lenny took a seat opposite, seemed at a loss what to say, and then started to talk about Alpha Global and the rents you had to pay in Century City. After a minute on that he ran out of steam. Then fell silent.

Golding touched at his tie.

"Mr. Mayot?"

Lenny gave him a rueful look.

"She thinks the guy's been in here," he said.

And he started talking. It took him about five minutes to go through the whole story: the phone calls, the barking dog, the picture on the wall.

"She thinks maybe last night."

Golding put his drink down on the coffee table.

"So—where is she?"

"Upstairs." Lenny jabbed a thumb at the ceiling. "I don't think she's coming down."

Something heavy hit the floor over their heads and they both looked up.

"I'm sorry, Mr. Mayot—"

"Lenny."

"Lenny. Tom Reynolds gave me the impression this was just—"

"Yeah, well it isn't anymore," said Lenny irritably, and he stood up. "This is the thing."

He walked over to the piano and pointed to a photograph of a young girl in skates. Golding came and stood next to him—spent a moment looking at the wall of photographs. He recognized Stepan Cusak from the magazine article.

The picture that wasn't supposed to be there showed a little girl in a blue dress.

"So this is her?" he said. "This is Ellen?"

It was obviously the wrong thing to say. Lenny moved his head around, his mouth working hard.

"No!" he managed to spit out eventually. "Jesus Christ. It isn't her and it's nobody she knows." Then he became still, looking hard at the picture. "Someone's just screwing with her head," he added in an undertone.

"Any idea who?"

Lenny considered this for a moment, then shrugged. Golding got the feeling he was holding something back.

"It just turned up," said Lenny. "Ellen noticed it for the first time today. Just now. We had a writer in here—Barbara Christian—she saw the whole damned thing. Great PR."

He pointed to another picture that was lying face-down on top of the grand piano.

"Whoever put this here put that one there—to make room, I guess. Nothing was taken as far as we can tell."

Golding lowered his face to the black lacquered surface. Two smeary marks were clearly visible.

"You haven't touched anything?"

"No. I figured they might be good for prints."

"You were right."

"I was going to call the police, but then I figured . . . You guys, you handle this kind of stuff, right?"

Golding nodded.

"Sure. We can dust for latents, do the whole scene. Grid search, fiber, fluids, everything. I just need to make a call. You're sure nothing's been taken?"

He looked up at the ceiling where the noise was coming from.

"She's going through her stuff. Underwear and suchlike. Make sure . . . you know, nothing's been handled."

Golding nodded.

"Have you checked the property for signs of forced entry?"

Lenny started patting at his pockets.

"No, I . . . like I said, this just . . . To tell you the truth, I have a thing I've got to do, and—"

"That's okay."

A woman's voice, straining for control.

They both turned.

She was standing at the bottom of the stairs. It looked like she had splashed her face with water and gotten some down the front of her silk shirt. Her green eyes were red as if she'd been crying. Lenny took a step towards her.

"Is there anything missing, honey?"

There was more iced tea for everyone. Lenny said he was there for her if she needed him, then left.

They started with the upstairs, going from room to room, Golding following behind, looking at all the windows and doors. He noticed motion detectors. Ellen explained that the alarm had been installed when the house was built.

"These are still working, right?" he said, pointing into a corner of the ceiling.

They were standing in the master bedroom.

"Sure. I mean, I think so."

"Do you set the alarm when you go to bed?"

She shook her head.

"I get up in the night. I've always been a light sleeper. I set the alarm off a couple of times when . . . when we first moved in here. I don't want to be punching in the code every time I get up for a drink of water."

She looked down at a big glass ring she was wearing.

"Anyway, I don't think he came in during the night."

"What makes you say that?"

She sighed, looked up at his face.

"Didn't Lenny go through all this?"

"If it's all the same to you, I'd like to hear your version, Mrs. Cusak."

She held herself in an empty embrace and frowned in concentration.

"Well, he called me again. I got home last night— maybe at eight o'clock. I took a shower, and when I went back downstairs he called. He said"—she shuddered, remembering the voice—"he said, 'She's so pretty in her blue dress.' No, wait. 'She's so pretty in that blue dress.' *That* blue dress, like he was referring me to the picture."

"So you think the picture was already on the wall?"

She nodded.

"Only you didn't see it?"

"I didn't notice it until it was pointed out to me this morning."

Golding thought for a second.

"So it could have been there for days."

"I don't think so. Maria dusts. She's real Catholic about dirt. She would have noticed the dime-store frame. And anyway—"

She looked at him levelly. Her thick lashes were damp from the tears. Golding felt something tighten at the base of his throat.

"Anyway what?"

"When he called me I think he was still here. On the property. I could hear next door's dog barking in the phone. Normally you don't hear it in the house so much because of the double glazing."

Golding looked out of the window, imagining the stalker sneaking around out there. The master bedroom looked directly out onto the empty swimming pool. He thought about telling her how visible she was from the road, then thought better of it. Something moving behind the pool house caught his eye. Yellow, shiny. Crime scene tape.

"Didn't the LAPD finish with that yet?" he said, almost to himself.

She shrugged.

"I think so. I just—I haven't gotten round to removing it."

He turned to look at her, and realized that she hadn't

been into the garden since they dug up the body. She was afraid.

"And this call, this was his second, right?"

"The second time he spoke anyway."

"Uh-hūh. What did he say the first time?"

Ellen took a deep breath.

"He said he was going to change my life."

"That all?"

"Yes."

"How did he sound?"

"Sound?"

"Angry? Aggressive?"

Ellen thought for a moment.

"I don't know. Not angry. A little nervous maybe."

"Nervous?"

Ellen shrugged.

"I don't know. I was half asleep. He sounded a little shaky. I'm not sure."

Golding resisted the temptation to go over it all again. What she was telling him didn't fit. The Ice Man's letters were so full of violence and hatred. They were gross, but simple. The calls, the placing of the picture, they were disturbing, yes, but in a very different way—a way he couldn't yet make sense of. *Someone's just screwing with her head,* her manager had said. What exactly did he mean?

"Anyway," he said, looking around at the airy, sunlit room, trying to strike a lighter note, trying to be a reassuring presence. "I guess you'd have heard if he'd tried to get in through here, right?"

She looked at the big bed.

"I don't sleep in this room," she said softly.

They continued around the floor, Golding making notes, checking locks. Everything was shut tight. When they came to the smallest guest room, he noticed her tense up. He looked in at the mess of clothes and scattered magazines. There was a smell of essential oil. Lavender. It was supposed to soothe you. Jackie used the same stuff. This was where she slept. It was the room where he'd seen her standing by the window.

"I think he got in downstairs," said Ellen. "I think he got in last night, sometime before he called."

Golding turned to face her on the landing.

"I went downstairs," she said. "When he called I got kind of scared, and when I went to find Maria she wasn't there."

"This is the maid, right? The one who likes to dust."

"She's more like a housekeeper."

They went back downstairs, and she led him through to the kitchen.

"This door was open. When I came in here looking for her I noticed it was open. She went out to look for herbs."

"And you think he got in then?"

"I had this feeling."

"Can I talk to Maria?"

Ellen checked her watch.

"She'll have gone now. She goes to the farmer's market Wednesdays."

He looked around the kitchen and noticed another door.

"Where does that lead?"

"To a kind of utility room."

They went through into neon light. Brick walls painted white. A cement floor. There was a washing machine and a freezer. Another door, this one leading to the garage. The dead bolt wasn't turned. Golding snapped it back and forth.

"These doors are normally locked, right?"

Ellen came forward under the striplight.

"Well, Maria's in and out of here a lot. To do laundry and stuff. But the garage door, I mean the big outside door, it's always locked. It locks automatically when you drive in."

Golding nodded.

"Right. On the same system as the gate. You open it with an electronic remote?"

"That's right. I don't even get out of the car. Doug insisted on it. He was real security conscious."

Golding smiled.

"I hate to tell you this, but there's a little black box you can buy in West Hollywood that'll open that garage door in about a minute."

She was watching him now, very still. Under the light her hair looked live, charged, lifting to her hand as she touched the top of her head. There were strands of red in among the yellow.

"These doors open on two basic frequencies," Golding continued. "Code's digital so chances are nobody's going to open it with his remote. But you get the right black box—we're talking subminiature computers that sequence twelve code combinations per second—and open sesame. Three hundred dollars a pop. Same thing for your front gate."

She pushed the hair back from her forehead. Her hand was trembling.

"Lenny says this guy, he can't go to the shops without taking a pill."

Golding put his head on one side.

"A pill?"

"*Yes.*" She was angry with him now, more petulant than angry. "How's he going to buy subminiature gizmos that . . . that—"

Golding held up his palms.

"Hold on a second. With all due respect, you don't know anything about him. We don't even know if it's the same guy that's writing the letters."

Ellen pressed her lips together.

"Well, thanks," she said. "That's very reassuring."

"I'm not trying to reassure you."

He looked away, remembering that Reynolds had sent him up there to do precisely that: reassure her. He took a breath.

"But you have these doors," he said. He went to the door that opened on the garage. "This one's kind of basic, but the lock on the other one's good."

"So I lock that, I make sure Maria locks that, and we're safe."

She wasn't safe. She was a beautiful woman in a big house in a town full of psychopaths. He wasn't going to lie to her. He went back to the door that led from the utility room back to the kitchen. It was a top-dollar steel door with a Medeco lock. He got down on his knees. Took out a credit card and slid it underneath. There was maybe a quarter of an inch of clearance. Too much. He got back up with a grunt.

"This door is steel," said Ellen, coming close, looking past him, "and it has a dead bolt. You turn the lock." She leaned forward and snapped the dead bolt over, touching his arm with her breast. "And there's no way you can open it."

The contact was fleeting, barely noticeable, but it seemed to tingle in his arm. Looking at her angry green eyes, he wondered if she'd even noticed.

"I'm not saying it's not a good door, Mrs. Cusak, but—but basically, unless it's a door that locks with a key from the inside, there are ways of opening it."

"Come on."

"Trust me. There are tools that'll do it, no problem. A firm called Intelligence Incorporated sells them. Look it up on the Net. There are tools that'll even—"

"I don't want to know."

She was backing away, returning to the safety of the house.

"Well, I'm sorry, but I think you need to know," said Golding, following her now. "The kitchen door's the same thing. In fact, all your exterior doors are vulnerable. Christ, you have a door through to the patio that has a pin tumbler lock. You might as well just leave that one open! And I'm not even talking about the glass everywhere. If somebody wanted to bust a window to get in, it would—"

He stopped himself. He'd gone too far. She wasn't ready for this, not yet.

They walked out into the heat of the early afternoon. He talked to her about changing the doors, about putting the alarm on, about things she could do without too much extra trouble or expense. It seemed to help.

"Maybe I should learn to use a gun," she said as they stopped by the edge of the empty pool.

Golding had a flash of Maddy Olsen saying the same thing. Standing on her patio, turning her clever dark eyes on him, asking him like it was a fun thing to think about. He had advised against it, too many people got shot by their own weapons. Either because of an accident or because the bad guy grabbed the gun.

"What do you think?" Ellen said, looking straight at him.

Golding shrugged.

"What did you tell Maddy Olsen?"

Like she was reading his mind. Golding swallowed hard, tried to look neutral.

"It turned out she already had a gun," he said.

He watched as she pushed a dry eucalyptus leaf with her foot, then he instinctively looked up through the trees towards the spot where he had parked only an hour ago.

"Dogs," he said. "Dogs are better than guns. They're warmer, friendlier. They can wag their tails . . ."

Ellen gave a theatrical shudder.

"Not for me. A cat maybe."

Golding nodded.

"Have to be a big cat."

"Or a small cat with attitude."

She looked for the crack in the pool but couldn't see any sign of it, and then realized what they had done by coming outside. A spell had been broken. The garden was hers again. She tried a smile but couldn't quite hold it.

"What do I do about the calls?" she asked.

"That's easy. You get a new line put in right away. I'll arrange a priority installation with the phone company this afternoon."

"But Lenny says I shouldn't do that. He says changing the number won't do any good."

Golding nodded.

"It won't. But that's not what we're gonna do. We give you a new number, but we keep the old one. Only we reroute it. That's what I'd suggest. No one calling will know that anything's changed, but the phone will be ringing in my office."

"In your office? Can you do that?"

"Absolutely. If this guy makes a traceable call we'll get to it right away. And everything he says will be taped for use as evidence."

"But what about—?"

"Of course you'll be advised of legitimate calls right away. Think of it as a kind of answering service."

Ellen hugged herself. It seemed like a good idea, but the thought that Golding and his people would be effectively screening her calls wasn't one she was comfortable with.

"Of course, if you prefer to keep the line here," Golding said, "that's fine. Just keep the answering machine on and don't pick up until you know who's calling."

"No." Ellen looked up at him. Lenny was right: it was time to put a stop to all this. "Reroute the line."

Golding smiled.

"Good. We'll also make sure you get Caller ID. If you hear from this guy on the new line, just hang up and get his number."

He watched her for a moment as she stood there looking down at the dry leaves in the empty pool, and was surprised to find himself feeling sorry for her. Despite her beauty, despite her fame, she was just a young woman, frightened and alone in a big house.

"Listen," he said. "Right now this guy probably seems like some kind of superman to you. You don't know who he is, you don't know what he wants, and you don't know how he's getting access."

She was watching him again, very still.

"But my guess—from the little I've seen, from this incident with the picture—is that for him the biggest thing is the sense of power he gets from doing this, the sense of control. You have to realize that power is important to him because generally he feels weak. This isn't the big bad wolf."

She nodded, but thinking about the guy's weakness didn't help.

Golding squatted down and tossed another leaf into the pool.

"This business with the photograph, what do you make of that?"

She shook her head.

"In these letters you've received, has there ever been any reference to a little girl, anything like that?"

"I wouldn't know. I don't look at them. I give them to Lenny."

"Oh."

He made a mental note to scan the letters for references.

"What about in your regular fan mail?"

Ellen shook her head.

"I don't get much of that anymore. Anyway, Lenny handles all the unsolicited correspondence, always has. I mean, stuff that doesn't come to the house at least. He passes on the nice ones."

"If you don't mind, I'd like to take a look at it. As far back as possible."

"Sure. You think—?"

Golding shrugged.

"You never know."

He took a last look around the garden. The breeze had dropped and from some nearby property came the hiss of lawn sprinklers. It seemed too peaceful, too orderly a place for madness and violence, too tasteful.

They were walking back towards the house when he saw the tape again. He walked around the side of the pool house. A tarpaulin still covered the hole where the woman had been found.

"This was a hell of a thing to happen," he said as she came and stood next to him.

"I know. I thought the house had a curse on it."

"I've been following it in the press. They don't seem to have any leads."

"No. Nobody knows anything about her."

He grabbed a handful of tape. It was tied to a stake that had been driven into the earth behind the low brick building.

"This guy," he said, "he's just a guy, okay? Probably some kind of nut."

"Oh great."

"What I mean is, he's probably got a history. Either of exposure or trespass, if not, you know, worse. Drugs, alcohol. There'll be something that somebody has written up in a report. His power—the only power he has right now—comes from his anonymity. It's like he's invisible. But if we look in the right places, my guess is we'll find that he's actually *highly* visible. Someone somewhere will have him on record."

"So where do you start?"

Golding nodded.

"I know a few places. You see, these people, most of these people, have histories of one sort or another."

He gave the tape a good pull and the stake came out of the ground.

"It's like a trail they leave," he said. "Like slime."

II

Hard News

11

Monday, August 2

"So let me get this straight," said Reynolds. "This guy, whoever he is, gets into the house—no sign of forced entry, no sign of . . . *anything,* and he puts a picture of Ellen Cusak on the wall?"

"A picture of a little girl that kind of looks like her. That looks like her when she was the same age."

Golding sat forward a little.

"There's this wall of photographs," he said, "pictures from when she was living in Kiev, and this picture, the picture of this . . . this kid, up there with the others."

Reynolds touched at his tie thoughtfully, then stood up. He went across to the window and looked down at the traffic crawling south on the Avenue of the Stars. Outside the morning was cooking up to a sticky eighty degrees.

"So what's your take on this, Pete?"

Golding shifted on his chair. He had spent the whole weekend running the facts through his head, and had come up with nothing coherent. He had started out with the assumption that the threatening letters were written by the guy who had gotten into the house, but the behavior seemed so different he wasn't sure what to think now.

"Well, the main thing is . . . the guy, this guy, he got in. If this is the Ice Man, the guy who wrote the hate mail—"

"If."

"Right, *if*—then we obviously have to take it very seriously. I mean it's serious whichever way you look at it, *whoever* got in."

Reynolds turned from the window.

"So basically you asked her to replace the locks," he said, returning to his seat, winding it up now.

"And set up the call monitoring, *and* told her to use the goddam alarm. She's got this expensive system but she leaves it off at night. And the maid isn't too careful about keeping the doors shut. That's how she thinks this guy got in."

"Oh? How did that work?"

"When the maid was out in the garden cutting parsley."

Reynolds' eyebrows popped up.

"Well, that would certainly explain why there were no signs of entry." He said it like he didn't believe a word. "The guy was obviously out there in the bushes with this picture under his arm, waiting for his chance. Then, when he saw the maid leave the door open, he snuck right in."

There was a long silence.

"Did you dust for latents?" Reynolds said eventually.

"Sure."

"Any prints on the frame?"

"Just hers, where she'd handled the picture."

"Just Cusak's?"

"That's right."

Reynolds looked down at his manicured nails, his lips crimped in a dubious pout. Golding found himself getting irritated.

"So what's on your mind, Tom?"

"Well, I'm just trying to see it from the intruder's point of view here. It seems like an awful lot of trouble to go to. I mean, apart from the risk."

He waited for a second, fixing Golding with his cold gray stare.

"What I'm saying is, once you're inside you're going to at least take something, right? Something valuable, or maybe a memento for the shrine. Underwear, soap, deodorant. Christ, if I'm the Ice Man, I'm going to take a dump on the carpet. At least. You're sure nothing was missing?"

"According to Mrs. Cusak, nothing was taken."

"If he wanted her to see the picture, why not just send it through the mail?"

"Power," said Golding. "He wants her to know he can get to her."

"I guess."

There was another long silence.

"You're saying this was a setup thing?" said Golding. Reynolds shrugged.

"But why?" said Golding. "Why would she bother?"

"Who knows? For the attention—for the publicity. Why do people do things? From what I gathered talking to Mayot, she's currently making a comeback. A body in the garden *and* a stalker—that's front-page copy for some papers."

"Come on. That's not her style."

"Oh really?" Reynolds shot him a skeptical look. "How would you know that? You only met her once, right?" He let this hang in the air for a second, then held up his hands. "Maybe it's nothing to do with her, maybe Mayot's calling the shots here. Who knows?"

"But why—why didn't she say something was missing? I mean if she wanted it to look good?"

"I don't know."

"I mean if she—"

Reynolds cut him off.

"Listen, we're just spinning our wheels here. What we need . . ." He stopped short, took a sip of cold coffee, made a face. "It would be a big help if Frank was around."

Romero was in New York giving expert testimony in a murder trial—billing the state five thousand dollars a day to pick apart the defense's insanity plea. It was a lucrative sideline for Romero, one that Reynolds resented slightly.

"How long's he away?" said Golding.

"Difficult to say with these things. Anyway, I know what he'd say."

"What?"

"He'd say we need to know more about this guy."

At seven o'clock Golding was still at his desk. From the end of the hallway, he could hear Reynolds talking on the phone. It sounded like he was getting a blow-by-blow account of the day's proceedings from Romero.

"So how much longer before they wrap it up?" said Reynolds, trying to sound breezy but coming across like an impatient hausfrau.

Golding buried his head in his hands. He had spent the entire afternoon wading through weirdness of one sort or another, and now he felt like a drink, or more exactly another drink. He had been sneaking sips of bourbon since six, trying to kill the jittery feeling of sickness that dealing with the material gave him. It was like kryptonite, like plutonium, like anthrax. It left him feeling diseased and, more than he would have liked to admit, vulnerable, as if these characters, trapped in their miserable fantasies, were actually in the room with him.

He preferred it when Romero did the reading, and then came up with a fancy term for whichever kind of monster they were dealing with. He preferred it when all he had to do was go into the field and confront the guy—it nearly always was a guy—put him straight, slap him with the restraining order. Within the profession there were those who had doubts about the effectiveness of restraining orders. There were people who saw them as provocative. That was okay with Golding. For him it was clear. You drew a line in the dirt. You drew a line in the dirt and invited the fucker to step over.

Ellen Cusak's sickmail made quite a stack for someone not in the top rank of celebrity: pages ripped from yellow legal pads or spiral-bound notebooks, floral-pattern stationery, absorbent paper towels, index cards—everything scrawled, scribbled and printed. Romero's dream was to tag each item and start a library like the one they had over at Gavin de Becker, the biggest of the L.A. agencies. De Becker's library was supposed to contain around 350,000 items: 350,000 examples of hatred, obscenity, delusion—love letters a hundred pages long, love letters stiff with semen, love letters signed in blood, hate letters stained with tears and shit. It made Golding's head ache just thinking about it.

Ellen's letters started in 1990, when she first appeared in front of the cameras, a year after she came out of nowhere to take silver at the Nationals. She got mail right out of the gate, of course, but the first spatter of

enthusiasm—requests for autographed pictures, etc.—
would have been dealt with in the normal way, and then
trashed. Only subsequently, out of the clamor of adulation, would the more intense and particular voices have
become audible. This was what Golding was looking at.

Six months after her climb onto the podium, three
sickos were already tracking her. One character
signed himself "Pierre." His short but flamboyant letters were posted either in Manhattan or in Paris. The
guy traveled, was maybe a businessman, and his thing
was footwear. The first sign that anything was wrong
was his repeated requests for Ellen's shoe size.
Through the spring of '90 his questions bloomed into
nuttiness. Where did she shop? Did she wear boots
off the ice? How did it feel being laced in so tight?
How sharp was the blade? What was it like when a
lace broke? Pierre knew a way of lacing the kind of
boots that had little steel hooks for eyelets. You held
the laces in one hand and zigzagged up through the
hooks. Top models used this method when they had
very high or thigh-length boots. Letter no. 35 flamed
into obscenity. He and Ellen fucked on the ice while
dancing a routine. "You slide on *my* blade"—"my,"
triple-underlined. In the next letter he apologized.
Then he told her she had hurt him, and for months
the letters stopped. Then started again. Paris and
New York. New York and Paris. He wrote good English but could have been French. He said the French
word for heel, *talon,* was like an eagle's foot. He
wrote and explained how her heel—always "heel,"
never "heels"—pierced his heart. He wrote and told
her about a wound he had to prove it. He wrote and
told her how the wound had become infected.

Compared to the Ice Man, Pierre was a cupcake. His

letters weren't angry or hateful, they were just sick. Golding bunched them together with a paper clip and returned them to Lenny Mayot's box.

The second guy was plain crazy. He signed his letters "Charlie Manson" and rambled between descriptions of satanic ritual and a music box that Ellen was supposed to live in. The letters were infrequent, and more or less illegible. They went into the box.

The third guy was obviously following Ellen's life in the papers. He wrote in slanting black characters that reminded Golding of driving rain. The guy signed himself "Bob." He kept referring back to Ellen's first routine, the first time he had seen her. It had "changed" his life. Golding vaguely remembered something of the performance himself. Taking time out from the letters, he went into the Web, looking for contemporary accounts, and found what he wanted in an archive service that carried back numbers of *Skating*. It was a retrospective piece written at the time of Ellen's marriage to Doug Gorman.

She still called herself Yelena in those days, was still known only as a promising young Ukrainian skater who had defected with her father during a trip to Helsinki. She'd had almost no exposure to the press, and the few brief interviews she had done had been faltering, her shyness obvious, her accent still strong despite the years in America. Most of the audience that day—most of the world—had never seen her skate. She had taken a couple of falls on the short program, and wasn't thought to be in the running for a medal. In fact, the whole contest seemed to have been settled when she stepped out onto the ice to perform the last dance of the night.

The music seemed to take forever to begin. Yelena waited motionless in the center of the rink, dressed in a simple blue tunic with red flashes and epaulettes, half ballerina, half military cadet. With her blond hair swept back in a short ponytail, her soft green eyes downcast, she was clearly beautiful. But more than that, she was different. She looked like something rare and precious that had washed up on a foreign shore. The audience slowly fell silent. People who were already headed for the exit stopped and sat down again. Photographers and cameramen who were getting ready to call it a night zoomed in, framed, and focused with sudden urgency. When the music still would not start, and Ellen glanced across at her father, a murmur of alarm went right around the arena.

Then the music did begin: the Brahms Hungarian Rhapsody in F-sharp Minor—a masterpiece that alternated at disconcerting speed between fast and slow passages, between exquisite sadness and wild gaiety. It was the kind of music that could drown a program, quite apart from the difficulties of tempo. But little Yelena Cusak didn't have to worry about how she interpreted the music, because for a few short minutes, she was that music, from the tips of her blades to the depths of her Slavic soul. Her skating was strong and fluid, her spins fast and precise, her jumps seemingly effortless, but that wasn't what was most compelling. There was nothing of the showman in her performance. Instead it seemed to come from deep inside her. A hunger that only the dance could satisfy. It was the voice of exile. It was the lost child yearning for home. By the end people were watching with tears in their eyes.

Commentators pointed out that, technically, Ellen's was not the most difficult program on offer that night, but for artistic presentation it was in a class of its own. Three of the judges awarded her a perfect 6, three of the others 5.9 It was enough to win her the silver medal, and bring her to the attention of millions upon millions of people who until that moment had scarcely known of her existence.

Presumably Bob had been one of those millions. He wrote that seeing Yelena skate was like a supernova going off in his head. He hadn't been able to sleep for days afterwards. Bob was clearly depressed. He wrote about his medication. He wrote about the lack of direction in his life. In his fifth letter he asked Ellen how come she didn't sweat. *I notice when you come off the ice that despite the extreme physical exertion, you do not appear to perspire. Is this because of the cosmetics you wear? Do skaters use the kind of cosmetics actors wear?* He wanted to know how much she weighed. He said he'd read somewhere that she weighed 118 pounds. *Is that right? Because to me you look lighter than that. I would have said 110 pounds or 115 pounds at the outside.*

In letter no. 27 he said he had bought a gun, and described himself as a bullet, moving too fast to ever be wholly in the present moment. He said that his dearest wish was to live only in the present, to spin in place the way Ellen did on the ice. But for a bullet things weren't so simple: *The next moment comes so quickly, and the next, and beyond all nexts, already almost now, but not quite now, the end, the target, my destiny.* The news of Ellen's marriage in '92 seemed to crush him. His letters got shorter, and more intense, squeezed out under the weight of bad news. Letter no. 83 talked about Prozac, and how it seemed to help him, but how it made him agitated sometimes. He referred to the Joseph Wesbecker killings in Louisville,

Kentucky. *Can you imagine that?* he wrote. *Just walking into a place and gunning everybody down?* Then, in January 1994 he sent a card. For Golding it was the spookiest thing of all. *We are one,* it said. Nothing else. He checked it against the rough chronology he had noted and couldn't get it to match up with anything. Then there was nothing for three years. It was as if Bob's oneness meant that he didn't have to communicate anymore. But in '97 he was back and weirder than ever. It was the same writing, the same slanting rain, the same signature, but there was a new strangeness. *I would never donate my body to science,* he said. *Would you?* He wanted to know if Ellen still had her appendix. He wanted to know everything.

The Ice Man's letters were the most blatantly threatening. They were also the most recent. Looking for something biographical to link them to, Golding saw that the letters dated from just after the shooting of the Ford commercial.

"How's it going?"

Bernie Ross, the newest recruit to the firm, was standing beside him, a slim, dark-haired guy with handsome features marred by bad skin. He was wearing his jacket, ready to leave, probably wondering if he should.

Golding gestured towards the boxful of letters.

"Romero's gonna think it's Christmas," he said.

12

Ellen watched the gates close and Maria's white Nissan disappear around the corner. It was a little before nine in the morning, the hillside above still a patchwork of bright vegetation and dark shadows. Clusters of cypresses and pines marked the course of the road that wound its way to the top for half a mile before turning down again into the San Fernando Valley. As the sound of the car died away, it struck her how still it was. She went over to the big steel door that led to the utility room and tried the handle, even though Maria had only just locked it—Maria had locked everything, right up to the windows on the top floor. On Golding's advice, Ellen had had dead bolts fitted to every exterior door.

Golding wasn't at all the way she'd expected him to be. She'd come across personal security types before at some of the glitzier show biz events Doug had taken her to. A few of the bigger stars—or maybe it was just the more pretentious ones—had turned up with bodyguards: big, sharply dressed men who seemed to relish their high-profile role and who clearly spent most of their time at the gym. Golding wasn't anything like that. He was smaller, to start with—edgier, shyer. He looked like he worked out, though, looked like he could probably handle himself if he needed to.

Maria had left the mail on the kitchen table. Ellen spread it out in a line: official-looking brown envelopes, three of them, different sizes, a couple of Hollywood trades in cellophane wrapping, both for Doug, a handwritten invitation of some kind from her friend Laura Mead, something from her accountant, something from the bank, and a small cardboard package the size of a book, the address typed on a label. She picked it up, weighing it in her hand, then realized what it was: the videotape of the breakfast show Lenny had promised to send her.

She opened the invitation first. Laura and Danny Mead were having a lunch party in a month's time. The cards had been decorated with blotchy potato prints. She instantly recognized the handiwork of their two boys, Joshua and Sean. Laura had written *Be there!!* in red pen along the top. It looked like it was going to be a fun occasion, and there was no danger—as there might have been at other times—of running into Doug. Ellen decided to call Laura there and then to accept.

Laura picked up on the third ring.

"So how *are* you?" she said. "What's happening in your life?"

This was Laura's standard entrée to the subject of men.

"Oh, you know."

"No, I don't. That's why I'm asking."

"Well, it's mostly hate mail and weird phone calls,"

she said, trying to sound relaxed about it. "But that's all over now."

"My God."

"It's okay now. Really." She could hear from Laura's silence that she was shocked. "Lenny got me some protection."

"Protection?"

"A private firm. Specialists. They sent this guy over to check my security arrangements."

"Security? You mean as in *bodyguard*?" Laura said it as if they were talking about something scandalous.

"Not a bodyguard, more like a—"

"Was he cute? Don't tell me: a hunk in a blue poplin button-down and a calf-leather shoulder holster. A lightweight suit, gray, with those little cuffs on the pants, black loafers." They were both laughing now. "Did he look like Costner?"

"Costner? Why would he look like Costner?"

"Well, you saw the movie, right? *The Bodyguard*?"

"Oh yeah, sure."

"Well?"

Ellen sighed.

"*No,* he wasn't like Kevin Costner."

"But he was cute?"

"Well"—Ellen thought about it for a moment—"I guess, yes, kind of."

"I knew it! And the butt? Does he have a nice butt?"

Butts were Laura's big thing—referred to alternately as asses, derrieres, buns, or tushes.

"Laura, I wasn't looking at his butt. We were talking about locks and call monitoring and psychopaths."

"I'll take that as a yes. Hey, and why not? They're all the rage—Princess Stephanie of Monaco, Madonna. Seriously, I can really see you with a strong silent type."

Ellen shook her head in despair.

"Well, you invite some strong silent types to your party and I'll give them a try."

"I'll see what I can do, but I have to warn you: my little black book isn't quite what it was. It's you single gals have all the fun."

It took Ellen another ten minutes to get off the phone. She made coffee and sat for a while thinking about what Laura had said. It was true, Golding was kind of cute, and actually not so unlike Kevin Costner, in a compact, sandy-haired way. She'd have liked to have him around, but not so much for that reason. The truth was: she'd have felt a lot safer.

She turned to the videocassette. On the label Lenny had written WATCH ME in thick black marker. She checked her watch. She had to leave for the meeting with Knapp-Weinstein in half an hour. She took her coffee through to the small sitting room that was home to the VCR and the huge thirty-two-inch television. At the time of the interview, all she'd wanted was to get it over with and be gone, but now she was curious to see how it had come out. Maybe Lenny and Barbara Christian were right: maybe the camera did love her.

This had always been Doug's room. It was here, lying stretched out on the black leather sofa, that he'd read or skim through the piles of scripts he was sent, talking them over on the phone for hours at a time; here that he'd gotten through the huge collection of tapes that at one time had lined the walls; here that he'd sat alone brooding, drinking himself into a stupor or a rage during the darkest days of their marriage. Most of his things were gone now—the old movie posters, the scripts, the tapes, the model *Star Wars* spaceship that had perched threateningly on the desktop—but the huge black television and VCR were still where he'd left them, items classified by her meticulous lawyers as "non-personal" for the purposes of the divorce settlement. All the same, Ellen hadn't actually used them in months.

She went across to the windows and raised the blinds. Doug had always kept them down, even when he wasn't watching the TV, said it helped him think— and the way he said it always gave Ellen a bad feeling, as if what he was thinking about was not his work but them, her. It got to the point that she was afraid to go into the room for fear of trespassing somehow, even though Doug himself had never told her not to. There was just an understanding—perhaps a misunderstanding—that what she asked of him was just a little too much, a little more than she had a right to expect. And it was only in his room, with his videos and his scripts and his black leather sofa, that he was free of it all. She still wasn't sure whether she *had* asked too much, whether her idea of marriage, of family, was somehow not reasonable at their age, not the normal thing. She just knew it had mattered to her more than anything else in the world.

She put the tape in the VCR, picked up the remote, and pressed PLAY. Smooth graphite blackness became a grainier void, flecked with white. She sat down on the edge of the sofa just as the phone rang.

The noise made her jump. It was louder than in the other rooms. She thought about not answering, letting the machine take it—in case it was *him*, in case he had found the new number. But then she remembered: it was going to be a normal day. She was back in control. Leaving the tape playing, she went to the desk and picked up.

"Hello?"

"Hi, Ellen, how's things? Still on for Knapp-Weinstein this morning?"

Lenny. On his car phone, it sounded like.

"Sure, sure. I'm leaving in twenty minutes."

For a second the signal broke up. On the TV the blackness gave way to a blurred blue-white. Clouds lurched into view.

"Great. That's great. Listen, I spoke to Barbara Christian last night. She's very excited about the book. She's gonna talk to Argyle this afternoon. If they give her the green light, we're in business. She really liked you, by the way. I knew she would."

White patio furniture, glass patio doors seen from outside, a couple of ghostly figures caught in the reflection. A man's cheerful voice, close by: *O-kay.*

"Lenny, are you sure you sent me the right tape? This looks like your home movie or something."

The camera swung around, the lens adjusting again. A wooden fence, a patch of brown lawn, in the middle a red plastic pedal tractor.

"Tape?"

"The tape of the breakfast show. I'm watching it now, but it's . . ."

The blurred round of a child's face, looking up into the camera, too close to be in focus. A young woman's voice in the background. *Come to me, sweetheart.* The camera zoomed out. It was a little girl, one year old or less. Wavy blond hair with a ribbon at the back. She was beautiful, as beautiful as the girl in the photograph.

"Oh, *that* tape," said Lenny. "I clean forgot to send it. Sorry. I'll get you a copy this afternoon."

The man's voice again. It was him holding the camera. Ellen knew that voice: *Okay, honey, go on. Walk for Daddy.*

"So what *are* you watching, Ellen? Ellen?"

A pair of pale arms came into shot, reaching out to the child. Jeans, a black T-shirt with a big white snowflake printed on the front. The woman's voice sounded far away. It said something like: *Show Momma what you can do.*

"Ellen? Are you there?"

The child was still clinging to a table leg. She looked up at the camera and laughed.

"I can't lie to you, Lenny, commitment is a big issue here. We can't take a punt with something like this. We have to be sure."

Abe Weinstein wrapped both hands around his right shin and rocked back in his armchair. He was younger than Gil Knapp, tall and slim with a neatly trimmed beard and glasses.

"It isn't just the shooting," Knapp growled from behind his desk. "There's all the publicity. Appearances. Interviews."

Lenny was nodding vigorously.

"I can assure you—"

"We'd need her on standby for six weeks minimum once the thing hits the stores. You don't get a second chance."

Lenny could feel a bead of sweat slowly working its way down his temple. As he'd hoped, Abe Weinstein was more positive about a Cusak video than his partner had been, but clearly not yet positive enough. In an effort to stoke their enthusiasm Lenny had mentioned that Ellen would be joining them at ten o'clock. It was now nearly half past and there was no sign of her.

"I can assure you," he said again, "Ellen loves this idea. In fact, it was *her* idea. She's back in training herself now, as well as coaching some juniors, and I swear she's never looked so good."

Weinstein nodded encouragingly, like someone who liked what he heard but needed to hear more.

"The video's her chance to make some of that . . . that special knowledge available to a wider audience."

Weinstein stopped nodding.

"Are you sure she's really interested in a wider audience, Lenny? I hear—I hear when she's not skating she likes to keep pretty much to herself, doesn't *like* publicity."

"I hear Doug Gorman's publicist had quite a bit of trouble with her," added Knapp. "They say she wasn't very supportive in that direction. Wouldn't do anything."

Lenny forced a laugh.

"Is that what Doug's telling people these days? Come on, guys."

"It's just what we're hearing is all," said Knapp.

"Well, if that's the worst Doug can say about his ex-wife—I could tell you a few things about *him,* you bet. Plenty of things."

Weinstein acknowledged Lenny's point with a nod.

"The fact remains that Ellen's a marginal call when it comes to this kind of merchandising—as things stand. She isn't the household name she once was. That means the marketing is all the more important."

Lenny shrugged.

"What can I say? Ellen wants to do the video and she wants it to be a success. Would I be here otherwise?"

Gil Knapp looked around at the office.

"I think the question is, Lenny . . . why isn't she?"

Bright lights slewed across the screen. An ice rink, the voices of excited children echoing, filling the room. In the middle distance small figures, black against white, drifted back and forth. Closer to the camera an Asian girl in a red suit executed a single toe loop, glancing back at the camera as she landed. Ellen leaned closer to the screen, trying to see if she could recognize the rink, recognize anything.

The camera panned unsteadily to the edge of the ice. She was waiting there, her back to the Perspex screen: the little blond girl in the blue dress, four or five years old now. She lifted a gloved hand and waved stiffly, then took off, skating past the camera and away to the far end of the rink, the autofocus losing and then finding her again. Slowly she completed a circuit and came to a halt where she had started. She did not smile, but stood there silently looking into the lens, as if waiting for Ellen to speak.

The phone was ringing. Ellen looked up distractedly, wiping the tears from her face with the back of her sleeve. After four rings the answering machine cut in: *I can't take your call right now. Please leave a message at the tone.* From the other room she could hear Lenny's voice, a tumble of anxious words. She turned back to the screen. The tape was finished. She picked up the remote, rewound it to the beginning, and, for the third time, pressed PLAY.

13

"Have there been any calls for me?"

Lenny Mayot's assistant, Sandra Reilly, flicked through her notepad.

"Abe Weinstein's secretary, confirming your meeting at ten—"

"Just had it. Anything else?"

"Er . . . Some guy selling a directory. He's going to fax."

"Great. That it?"

"Um . . . yes."

Lenny returned a grunt and walked through to his office, pulling off his tie as he went. The meeting had been a disaster, a humiliation. The video deal was dead. Ellen Cusak was still a face from the past, and worse than that, she was flaky, utterly unreliable. If Gil Knapp and his partner had had any doubt about that, they didn't now. Ice Magic might as well have happened yesterday. As he was leaving, Abe Weinstein had clapped him on the shoulder and said *Nice try, Lenny,* like he was some twenty-five-year-old kid who was new in the business.

Like he was some schmuck just trying his luck. It made him angry to think of it.

And after all that, Ellen hadn't even called to explain.

He was still sitting there, his fingers pressed against his throbbing temples, when the phone rang.

"Ellen?"

"Guess again, Mr. Mayot. Barbara Christian."

Lenny snapped into his upbeat, couldn't-be-better voice.

"Barbara, how are you? What's new?"

"I talked to Eve Kaufman at Argyle this morning."

"Oh yeah, yeah, how'd it go?" said Lenny, trying to sound like he'd forgotten about it.

"Well, Lenny, it's good news and bad news."

Lenny dabbed at his forehead with his shirt cuff. In his experience, good news and bad news meant bad news that stopped a few inches short of total disaster.

"Oh yeah?"

"Basically they think a sports bio like the one we envisioned would work for them. The female market is definitely the stronger in this area, and a winter sports star would fill a gap in their list."

"That's great, great," said Lenny, shutting his eyes.

"*But* they don't feel Ellen Cusak has really got the profile they're looking for. A few years ago, yes. But right now.... They feel she needs to be more in the public eye. One commercial and an ice tour. It's a start, but ... frankly, there needs to be more of an *edge* to this thing. I'm sorry, Lenny. Lenny?"

"Yeah, yeah, I'm listening. Well, that's too bad. Thanks for trying anyway, Barbara. I appreciate it." He was too tired to make a fight of it. What was the point anyhow? "I'll see you 'round, okay?"

He made to hang up.

"Lenny?"

"Yeah?"

"Lenny, listen. For what it's worth, I still think there's potential there. I told you I was excited about this project and I meant it. Ellen Cusak is a very interesting person."

Lenny shook his head in disbelief.

"Well, I'll certainly tell her you said so—if I see her."

"I mean her *life* is interesting. I want to know more. I think a lot of people would like to know more. They just need a push. Something to focus their attention. When I was up at the house last week, I could almost taste it."

Lenny sat back in his chair and sighed.

"The trouble is, Barbara, there are world champions and Olympic champions out there, title winners *in competition.* In a few years Argyle's readers'll be too young to remember Ellen Cusak."

"Screw Argyle. Those stupid little books aren't worth a dime. Like you say, they're for kids. I'm talking major hardcover. Depth and quality. That's what we should be aiming for."

Lenny couldn't help laughing.

"Well, Barbara, I'm aiming, I'm just having a little trouble seeing the target right now."

He heard Barbara's breath push against the mouthpiece. She was a fighter, he had to give her that. And she had a head on her shoulders.

"Lenny, all I'm saying is, if something breaks—about Doug, about the stalker, anything—will you talk to me first?"

14

The road begins to climb. He winds down the window, sucks in flower smells—always sweeter after a night breathing the other guys' sweat and cigarette smoke. The sun isn't up for another hour, so everything comes through in soft predawn blues that make it easy to believe in the old L.A.—the L.A. of orange groves and peach orchards, of abundant water and farmsteads. He's amped from the Benzedrine, his pulse going through hard and tight like knots in a cord, but he's skipping sleep today anyway, and he wants to be sharp for this, wants to get the most out of his new toy.

At the junction of Kenter Avenue he slows down, looking for the private patrol car that is sometimes tucked in behind a sprawling lilac bush. Once it followed him, tailed him all the way up the hill. He flipped on his nearfield interceptor and picked up a beacon of clean audio from the security guy's crappy two-way; listened as he checked out his license plate. He wonders at the people up here, spending all that money for the right to put an ARMED PATROL sign at the end of their driveway, as if an old fart in a Chevy Caprice was any protection.

Above the house he pulls off the road and makes his way on foot through the pines and scrub that cling to the side of the hill. Even in the near-dark he moves easily, noiselessly, the position of every tree and twisted root known to him. From the branches above him he hears movement—rustling, the stirring of birds and animals. Away to his right a jaybird explodes from the dense foliage and goes screeching down towards her house.

He opens his knapsack and takes out his most recent acquisition. Incorporating a third-generation gallium arsenide photo cathode yielding 1,200 micro amps per lumen, the night-vision goggles cost him two months' salary, so he handles them with care as he slips them over his head. Then he is laughing his ugly high laugh, pressing his hand against his mouth to stifle the sound.

It's beautiful. The world comes through with a weird underwater quality. But it's the seeing without being seen that he loves—that he has always loved. He has already tested them at home of course, even tried to use them in the games he plays with Nat, but this is different. He looks around at the bright spangled greens of the foliage, and then down at the house. On the second floor the third window from the right is marked with a brilliant green symbol; his symbol, his graffito, sprayed on the wall beneath the window in the special marker dye. Infinity. An eight on its side—invisible except to his four-thousand-dollar eyes.

He watches for a long time, imagining Yelena in her bed. He is so still the animals start to move again, rustling in the bushes around him. He is watching a large spider move over the ground when he sees the footprint.

At his feet, in the dirt, several footprints. Not his own. The realization is like a harsh light coming on. Someone has been here. A man. A man watching the house, watching *her*. He squats down, tracing the outline with his fingers, trying to stay calm, trying to hold back the anger. He looks around for more, finds another behind him, and another. Smooth soles, probably leather, but with a rubber heel, a zig-zag pattern running across it. He tries to picture the man, tries to picture him standing there. Some fucking psycho peeper trying to get a look at *his* Ellen. If he were there now, he'd kill him.

He pulls the goggles off his head and thrusts them back into the knapsack. Starlings scatter as he hurries to the car. He throws himself behind the wheel and sits, his mind in turmoil, struggling with his feeling of violation. This is a signal, a warning that he has waited too long. He reaches into the glove compartment and pulls out the .38, running the barrel down the side of his face, pressing it into his cheek, riding out his anger.

The sun is still below the horizon when he reaches the far side of the garden. He kneels down before the gap in the hedge, looking for more of the footprints. But there's nothing here.

He walks towards the house across the middle of the lawn, making no attempt to hide, but careful of the noise because of the dog. She sleeps in the small bedroom now, as far away as possible from her marriage bed, where she and the actor performed their fruitless lovemaking. But the phone has not moved. She will have to walk down the hall to answer it.

He stands beneath the shuttered window and enters

the number, calm now despite his thumping heart. He doesn't know yet what he will say. That is not the important thing. The time has come for her to speak. The time has come for her to open her eyes.

The line purrs once, twice, three times. There is a pause, then a hiss as the answering machine turns itself on. Yelena's voice: *I can't take your call right now. Please leave a message at the tone.*

But something isn't right. He kills the signal, dials the number again, holding the mobile away from his ear this time, listening instead for the sound of the phones ringing inside the house. There is no ringing. Only silence.

He stands there, looking up at the window, staring at the spot where he has made his mark, the rage building behind his eyes.

Back in the car, he dials again.

The hiss of tape. Yelena's recorded voice.

They are listening.

He takes a deep breath, lets it out slowly, speaks.

15

Golding arrived just after ten to find Ellen Cusak already installed in Lenny's cramped office.

"Thanks for coming over at such short notice," said Lenny, pulling a chair out from next to a filing cabinet.

"I needed to talk to you anyway," said Golding, sitting down next to Ellen, noticing the dabs of shadow under her green eyes. It looked like they were all set for some TV viewing. Lenny had pulled a big Sony out from under some shelving. He messed around with cables for a moment, then pressed a button to start the VCR.

"This came in the mail yesterday," he said, sitting back down. Golding saw fluffy clouds jerk into focus, white patio furniture. A home movie. "Ellen thought it was the breakfast show thing, and opened it by mistake."

Patio doors. A reflection. Then a guy's voice: *O-kay.* Golding recognized it immediately, felt the hairs come up on his arms. The stalker had sent a video.

He had seen videos made by obsessives before,

Romero had a stack of them. They started okay—in a sunny kitchen, maybe, or in a garage—then you noticed the M-16 leaning against the door and things got weird. He hoped it wasn't going to be too gruesome. He hoped the guy had made the mistake of filming himself in the bathroom mirror.

"We think it's . . ."

Lenny stopped himself mid-sentence, holding up a hand.

A golden-haired infant filled the screen. Then the same child just beginning to walk, holding onto the leg of a table, then—*wham*—the kid herself, the kid from the photograph. Lenny froze the image. Same girl, same dress. Lenny moved on. A rink somewhere. Shadows and voices. Golding checked Ellen's face to see how she was reading it. Her eyes were fixed on the screen as the little kid clumsily twirled.

For two minutes nobody spoke.

Then it was over. Golding looked across at Lenny.

"It arrived in the mail?"

"Wrapped in brown paper. Yesterday morning, isn't that right, Ellen?"

"It was in among the other mail," said Ellen as Lenny pushed a torn package across his desk. The address was typed but there was no stamp. It had been delivered by hand.

"I wouldn't be too hopeful of getting any prints off this," said Golding. "We'll have a better chance off the cassette, though, as long as you haven't handled it too much."

"Er . . . that's a copy," said Lenny. "I er . . . I figured you'd want to dust for prints, so I bagged up the original. I've got it right here." He handed it over, wrapped in a Ziploc bag. "So what do you think?" he said, flipping over his palms. "I mean what the hell is this all about?"

Golding looked at Ellen, wondering if she knew. She was still staring at the blank TV screen.

"The truth is, I've never seen anything like it," he said. "I mean, it seems so . . . well, for want of a better word, *personal*."

He took the remote from Lenny's desk and rewound the tape to the beginning, ran it again, freezing it as the camera panned past the patio doors. There was a fleeting glimpse of something reflected in the glass—a face, a woman maybe. He went back and forth over the same few inches of tape. A white woman. Then a woman's voice said: *Come to me, sweetheart.* The mother? Golding switched off.

"Do you recognize the man's voice?" he asked.

Ellen nodded.

"It's the guy who called."

Golding opened his bag and took out an audiocassette tape.

"Okay. Now I want to play you something. It came through on your old number this morning."

She was looking at him now. It was the first time he had really gotten her attention.

"So what . . . what is it?" said Lenny uncertainly.

"A message from the guy who sent the video."

"The Ice Man?"

"I don't think so."

Lenny looked at Ellen.

"Honey, I think it's probably best if—"

"I'd like Mrs. Cusak to hear it," said Golding.

She gave him a hard look like she was trying to figure him out.

"You might find it upsetting," he said, "but I need to know what you think."

"What she *thinks*?" said Lenny.

"It's okay, Lenny. I'm a big girl."

Lenny shrugged and folded his arms.

There was a long hiss as the tape fed through. Then a voice.

I'm sorry, Yelena. Sorry for what you did. . . . Disappointed. A long silence, the snap of a lighter, then a deep inhale. *It's not as if I did anything. Which . . . which I could have done.*

Silence. Lenny looked at the tape recorder like it was about to explode.

And it felt so right. You know? It felt so right to be there. I felt so . . . at home. And she looked so pretty on that wall . . . with—with the rest of the family pictures. Ellen shifted in her chair. *Did you like the tape, Yelena? Did you see her skate? She skates with your body and your soul. That way you have? I sent you the tape so that you could see her. So now you see her . . . Now you know.*

Breathing, just audible. A sound in the background. Like rain. Golding strained to imagine the face, got as far as male Caucasian, maybe in his thirties. He braced himself as the voice began to build towards anger.

We don't need these people, Yelena. They have nothing to do with this. They have nothing to do with us. Nothing. They're just trying to come between us, to keep you from the truth. You see, I see you, Yelena. I see you. Soft laughter. *I see you in a room with them.* Laughter again. *The weasel's there. Leonard Arthur Benjamin Mayot.* Lenny sat up straight. *Hello, Lenny. You wouldn't want to be kept out of anything. Little Lenny, nose in the trough.* A deep shuddering pull on the cigarette. *And the other guy*—the voice went tight, the mouth close to the mouthpiece, bumping the mouthpiece, the words squeezed and hard—*whoever he is. They don't—Yelena, for them you're just a thing, a commodity. Don't you see it? They dress you up, and paint your face like a—like fucking Cindy. Don't you see it, baby? Don't you see the way it's always been? The men. Always taking from you, fucking you up, starving you.* The voice, straining against a sob. *Well, the time is coming, the time is here, and I won't fucking allow it anymore. I WON'T . . . ALLOW . . . IT.*

Golding switched off the machine. The booming voice seemed to hang in the air.

Lenny drew a hand across his face. He was trembling.

"Pete. I want you to nail this son of a bitch. You've got to nail this fucking guy."

Tears stood in Ellen's eyes.

"Ellen?" Golding waited for her to look at him. "I know this may sound strange, but does that mean anything to you?"

"What's to mean?" shouted Lenny. "The guy's raving."

"He says he wants you to *see*," said Golding. "Does that—is there any way in which that . . . ?"

She shook her head.

"It's the freakin' Ice Man," said Lenny.

Golding felt his face grow hot.

"Lenny, this—"

"With the skates and stuff—it's the Ice Man. It's some freak with a skating obsession."

Golding sat back in his chair.

"Lenny, look at the time frame. If the girl wearing the skates is now—I mean, if she was filmed recently, then we're looking at pictures going back five, maybe six years. The Ice Man's been writing for two months."

"So he pulled out one of his old home movies. So what?"

Golding looked at the blank screen. Lenny was right,

of course. The fact that the movie showed a five-year-old didn't make it five years old, didn't prove that the maker had been obsessed with Ellen for that length of time. He considered her for a moment. There was stuff she wasn't telling him. He felt sure of it.

"Mrs. Cusak, he said something about men, about them starving you. Does that . . . ?"

"What?"

She pushed hair back from her forehead in a jerky, nervous gesture.

"Does that mean anything to you?"

She looked at him for a long time. "Well, I guess you read the papers, don't you?"

"It was reported in the press," said Lenny.

"What was?"

Golding had to wait a long time for the answer.

"I had some eating problems when I was younger," she said quietly.

Lenny cut in: "Come on, Pete. Is this about the psycho or Ellen?"

"I just—to understand where this character's coming from, I have to know what he could know. About Ellen."

"Look, the eating thing, it's not uncommon," she said, turning her eyes on him again. "Lots of athletes, lots of women athletes, go through it. Gymnasts, skaters. It's worse with skaters because . . . well, you peak very early. You reach your optimal strength-to-weight ratio at around thirteen. You're jumping your best at age thirteen. Then you start putting on weight, and your jumping goes to hell. I . . . when that happened to me, I stopped eating properly. I'm okay now."

Golding wasn't sure whether to believe her.

"But . . . this guy says 'the men' did it to you. Who? Your coach? Maybe your dad?"

Patches of color appeared high on her cheekbones.

"What are you trying to say?"

"I'm just—"

"Are you saying my father starved me?"

"No. I'm saying, could that be what he's talking about."

She looked at Lenny as if this was all his fault.

"I wouldn't know," she said.

Lenny put his elbows on the desk.

"Come on, Pete. The guy's just crazy. I mean—I mean listen, he says they make her look like Cindy Crawford. Ellen's not even a brunette."

"He doesn't say Cindy Crawford. He says Sindy. I think he means the doll."

"Oh . . ."

Ellen was frowning, remembering something.

"What was it?"

"At the shoot. There was . . . You know for the Ford commercial?"

"The four-by-four."

Ellen nodded.

"They wanted me to jump in this wig, like a blond wig. But it kept getting in my face when I jumped. So in the end we scrapped it. Anyway, I remember somebody did say I looked like a Sindy doll in that wig."

Golding sat up. "Do you remember who said it?"

She thought for a moment, then shook her head. "It was just a remark."

"But you didn't use the wig in the end?"

"No. Like I said. It was no good."

Golding looked down at the tape recorder. The Ice Man letters had started a week after the shoot.

"How did that go?" he said. "I mean the shooting of the commercial. Were there any problems? Disputes of any kind?"

"Not really. There was a certain amount of tension on the soundstage, but I don't think that's unusual. There's a lot of money involved, so there's pressure. People lose their tempers."

"Do you remember—did you lose your temper? Did you argue with anyone?"

She shook her head.

"Didn't the Ice Man start writing after the Ford thing?" said Lenny.

"That's right."

Lenny nodded significantly.

"That's quite a coincidence."

"Maybe that's all it is," said Golding. He looked down at his pen. "Now tell me about Bob."

Lenny looked puzzled.

"Who?"

"Bob. He's written to Ellen a lot."

"Oh, *Bob*. Jeez, that guy's been writing for years." Lenny caught the expression on Golding's face. "You think—you're saying Bob is this guy, Bob's the guy with the little girl?"

"I think it's worth considering."

"Come on, Pete."

Golding squared his hands on the table, trying to organize his thoughts.

"The Ice Man says he wants to hurt Ellen," he said. "This guy says he wants her to see, to look at how the little girl skates. These are very different things."

"Are they?" said Lenny, raising his voice. "Freakin' guy, he probably read some tabloid bullshit about fertility problems and now he's trying to mess with Ellen's head."

There was a tense silence.

Lenny looked across at Ellen, shrugged. "I'm sorry, honey."

She stood up. "Can I go now?"

She gave Lenny a withering look and walked out of the room.

They listened to the door slam.

"Jesus Christ."

Lenny buried his face in his hands. Then looked up.

"What can I say?" he said. "It's a touchy subject."

Golding could no longer hide his irritation. "Lenny, I've been trying to make sense of this little girl for a week and now you tell me Mrs. Cusak's had fertility problems. This is . . . I need to know about this."

Lenny slumped back in his chair.

"I didn't say Ellen had fertility problems. I said this guy might have read something, that's all."

"Read what?"

"Listen, Pete, even I don't know the whole story. Ellen's Ellen. She's a very private person, very inside herself."

"What story?"

Lenny sighed, shrugged.

"The Ellen and Doug story, I guess you'd call it. The 'Why couldn't-they have children?' story."

"Children? Wasn't she a little young for that?"

"Hey." Lenny shrugged as if it went without saying. He reflected for a minute, then stood up and went over to the watercooler. When he came back to his chair, it looked like he was ready to talk.

"You've got to see how it happened for her. Okay"—he held up a finger—"the big picture: 1989—Ellen wins silver at the Nationals. She's seventeen years old. They say that for a skater Olympic gold is worth from five to ten million dollars in endorsements. That's right. Five to ten million. Keep that figure in mind, Pete.

"When a kid like Ellen shows some star quality, looks

like a real prospect, there are plenty of people willing to handle her. Especially when the kid has Ellen's looks. So it's no surprise she got some pretty sharp representation very early on. Of course she had her dad and Sam Ritt to look after her interests, but after the Nationals, she was—how can I put it—*launched* on a fairly commercial trajectory. Then, before anyone knows it, she's the world's number one. *In two years*. And all this time she's being worked pretty hard, doing interviews, showing up at the right functions, getting invited all over town. And it was at one of these occasions that she meets a young actor called Douglas Gorman. She is nineteen years old: radiant, confident, funny. I know that may be hard to believe, but this is before everything happened, okay? Anyway, she's nineteen, Doug is twenty-three. And botta bing—it's love at first sight. Then, less than a year later—"

"Her father died."

Lenny raised an eyebrow.

"That's right. So you do read the papers."

"I've done a little research, that's all."

Lenny took a deep breath. "Dad dies. A heart attack. And he's everything she has. Not just of family but also roots. Sam Ritt, the coach, tries to take some of the strain, but basically it's down to Doug to stop her going off the deep end, because she's taking it real bad. They go through some tough months. Ellen's off the ice, and onto antidepressants. Then, out of the blue, they announce that they're going to get married in the fall, which comes as a big surprise, you know, because she's so young and Doug . . . well, up till now he was running with the brat pack—a hot pistol."

Lenny picked up a letter opener and considered it for a moment.

"Now, I don't know what Doug thought he was doing, but I think that for Ellen it was pretty clear. Marriage meant a home. It also meant a certain amount of privacy, a certain amount of protection from the media. You see the way she is now? Well, she was no different then. She was younger, she did what her agent told her, but basically that whole celeb glitz thing was not her. I think she saw herself in this nice house with Doug—candlelit dinners, walks in the park, you know. Doug of course took a different view. He didn't really understand why somebody, given the chance, wouldn't go to three parties every night. And then—and this is where we get to the fertility thing— she wanted to start a family."

"How old was she?"

"This is early on in the marriage, so—she's young, maybe only twenty-one."

"Twenty-one?"

"That's right. It's not what you would call normal behavior. I mean this kid—okay, she's had a rough time losing her pop and all, but basically she's got the world at her feet. The Lillehammer games are two years away—a possible multimillion-dollar medal, and all she wants to do is keep house and have a baby. Can you imagine the conversations she was having with her agent? I mean, I know this guy and he is *not* a sentimentalist. For him the baby is like a three-megaton warhead. What she just said about the strength–weight thing? Can you imagine what motherhood does to your triple toe loop?"

"Maybe she'd had enough."

"Sure, whatever. Anyway, the agent gives her some kind of ultimatum and she tells him to take a walk. End of relationship. She is now a housewife, and in a way it works pretty well for a while. She's around more for Doug. She can handle the late nights better. She can be more supportive and so forth. But with one thing and another, soon after she quit the ice the marriage started to go downhill."

"Gorman didn't want a child?"

"I don't know if it was like that. I mean, he was still crazy about her. Who wouldn't be, right? But somehow or other, for some reason or other, the child didn't come. So then someone spots Doug Gorman going into the Harper Trust—it's a fertility clinic down in Orange County—and the tabloids get hold of it. Macho heart-throb Doug Gorman was sterile or impotent or both. You know, the usual free-for-all. Guess you missed it, huh?"

"I didn't go that far back. Was there any truth to the stories?"

"I really couldn't tell you. Like I say, I don't get into this kind of stuff with Ellen. You saw yourself how much *she* wants to talk about it."

"Yeah."

"And that wasn't the end of it. Three years into the marriage Doug and Ellen went to an adoption agency. And guess what? No luck there either."

"They were refused?"

"That's right. The way I heard it, the agency didn't consider the marriage strong enough to provide a stable home."

"Ouch."

"You can imagine how Ellen took *that*. They tried again, twice. Meanwhile they're building this great house in Brentwood. Like *that's* going to convince the agencies the marriage is viable."

Lenny stood up and walked over to the door. He

asked his assistant for coffee, came back, and sat down.

"So, you see now what I'm saying about messing with her head?"

16

Barbara Christian came out of the video suite and almost ran into Greg Chalmers coming the other way with a tray full of coffee cups.

"Whoa, watch out," he said, swerving around her. "What's the rush?"

A couple of heads on the subeditors' desk popped up from behind their screens.

"Make mine black, no sugar," she said without stopping.

"Oh really?" Chalmers called after her. "Would you like a petit four with that?"

At her desk she riffled through her Rolodex and pulled out a card with HARD NEWS written in the top right-hand corner. She grabbed the phone, glanced over the top of the burlap screen, sat down again, and dialed.

The line buzzed once, then a terse voice said: "Fenwick."

"Adam?"

"Yes."

There was a lot of noise in the background, recorded

voices running at high speed, stopping and starting, what sounded like an argument close by.

"It's Barbara."

"No, no, *back*. Barbara?"

"Christian."

"Yeah, there. Right. Hi, Barbara, what's up? *No*. I don't want that. Lose all that. Sorry, Barbara. How are you?"

"Great. Listen, you got the Sunday show all blocked out yet? Tell me."

"Why, you got something?"

"It's a little weird, but I think you'll like it."

There was a muffled crunch as Fenwick covered the mouthpiece. Christian could just make out his voice, telling someone what to do. Then he was back again.

"Weird is fine. You got pictures?"

"Better than that."

"I like it already. What's the angle?"

Barbara held the phone close.

"Okay. You remember all those stories about Doug Gorman?"

17

The Ford commercial had been shot on a rented soundstage at Alameda Studios, eight miles north of downtown Los Angeles. The stage—one of the largest on the lot at 31,000 square feet—was equipped with an underwater tank that had been frozen a few weeks earlier for use in a feature film. The facilities available on the stage had made it possible to cut the production schedule to four days, something that would have been impossible at any commercial rink. They also made possible the kind of dramatic tracking and aerial shots that gave the commercial much of its impact.

Pete Golding arrived at the studios at one o'clock in the afternoon, having spent most of the morning at the West Coast offices of King Taylor Simon, the advertising agency responsible for the Ford campaign. The production manager on the Ford shoot, he'd learned at last, had been a woman called Sandy Richter. It was she who'd had overall responsibility for logistics and personnel, and if there had been any trouble behind the scenes she should have heard about it. As it turned out, she was back at Alameda that day, overseeing the production of a soft drinks commercial on one of the smaller stages.

Golding wasn't holding out much hope of a breakthrough as he pulled up at the barrier and wound down the window. The Sindy reference in the call was striking, but hardly conclusive. And the fact that Ellen Cusak had no recollection of being pestered by anyone during the shoot, or of even having a serious argument, made it an unlikely starting point for all the madness. Nevertheless, he had to check it out. He'd promised to find the stalker, track him down, make him stop. That was why Mayot had asked for him: he wanted action. But so far he had nothing. The truth was, he was beginning to feel out of his depth. It wasn't just that the letters and the calls didn't fit, that he couldn't put together a picture of the stalker that made any sense (Romero being out of town didn't help). Nor was it the guy's cleverness, the fact that he seemed to know about telephones and security. It was more a feeling that he knew a whole lot about Ellen Cusak, that the years—he felt in his gut that it had to be years—of watching her and studying her and thinking about her had given him a kind of head start. That might not have bothered Golding so much if he himself had managed to win her confidence, gotten her to open up a little. But that was proving very difficult. Just as Lenny Mayot had said, Ellen was a very private person, very "inside herself." But why was she that way? Had it ever occurred to him to ask? For a moment Golding saw her as he had that first time, standing by the window, looking out: her sad, beautiful face. He felt an urge to reassure her, to show her that she could trust him. He wanted her to know that she was not alone.

"Can I help you, sir?"

The security guard's flushed face was tilted to one side, eyebrows raised, as if the guy he was talking to was a little simple. His uniform was black, indistinguishable from a regular police officer's except for the badge. Golding reached into his jacket and pulled out his ID.

"Yeah, I'm here to see Sandy Richter. She's making a commercial on stage seven."

The guard took the ID, examined it closely, then handed it back.

"You expected?"

"Uh-huh."

The guard picked up a phone, said something into it, then pointed Golding towards an area on his right marked VISITOR PARKING.

"Just pull in over there, sir. Someone will be with you shortly."

Golding did as he was told. After a few minutes another guard appeared to escort him to stage seven, which was hardly necessary since the numbers on each of the hangar-size buildings were six feet high. Anywhere else, Golding would have found such heavy-handed security irritating, but this was a place where famous people came to work: household names, familiar faces, objects of fascination and fantasy, targets for the deluded, the abused, the self-loathing, the psychotic. The sheer scale of the place afforded some protection, the towering coffee-colored walls, the long empty alleyways. But not enough. The only thing he found surprising was that so far nobody had tried to search him.

He found Sandy Richter standing outside one of the production trailers that were parked beside the soundstage, a mobile phone in one hand and a clipboard in the other. She was in her early thirties, with shoulder-length red hair, nice-looking but for the dark circles under her eyes that bore witness to a career of long hours and high pressure. She wore a yellow silk blouse and gray slacks, which looked a little dressy next to the technicians and crew in their T-shirts and jeans.

"You work for Ellen Cusak?" she asked before Golding had had a chance to introduce himself.

"That's right. Pete Golding. Thanks for seeing me." He glanced into the cavernous interior of the sound-stage where a mocked-up school gymnasium was surrounded by a jungle of wires, cables, and scaffolding. The noise of drilling and hammering echoed in the darkness. "I know you must be very—"

"You bet," she said briskly. "We gotta start shooting in forty minutes. What was it you wanted exactly? They weren't very clear at KTS."

A young woman came hurrying out of the trailer carrying a checked dress on a hanger. Richter and Golding followed.

"It's about the Ford commercial you made here a couple of months back."

"Uh-huh." Richter looked at her watch.

"Mrs. Cusak started receiving threatening letters shortly afterwards."

"Who from, General Motors?"

"Well, that's the point. We don't know. There's a chance the person responsible was present during the shoot."

Richter stopped at the next trailer.

"No kidding. Here?"

Golding wondered whether to give her the full facts, decided against it.

"In one of the calls there was a reference to the way her hair was done."

Richter laughed, frowning in disbelief.

"You need Paloma." She rapped on the trailer door. "Paloma, honey."

From inside the trailer a hassled voice answered: *"Sí."*

"You been making those obscene phone calls again?"

There was a thump from inside and then a small Latin woman with curly dark hair appeared in the doorway holding a matronly gray wig.

"Say what?"

"I think anyone present during the Ford shoot could have seen it," said Golding. "You had Ellen Cusak in a long blond wig for a time, I was told."

"Hair extension," said Paloma. "Wha's going on?"

Before Golding could answer, a call came through on Richter's mobile. Paloma waited for a moment, then rolled her eyes and disappeared back into the trailer. Richter talked schedules with some guy called Arty. An electric trolley carrying a small party of tourists trundled past the end of the alleyway on its way to the back lot with its mocked-up Wild West town. Golding was wasting his time here, he knew it. And Sandy Richter knew he was wasting hers.

"Sorry about that," she said when she was finished, although she didn't look sorry. "So what exactly did you want to know?"

"Specifically, if you had any personnel problems during the shoot. I mean any incidents of, let's say, inappropriate behavior. Any complaints or—"

"Are you kidding? They never stop."

Golding ignored the humor.

"In particular I'm talking about reports of sexual harassment, that kind of thing. Maybe people on the set who shouldn't have been there: fans, autograph hunters, paparazzi."

Richter looked at him for a moment. It was clear she was rushed off her feet—and probably liked it that way, liked everyone to know she was the busiest bee in the hive. All the same, Golding had the impression she was taking him seriously at last. Maybe she had her own experiences of what sexual harassment could mean.

"We don't get much trouble from that kind of thing," she said. "I mean fans or whatever, not here. The security's pretty tight. There's a studio tour, but the visitors go around about ten at a time, and they're always marshaled. As for the other thing—"

"You mean harassment?"

"Right. You gotta remember we had a pretty big crew for that commercial, plus a hockey team. It got a little boisterous at times."

"How big are we talking?"

"Crew? Twenty or more, I guess."

"Twenty?"

"Sure, if you include electricians, wardrobe, makeup. Plus we had choreographers, two stunt guys, paramedics on standby, drivers. The whole enchilada."

Nearer thirty people then, plus the hockey team, plus the occasional visitor from the agency or the client, plus any of a thousand people who could have wandered over from one of the other stages just to take a peek. There was no way Golding could even begin to check them all. The best he could do was keep asking questions and hope something would shake loose.

"So . . . what about the film itself? I'm thinking there'd be people who'd have seen the dailies, the stuff you didn't use."

"You mean postproduction?" Richter said. "That'd be another . . . five."

"Did you do that here?"

"We did that time. Generally we farm it out, but time was the big issue on that project, and it helped doing everything on site. Plus they have everything state-of-the-art here: sound transfer, video mixing, telecine. The director didn't even have to leave the lot."

"But if there'd been trouble, complaints, you'd have heard about them, right?"

Richter shrugged.

"Maybe. But, like I say, things on that shoot got pretty hectic. Time is money here like you wouldn't believe. Second-for-second, that commercial cost more than *Titanic,* did you know that?"

Golding shook his head.

"It's not like everything's gonna grind to a halt because someone gets goosed in makeup. You know what I'm saying?"

Unless you were a star, Golding thought, a bigger star than Ellen Cusak.

"So what you're saying is anything could have happened, and no one would know about it unless it interfered with the shoot."

"I didn't say *no one*."

"Then—"

Richter smiled.

"You know what they say in the movies? If you wanna know what's really happening on a shoot, how it's *really* going, you don't ask the director or the producer. You ask the drivers. That's when you're on location. In this place you ask the studio security. They see everything."

Golding could see a couple of them standing at the corner of the next stage down. They looked big enough and mean enough to be cops, which made him wonder why they weren't.

"Yeah," said Richter, following his gaze. "They got some big fish starting work this afternoon. I don't know who."

"You think they'd talk to me?"

Richter shrugged.

"If you have a signed letter from the head of the studio, sure."

18

Saturday, August 7

Text and pictures—grainy, smear-streaked: Ellen mid-jump, arms crossed high on her chest, smiling, eyes closed; Ellen holding an armful of flowers, kissing gold in 1991 under the headline STELLAR CUSAK; Ellen stepping out of a limousine at the funeral of her father; Ellen at her wedding in Santa Monica.

Golding spent the whole of Saturday sitting at computer terminals, first in the office, then in a local library where he dropped thirty dollars using the Nexus database, picking up stories going back ten years. At the end of the afternoon he lined up a string of sixty articles and hit PRINT. He would have liked to go straight home and spend the evening sifting through them, but he was already committed elsewhere.

Jackie had called him a couple of times during the week, leaving messages on his answering machine at home. She didn't sound too good. Every time he had called her number it had been busy. Finally, on Thursday, he thought of calling her at work, but was told she hadn't turned up again. He left a message saying he'd come over on Saturday evening. Her Saturday evenings were nearly always free.

He pulled up outside her place just after seven, relieved to see all the lights on. She opened the door as he was coming up the path.

"Hey, big brother."

She was drunk, weaving a little on the threshold, her face flushed. Her light brown hair, which she tended to bunch up with a clip, had collapsed on one side.

"Hey, sweetheart."

He kissed her cheek, and before he could get in through the door she burst into tears, grabbing hold of him, clinging on tight, saying his name over and over.

Golding had to detach her hands from the back of his neck.

"What's up, sweetheart? What happened?"

She pulled back from him and wiped her face with the back of her hand. She shook her head, made an attempt to push some hair back into the clip, and then walked through to the kitchen. Golding looked around at the living room. The place looked like a bomb had hit it. There were clothes strewn everywhere. A big vinyl suitcase was open on the coffee table. He called out to her.

"What's happening, Jackie? What are you doing?"

She came back into the doorway holding a bottle of beer.

"I'm packing," she said, gesturing at the suitcase. "I'm moving out."

"Moving out? Where you going?"

"I'm going back to Milwaukee."

She was going back home. Golding couldn't believe it. It was the worst thing she could possibly do.

"Why?" It was all he could think to say.

Jackie shrugged and drank from the bottle. She saw him watching her and stopped.

"You wanna join me?"

"Sure."

They went through to the kitchen. Golding found a glass for himself and she poured him a drink. They sat at the Formica table. Golding noticed that John's ashtray had gone.

"Has something happened?" he said.

"He left." She blinked the tears out of her lashes. "He left on Wednesday morning. I called you twice."

Golding felt a flush of shame. She had called him, and he'd been too busy to answer, too busy looking after his celebrity clients.

"I called back, baby, but the line was busy."

She nodded, sniffed.

"I was talking to Mom," she said, wanting to change the subject. She wiped away her tears and tried to smile. "She's walking around now, Pete. With a cane anyway. The doctor says she's doing fine."

Golding stiffened up at the mention of his mother.

"You should call her, Petey."

"So he just upped and left," he said, ignoring her. He looked across the kitchen at the shelves where John had kept his old LP collection. The LPs had gone, so had the stereo. "Where's the hi-fi?"

"He took it."

"Son of a bitch." Golding stood up. "It wasn't his to take."

Jackie was staring up at him, a scared look in her blue eyes. He couldn't bear to see her scared. It was agony for him. He looked away from her, looked around for something of John's that he could tear or smash.

"Son of a bitch," he said again.

"He left other stuff," said Jackie. "He left the microwave and that *was* his."

Golding walked over to the sink and washed his glass under the tap. He went to place it on the draining board, but there were too many plates and cups there already, half of them dirty. The sink was full of filthy saucepans. He leaned forward, putting his hand on the edge of the sink, trying to think straight.

"But why go back?" he said. He turned to face her. "Jackie, you have to leave all that behind. You have to move on. We all do."

She looked down at her beer bottle.

"I have moved on, Petey." She lifted the bottle to her mouth and took a long drink. Then looked at him levelly. "You're the one who's stuck. You're the one who's in the past."

She stood up. Golding winced as she struggled to her feet. Her ankles were badly swollen. She was thirty-four and she had the ankles of a seventy-year-old. She came across to him and touched his face. For a long time they just stared at each other.

It was Jackie who broke the silence.

"Daddy's dead, Petey. He died a long time ago. What he did . . ." She closed her eyes for a second, shaking her head. "What he did died with him. Momma's on her own now. She needs me."

Golding grabbed her to him and buried his face in her shoulder. He clenched his eyes tight shut, wanting to believe her, wanting to believe that the past was the past, but she wasn't right. What their father had done would always be there. Not only would it never die, it would always be trapped in the present. It had happened almost twenty years ago, but as far as he was concerned, it was happening today—now.

Dad had lost his job. That was how it all began. It was such a banal thing, something that happened all the time. It wasn't even such a big deal since their mom was still working—going out every day to her job with the taxi company, where she handled the paperwork between stints on the switchboard. But in spite of that, after his father lost his job they struggled as a family.

Golding had always been very close to his father. They went fishing together, would go off sometimes for the whole weekend into the woods, finding pristine stretches of river, camping overnight. But that year, the year he lost his job, there were no weekend excursions. His dad would keep to the house, never leaving the couch from which he would sullenly watch the TV, criticizing the network news, the baseball players, the commercials. He'd start drinking in the morning and just drift through the day, dozing on the couch or wandering around the house aimlessly.

Jackie was sixteen years old. She had gotten past the stage of trying to cover up what was happening to her, what was happening to her breasts and hips. She was beginning to enjoy being a young woman. She had always been closer to Mom than Dad, but when she started into puberty they were even closer, almost conspiratorial. Golding could remember that even he felt excluded. Jackie confided less, spent more time in her room or out with her friends. Then one day, one day when Mom was out at work, something had snapped—that was the only way Golding could figure it—something had snapped, and the old man had raped her.

If he tried really hard, Golding could still remember things about the week it happened. He couldn't be sure about the day. There had been no big scene or row. It had happened when Jackie came home from school—she had told him that much many years later. There had been no explosion of anger or resentment, but something changed in the house. It was as if Jackie had been switched off. She had always been vivacious, playful, but after it happened she became quiet and withdrawn.

Then he raped her again. For three months through the summer of '81, he continued to abuse her, and nobody did anything. Nobody saw anything. Then Dad got taken on in the warehouse of a local brewery and the abuse stopped. Things got back to normal. The fishing trips began again, and with the exception of Jackie's new silence, the family went on as before. Looking back on it, Golding couldn't understand why nobody saw what was happening, why nobody did anything. He couldn't believe his mom didn't see what was going on—she and Jackie had been so close—he couldn't believe his father could have just pretended it didn't happen. It reminded Golding of those cartoon characters that ran out over the ravine and only fell when they realized what had happened, except that the moment of realization had never come for them. They were suspended in midair over the ravine, acting like everything was just fine.

It was from that summer that Jackie started to turn in on herself. She stopped going out, started to eat more, spent more time in her room. Five years later she was obese and ugly and so tangled up inside nobody knew how to handle her. And even then the family had continued to function. Then Golding had started to understand. Things Jackie said, the things she did, started to make sense. He left home. Instead of confronting his old man, he had left, abandoned her. He had never forgiven himself. By asking her to come out to L.A., he was trying to make up for the past, he was trying to be a good brother to her.

He let go of her and they separated. Jackie went back to her chair.

"But that house," he said quietly. "How can you go back to that house?"

She pressed her lips together, shook her head.

"She's selling the house. It's too big anyway. She's taking a little place nearer the mall."

Golding stared at the top of Jackie's head. For the first time he noticed strands of gray growing from the neat whorl of her crown.

He left after midnight with a sense that nothing had been resolved—a sense that nothing would ever be resolved. He got home feeling utterly exhausted, but when he lay down on the bed he found that he couldn't sleep. Thoughts of his father and home kept going round in his head. His father had died four years ago, and the day Golding heard about it, what he had felt most was anger; not anger that he had died so young— he was only sixty-two—but anger that he had never confronted him, had never done the right thing. The anger had never left him. Just thinking about the old man filled him with rage.

He gave up on sleep and walked through to the living room, where the Cusak file was open on the table. He picked out an article from a sports journal and read. He read for hours, picking through the text, circling, underlining. It started to get light outside. He read an article that said over half the women in sports like figure skating and gymnastics had eating disorders. They starved, they messed up their menstrual cycles, they had heart attacks. He read how a top gymnast had used anorexia and bulimia to control her weight, how she had gotten down to forty-seven pounds and then died of multiple organ failure. He learned that bulimics could be pathologically secretive, were able to vomit so quietly that it sounded like urination. In the same article, the writer, a medical doctor, recommended that coaches watch out for telltale signs like frequent eating alone, continuous drinking of water, use of laxatives, of feet pointing towards the toilet in a bathroom stall. It freaked him out. The image of Ellen defying gravity in a triple axel was replaced by Ellen as a frightened kid, alone and afraid in the dark—afraid of what her body was doing, afraid of what her father would say, afraid, above all, of failure.

At eight o'clock in the morning he tried calling Jackie. He didn't know what he was going to say to her. He just wanted to talk. But all he got was her answering machine. He thought about driving over there and seeing if she was okay, even picked up his car keys, but then decided it would just mean more heartache—for him, for her. She was not okay. Neither was he. He couldn't help her. When he'd had a chance to help her he'd done nothing, and now it was too late.

That was when he decided to put up the pictures. He put up a picture of Ellen on the sitting room wall. Then another. He supplemented the grainy printouts with a couple of glossy full-color pictures he had culled from the office file. One picture, shot through bushes with a zoom, showed Ellen beside the pool with Douglas Gorman. They were both laughing, and Ellen, dressed in a T-shirt and shorts, had obviously just climbed out of the water. The soft shadows of her nipples was faintly visible through the wet cotton. He told himself he was just being professional, that by seeing Ellen that way, he could get into the mind of the stalker.

He snatched a few hours of sleep on the couch and awoke from a hot suffocating dream just after midday, his head splitting. He washed, shaved, swallowed a couple of Tylenol, and then made more coffee.

The place was a mess—scattered clothes and printouts everywhere. He started clearing up but immediately became engrossed in an article from *Rink International*. Two hours later he was still reading. He brought the coffee in from the kitchen and installed himself at the table where the printouts now formed a neat stack. At a second reading a lot of the articles seemed weak. There was plenty of speculation about Ellen and Doug's efforts to have a child, but nothing concrete. An article in *People* magazine from 1993 described how Gorman had punched out a photographer in a parking lot. It turned out that the photographer had made some kind of remark about Gorman's virility. Touchy Douglas.

He read everything from beginning to end but didn't feel that he was any nearer to understanding her life. He felt that there must be stuff hidden, probably having to do with her years alone with Stepan. He looked up at the picture of Ellen winning gold in '91. She was nineteen years old. She'd had the world at her feet, but all she'd wanted was to get hitched and have a kid. Why?

He played the stalker tape again, focusing on the part where the guy started talking about the people around Ellen. *They're just trying to come between us, to keep you from the truth.* He wondered what that truth was, what reality Ellen Cusak was supposed to be hiding from. Then he realized that even if he knew, he'd be no closer to finding the guy. If he ever caught him, it would be around Ellen's house. That was the one place he knew the guy went. And it wasn't just to deliver his pictures. This guy was a watcher, Golding felt sure of that. *You see, I see you, Ellen.*

Playing the tape made him itchy. He decided to drive into the office to see if the answering machine had picked up anything more, anything that might give a clue to the guy's identity. He got as far as the front door when he realized that if he left the house he would end up driving over to Ellen's place. That was the way he had started with Maddy—sitting outside in the dark, telling himself he was doing it to catch the stalker.

He went back into the sitting room and put on the TV. Then realized how hungry he was. In the kitchen the best he could come up with was chicken soup. He hadn't been shopping for days. He was coming back into the room, chewing a piece of stale bagel, the hot soup on a tray, when he saw the girl.

She was on the ice in her blue dress, frozen mid-stride. Her face was pinker on his TV, but he recognized it as the same recording. She raised her gloved hand in a jerky slo-mo wave. He choked on bagel. The bowl slid from the tray, sending soup down the wall.

"Goddammit!"

He fumbled for the remote, brought up the sound.

Driving, rhythmic music. *Current Affairs* on speed. *Hard News:* bullshit tabloid TV. The picture of the girl was replaced by the set—two immaculately coifed anchors, a severe-looking Asian woman and a silver-haired man, smiling from behind a chrome and plastic console. The camera jumped in tight on the two heads as they started a punchy, back-and-forth lead-in: *Four years ago world champion ice skater Ellen Cusak sought to save her failing marriage to Doug Gorman by adopting a child.*

Unfortunately for the celebrity couple, no less than three agencies turned them down, unimpressed by the domestic arrangements at their luxury home in the Brentwood hills.

But why adopt in the first place?

Was the couple infertile?

Was Gorman impotent? The guy looked up through his elder-statesman eyebrows. *Until now the news media has been frustrated by the wall of silence around the Brentwood home. Rumors that the famously private Cusak was unable to bear children have remained just that—rumors. But tonight* Hard News *breaks through that wall of silence to bring you images of a little girl . . .*

Ellen as a young girl in a blue dress was flashed up next to the mystery child. Then they were back with the anchors, who allowed a moment to pass, as though speechless in the face of such clear evidence: this was Ellen Cusak's child.

Golding folded his arms. Tabloid bullshit.

The male anchor twisted to a new camera position.

Two weeks ago a mysterious intruder entered the Brentwood property where Cusak now lives alone. Nothing was taken, but a photograph of this child was put on the wall next to Cusak's family pictures.

A calling card? said the woman, raising an eyebrow.

Or something more sinister?

In the last couple of days, the intruder called again. This time to leave a videocassette, showing the same little girl . . . skating.

They ran the tape without interruption. It was eerie as hell. Golding took a piece of bagel out of his mouth.

Our experts estimate the age of the child to be between four and five years, which would mean this little girl was born at around the time the couple were hoping to start a family of their own.

They exchanged a look as if to share an obvious conclusion. Then the woman took up the narrative.

Cusak recently employed an agency to track down what she believes may be a stalker.

Someone who is obsessed with her ice-queen persona.

But is that the whole story?

Is that what lies behind these bizarre approaches?

Hard News *is used to asking tough questions, and tonight we ask: Is the "stalker" in fact someone from Ellen Cusak's past?*

"For Christ's sake," Golding said out loud. Where did they get this kind of crap?

Is this little girl Ellen Cusak's child?

The *Hard News* logo came up, with the corny sound effect of breaking glass and then a commercial.

Golding cut the sound. He couldn't believe it, couldn't believe how they could come up with such . . . *lies.* Lies that were surely designed to hurt. He pressed the remote to rewind, and then remembered that he wasn't watching a recording. The story might be bullshit, but the tape was real. Somebody had leaked it. But who? He remembered what Reynolds had said about Lenny trying to manufacture a comeback for Ellen, but it was hard to believe he'd be capable of such a betrayal.

He found his address book and called Lenny Mayot's mobile number, but there was no answer. Then he tried the office number and got Lenny's answering machine, but when the beeps came up he didn't know what to say. He stood up, his heart racing.

The phone rang.

"Hello?"

Nothing. Just the sound of someone trying to control

their breathing. For a split second he felt that this was the guy, the stalker.

"Hello?" His voice came out loud, aggressive.

"You . . . you shit, you piece of *shit*."

"Ellen? Is that—?"

But the line was dead.

He grabbed his keys and ran out of the house.

All the way over the Santa Monica Mountains, he kept up a constant monologue, shaking his head, swearing to her that it had nothing to do with him, swearing to her that he would never, ever, do anything to betray her. By the time he got on to Beverly Glen Boulevard he was exhausted, wrung-out—the sweat standing in beads on his forehead.

He pulled up in front of the property and the déjà vu hit him like a wave. He was back in front of Maddy Olsen's house, out of control, ready to do anything to save her. He remembered her cold smile when she found him sitting in the shadows. She told him he was like a little kid. She told him he was like a little boy that wants to protect a butterfly so much he ends up squeezing it to death.

A dog was barking next door. He wound down his window and sat for a long time, looking up the drive. Through the bars of the gate he could see one taillight of the Mercedes that was parked in front of the garage. He waited until he was breathing normally and then checked his face in the mirror. He got out of the car and pressed the buzzer. There was no answer. He pressed again. After what felt like a minute he heard Ellen's voice.

"Yes?"

He had been expecting the maid.

"Ellen—Ellen, it's me, Pete Golding."

Silence. He pressed the buzzer again. The dog went on barking. He was amazed the neighbors put up with it.

"Come on."

He pressed again.

"Go away."

Her voice sounded calmer than before. She was just angry now.

He put his face against the intercom. "Ellen, you've got to believe me, I never had anything to do with that *Hard News* bullshit."

"Yeah right."

She was listening to him.

"You have to believe me," he said, trying to keep the emotion out of his voice. "Can you—would you open the gate?"

There was complete silence. Then he heard the front door open. He peered up through the gloom and saw her walk into the driveway. She was wearing a black dress, ready to go out.

"You've got to believe me," he said.

She watched him for a long time, then reached up and touched at her hair.

"Why? Why should I?"

She was at least twenty feet away, but she spoke in a wary undertone.

"Because . . ." He didn't know what to say. He tried to smile. "Because I'm on your side." She looked him up and down and he realized that he must look like a complete slob in his old jeans and T-shirt. "It's just not something I'd ever do."

"So who did?"

"I don't know. It could have been . . . anybody. It could have been Lenny."

She slowly shook her head.

"Lenny's a friend," she said.

"Then maybe it was the guy. The Ice Man, or whoever it is." She looked over towards the barking dog. "Maybe it's part of his game."

She came down the drive until she was standing just the other side of the gate. She looked at his disheveled clothes and hair.

"What game?"

And Golding saw it in her eyes. Something off, something wrong, like *she* was the one playing games. It made him afraid for her.

"I don't know." They stared into each other's eyes. "Do you?"

She shrugged.

"Look—look, you shouldn't have driven over. I'm sorry. I'm sorry. It was just . . . a shock. I wasn't even watching really, and then I saw those pictures. It just freaked me out."

"That's okay." He smiled. "I understand."

"You didn't have to drive over."

"No—I did. I needed you to know that I'm . . ."

"What?"

"Well, that I'm around. Whenever you need me."

He put a hand on the gate, and she looked at it for a moment.

"Well, that's . . . that's good," she said. "That's nice to know."

She started to back away up the drive.

"I'm going to find out who leaked this," he shouted.

She turned, holding up a hand to wave good-bye.

19

Monday, August 9

Abandonment? What the . . . ? Are you insane? What did I just tell you?" Lenny gripped the phone so hard the plastic popped. "Ellen Cusak did *not* abandon her child for the sake of her career, or for any other reason—are you getting this down, Mr. . . . Mr. Schrader?— because she does not *have* a child. Okay? You want me to say it again?"

He looked up and saw Sandra Reilly peering around the door. Behind her the desktop switchboard was ablaze with flashing lights: a mob of reporters clamoring for the lowdown on the Ellen Cusak stalker story—a story that was mutating before his eyes into the Ellen Cusak child abandonment scandal. Sandra gestured helplessly. This wasn't something she was used to.

"Be there in just a second," Lenny called out, so that the guy on the line couldn't fail to hear him.

"So you think the video of the little girl is a fake?" Schrader came back, his voice all innocent curiosity suddenly, like he was only trying to understand it. "And the photograph too. Is that right?"

"Yes," said Lenny. "*No.* I'm saying—"

"You're saying *Hard News* faked the pictures?"

"No."

"Then who did? Who would want to do that?"

"Listen, listen"—Lenny brought his hand to his forehead, trying to see his way through the tangle of chop logic and half-truths, a tangle from which tabloid hacks like this one made their living—"I don't know where the pictures came from. I don't know who the little girl is, okay? And neither does Ellen Cusak. This whole thing's the work of some psycho who's been stalking her. *That's* the story here."

But even as he said it, Lenny knew that he was wrong. The stalker was *yesterday's* story. This guy wanted more than that, something newer, bigger. They all would. They'd keep on digging and connecting and insinuating—all the way to the Oval Office, if they could possibly manage it.

"Can I be clear about something?" said Schrader. "You've been Ellen's manager how long?"

"A long time," said Lenny, tugging his tie loose and undoing his top button. "Coming up to six years. So I know what I'm talking about."

"Ri-ight. So . . . given the likely age of the child, even assuming that the pictures are fairly recent, isn't it possible she was born before you were on the scene? I mean, she could be six, seven, eight years old by now."

Lenny sucked in a long breath. He could feel himself getting angry now. He would have put the phone down right there and then, but he had an idea Mr. Schrader would be quite happy about that. And then a few days later the world would read: *When asked about the child's parentage, Ellen Cusak's manager, Lenny Mayot, suddenly hung up. . . .*

"Let me ask you something for a change," he said. "If

you have a child, a normal, healthy child like the one in the video, why would you make applications to *three* adoption agencies? Does that sound to you like someone who doesn't want to be a parent?"

"Mmmm." Schrader sounded as if he had just sipped at an especially interesting Bordeaux. "We've had some thoughts on that. Could have been, you know, like a screen."

"A screen? What kind of—?"

"Or maybe guilt," Schrader added. "Maybe her husband didn't know anything about it. If it was a teenage pregnancy, the child could have been put out for adoption. All over before she hits the limelight. Then, later, she's overcome with remorse."

"This is crazy," was all Lenny could say. "This is . . . She was a skater, for God's sake."

"It's just what people've been saying."

"Oh really? What people are we talking about?"

"Oh, you know how it is, Mr. Mayot. I agree it seems a little bizarre."

As if that was a problem, thought Lenny.

"Listen to me, Ellen Cusak has been *paying* someone to find this guy. She wouldn't—"

"To find the child?" said Schrader. "She's paying someone to find the child?"

"*No,* goddammit!" Lenny was on his feet. "She is paying someone to find the stalker! The guy who sent her all this shit."

"But isn't that the same thing, Mr. Mayot? You find the guy, you're gonna find the little girl, right?"

Lenny didn't know what to say. All he knew was he was only making bad worse. He needed to take control of the situation before it was too late. That was supposed to be part of his job.

"Okay, okay, okay, Sam—it is Sam, right?"

"You got it."

Lenny sat down again, tried to sound calm.

"I'm gonna level with you. Because I don't want you making a fool of yourself, okay? And I don't want my client getting any more hurt by this whole thing than she already has been."

"Of course," said Schrader soothingly. "We're not trying to hurt anyone. We're just trying to get the story straight. Personally, I've always been a big fan of Miss Cusak's."

"Sure, sure, who isn't? Now this is off the record, Sam, okay? Okay?"

"Whatever you say, Mr. Mayot. Off the record is fine."

Lenny sat back in his chair. Could he trust the guy on this or not? Probably not. But at this stage of the game it didn't much matter either way.

"You wanna know why I *know* that kid isn't Ellen Cusak's child?"

"Uh-huh."

"Because I happen to know Ellen Cusak can't *have* children. She tried fertility treatment, the works. No joy. It's sad but true."

For the first time there was silence on the line. Mr. Schrader was momentarily out of questions.

"That's, er . . . that's tough," was all he could manage.

"You bet," said Lenny. "Very tough. Now you see what's going on here? This sicko found out about it somehow, and now he's torturing her with it, showing her what she would have had. I've seen his letters. This is not someone who wishes her well, I can tell you that."

Schrader let out a low whistle. Lenny hoped he was impressed.

"Seriously sick stuff, huh?"

Sandra was at the door again. She held up a sheet of paper with the words BARBARA CHRISTIAN URGENT written on it.

"I gotta run now," said Lenny. "You keep that to yourself, okay?"

And before Schrader could ask him anything else he put the phone down.

"Is she waiting?"

Sandra nodded.

"I'll put her through," she said, hurrying back to her desk.

"Yeah, thanks, and, er, Sandra?"

"Yes?"

"Shut the door, would you?"

Sandra gave him a nervous smile.

A moment later the phone rang again.

"Barbara?"

He had to fight the urge not to whisper.

"Lenny, before you tear my head off, I'm not responsible for the angle."

She sounded hurried, excited, anything but apologetic.

"Not respon—? I've just . . . Have you any idea what they're saying out there? I've been fighting fires for two hours already and it's not even nine o'clock."

"What can I say? News travels fast."

"News? This was supposed to be . . ." He leaned into the mouthpiece. "People were supposed to sympathize," he hissed. "Be intrigued. Tomorrow we're gonna have *Ellen Cusak child abandoner* all over the national press."

"If we make the nationals we'll be doing just fine. Lenny, this is just what we need."

"Are you crazy? Have you any idea how Ellen's gonna take this? She's gonna go ballistic."

"Oh, come on, Lenny, it's just a story. There's nothing to worry about if it isn't true. It, er . . . it isn't true, is it?"

"*No, it is not.* For God's sake, Barbara. This whole thing has gotten way out of hand. I thought you were gonna focus on the Ice Man. That was what we agreed."

Lenny heard the click of a lighter and a long inhale. If she was smoking, she couldn't be in her office. He wondered where she was actually calling from.

"I gave them the whole story, just like you told me."

"Then where did they get all that shit about someone from her past? About it being her kid?"

"*They* came up with that. Actually, I think it's a good angle. It's *much* more intriguing."

Lenny groaned.

"I can't believe this. I can't believe this is . . . Well, I'm telling you, Barbara, if anyone goes on the record saying—"

"I already spoke to Argyle, Lenny."

Lenny sat up.

"You did?"

"Eve Kaufman was on the line at six o'clock this morning. She was that keen."

"They want the book?"

Christian laughed.

"Oh yes. Hardcover. Color plates. The whole bit. You can forget about those little softcovers by the checkout."

"Just because—?"

"I'm not committing for a couple of days. Meantime I'm pushing out a revamped proposal to a few other houses. See if we can't get an auction going. We get the price up, that guarantees publicity. That's why I'm calling, Lenny. I want to know you're happy about that. I mean, if we go with another house."

Lenny wasn't fooled. He knew she would do the book the way she wanted whatever he said, unauthorized if necessary. This was just a courtesy call to keep him on her side.

"Sure, sure, whatever. But I can promise you, if Ellen finds out—"

"She won't. Not even the producer at *Hard News* knows where that tape came from. She'll never know."

Lenny shook his head. He had a feeling of having turned a corner somehow.

"I still don't think she'll do the book. Not now. Not after all this."

He listened to Christian take a long pull on her cigarette. He could almost smell the menthol.

"The book's her chance to set the record straight. She has to see that. All she's gotta do is be honest. I mean, what's there to be afraid of?"

Lenny swallowed. He hoped she was right about the tape. He already wished he'd kept it to himself.

"I don't know, Barbara. I don't know."

Christian's voice hardened.

"Come on, Lenny. That is what Ellen needs. She should be thanking you."

20

Golding called Lenny Mayot first thing Monday morning, waited until lunchtime, then called again. He wanted to talk to Lenny before Ellen did, wanted to preempt any complaints about his uninvited visit on Sunday night, wanted to make it perfectly clear that he had had nothing to do with the leaking of the tape. But Lenny's lines were busy the whole time. He finally got to leave a message on the answering machine on Monday night. Lenny returned the call Tuesday afternoon.

"I'm sorry, Pete, but it's been crazy here. I guess you've seen the stories in the press, right?" Several tabloids had taken up the *Hard News* Cusak's-mystery-child line. "I've had reporters all over me."

Lenny sounded elated but nervous, like a kid that's been given a pet snake for his birthday.

"That's okay, Lenny. I just wanted to be clear that I had nothing to do with leaking the tape."

Lenny chuckled.

"I'll be straight with you, Pete: I did give that possibility some thought. But then I figured . . . ah, what the hell. Ellen said you thought maybe the stalker had leaked it."

So Ellen had spoken to him about Sunday night. Golding hoped she hadn't been too critical.

"There are only so many people it could have been," he said. "I mean, who had copies of the tape? You, me, and the stalker. Right?"

Lenny sighed into the phone. It was obvious he had other things on his mind.

"This whole situation is crazy," he said.

"Tell me about it."

"We've been getting letters. A ton of stuff was sent to *Hard News* and they sent it on to me."

"That's real decent of them."

"Well, it's national TV. Big audiences. They told me it was normal to get a few crackpots writing in."

"Crackpots?"

"Yeah. Not all of the letters are written by Ellen Cusak fans."

"What do you mean?"

Golding closed his eyes, already pretty certain of the answer.

"Well—you know, there's what you would call hate mail."

"Great. That's just great. That's exactly what Ellen needs right now."

"Yeah right. I haven't told her about it. I think it's better not to."

Golding reflected that, as always, the person being threatened was going to be the last to know. They decided that the best thing would be for him to send the most offensive mail over just in case the Ice Man had been prompted to write.

"You never know," said Golding. "He may have gotten sloppy, given something away."

The letters arrived in a box late Tuesday afternoon, and there were more on Wednesday morning.

By Wednesday afternoon Golding had another interesting selection for Romero to file under "Hatred." The stuff oozed the sadness and frustration of nowhere lives and mood-stabilizing drugs. As always, various forms of 20/20 hindsight were at work. A guy from Wisconsin who signed himself "Chef" claimed to have known all along that the "Cusak Cunt" was a whore and a cheater. A woman wrote from inside a penitentiary to say that she had shot the motherfucking social worker that came to take her girls away, and that any woman who could abandon her child deserved to be burned alive. She signed herself "DOLORES" in capitals, the two O's drawn as love hearts. In a scribbled P.S. that plunged down to the corner of the page—Romero was going to love it—she wrote that she knew where to buy the gasoline. *Hard New*s had tapped into a vein of crud that ran right through the country.

But there was nothing from the Ice Man. Coming to the end of the stack, Golding realized that he was disappointed. Without any new development on that front, without any more calls or surprise packages from the stalker, he had no reason to be in touch. No stalker meant no Ellen.

Then there was an opening. Late Wednesday afternoon Sandy Richter called sounding contrite. After all her blithe talk at the lot, it turned out that something had happened during the Ford shoot.

Golding flipped open his notebook.

"I'm listening."

"There's this character, Jeffrey Grossman, a grip. He was kicked off the set after a complaint about inappropriate conduct."

"What does that mean?"

"Inappropriate? I couldn't really say. But it had something to do with Ellen Cusak, which is why I called. Apparently he was hanging around her trailer doing I don't know what."

"Hanging around? That doesn't sound too bad."

"Yeah, well, there's probably more to it. Otherwise I don't think they'd have insisted he leave."

Golding frowned. When he had asked Ellen if there had been any trouble on the shoot, she had said no.

"Was it Cusak that made the complaint?" he said.

"I don't know. Like I said before, the people you need to talk to are Alameda Security. They're bound to have gotten involved. If you like I can set something up there."

He took Santa Monica Boulevard east to the 101. He was glad to get away from his desk and the hate letters, but even with the Sebring's top down he couldn't shake the feeling of disquiet he had, a feeling that Ellen was keeping things from him, things he needed to know. Rather than feeling angry about that, he was afraid— for her. He wished she trusted him enough to tell him what the hell was going on. He knew that given enough time, she could. He had sensed it when they stood at the bottom of her drive. She had looked at him differently, seeing him as a person and not just a hireling. Something had been revealed, something that got them onto another level of understanding.

Alameda Security occupied a couple of offices at the end of a row of prefabricated buildings painted the

same coffee color as the big soundstages. He was ush-
ered into a room where a bank of TV monitors offered
views of the lot. A sour smell of men in uniform reminded him of every security firm he'd ever been in.

Joe Walsh, the man Richter had lined up for him,
turned out to be a jowly, close-shaven, cop's cop type,
who wore his black *Il Duce* uniform with pride. They
went into his office. Bullshitting about what a nice kid
Sandy Richter was, what a *quiet* kid Ellen Cusak was, his
hard blue eyes never left Golding's face.

"So how's Tom Reynolds?" he said when he was installed behind his desk. "Is he a millionaire yet?"

It was clear that as soon as he had gotten off the
phone with Richter, Walsh had made a few calls of his
own, just to be sure who he was dealing with.

Golding shrugged. "He's getting there, I guess."

"I knew Tom before he set up the TMU. Did you
know that? Oh yeah. I had twenty-five years on the
force before I landed this job."

He made a how-about-that sweep with his hands
that took in filing cabinets, diplomas, an LAPD pen-
nant, and a wall of signed photographs that showed
him clutching the hands of some of the stars that
made Alameda Studios such a magical place. He had
obviously never gotten over the fact that he was responsible for the safety of stars like Harrison Ford
and Clint Eastwood. The LAPD reference was just in
case Golding thought he wasn't for real.

"Must be great rubbing shoulders with the rich and
famous," said Golding, hoping he sounded sincere.

Walsh shrugged.

"It is. But I have to say I do miss the action." He shot
Golding a look. "You'd know all about that, though."

Golding had yet to meet a law enforcement type who

could resist bringing up the shooting of Arthur McGinley. He shrugged and tried to think how to move them on.

"From what I understand, you had a little action of your own recently. Sandy mentioned you'd had to deal with somebody on the set of the Ford commercial."

"Oh yeah. That was nothing."

"I'd really appreciate it if you could tell me what exactly happened."

Walsh planted his elbows on his armrests and pushed himself up a little.

"Before we get into that, maybe you could . . . ?" He made a little give-it-up gesture with his right hand.

"Well, I guess Sandy probably explained to you that Alpha Global was retained to deal with some problems Ellen Cusak has been having recently with—"

"The stalker? This guy's been breaking into her place?"

The door opened and Walsh turned to look at a smiling, red-faced guy with a buzz cut. He had a soda in each fist.

"You guys interested?"

Walsh held up his hands and caught a Pepsi.

"How about you, Pete?"

"I'm fine, thanks," said Golding.

"Oh, Hal," said Walsh, "do me a favor and ask Hughie to step in, would you?"

"Sure thing."

Hal gave Golding a hard look and then closed the door.

"So are you saying Grossman's the guy?" said Walsh, pulling the tab.

"It's a little more complicated than that."

"So . . . I'm listening."

He wanted the whole story.

"Well, doing the job you do, you know how it is, Mr. Walsh."

"Joe, please."

"Sure, Joe. Well, Mrs. Cusak has been the focus of unwanted attention for a long time. This is going back over many years. Recently, after the Ford shoot in fact, she started to receive obscene and vindictive letters from someone signing himself the Ice Man. That's what I'm focusing on here today. Whether or not the Ice Man is also the intruder everyone is talking about is another issue."

Walsh smiled and sipped his drink.

"I got to say I'd have trouble seeing Grossman as a B&E wizard."

"Oh, why's that?"

"Well, he's the kind of guy leaves a trail. You know what I'm saying? A real slob. Plus he weighs in at around two hundred pounds. He isn't going to be crawling in through the air vents."

"I understood from Sandy Richter that he was asked to leave the set of the Ford commercial."

"That's right, he was."

Golding nodded, waiting for more.

"One of my people found him jacking off in Miss Cusak's trailer." Walsh watched for a reaction, sipped his soda, then went on. "Fortunately, Mrs. Cusak wasn't in there at the time. Her makeup lady walked in and found the slob pulling his pud over one of those sparkly leotard things she wears. Evidently Grossman fished one out of the laundry basket, and I guess the smell was just too good to resist."

There was a knock at the door, and another uniformed guard walked in.

"This here's the guy who found him," said Walsh. "Hughie, this is Pete Golding. He's following up on that thing with Jeff Grossman. Seems he's been making all kinds of trouble."

They shook hands. The guard had short dark hair and deep-set eyes.

"What kind of trouble?"

"Obscene letters," said Walsh before Golding could answer. "To Mrs. Cusak. Says he's gonna cut her face off. All kinds of vindictive shit."

"No kidding."

"He may even have broken into her house."

The guard let out a low whistle, then looked Golding up and down. "You a cop?"

"Pete's working for Mrs. Cusak. Hughie, just tell him what you saw in the trailer."

"Mrs. Cusak's trailer? Oh yeah. Well, I was outside when I heard this scream. From the makeup lady."

"That'd be Carol Hershey," said Walsh.

"Uh-huh. So I went in, and Grossman was there kind of . . ."—he glanced at his boss, as if unsure of the appropriate language—"exposing himself. He had all Mrs. Cusak's clothes out. I told him to get the hell out, and he got nasty."

"He hit you?" said Golding.

The guard shifted his weight from one foot to the other.

"It was more like a scuffle. I reported the matter to Mr. Walsh." He shrugged. "That's it."

"Did you tell Mrs. Cusak about it?"

"Uh-huh. I mean, she found out. From Carol Hershey."

"Was she upset about it?"

The guard nodded slowly.

"Mrs. Cusak? I think so. That kind of thing isn't supposed to happen on the lot."

"You can say that again," said Walsh. "I talked to the guy in here for a couple of minutes until he cooled down, and then we walked him to his car." He smiled. "Kinda stacks up, right? Come next door and I'll give you the scumbag's details. Thanks, Hughie."

They walked into the next room, where Hal and two other guards were drinking sodas in silence. Walsh pulled up a file and took out a copy of the complaint.

"There was no formal complaint. Carol Hershey, the makeup lady, said she didn't have the time. I sent a report to the guy's agency, though, and another to his union."

The guards were all looking at Golding. He could see they were wondering what it was like to shoot someone dead.

Temple was a side street off Marr between Venice Boulevard and the Del Ray Yacht Club. The sun was almost down when Golding pulled over and parked. The street had a quaint European feel but was otherwise typical L.A., with a wind chime tinkling somewhere and the smell of fried food. Grossman had the ground floor of a converted stucco-fronted house. Golding sat for a long time, looking at peeling paint and unchecked crabgrass, trying to decide what to do. A check with one of Reynolds' many contacts at City Hall, had revealed a misdemeanor jacket for Jeffrey Taylor Grossman that included drunk driving, possession of a controlled substance, and two sexual-exposure charges that went back to 1992. DMV had faxed the picture from the guy's driver's license. Grossman was a two-hundred-pound weenie wagger with a tiny trumpet-shaped mouth and innocent eyes—the kind of scumbag Golding dealt with all the time. Normally he'd have been across the street and pounding on the door in a minute, but normally there would have been no problem linking the subject to the complaints. Until he could get hold of some reliable handwriting samples, he wouldn't have anything that linked Grossman to the letters, the B&E, or the tape of the girl. There was absolutely no point in going up to the door and asking if he was the Ice Man. Grossman would be just as likely to tell him to go fuck himself, and then he'd feel obliged to punch him out. The best he could hope for was to get inside the house. If he could take a look around, see if there was anything concrete that linked Grossman to Ellen, then he could put a little pressure on the guy. He wished he had the fake police ID he'd taken from Raymond Lubett. He stood slightly more chance of getting over the threshold with a badge. He was thinking about driving home to get it when he saw the guy shambling along the street with a bag full of groceries.

He was wearing black jeans and a stained white T-shirt that snagged on his gut. Golding checked the DMV picture and got out of the car as Grossman reached his front door.

"Mr. Grossman?"

The door was open, the key in the lock. He took a long time turning around.

"My name's Pete Golding."

Grossman touched his belly with his long yellow nails, seemingly unfazed. Golding leaned forward a little, getting right into his face.

"Mr. Grossman, can you hear me?"

"I hear you fine."

"I wanted to ask you a couple of questions."

"You a cop?"

Golding smiled. "Why? You done something wrong?"

Grossman didn't budge. A smell of garbage and bug spray drifted along the passageway, but it was too dark to see anything. Golding knew he had to jerk the guy's chain if this wasn't going to just fizzle out.

"I'm investigating an indecent exposure complaint," he said.

Grossman made a bobbing movement with his head. "I don't know what you're talking about."

"Sure you do. I've just been up at Alameda Studios, talking to Miss Carol Hershey. She's still very upset."

Grossman's face went bright red. "Didn't I—haven't I paid for that already?" He was trembling all over.

"How's that, Mr. Grossman?"

Grossman pushed the hair back from his face and stepped into the house muttering. Then he turned in the doorway. "The fuckers, they called my union. They took away my card. So how am I supposed to work now?"

Golding smiled. "What do you expect, Jeffrey? You go around exposing yourself, you're going to get into—"

"I WASN'T EXPOSING MYSELF!" The voice blasted out of him. "I was . . . I was . . ." He struggled to gain control of himself, clutching at his chest. Then his eyes narrowed. "This is that Cusak bitch, isn't it? She's the one behind this." He looked at Golding, nodding. "Hershey was cool about it. She knew I didn't mean to scare her. It's *fucking* Cusak. The cunt wants to destroy me."

Golding found himself moving forward, but Grossman pushed the door against him. For a moment they struggled on either side of the flimsy panel, but Grossman was too heavy. It slammed shut.

Golding stood in the crabgrass, momentarily stunned.

He could hear Grossman gasping for breath on the other side of the door. Then he was sobbing.

"I'm warning you," he said. "I'm warning you to keep away. You try to come in here and I'll blow your goddamned face off."

21

Thursday, August 12

Ellen pulled her sports bag off the shelf in the utility room and carried it through into the kitchen. With a change of clothes and her boots it was already jammed. She wasn't sure if the bottle of wine she planned to take to Tina's parents was going to fit. It was a Château la Nerthe '92, a bottle left over from Doug's wine-buying days, when he was full of enthusiasm for one of his restaurant ventures. She was meeting Tina at the rink at eight, and after their session they were supposed to be going back to her parents' for supper. She was looking forward to it, but couldn't help feeling a little anxious. She hoped the Tuckers weren't going to be too formal about it. She just wanted a nice relaxed evening. Beyond that, she was curious to see what kind of domestic setup produced an athlete like Tina. She pushed in the bottle and closed the zip with a struggle.

She was on her way out the door when the phone rang. It was Tina.

"Hi!" Ellen lowered the bag to the floor. "I was just setting out for the rink."

"Oh." Tina sounded tense.

"Is everything okay?"

"I can't come tonight."

"Oh . . . okay. Why?"

"My mom—Mom says I need to stay home to finish an assignment."

"Really? I thought you were on top of all that."

"I am, but . . . well."

"So supper's—"

"Not happening," said Tina gloomily.

And then Ellen understood. Tina's parents had seen the *Hard News* item, or had heard about it, and now they didn't want their daughter mixed up with her.

"So, I guess, I'll be in touch," said Tina. It sounded like she might start crying any second. Ellen felt a squeeze of pity for her, then anger. The parents had taken this decision, but they didn't have the guts to talk to her directly.

"Tina?"

"Yeah?"

"Can I talk to your mom?"

"Oh." Tina sounded startled. This was obviously not part of her script. "Hang on a second." There were some muffled noises, and then Tina was back. "Sorry, Ellen. That's not—it's impossible."

"What's up? Isn't she there?"

"Um . . ." But Tina couldn't lie to her. Her mom was there, but she didn't want to come to the phone. Ellen heard her sniff. "I'm sorry," she said.

Ellen gripped the phone.

"Tina?"

"Yeah."

"Good luck, honey."

She put down the phone and leaned back against the wall.

She was putting the wine back in the rack when the phone rang again.

It was Lenny this time, sounding agitated, almost euphoric.

"Guess what?" he said. "Pete Golding tracked down the Ice Man."

He came around a half hour later, still buzzing.

"Can you believe it?" he said. "A goddamned grip."

From her corner of the sofa Ellen watched him pace back and forth in front of the French doors, swirling ice cubes in his empty glass. Outside in the garden the lights were on, making silhouettes of the overarching trees. An ocean breeze rocked the branches, shadows shifting over the ground.

"The guy's got a rap sheet as long as your arm. It's amazing he lasted as long as he did. I tell you, I wouldn't want him on a closed set."

He stopped pacing for a moment and looked around, noticing for the first time that Ellen was in her training clothes. He smiled.

"How's it going with Tina Tucker? She gonna make the Junior Pacifics?"

Ellen shrugged.

"I'm not sure we're going to be working together anymore."

"What?"

"She called just before you did. I was supposed to go over to her house tonight after training, but . . . I don't know, she had to stay home for an assignment."

Lenny didn't know what to say. He could see what was going through her mind.

"Gee, I'm . . . That's too bad. Still, kids've got to study sometime, right? Maybe she's been getting bad grades."

"She's been getting *good* grades," said Ellen. "Her mom said it herself. Come on, Lenny, that's not the reason."

Lenny nodded grimly, then came and sat down on the sofa.

"Ellen honey, the Ice Man is the reason. That's what this is about. But it's not something you have to worry about *anymore*. I told you Pete Golding would deal with it, and that's just what he's done. It's over, Ellen. I promise you. We've got this scumbag where we want him. He puts a foot wrong and he's gonna be sorry, I mean it."

"How can you be sure it's him? I don't think I ever even spoke to the guy."

"It's him all right. He thinks you're trying to *destroy* him. He told Pete that, came right out with it. He thinks you got him thrown off the lot."

"But that's crazy."

"Sure, but it happens all the time. Some guy thinks you took his parking space and six months later he's trying to burn your house down. You should hear some of Tom Reynolds' stories. What seems trivial to you or me can seem like a very big deal to someone with a fragile ego. Plus Grossman was whacking off in your trailer. Why *wouldn't* you get him thrown off the lot?"

"What does Golding say?"

Lenny hesitated.

"He thinks . . . Yes, he thinks this is our man. He's gonna get some samples of Grossman's handwriting from the agency. If they match the letters we should have enough for a restraining order. After that he comes within a hundred yards of you and we grab him for contempt of court."

Ellen looked past Lenny into the garden. The wind

was tugging gently at the open shutters, the faintest draft stirring the drapes. She knew she should feel safer now, but she didn't. Since the *Hard News* story she'd felt besieged, surrounded. Some of the hate mail had gotten through to the house. A three-line letter, neatly typed, from a woman in Wichita, Kansas, who described herself as "barren" told her she was no better than a whore. Another, in a scented pink envelope bordered with flowers and mailed from somewhere in Salt Lake City, began *Dear Filth*. A third contained nothing but an old photograph of her in mid-jump, torn from a skating magazine. In ballpoint the sender had drawn a dagger on the ice beneath her, the point upward, ready to impale her. The line of her vulva was crudely scored into the paper, together with wavy lines running down her thigh, presumably meant to represent blood. On the handle of the dagger was written the word PREY. And now, to cap it all, Mrs. Tucker didn't want her daughter going near her. It felt like she had a world of enemies. The Ice Man was just one of them.

She got up and went to fix herself another drink. She was surprised to see that the bottle was almost empty. She had only opened it at lunchtime. She found it helped, the warming sensation in her stomach, the hazy blanket it slowly wrapped around her senses. It made a change from the Prozac.

She lifted the bottle, offering Lenny a refill.

"Not for me," he said, smiling a tight smile. "Gotta drive."

She felt him watching her as she poured out a half glass. She took a sip and turned back.

"So what about the little girl, Lenny? Who's the little girl?"

*   *   *

The framed photograph had come back from the laboratory in a resealable plastic bag tagged with a serial number and a date, like a regular item of police evidence. Golding propped it up on his desk and sat in the empty office looking at it, trying to make it fit what he had learned. Jeff Grossman had tangled with Ellen Cusak—or thought he had—and a few weeks later stumbled on a picture, then a video, of a child that looked enough like her to cause trouble. How could that have happened? According to the personnel files at King Taylor Simon, Grossman was single and had no children of his own. Did his interest in Cusak go back beyond the Ford commercial? Had he been hoarding the pictures for years precisely because they did look like Cusak? Golding had already listened to the recorded message again. The voice on the phone didn't sound like Grossman. But that didn't mean much. It was one thing talking to an answering machine when you were prepared, when no one was talking back; another to be confronted on your doorstep by a total stranger talking indecent exposure. Maybe Grossman had been stalking Ellen for years, had wangled his way onto the Ford shoot because he knew she'd be there. The possibilities went round and round in his head, connecting for a moment and then breaking apart, never settling into a pattern that he could recognize or believe in.

He took a mouthful of tepid coffee. He knew he should go home, cook a meal, watch some TV. He knew he should step back now. But somehow he couldn't make himself do it. He wanted to drive up there to the house, to be where he could make a difference. But that was how he'd felt about Maddy. That was where it had started to go wrong. He couldn't let it happen again. If she needed him, she could call. He wondered what she was doing now, what she was feeling.

He closed his eyes, trying to empty his head of everything but the ambient noise of Century City, the ceaseless motion of temperature-controlled air, of traffic, the distant whoop of a siren. He pictured himself in Ellen's garden, looking up at the bedroom windows, watching for her shadow against the pale yellow drapes. He saw the square of freshly turned earth by the pool house. He heard the dog next door barking at the scent of an intruder. The woman in the ground had still not been identified. There would have been something in the press if she had. That made two people—two people in Ellen Cusak's life with no name, no family to claim them, no past. Two uninvited guests.

Tom Reynolds came out of his office, pulling on his jacket.

"Still here?" he said.

Golding sat up.

"Just waiting for those handwriting samples. Sandy Richter promised to send them over."

"Right, right."

Reynolds' eyes scanned Golding's desk as if he didn't quite believe that was the whole truth.

"I put in a call downtown for you. There's a graphologist called Hansen we used to use for that stuff. Dr. Carl Hansen. He's giving evidence right now, but he'll help out." Reynolds paused. "No hurry, is there?"

Golding shrugged.

"No, I guess . . . I just wanna see for myself."

"Uh-huh. Right. You, er . . . You think this Grossman character's a threat? You think he might try something?"

Golding sucked his teeth. There was something in Reynolds' demeanor he didn't like. It wasn't just the skepticism. It was as if he had something to say but wasn't sure if now was the time to say it.

"I don't know. He isn't what you'd call wholesome, but . . . on balance probably not."

Reynolds smiled. He liked nothing better than to be proved right.

"Like I said all along, these obscene-letter guys are all talk and no action. They blow off steam, but that's pretty much as far as it goes."

"That's right, you did say that. But this one got into her house."

Reynolds' smile vanished. He tugged at his cuff and turned to go.

"Yeah, so she says, Pete. So she says."

A line of storm lanterns outside the Old Neptune fish restaurant cast a hazy white light across the street. R&B music and the muffled babble of voices hang in the air. A couple go by holding hands, the girl in jeans, long brown hair, the man talking, joking. They stop, lean against the next car down, she reaching up to kiss him, revealing the bare skin of her waist.

From behind the windshield he watches them, watches the girl as she slides her tongue into the man's mouth, her hands on either side of his face. He watches their writhing, aware at the same time of the neon reflections patterning the hood of his car, the R&B music, the muffled voices, the gentle pulse of the dashboard clock. He feels himself drawing nearer to *her,* to Yelena, entering with one decisive step a world inhabited by the two of them alone.

He slams the door shut behind him, catching the couple by surprise.

"Sorry, officer," the girl says, covering her smiling mouth.

The man glances back self-consciously, mutters something, and leads her away. He watches them disappear into the darkness, then crosses the street towards Temple. Turning the corner, he smells the warm, fatty air of the Old Neptune's kitchens, hears the shouts of the waiters and kitchen boys, the buzz of the fans. A big white pickup with oversize tires cruises by on Marr, subwoofer pumping out rap from behind tinted glass.

Temple is a cul-de-sac. Just a hundred yards long, it stops at a rusty wire-mesh fence on the edge of a vacant lot. At the far side of the lot a painted sign reads E-ZEE BUDGET PARKING. Stunted palms push up through broken cement, obscuring the handful of yellow streetlights. From the low-rent houses dim rectangles of light—yellow, red, orange—color the darkness.

He stops outside number 16, sees the white plastic numbers nailed to the mailbox. A Spanish-style house, paint peeling, a chunk of stucco fallen away at one corner. He walks up the path, feeling the breeze on his damp forehead, feeling his heart pumping in his chest. At the door he puts a hand behind his back, feeling for the hard edges of metal beneath his shirt. He reaches for the doorbell. Sitcom chimes from inside the hall. He waits, hearing other music now, the rolling drawl of good ol' boys in song.

Rattling from the other side of the door.

"Who is it?"

Jumpy, defensive.

"Jeff? Jeff Grossman?"

"Who *is* it?"

Louder. A pinprick of light appears in the middle of the door as the man on the other side looks out through the fish-eye.

"It's me. Open up."

"What do *you* want?"

"I want to talk to you. 'Bout a guy called Golding."

"Never heard of him."

"Works for Ellen Cusak. . . . He's been round at the lot, making accusations. Got some people pretty pissed."

A moment of silence. The door opens a few inches, still on a chain. Grossman's face, little-boy eyes sunk in a bloated, unshaven face.

"I didn't do a goddamned thing. I told him that. I told your *boss* that." A nicotine-stained finger jabs out from the darkness. "That Cusak bitch is a fucking liar. She's *sick*."

He feels the heat rising in his face.

"And they went and wrote to my fucking union."

"Well, that's why I need to talk to you, Jeff. Joe Walsh thinks we may have been a little hasty. Thinks we have to present a united front before this all gets out of hand."

Grossman's mouth twists into a sneer.

"A united front? Are you crazy? I haven't worked for two months thanks to that motherfucker. An' the agency still owes me three days' pay. What's the bitch saying now? Joe Walsh tried to grope her in the can?"

"We have to discuss compensation, obviously." He looks at Grossman steadily. "For loss of earnings, damage to reputation, standing in the professional community. Plus the emotional trauma. That kind of suffering is hard to put a price on, right? But Cusak has deep pockets. She can afford it. Of course we have to get the story straight first, Jeff. That's what we have to do right now."

Grossman smiles a lazy smile, slides out the chain, and steps back from the door.

"Better come in."

As he steps into the hall he sees the .45 magnum Grossman is holding by his side.

"Not taking any chances, huh?"

Grossman looks down at the piece.

"Lotta scumbags down here," he says. "Gotta watch yourself."

"Who knows? Who cares? The guy does drugs. He could have gotten that tape from anywhere." Lenny touched at his throat. He felt warm. "The point here is—"

"They're saying the child's mine," Ellen said. "Everyone thinks the child's mine."

"They don't . . ." Lenny shook his head in despair. "All that . . . It's just bullshit, tabloid bullshit. It's entertainment, ratings. This week's paychecks. Next week they'll . . . No one actually *believes* it."

"Tina's mom believes it."

"Ah, she'll soon come around. You know how mothers are when it comes to their kids, they . . ." Lenny winced. "And if she doesn't there are plenty of other young hopefuls who'd . . . who'd *kill* to get a little coaching from you."

Ellen took a mouthful of wine and looked up at the wall where the photographs were hung. Her dad in a cable-knit sweater, hair swept back, smiled at her from the side of a rink. It was in Kiev. She used to go down there in the afternoons and practice her school figures on one of the little strips of ice reserved for skaters in

training. In those days everyone had to learn figures—
that was what the tests were based on: figure-of-eight
patterns of different sizes and configurations, dozens of
them, each one traced and retraced, right foot, left foot,
outside edge, inside edge, forward, backward, over and
over and over, until her legs ached and the ice was pat-
terned as if by some giant calligrapher. Hour after hour
she would practice, her father standing there watching,
his arms folded, only speaking to correct her posture or
her technique, never taking his eyes off her, his gaze always following her, tracing over and over the figure of
eight. To this day she couldn't skate without feeling him
watching her. She wondered if he was watching her now.

"Anyway, this whole business, it's all the more reason . . ." Lenny leaned forward, rubbing his finger along
his forehead. He felt suddenly weary. "All the more reason, Ellen, to do this biography. I had a call from Barbara Christian today. Argyle has made an offer. I think
this is an opportunity we have to take. I think—"

He was interrupted by the phone. He sighed and sat
back on the sofa, waiting for Ellen to pick up. But she
didn't move.

"Ellen, are you . . . ?"

She turned, looking at the phone now as if it had
nothing to do with her.

"What's the betting that's Pete Golding?" Lenny said.
"He promised to call if he had more news. . . . Why don't
I . . . ?"

He got to his feet and lifted the receiver.

"Yeah, hello?"

At the other end of the line a sharp intake of breath.

"Pete?"

Music in the background. A TV or a radio. Country
and western.

"Hello? Who is this?"

Lenny met Ellen's stare.

A man's voice, tense, hostile: "I want to speak to Yelena."

"Yel—?" Lenny's expression darkened. "I *said* who is this?"

For a moment nothing, then: "I know who *you* are, Lenny. Leonard Arthur Benjamin Mayot." A little tut-tut sound. "It was you sold the video, wasn't it, Lenny? Had to be you."

Lenny's face flushed, caught Ellen's questioning look, turned away from her.

"Does Ellen know about that? Does she, Lenny?"

"Now, now you listen to me, you sick son of a bitch."

His heart was suddenly beating so fast he could hardly breathe.

"I want to speak to Yelena."

"We're onto you, buddy. You sick psycho fuck! You ever call here again, we're gonna nail you to the fucking wall, you—"

"I WANT TO SPEAK TO *YELENA*!"

Searing rage. For a moment Lenny was too stunned to speak. In the back of his mind he had an idea that he was supposed to keep the guy on the line, make it easier to trace the call. But then he realized that wasn't necessary. Caller ID was instantaneous. He took a deep breath, trying to stoke up some anger, some comeback.

"Well, get this, you sick freak: there's no way that's *ever* gonna happen. So you may as well go whack off on the beach like all the other sickos. Okay?"

He slammed down the receiver, then lifted it again. Ellen was beside him.

"Lenny, what—?"

"Yeah, yeah, it was our friend again. Sick bastard." Lenny was shaking, out of breath. "You got something I can write on?"

"Sure, why—?"

"Caller ID. Worth a shot."

He dialed, reaching into his jacket for a pen. After a couple of seconds a computerized female voice calmly read out a ten-figure number. Lenny scribbled it down along the top of a magazine.

"Bull's-eye! We've got him now. That son of a bitch. I'm gonna call Golding. We're gonna nail this guy. Right here, right now."

"Lenny, wait a second. I don't want—"

"Come on, honey, you crazy? This is the chance we've been waiting for. Gimme the number."

Ellen hurried into the kitchen, fetched Golding's card from the refrigerator door.

Golding picked up at once.

"Pete? This is Lenny Mayot. We just got another call from the Ice Man."

"Same guy as before?"

"I'd know that voice anywhere."

"You at Ellen's place?"

"You betcha. But this time we got his number. You ready?"

"Speak to me."

"Area code 310, number 822-3431. You got that?"

"Got it. 310, that can't be far from here. That's . . ." There was the sound of shuffling papers. ". . . Grossman."

Golding turned the corner into Temple twenty minutes later. Grossman's place was halfway down on the right-hand side. He drove slowly past, looking for signs of life, then did a U-turn at the end of the street and parked about fifty yards short of the house. The air was thick and humid, despite the onshore breeze. He was already sweating beneath his jacket. Dried-out palm fronds crunched beneath his feet as he stepped out onto the sidewalk.

The main question was: did Grossman have a gun? There was only one specific reference to firearms in the Ice Man letters—most of the violence they described involved cutting and slicing— but his last explicit threat, to Golding himself, had been one of shooting. He knew what Tom Reynolds would have said: that they should wait for the restraining order, then serve it on the guy, if necessary with police backup. But Golding wasn't going to do that. After all the trouble he'd taken to conceal his identity, Grossman was suddenly using his own phone. That suggested he was getting desperate, that something had changed. Maybe his visit had tipped him over the edge. If he already considered his own life a write-off, he might decide to write off Ellen's as well. He had seen that before. He had seen it with Arthur McGinley and Maddy Olsen: *If I can't have you, then no one will have you.*

The blinds in the front room were pulled down halfway, but the lights were out. Peering in through the filthy glass, Golding saw a dark-colored sofa with wooden arms, one of the cushions split, what looked like piles of videotapes and magazines on the floor, a photographic tripod, a cardboard packing case with screwed-up newspaper spilling over the sides. Somewhere in the building a TV was on: applause and whistles, then uproarious laughter.

Golding moved around the side of the house. An old wooden fence, bowed over by a straggling oleander, separated the property from the one next door. The branches brushed against his face, catching on his sleeves. The garbage smell was stronger here. Old milk cartons and food packaging that hadn't made it to the street were strewn on the ground. An old loudspeaker with the fabric torn off the front was propped up against a drain. The sound of the TV grew louder as he approached the back of the house.

He'd gotten Grossman all wrong, there was no doubt about that anymore. It was tempting to think someone like that, someone as screwed up as that, had to be stupid, unsophisticated, incapable of complexity or cunning. But it didn't work that way. Grossman used hate mail to vent his frustration, his anger, but then, just like Lenny Mayot said, he'd moved on, found a more satisfying angle, become more creative. His warped personality was flowering in the role of Ellen Cusak's torturer.

He came slowly around the corner, his hand over the front of his jacket, ready to draw. This was trespass, way over the line, but it was a little late to worry about that. The yard was small, at most forty feet from end to end. From the nearest window horizontal strips of light shone out into the gloom. A couple of yards along, concrete steps led up to another door.

He was almost at the window when he sent a tin can flying, bouncing across the hard ground. He dodged back into the shadows, certain he must have been heard. Then stood with his back to the wall, listening for the sound of the door, listening for Grossman's voice. But all he could hear was the TV, music now, a jingle: *The name you can trust.* Then more music, sweeping Hollywood- style. He edged back to the window, looking now through lopsided venetian blinds. A desk lamp, shade turned towards the outer wall, shone in his eyes. He moved further along, catching now the blue rectangle of the TV, a squad of ice hockey players slamming into each other, a four-by-four sweeping across a wet track.

The Ford commercial. Ellen's commercial.

And then he saw him, back to the window, stretched out on his La-Z-Boy: Grossman. He was rocking slightly backwards and forwards, his head making little jerking movements as Ellen Cusak executed her perfect triple lutz, the picture freezing for an instant on her brilliant champion's smile.

Golding felt a wave of disgust.

"Jesus Christ."

He stepped away from the window, decided to go right in the back, catch the son of a bitch with his prick in his hand—why not? Better a prick than a gun. He pulled open the screen, tried the door. The slob hadn't locked it.

The kitchen was dark except for a dim yellow strip above the range. Packaging and dirty plates littered every surface. Crushed beer cans spilled out onto the floor from a bulging plastic sack. He moved through into the narrow hallway, watching his feet, trying not to trip on anything. The TV was on loud, the sound reverberating through the plasterboard walls. He placed his hand against the lounge door and gently pushed.

"Having fun there, Mr. Grossman?"

The figure in the recliner twitched, didn't turn around. The right arm was extended, shaking, reaching for the phone on a glass side table. Over the singsong melody of another commercial came a wheezing, rattling sound. It suddenly hit Golding that the guy was having a seizure. Maybe drugs, maybe shock. He crossed the room, saw it: on the floor, on the chair, Grossman's T-shirt caked in it. Blood.

"Jesus. What the—?"

A sucking, tearing sound. Grossman's body convulsed. The whole side of his face had been shot away. Where his right jaw had been was a dark bloody mass, fragments of teeth and bone peeking through the massive wound. Golding stumbled back, knocking over bottles, glasses. For a moment he thought he was going to vomit, at the same time seeing in his mind's eye the barrel of the gun beneath Grossman's jaw, the hard gleaming metal pushed up hard into the soft flesh, the head burst like a big bloody fruit. He scrambled over to the phone, knowing as he punched in the number that it was already too late.

III

Erotomanic

22

"They kept you there how long?"

Tom Reynolds turned from the window and frowned at Golding's rumpled clothes. The kind of guy who could spend four days on a stakeout without even loosening his necktie, Reynolds hated to see his staff sloppy, even when they had an excuse.

"Nine hours." Golding looked at a brownish stain on his sleeve. "I didn't even get a chance to go home and change."

"Who caught the case?"

"Guy named Wolpert. Detective James Wolpert. Pacific Division."

"Never heard of him. Nine hours. Jesus. What did you find to talk about?"

"They wanted to know what I was doing at Grossman's house."

"And?"

"I told them I was working for Ellen Cusak."

Reynolds turned back to the window. Golding could see where this was going and he didn't like it. He was tired and he needed coffee.

"So they figured you did it," said Reynolds, still looking down at the traffic.

Golding waited for Reynolds to turn, waited until he could look him in the eye. Then he shook his head. "No way, Tom."

"But they think so, right? I mean you shot scumbags before."

"One scumbag. In self-defense."

Reynolds came back to his chair.

"I didn't shoot Grossman," said Golding. "I found him in a recliner with half his face in his lap. Christ, I was the one called 911."

Reynolds nodded.

"Must have been quite a shock, finding the guy like that."

Golding shrugged.

"So this . . . Detective Wolpert—did he buy your story?"

"Not really." Once he'd realized who he was dealing with, Wolpert had been all over him, had obviously thought he was some kind of vigilante. He'd been reluctant to let him walk away. "But I can see the way it must have looked. I was covered in the guy's blood when they walked in."

"Oh?"

"I tried to stop the bleeding. So when the cops came in the door, I'm standing there . . ."

"Christ."

"Plus they did my right hand for powder residue. It came up positive."

"What?" Reynolds stood up again.

"Tom, I was down at the range yesterday. They're going to check that. Wolpert told me not to leave town."

"Oh boy." Reynolds ran a finger along the edge of his desk. "Did Grossman leave a suicide note?"

"There was an Ice Man letter ready for mailing. No suicide note. The gun was registered in his name."

"Any sign of a struggle?"

"Nope. No sign of forced entry either, but the kitchen door was open when I got there. If somebody had wanted to sneak in, it wouldn't have been a problem."

"You think somebody snuck in, whacked him?"

"I don't know."

Reynolds smiled. "No, but you got that look, Pete."

"There was a call to Ellen—to Cusak's house at around nine-thirty. Lenny Mayot picked up. He was certain it was the guy who made the phone call we taped—certain it was the same voice."

"Right. So that voice was Grossman's voice."

"Maybe. The thing is, I talked to Grossman the day before he was killed. And I thought his voice was different."

Reynolds sat down again, more comfortable now that they were speculating about the case.

"Well, you know how those things are. How many times you seen a witness fold on voice-recognition testimony? It's hard to be absolutely sure. Anyway, the call came from Grossman's house, right?"

"That's right."

"So what more do we need to know?"

"He phoned up and then shot himself," said Golding as if it was the stupidest thing he'd ever heard.

"Why not?"

"He'd written one of his firecracker notes. Four pages of hot stuff. I think he was planning to mail it."

"Maybe not. He went to all the trouble of finding Cusak's new number, wanted to tell her about the great letter he's sending. But when he phones her house he gets Mayot. He's so depressed about it he shoots himself." Reynolds registered Golding's expression and held up his hands. "Okay, I'm being flippant, but Pete, you're not telling me it couldn't be something like that. Obviously Grossman was disturbed. You said yourself he was depressed—losing his union card."

Golding looked away.

"Anyway," said Reynolds. "They think you did a great job."

"What?"

"I just got off the phone before you came in. Lenny Mayot. He says Mrs. Cusak is delighted that the situation has been successfully resolved." He brought his hands together and rubbed. "So Alpha Global does it again. Under the circumstances, I think you should take the morning off."

"I'm fine," said Golding. The thought of going back to the house and taking the Cusak pictures down was not very appealing.

"No really," said Reynolds. "Take my advice. Go have a shower, eat a long lunch. You could use a little downtime."

What did *that* mean? Golding tried to hold his gaze, but Reynolds was already moving on to the next thing. He pulled a file out of his desk.

"I've had a request from Linda Farrar—you know, the producer? She's putting together some kind of event at the Hillcrest. She wants us to organize security."

Reynolds was trying to be cool about it, but Golding could see he was delighted. It was precisely the kind of business Reynolds was always hoping for. It wasn't as messy as chasing sickos around, and there was a clear beginning, middle, and end. Reynolds' long-term dream was to head up an Alpha Global security services arm, and leave the personal threat management side of things to Romero.

He pushed a sheet of paper across his desk with a drawing of the Hillcrest Country Club on it. Golding didn't even look.

"Can't you put Denison on it?"

"Roy's busy."

"What about Bernie?"

"He'll go with you, but he doesn't have the experience to take charge. I want you to handle this." Reynolds gave Golding a tight-jawed stare. "You got a problem with that?"

"What did you say to Lenny Mayot?"

"What do you mean, what did I say?"

"About closing the case."

"I said, great. If you're happy we're happy."

"But this . . . we can't be sure Mrs. Cusak is out of danger."

"Come on, Pete. You said yourself Grossman was the letter writer. There was an Ice Man letter all set for mailing."

"That's right. But we still don't *know* if he did all the other stuff: the picture, the video, the phone calls."

"Frankly, Pete, I don't see how it matters one way or the other. It was the Ice Man letters we were brought in on."

"But we have to consider the possibility—"

Reynolds interrupted: "No we don't. We don't because the client doesn't want us to. The client said thanks, the check's in the mail."

"At least we have to keep up the call monitoring. We can't walk away when we don't have all the facts."

"Ellen Cusak is not our client anymore. To go on

watching her and listening to her calls would be an invasion of privacy. As of now."

"It's for her own protection."

There was a moment of complete silence. Reynolds nodded once and then looked away.

"You know what, Pete? I'm getting a really spooky feeling of déjà vu." He looked back. "Are you hearing me, partner? I'm recalling a certain young woman named Madeleine who called me up, agitated, spooked, because a guy was hanging around outside her house."

Golding felt his face go hot. Reynolds was pointing at him now.

"So Pete, I want you to listen to me. I'm not asking you. I'm *telling* you. I want you to go home, have a shower, put on a clean suit, and come back this afternoon ready to work on Linda Farrar's party. I'm telling you to *let this go.*"

23

Saturday, August 14

He ran for an hour on the beach at Santa Monica, then walked for another hour along the water's edge. Reynolds was right, of course. Alpha wasn't a public service. It had no duties beyond what it was paid to do. And as of Friday morning Ellen Cusak wasn't paying it to do anything. There were no bonus points for getting involved, there was only trouble. So Cusak's old phone number had been disconnected. Her old mail would be boxed up and sent back, or destroyed. And Peter Golding would stand guard over Linda Farrar's party guests. Because that was his job.

He was back in the car, waiting at the junction with Sunset when he decided he had to speak to her. Brentwood was only a couple of miles away. He would just drop by and explain it to her in person. And that would be that.

She was standing in the driveway, just as she had been the last time he'd seen her. Only this time the gates were open. The Mercedes with its punched-in fender was in the drive, the trunk open. Ellen was dressed in blue jeans and a white cotton shirt and was carrying a small suitcase. Golding climbed out of the Sebring, his heart beating double-time.

"Hey there."

Ellen turned, squinting into the sun.

Golding pointed back over his shoulder at his car.

"I—I was down on the beach, and I . . ."

She gave a little crooked smile.

"If this is a professional call, Pete, you should know that the account is closed. You people are expensive."

She looked at his clothes.

"If it was professional I'd be wearing my suit," he said.

"Then I'm glad it isn't."

For a second he thought he'd heard wrong.

She registered his look and pointed at his sweaty Lakers shirt.

"Glad for you, I mean. You always look too hot in that blue suit."

He held her look, feeling the heat rise in his face. Even though he had pictures of her all over his walls, there was something surprising about her beauty when you got up close. He remembered what Lenny had said about the way she was when she married Doug Gorman—radiant, confident, funny. It wasn't so hard to imagine. She was obviously relieved to be finished with the Ice Man.

"I heard what happened with Jeff Grossman," she said. "It sounded horrible."

"Yeah, it was."

"I can't help thinking if maybe I hadn't—"

"No way," said Golding, cutting her off. He shook his head. "It had nothing to do with you, Ellen. Nothing. Grossman was on his own trajectory. You have to believe that."

She nodded, looked down at the suitcase in her hands.

"I guess. I mean, I never even spoke to him."

"Exactly."

She hunched her shoulders.

"It's just so . . . sad." She shook her head. "Don't worry about me. I'm okay." She put the case into the trunk. "Is that why you came up here? To talk about Grossman?"

"Kind of. I wanted to make sure you were properly debriefed."

"Debriefed?" Again she looked at his shirt. "What does that mean?"

Golding smiled.

"Sorry—that's my boss, the way he talks. I mean, I think you should have the full picture."

She pushed open the shutters in the sitting room and brought him iced tea in a tall glass. There was no one else in the house. It was almost uncomfortably quiet.

"Did you talk to Tom Reynolds yourself yesterday?" he said.

"Lenny did that. He was really excited about helping to catch the guy. Of course, he didn't know how it was going to turn out."

"And he told you everything's taken care of?"

"Uh-huh." She sat down on the sofa. "Why?"

"I just—I felt I had to come up here in case . . ."

He didn't know how to go on. Already her sunny mood was evaporating.

"Do you think . . . do you think it might not be over?"

He sat forward a little.

"Ellen, we *know* Grossman wrote you all those hate letters—they found one in his house—but that doesn't mean he was responsible for everything that's been happening: the calls, the photo, that videotape. Personally, I don't think it stacks up."

She was very still.

"Why not?"

"Because in my experience nobody goes to that much trouble unless they're obsessed. In this case . . ."—he hesitated—"obsessed with you. The way he sounds, the way he acts, it's clear this guy thinks he has a relationship with you of some kind. How can you say you're *disappointed* with someone if you don't have some kind of relationship? That's the behavior of an erotomanic."

"Erotomanic," she said. Her hands were pressed together between her knees. "I think Lenny said something about that."

"But if Jeff Grossman was obsessed with you, Ellen, he did a primo job hiding it. The police didn't find a single press cutting in his house, a single photo, nothing. Normally, these guys have like a shrine. There wasn't even any evidence that Grossman was interested in skating. As far as we can tell, he didn't own a video camera. And he certainly didn't have any children."

Ellen stared, silent. He hated giving her the bad news, but if he didn't, who would?

"You see my point?" he went on. "Grossman may have had a crazy grudge against you, but that's not the same thing as—"

She was suddenly on her feet. For a moment Golding thought she was going to run out on him. Then she went over to the French doors, pressing her hands against the glass.

"You're saying . . . you're saying he's still out there."

"Maybe."

"Is this what your boss thinks? Is this what Tom Reynolds thinks?"

Golding looked down.

"I don't know. I guess . . . I guess he thinks you don't have anything to worry about."

"And you think I *should* worry."

"I think you should be careful," he said, standing up. "That's all. I'm not trying to scare you, Ellen. I just think you should be aware."

"I'm sorry," she said, turning from the window. She tried to smile. "It's not your fault. You're just doing your job, right?"

Golding found himself at her side. He wanted more than anything to hold her. It felt like the most natural thing to do. But she would just think he had made everything up as an excuse to come up there. She had to know he was serious about what he'd said.

"I'm getting out of here for a couple of days," she said, looking out again at the garden.

Golding wondered if she was going alone, realized she almost certainly wasn't—then understood that that was the point of her remark.

"Where are you headed?"

"Lake Arrowhead. Sam Ritt's invited me up there."

"Sam Ritt?"

Ellen studied him for a moment.

"Sam's my old coach. He wants me to help choreograph a couple of programs."

"Great. That's great."

"It'll get me out of this place anyhow. That's the main thing."

"You don't like it here?"

She shook her head.

"Not anymore. I'm trying to sell it, as a matter of fact. I just can't find any buyers right now."

"Are you leaving town?"

"I don't know. Maybe. All I know is, I've had enough of ivory towers. I want to come down and mix a little. Some neighbors I can actually talk to would be nice. I met thousands of people through Doug and his work. But it wasn't until we split up I realized they were contacts, not friends."

Golding wondered if what she said was all true, whether she wasn't saying it just to make him feel better, trying to close the gap between them.

"You aren't gonna miss all those gala occasions? The premieres? The photo ops?"

She smiled.

"You're kidding, right? That was all just business, Doug's business."

"So what do you like to do?"

"Me, I'm happier with a pizza and a movie; preferably a funny one where nobody gets shot."

"Well, if you're ever at a loose end . . ."

He had wanted it to sound like a throwaway, but it came out dorky and intense. She looked away, and he realized he'd made her uncomfortable.

"Ellen?" He waited for her to look at him. "Seriously, about this whole situation. If anything happens, anything at all, I want you to call me, no charge."

She smiled and nodded.

"Thanks, Pete. Thanks a lot."

24

Tuesday, August 17

Douglas Gorman had been placed at the end of the table where everyone could see him. There were fifty people at Linda and David Farrar's tenth anniversary dinner, and although he was one of only two or three who might have been recognized in the street, among the rest were enough studio executives, agents, producers, and directors to represent a significant slice of the moviemaking establishment. Nevertheless, as he stood outside the dining room in his rented tuxedo, an earpiece jammed into his left ear, a microphone clipped to his lapel, Golding couldn't help thinking the presence of extra security at the event was unnecessary, an affectation on Linda Farrar's part, at best a gesture designed to flatter the egos of her guests. The Hillcrest Country Club was about as private a public place as you could find in the city of Los Angeles. That was what the members paid their five-figure dues for.

Despite Reynolds' instructions, Golding had tried to get hold of Lenny Mayot several times. If Mayot could be made to see that there could still be danger, maybe he would talk to Reynolds and get Alpha back on the case. But according to Lenny's assistant, he was out of town until the end of the week. Golding had left messages, but the messages had been ignored. As far as Mayot was concerned, the case was closed. The Ice Man letters were what had upset his client in the first place, and the Ice Man, a.k.a. Jeffrey Grossman, was dead. The fees had been paid and even the press had moved on, thanks in part to the police, who had deliberately kept Golding's name out of their official statement. Never mind that the police had found no shrine at Grossman's house, or any indication of a long-standing interest in Ellen Cusak. Never mind that there had not been so much as a single skating magazine among the stacks of pornography. Everyone was too anxious to get on with their lives to worry about such details—and anxious for Ellen to get on with hers. What Lenny wanted was to *reassure* her, so that he could get her back to money making, to making his ten percent count for something. As if nothing had happened, as if everything was back to normal.

But everything was *not* back to normal. Golding was certain of that. Ellen still needed him, perhaps now more than ever. She had to see that, to sense it at least. She had to understand.

Lying awake at night, he thought about her a lot. He'd tried to think his way into her head, to see her life through her eyes, but it was hard. There were too many blanks, too many pages in her story that were unknown to him. And then he would awaken with a start, seeing only Jeff Grossman, stretched out on his La-Z-Boy, convulsing in death while Ellen Cusak, costumed and painted, skated and spun on the TV screen before him.

Finally, on Monday night he had called Ellen's number and left a message. They were showing *The Apartment* at a small theater in Burbank that Thursday night, he'd said. Maybe she'd like to come along. So far she hadn't called back.

Golding hadn't seen Doug Gorman's name on the Farrars' guest list until a few hours before the party. In the flesh he looked older than Golding had expected, and at least a couple of inches shorter. His sandy-colored hair, which he normally wore long, was clipped short, and he looked tired—older, if anything, than his thirty-one years. According to Al McMichael, one of the bodyguards Alpha had hired for the evening, he was in the middle of a six-week shoot in Prague and had flown back specially. The exotic-looking brunette at his side was some Czech model turned actress in the cast. Golding wondered how much Gorman knew about his ex-wife's recent troubles, and how much he cared. He had a strong feeling the truth, in both cases, was, not much.

By half past ten he was tired of playing Secret Service man while Ellen's ex had a good time. Over the sound of the jazz quintet he could hear Bernie Ross and the two freelance security guards reporting to each other on the status of the driveway and the emergency exits, taking the whole thing very seriously, probably just for his benefit, so that he could report back to Reynolds what an ace team they were. He flipped up the microphone and told Ross to take his place while he went and checked something out. Ross arrived almost at once, looking like he was all set to wrestle someone to the ground.

"Do we have a problem?"

The Farrars were on their feet now, leading off the dancing to the strains of "Moon River." A smattering of applause went up from the other guests.

"Yeah," said Golding. "If anyone tries making a speech, shoot them."

The Four Roses was under the dashboard in a brown paper bag. He took a long pull, then another. He felt too drained to work, too churned up inside to rest. He looked out across the landscaped grounds to the stream of headlights on Pico. He didn't want to be here—he felt it then, how much. It wasn't just the assignment, the tedium of it, the second-class manservant status. He wanted to be with her, with Ellen. That was what made it hurt. It was no good trying to kid himself anymore. *That* was what had really changed.

He picked up the car phone and started punching in Ellen's number. She'd told him she was going away for a few days. Maybe she'd just got back and had tried to call him. He could say he just wanted to check that she was okay, that she hadn't received any more threatening letters or weird calls. And she would tell him, no she hadn't. Everything was fine. And she wouldn't say a thing about his message or the movie. Or at best she would say thank you, but that she couldn't make it— knowing all the time that this was the real reason he had called. He could picture perfectly that moment of mutual understanding.

He put down the phone. It was no good. He was behaving as if they had a relationship: Ellen and Pete, Pete and Ellen. But they *didn't*. If it hadn't been for the stalker, their paths would never have crossed. And now that the stalker was gone, that was the end of it. She had no use for him anymore. Why would she want him anyway, when she was used to celebrity heartthrobs like Gorman? He had been deluding himself to imagine that she felt anything for him. *I've had enough of ivory towers.*

Maybe that was true, but it was a long way from the top of Brentwood Heights to his end of Van Nuys.

He sat for a long time looking up at the clubhouse, wondering how it was he'd ended up there, living, working, dreaming in the shadow of two worlds, one of fame and riches, the other of madness and despair—two worlds that could hardly have been more different, but that somehow complemented each other perfectly. Of course there were people who thought it was all quite wonderful. His friends used to ask him whisperingly if he'd met anyone famous recently. He'd taken to mentioning anyone he thought they'd get excited about, regardless of whether he'd seen them or not. He didn't have to elaborate because there was such a thing as client confidentiality.

He looked down the neck of the bottle at the dark, sweet-smelling liquid. It would be easy to dive in, drown in it for a while. He had done it before. But in the end it always made things worse. He would despise himself for being drunk, even as he was getting there, even as he was slowly sinking into oblivion, but that wasn't the worst of it. He would wake up the next morning knowing he was another step closer to the dark, lonely hell of the paranoid, the psychotic, the damaged, the abused— the very same screwed-up monsters who kept Alpha Global Protection in business. It was out there waiting for him, that place. Sometimes it felt like all he would have to do was step inside himself, turn his back on the judgment of the world, and he would be there.

He heaved himself out of the car and began to empty the remains of the bottle onto the asphalt. Remove the temptation, that was the only way. The whiskey was still splattering around his feet when he realized that someone was watching him.

"I admire your willpower."

Golding saw the glow of a cigarette, a plume of smoke pushed out into the air. It took him a moment to realize that he was looking at Douglas Gorman.

"Filthy habit, I know," said Gorman, stepping out of the shadows. "I just don't seem to be able to . . ." He gestured back towards the building. "You'd think they'd have a smoking area in there."

Golding didn't know what to say. It occurred to him that Gorman could report him, probably get him fired. Reynolds took a dim view of drinking on the job.

Gorman put the cigarette back in his mouth and extended his hand.

"Doug Gorman. It's Pete, right?"

"How did you know?"

"Oh, someone in there pointed you out. You know, the . . ."—he shrugged apologetically—"the Maddy Olsen thing."

Golding nodded silently, wondering what Gorman wanted from him: deep background for his next role? *I just wanted to ask: What does it really feel like to kill someone?* He locked up the car and began walking back towards the clubhouse.

"Oh right. Well, I've got to be getting back," he said, barely managing politeness.

"Is it true you've been working for my wife? I mean, my ex-wife?"

Golding stopped. So that was it.

"I'm afraid we're not permitted to reveal the identities of our clients, Mr. Gorman. It's—"

"Oh come on. I spoke to Ellen this morning."

This morning? That meant she had to be back already.

"Then why are you asking?"

"Because I want to know if she's gonna be okay. I want to know if this thing's all over."

Golding looked into Gorman's face. He saw concern. If it wasn't genuine, it was a great piece of acting.

"All right. Yes, I have."

"And *is* she going to be okay? Is this thing all over with?"

"I wish I knew."

Gorman studied him for a moment.

"I'm sorry, would you . . . ?"

He offered a cigarette. Golding looked at it. Sometimes he wanted to smoke, sometimes he didn't. Right now he did.

"I only heard about this yesterday," Gorman said. "They say some guy . . . a technician, shot himself."

"That's right. Name was Grossman."

"Wasn't he the guy? The stalker?"

"Is that what Ellen told you?"

Golding accepted a light.

"She didn't really want to talk about it, not much. She wanted to forget the whole thing, she said. I had a feeling she wasn't telling me everything, though."

"Yeah, I've had that feeling, from day one," said Golding, taking a deep drag. "It's made my life—my job a lot more difficult."

"You think there's someone still out there?"

"Someone, maybe."

"And he'll come after her again?"

Golding hesitated.

"In my opinion, yes."

"But you still have no idea . . . ?"

There was a noise from outside the clubhouse: a woman's laughter, a man singing a line of some old crooner's song, the clunk of limousine doors.

"I think it's someone who's known her a long time," said Golding. "That's what I think."

"Known her?"

"Known *about* her. Years. Maybe even longer than you. I think he's been patient, very patient. And he's got a plan. This isn't your typical freak."

"What makes you say that?"

Golding looked Gorman in the eye, saw fear there. Was he thinking about Ellen, or was he thinking: *This could happen to me?*

"This guy knows something. He *has* something. It's kept him going all the time. I don't know what it is, but if I could find out, I could find him."

Headlights swept across the parking lot as the limousine turned towards the gates.

"Is there anything I can do?" said Gorman.

Golding considered the handsome face for a moment.

"Sure," he said. "You could tell me about your ex-wife."

They took a seat in a corner of the clubhouse bar. Golding ordered mineral water, Gorman scotch and soda.

"It was a crazy thing to do. I knew it at the time." Gorman put down his glass and hung his arms over the back of the green-and-cream-striped couch. "I said to myself: I'm twenty-three years old. My career is just taking off. There's no way I should be getting married. I kept waiting for someone to tell me I was crazy. My dad, my manager, *someone*. But you know, no one did. All anyone said was: that's wonderful, you're a very lucky guy, congratulations."

"You're telling me you didn't want to marry her?"

Gorman shook his head.

"I don't know. I wanted *her*. I was in love. And then I started thinking . . ."

"What?"

"I thought maybe stability—you know, beautiful wife, a home, all that—was just what I needed. Keep me out of trouble. A lot of relationships in my business, they're not . . . you know . . . they don't last. But Ellen wasn't *in* my business. I started thinking it could work. And then . . . well, after her dad died it . . . it felt like the right thing to do."

He shrugged and looked away across the barroom. It felt strange to Golding hearing him talk in this way, hearing him talk so openly about his marriage, his feelings, to a near stranger. It was the kind of thing Golding himself would never have done. It crossed his mind that he was listening to a performance, a little speech that Gorman had worked out for himself, ready for anyone who asked.

"Tell me about him, about her dad."

"Stepan Cusak?"

Gorman shifted in his seat. Golding had the sense that they were departing from the script.

"How well did you know him?"

Gorman smiled and shook his head.

"I didn't. Not really. To tell you the truth, he made me kind of nervous."

"He didn't like you?"

"Probably not. Well, I was taking away his little girl. What do you expect? Plus I was in the movies. We're not supposed to be good husband material. We take drugs and go to orgies, right?"

"Did he try and stop the marriage?"

"No, no, nothing like that. He just used to . . . to watch

you. You know, if the conversation lapsed for a moment, you'd sense him watching you, sizing you up. And look, I'm an actor. I'm supposed to be used to that kind of thing, right? But I wasn't used to that, no way. It was like everything you said was a sham, a front, and he was sitting there looking right through you."

Golding could picture the difficulties. Stepan Cusak was a very determined man, that much was clear. He had made huge sacrifices to achieve a better life, both for himself and for his daughter. To him Doug Gorman must have seemed impossibly lightweight, pampered, ignorant even of the ways of the world.

"Did he starve her?"

Gorman straightened up.

"Starve her?"

"That's what the stalker said. The men in her life starved her so she wouldn't lose her edge on the ice. I figured he meant her father."

This required a little thought.

"Well"—Gorman pushed out his bottom lip—"it turned out . . . yes, she had an eating disorder. A form of anorexia. I didn't even know about it until later. It came and went."

"Even after you were married?"

"Less. She put on a few pounds then actually."

"What about drugs? Had she ever taken growth suppressants, anything like that?"

"If she did, she never told me."

"What about sexual abuse? Do you think it's possible . . . ?"

"Whoa, whoa, wait a minute." Gorman looked shocked. "You're getting the wrong idea here. If Ellen has problems, I don't think you can pin them all on her dad. He was a strong kind of guy, and I know he meant the world to Ellen—more than I ever did. I came to realize that pretty quick. But she *wanted* to be a champion, you bet. And you don't get to be a champion unless you're prepared to make sacrifices."

"Go on."

"Well . . ." Gorman shrugged. "You spend your whole life on the ice. And when you're not on the ice, you're too tired to do anything else. And if you want to study on top of that—and Ellen did, she had to—you can pretty much kiss good-bye to a social life." Gorman took a mouthful of whisky, wiped his mouth with his fingers. "As a matter of fact, that *is* Ellen's problem, if you ask me. She never really had any friends, I mean close friends. She pretty much still doesn't. You must have seen how she is. She doesn't . . . I don't know how to put it. She doesn't know how to *connect* with people, not really. She's a loner."

"You think she paid too high a price?"

"Don't you?"

Golding shrugged.

"Did you encourage her to give up competitive skating?"

"Me? No way. At the time I thought it was just great, just wonderful. She was the one whose priorities changed. Soon as we were married she wanted a family. A *big* family. And that was all she wanted."

"Any idea why she was in such a hurry?"

"Sure. Her dad was all the family she had. And suddenly he was gone. She wanted stability. Plus . . . plus she was worried."

"About what?"

Gorman took a sip of his scotch, swallowed. They were well off the script now, Golding could tell. But it was too late to be coy.

"You didn't hear this from me, okay? Ellen would be

really upset. I mean, I don't even know why I'm telling you this."

"Because it might help."

Gorman sighed.

"Like I said, she had this disorder. Maybe she had used drugs, I don't know. But it messed with her system, you know what I mean? She used to go three, four months at a time without a period. When she was nineteen, the year she was world champion, she didn't menstruate *at all.* I think she was scared she had a major problem, and as soon as she lost her dad she couldn't think of anything else."

"And did she have a problem?"

"You bet."

"I read—"

"Yeah, I know. The tabloids started saying it was me. I was sterile. I was impotent. I guess they thought it was kind of ironic, given the roles I was doing. Anyway, it wasn't true, and I know that for a fact, believe me."

Golding fell silent for a moment. He'd wanted, hoped that the stories about Doug Gorman had been true. He didn't want Ellen to be the one who couldn't have children. Yet how was it the stalker seemed to *know* that was the truth, when all the press stories had said just the opposite?

"You tried fertility treatment?"

"The works, including IVF. No luck. Ellen couldn't carry a baby to term. Embryos were as far as it went."

"What about a surrogate mother? Couldn't you arrange that?"

Gorman shook his head.

"I didn't . . . I've always thought that was kind of strange. Having some other woman carry your child. You know what I mean?"

"I guess."

"And I'd heard things. How these situations get out of control, get complicated. I heard about this woman, this surrogate, who didn't want to give the child back. So . . ."

"So you said no?"

Gorman shrugged, looked away.

"We talked about it. I explained my feelings, and in the end I think Ellen—I think she understood."

"But if it had been up to her, she would have tried surrogacy?"

"I guess. Probably. You'd have to ask her. Anyway, then we got into the adoption thing."

"Right. And you were happy with that?"

Doug shrugged hopelessly.

"I guess. Not completely, but . . . I mean, once she started looking at all the poor lost orphans around the world, it became a kind of obsession. It was weird. I could see we were going to end up adopting a whole bunch of them. Frankly, I was glad when the adoption people said no."

"You were?"

"Yes. It meant I didn't have to."

25

Wednesday, August 18

"Twenty-nine, thirty, thirty-one . . ."

The boards give with a gentle pull, scattering the cockroaches that thrive in the crawl space under the house. He squats, breathing in the sour smells of decay, and beyond that the oilier smell of the guns and the C-4 explosive. He got the C-4 through the same guy that sold him his other toys, a flaky survivalist type who thought McVeigh had his reasons for doing what he did in Oklahoma, and that some of them were good. He was pretty sure he had been ripped off on the deal—the guy bitching about how hard it was to get hold of the stuff, how he'd had to go all the way to North Carolina—but he'd paid the money anyway, taking the decision right there to make his own bombs his own way. He bought the books through the Net and made up his own mixtures in the back kitchen while Nat was asleep. There are two bags of ammonium nitrate fertilizer and a barrel of nitromethane directly under his room now, the whole package bound together with duct tape and wired to a detonator he plans to push up through the floorboards so that kingdom come will be within easy reach of his bed. He considers the whole deal for a couple of seconds, a half smile on his lips. One way or another he will get his happy end. Then he works his way into the darkness, pushing himself forward with his elbows and knees.

This house is too small to play the game properly: just the two bedrooms at the front; the sitting room, kitchen, and bathroom at the back. But the modifications he has made have improved it, have in fact changed the nature of the game. When Nat sends him into the yard to count, before he even gets to thirty, he is pulling off the loose siding beneath the kitchen window at the back of the house.

Needles of light pierce the darkness below the house. In some places he has opened up holes with his knife.

In his room the TV is on. A commercial break throws flickering light over the picture-lined walls. *The world's favorite airline*. He presses his face against the musty boards, straining upward, his weight supported on his elbows. He can just see the photo of the Turner's syndrome girl, pinned up over the air conditioning unit—can see the weblike fold on each side of the neck, can see her blank, canceled eyes. A baby roach skitters across his forehead and he rolls away, moves across to another vantage point.

Looking up through a gap in the boards that run the length of the hallway, he listens for Nat. Over the muffled sound of the commercials he can hear her talking to herself. She can't decide what to do—can't decide whether to get on top of the wardrobe in her room or under the kitchen sink, where she can hide behind the curtain. He loves these secret moments, the moments when she thinks she is alone.

She comes out of her room and walks directly over him. He bites his tongue, eyeing the shadowy fork her legs make in the gray bell of her skirt. He knows what she is doing. She is looking at the padlock on his door. She wants to know what's in there.

26

Wednesday, August 18

First thing Wednesday morning Golding drove over to Jackie's place. She had spent the past ten days making arrangements for the move back to Milwaukee. They'd had a couple of long conversations on the phone in which Golding had tried to persuade her to stick it out just a bit longer, but she was adamant: Mom needed her, and there was nothing, apart from him, to keep her in L.A. He still disagreed with what she was doing, still saw it as a sliding backwards into negativity, but he wasn't going to part on bad terms.

He arrived at her front door at eight o'clock carrying coffee and donuts.

"Hey, big brother."

She stood back and let him into the house. He was surprised to see that it was clean and tidy. All of her personal possessions were gone.

"Nice place, I'll take it," he said, smiling.

Jackie considered her handiwork for a moment.

"Yeah, it's not too bad actually. I could live here myself."

He handed her a coffee and opened the donuts on the table.

"Really? So you changed your mind?"

Jackie took a donut and bit into it hungrily, shaking her head.

"No way."

They filled the next few minutes with talk about how long it would take the Greyhound to get to Milwaukee, about where she'd have a chance to rest and stretch her legs.

"You know, I'd have bought you a plane ticket," said Golding.

"I know you would. But this is fine. I kind of like seeing the land roll past, and I'm in no hurry." She frowned and looked down at her joined hands. She had gotten sugar around her mouth. Golding reached across and brushed it away. When she looked at him there were tears in her eyes.

"What's up, sis?"

She shook her head.

"I just hate good-byes," she said, trying to smile. "Do me a favor, will you?"

"Anything, baby."

"When we get to the bus terminal, don't wait until I get on the bus. Just let me out and leave."

He nodded, suddenly unable to speak. They both looked at the floor.

"Petey?" He looked up. She was staring at him with her beautiful blue eyes. "Are you going to be okay?"

He shrugged, confused by the question.

"Sure. Sure I am." She nodded, but he could see she was not reassured. "Why wouldn't I be okay?"

She looked back down at the floor.

"One of the girls—at work—she showed me a magazine . . ."

"And?"

"Talking about that Grossman guy." She looked up, this time fixing him with a hard stare. "That wasn't you, Petey?" Her voice was barely audible.

"What? What wasn't me?"

"That wasn't you that killed him?"

Golding felt himself go cold.

"No. No way. He was dead when I got there—dying anyway. You shouldn't believe everything you read."

She nodded, seeming to accept his answer.

"Okay," she said. "Okay. Forget I said it. I just worry sometimes."

"Hey, don't worry about me," said Golding, unable to keep the annoyance out of his voice. He stood up and looked at his watch. "What time's your bus?"

"Eight fifty-two."

"So we'd better roll."

Jackie struggled to her feet. He watched her shuffle through to the back of the house. She returned a moment later with her blue vinyl suitcase.

"You do believe me, don't you?" he said.

She looked at him then, and put her case down. She crossed the small space and took him in her arms.

"I just worry, Petey. That's all. I don't want anything to happen to you."

He pulled away. There was something in her expression, a kind of pitying look that he found unbearable.

"Nothing's going to happen to me," he said. "I'm fine. You should worry about yourself for a change."

This came out a little harder than it was meant to. Jackie nodded once, twice. She put her head on one side.

"Oh?"

"Come on." Golding knew he had said the wrong thing. He reached for the suitcase. "Let's not argue."

"No." She was still looking at him, her head pushed over at an angle. "I want to hear it. Why should I worry?"

A big truck went past outside, making the windows rattle.

"I'm not a victim," she said quietly. "I'm not a victim because I choose not to be."

Golding made another attempt to reach the suitcase, but she was blocking his path now.

"I'm not the one who can't forget. I'm not the one who can't . . . I'm not the one who doesn't speak to his mother."

Golding felt his throat go tight.

"You know why I don't speak to Mom," he said.

"No, I don't. Tell me."

He couldn't tell her. Just thinking about it was like drowning. He could never talk about it. She knew that.

"That's why I worry," she said. "I worry because you bottle it up. Sometime it's going to come out and you're going to hurt somebody. And you're going to hurt yourself."

27

White patio furniture. The glass doors seen from outside. A home-movie-style pan catching ghostly figures in reflection.

Golding set up a loop on the VCR and scanned that moment thirty times—forty, *fifty*, started to see a woman's head. When the male voice said *O-kay*, he mouthed the word, tried to imagine Grossman talking like that, but knew it was the other guy, the guy Reynolds called Videoman, the guy he didn't want to name in case it clouded his thinking. Slumped on the couch, sitting at the table, standing in the doorway, he knew he was watching something strange, something that came out of deep strangeness, but the surface gave no clue to its depth. It was banal, ordinary.

He didn't want to think about Jackie, didn't want to think about what she had said. They had driven to the Greyhound station in silence. He had let her out and pulled away without a word. Then he had gone into the office and tried to concentrate on work, but he wanted to be with the material—the files, the pictures, the film that evoked Ellen's presence. He wanted to help her because he could.

The wooden fence. A patch of lawn that needed water. In the middle of the lawn a kid's toy tractor.

He watched the film late into the night. A pair of pale arms reached for the little girl. The woman's arms. When the kid's face flared into focus, he squinted at the light and hit freeze-frame. The whole room was lit by the flickering face. Pink light washed over the images of Ellen he had tacked to the walls. Dopey from lack of sleep, his eyes registered the strange new colors: her green eyes black, her red mouth gray, the gray lips parted over pink teeth. He scanned forward and back, forward and back. When the film was finished, he stared at the blank screen, lost in thought.

The talk with Gorman had left him with an impression of deeper understanding, but it wasn't a comfortable feeling. Deeper was darker, and reflecting on Ellen's childhood, the early years of struggle under the watchful gaze of her father, he entered his own personal darkness, until it seemed to him that their lives intertwined.

Before talking to Gorman, he had more or less decided that Ellen had been starved as a child; probably not in an obvious way—he couldn't imagine Stepan withholding food—but he could see how the pressure to succeed, to jump, to spin, might lead to crushing anxiety about weight, which in turn would lead to a kind of coerced deprivation. Now, in his long nights of brooding thought, he wondered if something else had been at work, something more tangled, more painful. Anorexia was sometimes linked to abuse. Sometimes little girls refused to grow up, desperate to keep the love of the father. What had been the nature of that love? He dug out a picture of Stepan, tried to see the staring, contemptuous eyes that Gorman had described, but in a trapdoor moment of recollection saw his own father's eyes—eyes he came to think of as being the color of leather, eyes thickly fringed with dark lashes, sensitive, furtively watchful.

He found a bottle of bourbon under the sink and twisted off the cap, told himself that just one glass would be enough, and took a slug direct from the bottle just to make sure that was so.

He ran the tape, saw the black T-shirt with the snowflake motif, heard the woman say *Show Momma what you can do.* A warm sunny afternoon in the garden. The snowflake jarred. He tried to make it make sense, trying at the same time to shut out his father's eyes, to shut out his father's voice. He took a long pull at the bottle, remembering Jackie's face the day he told her he was going to leave home.

The clunk of the VCR switching off brought him back to reality. The bottle was half empty. He stared at it for a moment in disbelief, then jerked up onto his feet, the blood banging through his heart. He was angry as if someone had forced him to drink. He walked through to the kitchen and pushed the bottle back into the cupboard. When that was done, breathing the fumes of spirits, he caught his reflection in the window and saw the fleeting image of the woman's head as it was reflected in the patio doors. He turned his head the way she held hers. Who the hell was she? The kid's mother? So why would she allow her child to be shown on TV? Why would she let *Hard News* tell bullshit stories of abandonment? Why would she allow them to say that it was Ellen's?

Because it *was* Ellen's?

He bent forward, twisting to drink directly from the faucet, trying not to go at this too hard, trying to let the thoughts come. From the first time he had seen the picture of the little girl, the framed picture left at Ellen's house, he had more or less accepted the idea that what this was, what this whole business came down to, was a kind of sadistic joke. It was like Lenny said: someone was screwing with Ellen's head. *They* knew she couldn't have a child, *they* knew how much she wanted one, and so they were torturing her. Either that or it was the product of plain delusion: some crackpot with a kid that resembled the young Ellen Cusak who was living out a bizarre fantasy. Even when he saw the *Hard News* story it never occurred to him there might be another explanation. Ellen was sterile. So the story had to be bullshit. But there was sterility and there was infertility.

Now, wiping his mouth, staring blankly at his reflected face, he went back over what Gorman had said. *Embryos were as far as it went.* Ellen was unable to carry a child, but she could conceive. She could make an egg. She and Doug could make an embryo. She had been ready to seek out a surrogate, would have done it if it hadn't been for Gorman and his fear of—what was the word he used?—*complications*? He tried to imagine how it would have been for Ellen to have her overwhelming maternal drive checked like that. It would have been understandable if, in her distress, in her desperation, she had decided to go behind Gorman's back, behind everyone's back.

But how would she have done it? Without Doug's consent there was no way she could get a respectable medical establishment to handle it for her. The child's father had rights. She would have had to find not just a willing surrogate—someone prepared to bear her child—but a doctor prepared to break all the rules, prepared to risk losing his livelihood if anyone found out. Where would she have found someone like that? She couldn't have put an ad in the paper, that was for sure. And besides, if this had all happened six years ago, why had Ellen never received the child? Why send the pictures now? Was it a question of money? Of blackmail? *You see, I see you, Ellen.* Was the child even alive? The thoughts crowded in, none of them making much sense. Suddenly he wished he weren't so drunk. He needed to think clearly and in straight lines. But it was impossible. Every idea spun him around, left him disoriented so that even the things he thought he knew seemed doubtful, ambivalent.

He went back to the tape, too drunk now to really focus. The white lake of the rink. The voices of excited children echoed. Dark forms drifted over the ice. Then he saw the little girl in the blue dress. He froze the image.

"Who are you?"

In the blur of drunken emotion, he imagined she was Ellen, imagined her trapped in some trailer-park life, struggling to get by, careful not to take too much bread at suppertime, conscious of her father's gaze as she reached for more. He pressed the button that let her go, and watched her make her slow circuit on the ice, one foot, then the other, a perfect figure of eight.

Los Angeles baked in the August heat. He did his job. Reynolds was watchful, but more relaxed with Romero around. Romero was too busy to give an opinion on whether Grossman was the stalker. Too busy or too smart. Golding felt that Reynolds had told him to change the subject if ever it came up.

He did his job. He and Roy Denison served a re-straining order on a Mexican kid called Rico who had a thing about a soap star called Carmencita. He had a couple of very long talks with Detective James Wolpert of the Pacific Division. Outside of office time he bought tabloids, scanning for Ellen stories. He recorded news items on the VCR. He resisted the temptation to go over to her house. Bernie Ross told him that *Hard News* had set up an 800 number after their item on the stalker: people were to phone in if they thought they knew who the little girl in the blue dress was. He called to check it out, then called the studio where *Hard News* was pro-duced. He was told there had been thousands of calls, from all over the country, and that, no, he couldn't have the list of callers. *Hard News* journalists were running down any "promising leads."

NBC aired a long piece on stalkers that used Gross-man's death to get into the subject of violence in the workplace. It wasn't just celebrities that got stalked, it was managers, checkout clerks, waitresses. It told the story of Robert Fairley and Lorna Block. They worked in the same Silicon Valley firm. Fairley harassed her big-time until, in the end, the management had to fire him. He came back with guns and killed seven people, including Block. A grim-faced profiler interviewed him in jail, asked him if he'd had relationships like that before, and the guy said, "One-way or two-way relationships?" Because for him a one-way relation-ship, a relationship where there was no reciprocation, was still a relationship.

A week after the Grossman killing he woke before dawn, feeling restless. He knew he had to do some-thing, make a break somehow, clear his head for a while. He thought about driving over to the shooting range that evening, but when he saw his face in the bathroom mirror, the putty-colored skin and the deep shadows under his red eyes, he knew that what he really needed was physical exercise. He had been neglecting his body, eating junk food and sleeping irregular hours. He called the office and told Romero he was taking the morning off. Then he put on jogging pants and battered Nikes, pulled a clean T-shirt out of the bottom of a drawer, and went out of the house jingling his car keys.

A kind of fake country freshness hung in the early-morning air. He took Beverly Glen over the mountains to Sunset, then made his way west toward Ocean Park.

A stiffish breeze was blowing in over the breakers as he jogged north towards Malibu. He was surprised how empty the beach was. He passed a solitary couple walking hand in hand and a Chinese guy in a gray suit tossing bits of bread up to the big herring gulls. About a hundred yards out, some kids with wet suits and boards were trying to catch waves, and beyond them, almost on the horizon, he could see seals twisting and diving.

Forty minutes later he was ready to pass out. The sweat was pouring off him as he walked onto the terrace of Angelino's, a budget restaurant sandwiched between the highway and the beach. It had just opened. He ordered a large OJ and leaned back in his molded plastic chair, wondering when his heart was going to slow. The waiter came back with an empty tray under his arm.

"I'm really sorry, but the juicer's on the fritz. It's getting fixed, but I thought you might like to order something else."

Golding shaded his eyes against the light, said he was in no hurry.

"There's the paper if you want." The guy smiled, com-

ing on to him a little. He pointed at a badly folded copy
of the *Los Angeles Times* on the seat opposite.

It was starting to get hot on the terrace. Golding
looked around for an umbrella, but they hadn't gotten
them out yet. He squinted at the distant surf, trying to
pick out the black dots of swimming seals in the hard
glitter of sunlight. Then, when he realized that it really
was going to be a while before he got his freshly
squeezed OJ, he grabbed the paper.

The front pages were all taken up by water rights disputes. The federal government's interior secretary was
trying to make Californians live with 4.4 million acre-
feet of water a year, instead of the 5.2 million it was
sucking out of the Colorado River. He turned to the
sports pages to check out the basketball results and
then went back to the beginning. He was looking for the
weather forecast when he saw the article—a half col-
umn on an inside page, topped by a headline—
STRANGER IN CUSAK'S GARDEN.

"Sir?"

He read the headline twice. But he couldn't believe it.

"Sir?"

He looked up. The waiter was standing over him
again.

"The machine's dead. That's what they're saying now.
Is out of a carton okay?"

"Sure. Whatever."

He went back to the paper, and for the next two minutes was completely oblivious to his surroundings. It
wasn't what he'd thought, though. The stranger in
Ellen's garden turned out to be the corpse her maid had
found in July. The article explained how LAPD were
getting nowhere with identifying the woman and so
had decided to call on a specialist to work up a three-

dimensional likeness. Sketches by the police artist had produced no viable leads, so they wanted Dr. Marcia Gallo to produce an actual head based on the skull of the victim.

Marcia Gallo and her associate Dr. Colin Slater make no bones about the difficulty of getting results. "It's really a tool of last resort," said Gallo, who claims nevertheless to have a 70 percent success rate with past reconstructions. Based at CSU's Anthropology Department at Monterey Park, the forensic sculptor and physical anthropologist work together to construct the facial features on the basis of the underlying cranial architecture. The partially mummified condition of the skeleton is going to make Dr. Gallo's job a lot easier. "We're pretty clear about race, sex, age, and weight, and that's obviously a big help," Gallo said.

The abundance of detail has been of little help to Detective Larry Hagmaier, who is leading the case. Fingerprints taken from the body have yielded no matches, while the clothing—the woman was fully dressed in clean clothes, evidently postmortem—indicates only the broadest socioeconomic parameters. The fact that she was dressed for cold weather continues to baffle LAPD. Was she killed out of state—maybe in the mountains? Or was she on her way there when she met her assailant? Detective Hagmaier has considered all the permutations but has so far been unable to develop any viable leads.

Golding read the passage twice, then stood up. It was like a light coming on. He started to run.

"Hey!"

The waiter came out of the restaurant with his juice, but Golding was already getting into his car.

He drove fast, hitting speed dips at intersections, taking chances on yellow lights. *Dressed for cold weather.* The phrase kept going round and round. She was dressed for cold weather, but it had nothing to do with the mountains, nothing to do with mountains at all.

Back at the house, he pulled out the fat file he had accumulated on Ellen, and started to riffle through articles looking for the more detailed pieces dealing with the discovery of the corpse on her property. There were several mentions of the warm clothing, but for some reason nobody had made the obvious connection with Cusak herself. Early on someone had said that the corpse had gone into the ground before Cusak and Gorman had moved in, and after that nobody, even in all the welter of speculation, had bothered to make the link with the couple. But maybe there was a link.

He checked dates, scribbling a rough time line on a scrap of paper. The foundations of the house were laid down in October '96. The actual decision to buy was taken sometime in late '95. As far as his Nexus search had shown, there had been no less than three articles on the planning of the house published in '96, one of which, in *Design* magazine, showing an artist's impression of the way the house would eventually look. Golding spread the pages on the floor. There it was, Doug and Ellen Gorman's dream house in Brentwood, all done up in artistic washes of color.

He went back to the corpse stories, laying the paper out on the floor until the whole room was carpeted. According to the coroner, the body had been in the ground for at least three years, maybe four. Whoever buried the body could have known what was planned there. It was perfectly possible.

The body was dressed for cold weather. The killer had

stabbed her—thirty-two times according to the reports—and then dressed her warmly. Thermal underwear, thick socks, boots; the works. Not for the mountains, not for a ski resort, but for right here in L.A., for an ice rink. Winter clothing in summer weather, just like the woman on the tape. The snowflake in the sunny garden. He sat back on the floor, trying to make sense of it, trying to make out of what it was that loomed just below the surface. Then another thought occurred. He scrabbled back through the papers until he found the report on the police autopsy. *The muscle attachment areas are well developed, particularly in the legs, leading the police to suspect that this person may have been a serious athlete at one time.*

An athlete, yes, but not the usual kind, not track or field.

He stabbed on the TV and the VCR, let the tape run, hardly able to sit still as the images moved on the screen. Beneath the excitement he felt a rising tide of unease, of fear.

The woman leaned in to pick up the child. The snowflake on her T-shirt. Then the rink. He rolled back to the patio doors and scanned back and forth, froze it on the spectral image reflected on the surface. . . . He'd bet money that the lady in the T-shirt was a skater.

28

Friday, August 20

"**S**o here we are, ladies," Lenny said, raising his glass of Sapporo. "Another week over. We're still alive. The city's still standing. And no one's suing us for professional misconduct."

"Three out of three!" said Sally Nicholson, clinking her glass first against his and then against Ellen's. "Mind you, we still have the afternoon to go. Maybe we shouldn't count our rice cakes."

Lenny held up his left hand as if he were taking an oath.

"My mobile is switched off. My answering machine is disconnected. As far as this working week is concerned, you can bring on the fat lady right now."

"Aah," said Sal. "So *that's* why I'm here."

"Oh, Sal." Lenny grinned as he took a sip of beer. "Will you listen to her? Three kids and she wants to look like . . . like . . ."

"Like a figure skater," said Sal, giving Ellen a sideways glance. "That's what I want to look like. You're in disgustingly good shape, Ellen. I demand to know your secret."

"Too bad," said Lenny, wagging a finger. "You'll have to wait for the video. All will be revealed."

"A fitness video?" said Sally. "What a great idea. Ellen was always a natural for the camera."

Ellen smiled, acknowledging the compliment but not feeling it. Sally Nicholson was an old friend of Lenny's who worked on syndication at HBO, a bustling thirty-something with bobbed brown hair and a big ruby-red smile. Normally lunch with a television executive would have meant business, but Ellen had met Sally before and got along well with her. Besides, Lenny had promised that the occasion would be strictly for fun, and to emphasize the point had booked them a table at Yamashiro, a Japanese restaurant in the Hollywood Hills that he only went to in his free time. The place was famous for its panoramic view of the city, which stretched all the way from downtown to the sea. From where she sat, Ellen could see the neatly spaced procession of aircraft descending toward the runways of LAX. She couldn't helping remembering her own first flight to the West Coast, her father staring with troubled eyes at the snaking wonder of the Grand Canyon, her own disbelief at the scale of a city that seemed to go on forever. She remembered how her father had turned to her as they came in to land and said: *Here, Yelena, we speak English.* And how he had done just that forever afterwards, refusing even to acknowledge her, for the first few years at least, if she addressed him in anything else. She wondered how many thousands, how many millions of people had said the same thing as they arrived in this particular promised land.

"So are you in training now?" Sal asked.

Ellen looked around, took a moment to register the question.

"No, no . . . Not really. I'm skating. I've got a show to do this fall. But I'm not going back into competition. I'm too old, for one thing."

"Oh, shame," said Sally. "And I thought you were all ready for a comeback."

"Never say never," said Lenny. "Elaine Zayak did it. But right now, Ellen's got enough on her plate. Things are really looking up at last, Sal, I gotta tell you. At last our way is clear."

Ellen got the feeling Sally had been briefed on her recent troubles, and had been chosen for the occasion as someone who could be relied upon to be supportive. But she didn't mind. Even with bidders coming forward for the video deal and rehearsals about to start for the *Nutcracker* tour, she was grateful for anything that would take her mind off the past few weeks. She had gotten back the night before from Lake Arrowhead, having spent longer up there than she'd planned, and found Lenny's invitation on the answering machine. She'd also found a message from Pete Golding, asking if she wanted to go to a movie. She'd been surprised at first, but not entirely displeased. It was too late to catch *The Apartment,* but she planned on calling back soon and making a counterproposal. She wasn't sure where things would go from there, or if they could possibly work, but she was a free woman now, she reminded herself, and there were lots of things about Pete she liked.

The food arrived, an array of small, fragrant dishes in black lacquered bowls. Lenny and Sally made appreciative noises, and then they all three began politely picking with their chopsticks at whatever was nearest them. Halfway through the meal, Lenny insisted on ordering sake and keeping everyone's cup well filled. Sally in particular seemed to appreciate it.

"You must've felt like someone up there didn't like you," she said, after the small talk was exhausted, "what with all you had to put up with."

"The press," said Lenny, shaking his head. "Assholes."

"How on earth did you cope? I mean, I'd have run away. I'd have left town."

"Sally, you'll never leave town," said Lenny. "You'd be afraid of missing a premiere."

"Oh, I wish. Seriously, though—it must have been hell."

Ellen tried to look comfortable with the question. She could sense Lenny's attention focusing on her, seeing how she would respond, how screwed up by the affair she really was. She took a mouthful of the sake.

"Well, I have just spent five days at Lake Arrowhead."

"Yes," said Lenny, "but Sal means before that. When the shitake was really hitting the fan."

Ellen shrugged.

"I thought about leaving. Actually, I almost did leave. But then I thought: why should I? Why should I let these people make an exile of me?" She put down her cup. "This city is my home."

She saw Lenny smile as he looked down at his plate.

"Good for you," said Sally. "Good for you."

"Ellen's a fighter," said Lenny. "You don't get to be a world champion if you fold when things get tough."

"Too right," said Sally, beginning to sound like the sake was getting to her. "But that stuff about the kid. I mean, that was nasty."

"Crazy," said Lenny. "Crazy *and* nasty. Do you know,

Sal, since that show *Hard News* has had calls from about three hundred people claiming they've seen that little girl."

"Three hundred?" said Ellen. "You mean, they know who she is?"

Lenny laughed and shook his head.

"Three hundred *different* people in three hundred *different* places."

"Wow. That's scary," said Sally.

"Oh well, not really. Now, the Ice Man"—Lenny raised a finger, getting into his stride now—"*he* was scary. I've got to be honest: he put the fear of God into me."

"You met him?"

"No way. I talked to him, though, on the phone. That was enough. My word on weirdos: leave 'em to the pros."

Ellen touched Lenny on the arm.

"Lenny, maybe one of those three hundred people— *some* of those three hundred people were right. Maybe they have seen her."

Lenny looked perplexed.

"Sure, Ellen. But, er . . ." He shrugged. "Who cares? I mean, she's just some kid, right?"

Sally was watching her. For a moment no one spoke.

"Yes, of course. I guess I'm just . . ."—Ellen looked down at her hands—"curious."

Sally smiled tactfully.

"Sure. *I'm* curious as hell. I mean, what did you do? I heard you had to hire bodyguards and stuff."

"Not bodyguards," said Lenny. "Specialists. The best. You ever heard of Pete Golding?"

Sally's eyes widened.

"Pete Golding? Wait a minute. He wasn't the guy in the Maddy Olsen thing?"

"The same."

"Shot that guy on the porch?"

Lenny nodded smugly.

"Pistol Pete, shoots to kill, never missed, nor he never will."

"Oh, knock it off," said Ellen. "I don't know how you can joke about that sort of thing."

"I'm just saying . . ." Lenny talked through a mouthful of food. "I'm saying with these crazies, with these *extremely dangerous* people, you don't get very far saying please and thank you. It doesn't work. They're crazy. And armed."

"So?"

"So sometimes it comes down to them or you." He tapped Ellen on the shoulder. "I mean *you*."

Sally's voice dropped to a whisper: "Jesus, Lenny, you're not suggesting this Golding guy shot Grossman too?"

Lenny held out his hands with a slow-motion shrug.

"Sal, we may never know. All I can tell you is the police questioned him for most of the night. And the tabloid press . . . but that's another matter. As far as I'm concerned—"

He was interrupted by his mobile phone. With an apologetic grimace he pulled it out of his pocket.

"Lenny, I thought you said you'd—?"

"I'm sorry, Sal. I thought I had. I'm sorry, I'll . . . Hello? Jack! How're you doing?" He covered the mouthpiece. "It's . . . it's a client. I'll take it outside. Be back in just a second."

He got up and walked away towards the hallway. The

two women watched him go. For a few moments they ate in silence.

"So," said Sally at last. "I guess hiring Pete Golding was Lenny's idea, huh?"

Ellen nodded.

"I didn't really know anything about him at the time. I mean, he seemed perfectly—"

"Frankly, I'm surprised. I mean, Lenny's right of course: these people *are* dangerous. They can be. But all the same . . ." Sally picked up a shrimp and dipped it in a bowl of red sauce. "I actually met Maddy Olsen. A few times."

"You did?"

"She's a friend of a friend really. Kimberly Ross? Well, we used to be neighbors, and she's known Maddy for years. They were in high school together."

Ellen didn't like Sally's expression. She had become very serious.

"And what did she say?"

Sally brought the shrimp close to her painted lips, considered it for a moment, then lowered it again.

"Well, she needed help, no doubt about that. I mean, that McGinley guy was seriously bad news. He gave her a ride home once—when she was working in reception at this publishing company in Florida? That was the only time they were ever actually out together, in any sense at all. But as far as he was concerned, that meant they were destined for each other. He called her, wrote to her, sent flowers *every day*. And that was just the beginning."

Ellen pushed her hands into her lap. She felt suddenly cold.

"She got another job, but he found out where and kept turning up there after work, telling everyone he was her fiancé. Can you imagine? If she arranged to meet her friends in a bar, he would turn up and introduce himself. It happened three times before she realized he was tuning into her mobile phone."

"There are machines you can buy," Ellen said softly, "scanners. They told me about that."

Sally popped the shrimp into her mouth, dabbing at her lips with her napkin.

"Right. So she moves across town. Changes her number. He's onto her in a *week.* A guy comes round to see her, an old friend, finds McGinley outside. He says: *You come near my wife once more, I'm gonna kill you.* Like, she's his wife now."

Ellen didn't want to hear any more, but Sally was enjoying herself too much to notice.

"They get a restraining order. He violates it three days later. So they grab him for contempt of court. But they don't put the guy away because he hasn't any previous convictions. Know what the judge says? He says, why don't they consider *counseling* to help them sort out their problems? *Their* problems. Can you believe that?"

"I thought . . . I thought McGinley had been in jail."

"That came next, after he followed Maddy here. He found another guy on her doorstep and put him in the hospital. They sentence him to eighteen months. He serves six. When she hears he's getting out, that's when she hires Golding."

"She knew he'd come back."

"She was moving *again,*" said Sally. "She wanted help to hide. To do it right. And she wanted McGinley put away again if he came near her. Golding took care of all that, set up her security and everything, talked to the police. He even offered to train her to use a gun. He took the whole thing very seriously."

"Isn't that what she was paying him for?"

"Sure. But it didn't end there. He started . . ."

A waitress arrived and began loading the empty dishes onto a tray. Sally looked on, smiling, determined, it seemed, not to be overheard.

"Started what?"

"He started calling her all the time, checking up on her. It was like he couldn't go to sleep at night without knowing she was okay. Then one night she found him sneaking around outside her house."

Ellen felt sick. She pictured the grounds of her own house, the sense of fear, of violation she'd felt knowing that someone had been there, watching, knowing that they had been so close.

"Creepy, huh?" said Sally, reading her expression. "So she tells Golding's boss she doesn't want him on the case anymore. She doesn't want their help at all. You see what I'm saying here?"

Ellen focused on Sally's expectant face.

"What? This was . . . *before* McGinley showed up?"

"Exactly. Press never found that out, and Maddy didn't tell them. But Golding wasn't working for her the day of the shooting. He was just out there. Uninvited . . ."

"Oh God."

"Uh-huh. And that wasn't the end of it. He kept on wanting to see her even after that. You know what Maddy said? She said Golding was just as bad as McGinley. As far as she was concerned, they were *both* stalking her."

Sally straightened up. Lenny was striding across the room towards them, tucking his phone back into his jacket pocket.

"I know they say it takes a thief to catch a thief," she said while he was still out of earshot, "but if you ask me, Pete Golding's a very scary guy. Like, once he gets a little piece of you, he never lets go."

29

Ellen ran a hot bath and stretched out, breathing deeply as the water slowly relaxed her aching muscles. After the lunch at Yamashiro she had collected her skates and gone straight down to the Pickwick Rink with a Walkman and a stack of cassette tapes. She'd wanted to try out some musical ideas she had for one of Sam Ritt's programs, but more than that, she'd wanted to stop herself thinking about what Sally Nicholson had told her.

The story about Maddy Olsen was disturbing. She hadn't said anything, but she was angry with Lenny for putting her under the protection of someone as dangerous, as downright screwed-up, as Pete Golding. And at the same time, she was angry with Sally for telling stories about him, as if Golding were a friend. It was confusing. She'd skated for hours, trying to concentrate on the music, trying to find the shapes and patterns that gave expression to it, until she couldn't skate anymore. But through it all her mind kept drifting back to Sally Nicholson leaning across the table, her red lips glistening, telling her how Pete Golding was no different from the stalkers he went after.

Maria was downstairs in the kitchen, singing snatches of some Cuban ballad about love and gardenias. Her voice drifted up through the empty house, stopping abruptly as she lifted or squeezed or bent down, and then going on again, although never from the same place. Ellen sunk further into the water, thinking now about Maddy Olsen and what it must have been like for her, having Arthur McGinley stalk her all that time, having Pete Golding shoot him dead on the steps of her porch. Olsen was pretty. She had delicate dark features, a cute retroussé nose, and a sassy character. At least that was the way she came over on TV. Ellen wondered what she'd said to Golding when she found him sneaking around outside her house. She wondered what he'd actually been doing there—trying to spy on her? Or did he sense, did he simply *know,* that McGinley was going to try and kill her? *It was like he couldn't go to sleep at night unless he knew she was okay,* that was what Sally had said. Maybe that was just how it was.

Yet Golding hadn't called her, apart from that one time. Since then she hadn't heard a word. She was surprised in a way. She thought about how she had been planning to call him back and shuddered.

She put her head under the water and rinsed the shampoo from her hair. The Doberman next door was barking. The noise stopped, then started again, closer this time. She felt a flutter of panic, pushed her hair back with her hands, squeezing out the water, listening. Maria had stopped singing.

She climbed out of the tub and wrapped herself in her robe. It was probably nothing to worry about, and she was damned if she was going to start getting paranoid. Standing next to the window, she could hear a man's voice. It was her neighbor. It sounded like he was shouting at his dog. The animal whined, then fell silent.

She was crossing the landing, towel in hand, when she heard Maria scream.

Glass shattered. There was a sharp crack as something heavy hit the kitchen tiles.

"Maria!"

She ran down the stairs. Maria appeared in the kitchen doorway, holding her face in her hands.

"I'm sorry, Mrs. Cusak. I saw . . . I saw someone"—she pointed behind her—"outside."

Ellen looked into the kitchen. There was glass all over the floor, an upturned saucepan in the middle of a spreading pool of soup.

"Mr. Bennett? Was it Mr. Bennett, the man next door?"

Maria shook her head. She pointed to the kitchen window.

"I look up. A face. A man's face. Not Mr. Bennett."

They stood looking at each other for a moment, then Maria went back into the kitchen to get her knife.

"Should I call the police?" she said.

The thought of Los Angeles' finest turning up on the doorstep was not very appealing. Ellen thought of Golding, then realized that it might *be* Golding who was sneaking around out there. In a spasm of anger she yanked open the door.

"Mrs. Cusak?" Maria was frantic.

"No, goddammit. I've had enough."

They both looked out. The security lights had come on. Ellen listened hard. There was nothing. She imagined whoever it was still standing there beyond the range of the lights, watching the house, holding his breath, rigid with excitement. But surely if he was still there the dog would be barking.

Then she saw it. A large brown envelope on the doorstep. It was marked with thick black lettering: YELENA.

There was a black-and-white photograph inside, about eight inches by ten. But it had been produced by no kind of camera that Ellen had ever seen. There were reference numbers along the top edge and several columns of ghostly horizontal bars running down the page. The translucent quality of the image reminded Ellen of an X ray. Pinned to the photograph was a single page torn from a Yellow Pages phone directory. A small ad had been circled in black. It read: EMERSON NEALE—*Complete Family Planning and Diagnostics Services—In confidence.* The address was in Santa Monica, just a few miles away.

She pulled the directory page free and found something else, a note, written on thin paper using a manual typewriter. Several of the letters punched right through. It began: *There's none so blind as they that WILL NOT see.*

She stood under the bright kitchen lights, her hands trembling as she read. Maria swept the last of the broken glass into the corner.

"You want I call the police, Mrs. Cusak?" she said.

Ellen looked up, distracted.

"Mrs. Cusak?"

"What?"

"You want I should call the police?"

Ellen looked at the note again, shaking her head.

"No," she said. "No. Don't call anyone."

30

Monday, August 23

The white patio furniture and the glass doors—the glass doors becoming the surface of a frozen lake, and trapped beneath the ice a woman's face, the mouth a ragged black hole.

Golding awoke bathed in sweat. He fumbled for the digital alarm, saw that it was five a.m. He had slept maybe three hours. He turned over and pulled the covers up, trying to cut out the dawn light. But it was no use. The head was there now. He couldn't stop thinking about it, had spent the whole of Sunday thinking about it, wondering if the one taking shape under Dr. Marcia Gallo's skilled hands was the same as the one on the tape, wondering if it was a face Ellen had known in life.

Standing under the shower, he realized what he had to do.

He spent Monday morning hunched over in his cubicle, keeping his voice down, phoning up a storm. An ex-cop friend working in a small firm of PIs in Santa Monica told him that Detective Larry Hagmaier had been close to Captain Neil Blackwood before Blackwood made area commanding office of the Van Nuys Division. Blackwood and Reynolds were long-time golfing partners—Golding even remembered meeting the old man a couple of times at the office. He called Blackwood in the afternoon, gave him Reynolds' best wishes, and then told him he needed to talk to Detective Hagmaier.

"I want to get a couple things straight about this corpse they dug up in Cusak's garden," he said. And then, into the silence: "I think I may have a lead."

"He could use one of those, I guess." Blackwood sounded preoccupied. He rustled some papers and then said he hadn't spoken to Hagmaier in a while and that he would give him a call. "How's Tom?" he said. "Is he around?"

Golding looked down the corridor to Reynolds' office. The door was ajar and he could see the back of Roy Denison's head nodding in agreement. "I'm afraid not," he said. "Guess he must be out with a client."

Blackwood sighed into the phone. "Could you tell him next Thursday's good for me . . . Pete, is it?"

"That's right. Golding. Sure, I'll tell him."

He called Hagmaier an hour later. He sounded stressed-out. His initial coolness disappeared at the mention of Blackwood's name. Golding hustled.

"I'm sorry, Detective Hagmaier, Neil Blackwood said he was going to call you." He pretended to be puzzled, though he knew Blackwood wouldn't have made the call a priority.

"Well, that's Neil," said Hagmaier, chuckling to himself, and without any prompting he told a story about how Blackwood had failed to show for a conference one time because he'd made the cut in an amateur golf tournament in Orange County.

"He shot this great round and squeezed through to the final twenty. Then forgot all about the speech he was supposed to give."

Golding laughed along.

"I haven't seen Neil in . . . Jeez, it's been a while. How's he doing up there?"

"Up where?"

"Van Nuys."

It was clear Hagmaier thought that he and Blackwood were best buddies. Golding didn't try to set him straight, but didn't push his luck either. Instead he got onto the subject of the Jane Doe in Cusak's garden. Hagmaier tightened up.

"Oh yeah? What's your interest in that?"

"We've been doing some work for Mrs. Cusak, and I think I have some information that might be of use to you."

"What kind of information?"

"A possible lead."

Hagmaier didn't sound impressed.

"And what about you? What do you get out of it?"

"Clarification. I was hoping for a little more detail on the case. Plus I'm real interested in this reconstruction work Dr. Gallo's doing for you."

For a second Golding thought he must have said something wrong.

"Okay, okay," said Hagmaier eventually. "If Neil says it's okay, okay. I'll talk to you, but I ain't going through the file in some bar."

Golding hunched even closer to the phone. "Tell me where to go. I'll meet you anywhere in the city."

Hagmaier thought about it for a moment. "I finish here at eight. Why don't you come up here after that?"

"Where are you at?"

"Tell you what: on second thought, why don't you come by my place? We can go through it there."

At just after seven o'clock Golding came up out of the Century City parking lot into evening sunlight and eased himself into the southward-flowing traffic on the Avenue of the Stars. He reached Pico and made a left. Despite the fact that everything was going smoothly, he couldn't quell the jittery feeling in his gut. For one thing, he was way out on a limb approaching Hagmaier. At some point, maybe next week, Blackwood might mention his call to Reynolds, and Reynolds would go nuts. He'd think he was just obsessing on Cusak, trying to worm his way back into her life. But beyond that, he worried where all this was leading, felt in his gut it was nowhere he wanted Ellen to be.

Oakhurst was a quiet, tree-lined street with neat brick-and-stucco-fronted bungalows each with their own patch of sloping lawn. Hagmaier opened the door of 237 as Golding pulled up at the curb. He was a tall, fit-looking man with a full head of gray hair.

"I really appreciate you seeing me," said Golding as he came up the drive.

"Yeah, well, Neil called just after we talked," said Hagmaier.

Golding nodded, trying to look unconcerned.

"So that's all okay," said Hagmaier. "I didn't realize you worked for Tom Reynolds. Neil tells me he's pretty handy around the green." They walked through to the kitchen, where Golding saw the case folder open on the table. It contained a stack of paper at least three inches thick. "You play much?" said Hagmaier.

"To tell you the truth, the job keeps me kind of busy."

"I hear that," said Hagmaier. He opened the refrig-

erator and pulled out a couple of Buds. Golding saw
the brightly lit, more or less empty interior. Hagmaier
lived on his own. "Still, pretty lucrative work, I guess.
With all the sickos in this town, it must be a growth
industry."

"I think Tom's doing okay."

Hagmaier handed him a beer and they drank.

"So, you a cop before?" he said.

"I started out as a private eye. Got my license in '82."

Hagmaier nodded, but it didn't seem to make much
difference either way. Golding wondered if he knew
about the Maddy Olsen case; couldn't believe he didn't.
He looked down at the case folder, hoping to see something new, maybe a photograph of Marcia Gallo's work.
He gestured at the pile of papers.

"So . . . how's it going?"

Hagmaier shrugged. "To tell the truth, this case—
well, it's kind of run out of steam."

They sat down at the table, and Hagmaier started to
leaf through the papers, telling the story of the case. They
had managed to get fingerprints. They had bounced the
fingerprints around just about every database in the country. They had instituted two separate canvasses of people
in the neighborhood. They had traced and interviewed
fourteen of the seventeen people involved in the construction of the house. Trying to work up the warm-cloth-
ing angle, they had talked to meatpackers, frozen food
companies, seafood specialists, fishmongers, anyone who
might use refrigeration equipment.

"We even looked at libraries," said Hagmaier. "You
know some archives with film negatives and prints work
at low temperatures, so we thought . . . but no. We came
up with nothing."

He took a long drink of beer.

"I read about how you brought in Dr. Gallo to make a head from the skull," said Golding.

Hagmaier pulled a face.

"Sure, that's right, but only because we don't know what else to do. We put out a sketch." He pulled a photocopy out of the file. Golding had one just like it on his bedroom wall. It didn't even look real. "But the response hasn't been very helpful. This Dr. Gallo approached us. She seems pretty keen, so . . ."

"How far has she gotten?"

"Well, you know they do this thing with little blocks that correspond to the average thickness of the soft tissue over specific points on the skull. Right now it doesn't look like anything much."

Golding tried to hide his disappointment. He wasn't going to get any further with the head.

Hagmaier riffled through the wad of papers. "Anyway, any new angles, I mean any legitimate new information, would be very useful to me." He paused and gave Golding a hard look. "But before we get into that, I wanted to understand where you're coming from."

Golding cleared his throat.

"Well, like I said on the phone, I want to get some more detail—"

"Sure. But why?"

"I have a feeling there might be a link between your corpse and something I'm working on."

Hagmaier scratched his chin. "The Cusak thing?"

"Yeah."

"I thought that was all over. I thought the guy got killed."

"I'm not so sure." Golding tried to hold Hagmaier's hard cop's stare, but he couldn't manage it. He looked away. The last thing he wanted to do was to get into a discussion about the video, about the possibility that the woman on the tape was the woman in the ground. Anything that linked Ellen to the corpse had to be kept out of the light. He had already decided that the way to get Hagmaier on his side was to throw him some bait early on. He decided to go for it. "I was wondering if you'd considered the possibility that the unidentified woman was dressed for a rink."

Hagmaier took another sip of beer.

"People go to the rink," Golding went on, "they put on warm clothes. Especially if they're going to be down on the ice."

Hagmaier shrugged. "It's an idea," he said casually, but it was clear from his expression that it wasn't one he'd considered. "Like I said, we thought about all the cold places a person could work. But ice rinks . . . that's a little more exotic."

"According to the press reports, the coroner felt this lady might have been an athlete. Is that right?"

Hagmaier nodded. "Might have been an athlete *once*. This lady was in her late twenties, remember."

"So why not a skater?"

"Like Cusak you mean?"

"Yes."

Hagmaier smiled "Is that the link? Between our dead lady and your assignment?"

Golding shrugged.

Hagmaier sipped his beer.

"Yeah, well. Like I said, our lady's too old to be a skater. You've seen these kids. Tara Lipinski's barely out of diapers."

"Sure but your lady could have been a skater in the past," said Golding. "Maybe she was a coach."

"A coach?"

"It would explain the warm clothes. The coach stands around on the ice. It gets cold. I was just thinking it might be a useful lead. She was dressed to go to the rink. She was on her way there, or on her way back. So the rink's more than likely going to be in L.A. or maybe somewhere like Lake Arrowhead. That's only a two-hour drive away. I mean, how many rinks could she have been going to? Ten, maybe? Less? Wouldn't take too long to phone around. Ask if any coaching staff stopped coming to work three years ago."

Hagmaier pushed out his bottom lip.

"It's a thought." He watched Golding for a moment. "Of course that would make it quite a coincidence, it being buried on a skater's property."

"I thought about that," said Golding. "But the timing's wrong, isn't it? Cusak and Gorman didn't move in until September '97. And as I understand it, this body's been in the ground at least since '96."

"Kind of makes you think, though."

Golding wasn't sure he wanted Hagmaier to think.

"Now I recall," said Hagmaier, "I'm pretty sure there were articles about the new house in the press, way before it was built. Someone could have known Cusak was going to be living there."

Before Golding could say anything, Hagmaier stood up and walked out of the kitchen. He came back with another folder.

"Press," he said, thumping it down on the table. He pulled out the article from *Design* magazine with the drawing of the house. "It's from the original architect's drawings."

Golding stared at a smudged pencil mark in the middle of some open space. "What's that?" he said.

"I guess that's the position of the body," said Hagmaier, looking at the drawing. "Probably Kronin, my partner. He's always marking stuff up."

"Yeah, but it's way off, right? I thought the body was behind the pool house."

Hagmaier shook his head. "It's the pool that's wrong. They moved it down to here."

He pulled out some more drawings. These were grid sketches of the crime scene, with compass orientation and measurements. The pool and the pool house were in the right place.

Golding hadn't noticed it before. The pool in the original drawing was further up towards the southern boundary of the property. There were some big eucalyptus trees down there. Ellen and Gorman must have decided there would be too much shade on the pool, so they brought it up nearer the house.

"So let's just consider this for a moment," said Hagmaier, sitting back in his chair. "What we're saying here is that somebody, some third party, may have seen these drawings and decided to put an ice-skating coach in Ellen Cusak's garden? I know what my partner would say." He smiled. "He'd say it was the biggest crock of shit he'd ever heard."

They both laughed, Golding relieved to see him taking it so lightly.

"Hey, what can I say?" said Golding as Hagmaier went over to the refrigerator and pulled out a couple more beers. "I'm as puzzled by all this as you are."

"And you don't know the half of it," said Hagmaier, sitting back down. "There was stuff we held back from the press that . . . well, it's all kind of strange."

"Like what?"

Hagmaier considered his beer for a moment.

"Well, you know we hold things back to filter out the

sickos that call in saying they did it. We ask them about ligatures, specific wounds, disposition of the body, stuff like that."

"Sure. But in this case . . . ? I mean the press reported the position of the body, right? They said you thought maybe this lady was sitting up."

"Sure. Not that I did. Not that I do."

He pulled out a couple of photographs of the crime scene. Golding recognized the back of the pool house. The partially mummified body was at an angle of thirty degrees from the vertical in the disturbed earth, the legs drawn up a little, the hands on the knees. It wasn't like a fetal position.

"No," said Hagmaier. "I think she was just dumped. You dig a hole the right shape and the corpse is going to be a little upright, but beyond that—I mean this could have been a thing with rigor mortis. You kill somebody— let's say in this case: the guy stabs our lady. For a few hours she's going to be flaccid. She'll flop around. Okay. He cleans her up. He dresses her. Gets her in his car. Maybe he's driving around for a few more hours, looking for a place to dump her. By this time she's starting to stiffen up. At the end of twelve hours, I mean from the time he killed her, she's stiff as a board."

"You think she stiffened up in a seated posture?"

"Or maybe he threw her in the trunk. That might give you something like this."

"So what did you hold back?" said Golding, still looking at the pictures.

"The glasses."

Golding looked up.

"The what?"

"This lady, she was buried with her glasses on. Serratosa, the coroner, was pretty sure of that. There was residual material on the frames consistent with them being in place as the body mummified."

Golding shook his head.

"Go figure," said Hagmaier. "But there again—if he was driving her around and wanted her to look normal, maybe he put the glasses on her to . . . Hell, I don't know." He sipped his beer and looked at the pictures. "Sounds stupid, but it was the glasses that got us thinking about librarians."

"Librarians, right."

"And there was one other thing we held back," Hagmaier said, closing up the file. "The parturition scars."

Golding frowned.

"The what?"

"The parturition scars on her pelvis. Sometime or other this lady gave birth."

31

Emerson Neale was housed in a modern low-rise building that looked out of place on the sunny residential street. It was set back from the road at a junction and partly concealed by spindly satin bark trees as though ashamed of its blank corporate facade. Looking at her reflection in the smoked-glass windows as she walked up the path, Ellen felt like she was stepping back into her miserable years of treatment. The whole experience came back in disjointed nightmare flashes: the initial diagnosis of a luteal phase defect, the examinations, the drugs; later on, the surgeon's cold gray eyes as he administered the anesthetic. As she went through the heavy double doors she realized that she was trembling.

The pretty Asian receptionist asked her to take a seat. Dr. Leane would only be a couple of minutes. Avoiding the eyes of the other quietly waiting woman, Ellen grabbed the first reading material she saw and found herself scanning the glossy pages of an Emerson Neale brochure. A page entitled "EN Parentage Testing" showed the whole range of services from home collection kits to a "certified chain of custody"—she savored the choice of words. Some tests had gruesome requirements like mother/alleged father/fetal tissue or mother/alleged father/amniotic fluid. She wondered how you got the alleged father to show up. Maybe you didn't have to. Maybe a stolen hair was enough. EN were also ready to provide "distinguished" experts, people ready to defend you in a court of law. A footnote stated that the clinic's tests were "carried out by experienced technologists using state-of-the-art inheritance determination, offering above 99.9 percent accuracy." In other words: don't say we didn't warn you if we get it wrong.

She had paid EN $495 up front for a comparison of the shadowy DNA print that had come to her through the mail, and cells scraped from her mouth by Dr. Tod Leane on Monday morning. Now she was back to learn the truth.

It was insane, of course. As crazy as the badly typed note that had come with the DNA banding shot. The note read like some kind of weird horoscope. *Your need reaches a crisis,* it said. *Natalia needs too, as much as you if not more. Doubts persist and should be set against the proof. Doubts persist but the proof is the proof. See it but see beyond it. See with your heart.*

She had stood there staring at the paper that fluttered in her trembling hands. Scariest of all had been the fact that she wasn't surprised. Not for a minute. As if she had always known. She realized that she had never believed anything Lenny had said about Grossman. It didn't matter how vile Grossman had been, he had remained outside her life, as much outside as this man was inside. He was inside her head, inside her life. Like someone in a trance, she had telephoned Emerson Neale. Like someone in a trance, she had somehow gotten through the next three days, waiting for the moment to arrive—the moment in which she finally understood. *Doubts persist.* But actually the defining character of her consciousness during those three days was certainty. She had begun to feel, had felt increasingly, overwhelmingly, that something big had happened, something wrong. She kept crying. Standing in the bathroom trying to get ready for another impossible day, she would burst into tears like those people she had read about in magazines who came through major surgery with an irreparable sense of violation.

On Tuesday morning she found that despite the Prozac she could no longer cope. She drank, she tried to sleep. And then, first thing that morning, the phone had rung.

A door opened.

He was standing in front of her, a puzzled smile on his tanned face.

"Ms. Cusak?"

It came to her in a flash that he knew who she was, that he had seen her face on TV or in the papers. There was nothing she could do about it either way. She followed him through to an office that smelled of antiseptic and roses. A window looked out onto lush vegetation. She saw a paving stone in thick grass, the branches of a towering ficus. Her heart was hammering.

The doctor sat behind his desk and waited for her to make herself comfortable. Then he was smiling again. He started to talk about the work they did at Emerson Neale, how sensitive they had to be, how discreet. Ellen struggled to make sense of his words, realized that he was inviting her to confide. She stiffened as he picked up the DNA print that had come through the mail.

"Presumably you went elsewhere to have this done," he said. "I was wondering if perhaps the other clinic, hospital . . . whatever, had already made a comparison for you?"

She shook her head. When he saw that she wasn't going to speak, he put the print back down.

"They've used a pretty common probe to pick out a couple of sites that serve well for the purposes of comparison, but beyond that they do nothing to identify the individual concerned. I presume we're talking about a child. Your child?"

Ellen looked away from him, had a vague impression of certificates, of photographs on a pale blue wall. It felt like she was falling backwards, and for a moment she thought she was going to pass out. Through the buzzing in her ears, his voice droned on.

"It's none of my business of course, but I was curious to know how long you waited before questioning his or her true identity. Has something arisen? Some question regarding the birth, or the postnatal arrangements?"

She heard herself say no.

"So . . . ?" He spread his hands. Then, seeing her distress, he frowned—tried a change of tack. "I want to tell you something that may . . . it may help. The feelings of guilt that are typically associated with this sort of experience, this kind of rejection, are entirely natural. Having these doubts does not make you a monster. Three years ago a young woman—"

She held up a finger. "So . . ." She didn't know how to put it. She tried to think of what the words were but they seemed beyond her grasp. "So there is no doubt," she said finally. "No *doubt*. This is my daughter."

He shrugged. "Well, regarding the sex of the child—as I said before—"

"But it is *mine*," she said emphatically.

"Yes. For the purposes of real life, for the purposes of this particular situation, it's meaningful to say there is no doubt. None whatsoever. This sample comes from your offspring."

She didn't know how she had left the room, or how she had gotten into the street. Seething, roiling impressions cut her off from the sounds of traffic. She was walking fast, fists clenched, head down. Stepping into the street at an intersection, she brushed against a speeding car. It brought her up short. She realized with absolute clarity and detachment that she had almost been killed. She stepped back onto the sidewalk, shaking convulsively. An old lady took her by the arm, asked her if she was okay. She stared into the woman's kindly blue eyes.

"I don't know," she said.

32

"Detective Hagmaier's out of town today. You want to leave a message?"

Golding guessed he was talking to Hagmaier's partner, Matt Kronin, but decided against introducing himself.

"No, no thanks. Is he going to be back tomorrow?"

"Should be. Who's calling?"

"The name's Golding. I'll, er . . . I'll call back."

"Is that like Gold with an I-N-G?"

There was no sign of recognition in Kronin's voice. Golding wondered whether Hagmaier had told his partner about their meeting. Maybe he wanted to take credit for the skater idea, or maybe he just didn't think it was worth mentioning.

"That's right. He's got my number. Thanks."

He put the phone down. Hagmaier had said he'd call if the skating-rink canvass turned up anything, but three days had gone by and Golding hadn't heard from him. If they had come across a missing person fitting what they knew of the woman in the ground, he wanted to know about it—before the press, before *Hard News,* above all before Ellen. He wanted to be the one to warn her, to be there when she needed him most.

It had been a long couple of days. The noontime temperatures were spiking at ninety-five degrees, and a dirty chemical haze had descended on the city, bleaching the color from the empty skies. The newspapers warned of brushfires in the Santa Monica Mountains and water restrictions in the San Fernando Valley. On Tuesday Reynolds had gone out of town for a threat management conference in Palm Springs. That morning Mrs. Sayers, one of his new clients, had called, almost hysterical, saying her ex-husband had been round to her house and killed her dog. When Golding had turned up he found the animal still lying crushed on the driveway, a pink bloom of intestines spread out beside it. Tuesday evening he'd crawled home on a choked-up freeway, thinking of Ellen gliding over the cold ice, distant and beautiful. At night he thought of the woman in the garden, the woman who might have been a skater, the woman who had given birth. He watched the video of the little girl and knew he didn't want to be right, didn't want a woman who had been stabbed thirty-two times to be connected with Ellen Cusak. Staring at the face reflected in the patio windows, he told himself that he could still be wrong.

Late Tuesday night he'd driven out to Von's to stock up on food and coffee. At the back of the store he'd come across a video called *Ice Dance Champions* that included Ellen Cusak's world-title-winning program. It was on special offer at $5.99. He took it home, fast-forwarding through the credits and the first routines, and there she was, standing motionless on the ice. The camera slowly zoomed in on her perfect, unlined face, a face

that expressed intense concentration on the moment,
and at the same time preoccupation, like she was thinking of something else. Nineteen-year-old Yelena Cusak,
about to dance her way into history.

The music was Rachmaninoff, from the Rhapsody on
a Theme of Paganini, the program a mixture of skittish
brilliance and extraordinary grace. She threw off dou-
bles and triples as if they were minor ornamentations.
Her spins were more than fast and steady, they were
sensuous. She glided through the slow sections with all
the grace of a ballerina. At the end, with the applause
erupting around her, she looked up and, for the first
time, smiled. Golding watched it again and again. He
watched Yelena and then watched the people in the
crowd watching her. He remembered what one of her
crazy fans had written in a letter, that seeing her skate
was like a supernova going off in his head. He wondered if Bob had been there in the crowd the night she
won the world championship. He wondered where he
was now.

That night he'd dreamed of Ellen and Maddy Olsen:
Ellen on Maddy's porch, Maddy's porch leading onto
Ellen's garden, Arthur McGinley's body lying in a shal-
low grave, there behind the pool house. Reynolds was
there, crouching over the body while the forensics people took photographs. He stood up, fixed Golding with
a look of disgust, told the other cops to take him away.
They were going to lock him up in Atascadero State
Hospital with all the other psychopaths, keep him there
for the rest of his life, with no one to love or care for.

He awoke in the predawn darkness and lay there, still
seeing Arthur McGinley's face. The memory was almost
as bad as the nightmare. McGinley had been at the
door, the shotgun at his side, when Golding had chal-

lenged him. He had turned slowly. Golding would never forget his eyes, the hopeless, vacant eyes of a man who had come not just to kill but to die. They were the eyes of a man whose obsession, whose love, had driven him to a point of no return, to a place where the sole consolation was death. *Put down the weapon and step back.* Golding's voice had echoed in the empty street. McGinley had blinked, taken a step to his left, raised the Mag-19 and fired. Golding had felt his gun jump in his hand, had seen McGinley twist and fall, Maddy in the doorway, screaming and screaming. He knew that sound would stay with him for the rest of his life.

Wednesday morning he was late for work. Reynolds was still out of town, but Romero was there, irritated at having to take more than his share of calls. Finally Reynolds showed up at three o'clock, and then disappeared again for his round of golf with Captain Blackwood. Golding wondered how long it would take Blackwood to get around to the subject of Hagmaier's unsolved case, and his interest in it. He had a feeling Reynolds wasn't going to be too understanding when he found out.

After his fruitless phone call to Hagmaier's office, he went down to the library on Blay Street that had a Nexus database. It was fine by him if the LAPD didn't want to pursue the skating angle, but he had to. He pulled up every story dated after 1995 with the word *skating* or *skater* in it, and then told the machine to look through these for the word *disappeared* or *missing* no more than twenty words away. There were hundreds of positives, but after an hour of searching, he could find only three that referred to actual missing persons. One of these was a twenty-year-old boy from Buffalo, New York, who had won an amateur medal for speed skating; the other two were teenage girls, one from Ohio, the other from Seattle, who skated as a hobby. Neither of them was old enough to have been Hagmaier's lady.

He was about to log off the system when another idea came to him. There was something else he could try: he could look for the word *disappeared* or *missing* in stories mentioning Ellen Cusak. It was possible, given the line of their inquiries, that the police had failed to make a connection. It seemed to him that they'd not really investigated Ellen's past at all. But then again, what if someone in her life had suddenly vanished in 1996? What was he supposed to do then? Tell Hagmaier? Tell Ellen? What was the point of telling her if she already knew?

He did the search. It came up with one story from 1993. It had appeared in *International Figure Skating* magazine in April. It was a discursive, almost flowery article about America's prospects, centering on the Nationals, a contest that had seen Ellen crash to fourteenth place, her worst-ever performance. The article enthused about the exciting new talent rising through the ranks, but devoted a mournful paragraph to the onetime champion.

Despite hopes of a return to form, Ellen Cusak's performance continues to disappoint. The skater who, perhaps more than any other, brought grace and artistic excellence to the ice dance form, today struggles to bring either conviction or technique to her competitive skating. Those who remember Cusak's mesmerizing performances of just a few years ago may ask themselves what is missing, what can have changed in so short a time? The answer, of course, is that a lot has changed in Ms. Cusak's life, a transformation from child to woman in every sense of the word. It must be our hope that she may yet recover the inner strength, the clarity and assurance that once made her the worthiest of champions. Certainly her many thousands of devoted fans—fans who crowd the rink-side at her every appearance, watching and waiting for that longed-for rebirth—will continue to believe.

Golding stared at the screen. He had seen the piece before. It was among those he kept at home, although he had never bothered to read it thoroughly. He had a powerful feeling of having missed something, of something important reaching out to him through the fog of unanswered questions. He scrolled up to the top of the article. It was written by somebody called Charles Sanderson. He tried to think himself into Sanderson's head, see what he'd been seeing when he wrote that paragraph. What he saw was the fans, *who crowd the rink-side at her every appearance*.

And then he had it.

The rush-hour traffic was solid on Bundy, and it was twenty-five minutes before he pulled up outside Ellen's house. He'd called from the car, but nobody had picked up. The sun was already going down over the ocean as he crossed the road and pressed the buzzer beside the gates. Automatically a light went on over his head, but the intercom remained silent. Nobody was home. It occurred to him that maybe Ellen had gone away again, was taking a holiday, celebrating the successful conclusion of her business with Alpha Global Protection. It was what a lot of people would have done, feeling they were in the clear at last, feeling they were out of danger.

He walked around the western side of the property, trying to peer into the garden through the thick barrier of spruce. Standing on tiptoe at one point, he glimpsed blue—the pool probably—but it wasn't enough. He needed to see the garden, he needed to be *in* the garden.

He had never been convinced by Detective Hagmaier's ideas on the disposition of the body, although he couldn't have said exactly why. With his experience in homicide investigation Hagmaier certainly knew a lot more about rigor mortis and the logistics of corpse disposal than he did. But for Hagmaier the significance of the construction site lay only in its convenience: an area of already disturbed earth over which turf was due to be laid. The killer had simply seized the opportunity for a quick burial. But if he was in a hurry, why the elements of ritual—the placing and orientation of the corpse, the glasses? Hagmaier passed over those elements as incidental, probably because ritual would suggest delusion or insanity on the killer's part. Like cops the world over, Hagmaier was doubtless sick of seeing murderers escape justice because experts decided they were not responsible for their actions. But in this case he was wrong. Golding could see that now. The killer had dressed his victim in her own clothes, not just enough clothes to cover her or hide her wounds, but a complete winter outfit. And he had placed the glasses on her face before shoveling in the dirt. If all he'd wanted to do was dispose of her personal effects, he could have tossed them into a plastic sack and left them out for the garbageman. It was a specific need he was answering, a duty he was performing, a duty that made the choice of site anything but accidental. All Golding had to do was check out the spot to be sure.

He was halfway along the fence when he noticed a patch where the spruce trees seemed to be dying.

Through the skeletal branches he could see the back of the pool house and the terra-cotta roof tiles of the house. Running through the middle of the hedge was a chain-link fence, and squatting down, he saw where the bottom had been pulled up from the ground, rolled up at least two feet—far enough for a man to crawl underneath. He cursed his own stupidity. He had been so focused on Doug Gorman's high-tech security arrangements, his remote-control gates and his remote-control garage doors, so anxious to dismiss them as a means of protection, that he hadn't even thought to check the perimeter. But this was where the intruder had entered. He had used poison, thinning some of the spruce at a spot mostly hidden from the house, then forced a gap in the fence. It was less likely to attract attention than opening electronic gates. It was the kind of trouble someone would go to only if they planned on visiting again and again.

He eased his way through. From inside the garden the damage to the hedge was almost invisible. He walked around the side of the pool house and looked up at the main building. It was just beginning to get dark, but no lights were on. Behind him the police tarpaulin covered the hole where the mummified body had been found.

He didn't have the article from *Design* magazine with him, but he could picture the architect's illustration perfectly. The house was drawn from a distance and from a few yards off-center, the pool in the foreground, the nearby eucalyptus trees framing the view. Where he was standing now was too close, the perspective wrong. He took a few paces back, then a few more, trying to recapture the angle until, in his mind, he could put the pool and the pool house back where they were first meant to be, where the killer believed they were going to be when he buried his victim: *behind the body, not in front of it.*

In the gathering darkness he hurried back to the tarpaulin, stooped down, and yanked it back. The excavated pit was just as Hagmaier and his team had left it. It looked like two big steps cut into the sandy soil. The orientation was just as he had expected, not random, not hurried, but perfectly, fanatically deliberate. Because they were *both* of them fans—it came to him then in a rush—a couple united in their obsession with the same person. Who else could Ellen have turned to when Doug Gorman stood in her way? Who else would have borne a child for her, have broken whatever rules she asked them to? Who would have done all that and then kept her secret? Who but her most devoted fans?

At that moment the security lights came on. He froze, squinting, trying to see past the glare.

"Ellen? Is that you?"

A figure was watching him through the French doors. Then it was gone.

"Ellen?"

He heard a door open, the kitchen door. If it wasn't Ellen he was in big trouble. Anyone else would probably call the police. He thought about running.

"What the hell are you doing here, Golding?"

Ellen came striding down the lawn towards him, dressed in a dark blue jacket and jeans.

"Ellen, you have to listen to me. I know—"

"You've no right to be here. You're trespassing."

"Ellen, listen, you have to tell me . . ." He saw the revolver. A compact black .38. He couldn't believe his eyes. "Jesus, I thought you said—"

"It's Doug's. Now I want you off my property. Now."

She jabbed the gun at him.

"Ellen, listen to me. I know what this is." He pointed down into the pit. "I know what it means."

"What the hell are you talking about?"

Before she could stop him he jumped down.

"What are you *doing*?"

She was almost screaming.

"She was buried sitting down, right here." He planted himself just where the corpse had been sitting, his hands resting in his lap. "Today all she can see is the back of the pool house because you and your husband moved it, remember?"

"I'm not interested."

"But if you'd stuck to the original plans, she'd have been looking up at the house, wouldn't she?" He pointed. "She'd have been looking right up into your bedroom."

Ellen hesitated, looked over her shoulder at the big picture window.

"You—you're out of your mind," she said. "I know what this is. I know what you're doing. You want—"

"She was dressed in winter clothes, Ellen. He put them on her *after* he killed her. He even put her glasses back on."

She shook her head, not wanting to hear any more.

"It's what she wore at the rink, isn't it? It's what she wore to watch *you*. We're talking about one of your biggest fans. Someone who'd do anything for you."

"You're crazy. You're as crazy as—"

"What happened, Ellen? Did the guy get jealous? Did she? What went wrong? Didn't she want to give up the child?"

"This is insane!"

Her eyes were full of tears, but Golding couldn't stop. He wanted her to know that he understood, that they were in this together now.

"He killed her, and then he wanted to make it up to her. So he put her where she'd most want to be: where she could watch you night and day. Why didn't you call a halt to it then, Ellen? Were you afraid you'd never get the child?"

She was pointing the gun at him now.

"Now get out. Or I'm calling the police. I'll do it, Pete, I swear."

"I'm only trying to help you, Ellen."

"I don't *want* your help."

The gun was shaking in her hand. Slowly he climbed out of the pit.

"Is it Bob?" he said.

"Get *out*!"

But he couldn't help himself.

"Jesus, Ellen. Don't you understand? This man's a killer, a fanatic. You can't reason with him. You can't *deal* with him. Not then, not now. You can only—"

"Kill him? Is that it? And you can arrange that for me?"

"That *isn't*—"

"And then I'll be grateful, right? The way Maddy Olsen *wasn't* grateful. Is that the plan, Pete?"

Golding straightened up. For an instant he saw Maddy's face, the look of horror, of revulsion, McGinley dead at her feet.

"You don't know what the hell you're talking about."

"*Everybody* knows, Pete. Everybody knows how you kept on sneaking around the house even after she fired you. Christ, you were worse than McGinley."

For a second he was speechless.

"Worse than . . . ?" He had to swallow to clear his throat. "Is that what people are saying? Well—" He pointed at her, his hand trembling with rage. "Well, for your information we were lovers, Ellen. *Lovers.* That's right. At least I thought we were. We screwed a few times, and I got it into my head that it meant something. Then, when she was tired of me, she showed me the door. And I couldn't take it because it seemed a little harsh, it seemed a little fucking harsh, and I still—I still *loved* her."

He lowered his hand, took a moment to get control of himself.

"Now maybe that makes me a fool," he said, "but it sure as hell doesn't make me a *psychopath.*"

He stepped back away from the hole, stumbled, turned, then set off towards the driveway.

IV

Infinity

33

Thursday, August 26

Dr. Richard Thomsen put down the phone, and for a moment sat staring at his office, taking in the upholstered furniture and the abstract art, the filing cabinets and the wall of certificates that showed how far he had come since medical school. Out of nowhere he found himself wondering how the building would fare in an earthquake; what the chances were that the room and its contents would end up in the middle of Newport Center Drive. He had a vision of clients' files blowing along the road that for a second was so vivid, so real, he had to shake his head to clear it. He got up and walked across to the window. In the distance the San Diego Freeway, invisible behind landscaped hills, made a brown smudge on the air. He pushed back wiry hair from his deeply lined brow and tried to suppress a growing feeling of panic. He told himself that he had always known this moment might come, but somehow foreseeing wasn't the same as being prepared. He watched a military transport drift down into El Toro air base and then went back to his desk.

He punched the intercom. "Janet? Tell Dr. Kelner I want to see him right away."

Henry Kelner walked into his office fifteen minutes later looking tanned and relaxed, if a little peeved. He was fifty years old and only two pounds heavier now than he'd been when he left medical school.

"I'm in the OR at eleven o'clock," he said blandly, his gray eyes registering Thomsen's red face and the perspiration under his arms. "Couldn't this wait until after lunch?"

"I just received a call from an ex-client of ours," said Thomsen, motioning for his colleague to sit down.

"Oh?"

"Ellen Cusak."

Kelner nodded, but it didn't seem to mean much. His memory ran from tax year to tax year; beyond that the past was a series of points on his earning curve.

"She was admitted here . . ."—Thomsen looked at the file that was open on his desk—"in the fall of '93."

Kelner narrowed his eyes, remembering.

"That wasn't . . . ?"

"Yes, it was. Just before we had our little problem." Again Thomsen paused. Kelner shifted in his seat. "She's coming down here to see us. She'll be here in about an hour in fact."

"Why? What does she want?"

"She's got this peculiar idea in her head. Or I should say, someone has *put* this peculiar idea in her head."

"What peculiar idea?" snapped Kelner, unable to hide his agitation now.

Thomsen leaned forward slightly and lowered his voice.

"She seems to think she has a child."

*   *   *

MacArthur Boulevard was spookily empty after the freeway. Golding hung back as far as he could, keeping his eyes on the Mercedes roadster that rippled and shimmered up ahead in the heat haze. After he left Ellen's house the day before, he had driven home cursing himself for his stupidity. He had done the one thing he had wanted above all to avoid: he had alienated her. He had spent the night struggling to empty his head, struggling to find sleep, but at four in the morning had given up. In the early-morning light he made filter coffee and drank until his hands were shaking, then drove over to her place, where he took up his position above the house. Watching the light grow in her secret garden, he knew he had entered a new and dangerous phase. He also knew he was powerless to do anything about it, and that, just as with Maddy Olsen, he would only be able to help by being there, by being close.

He cut between lanes, careful to keep a couple of cars between him and the Mercedes. They were speeding towards Corona Del Mar Beach, the needle flickering between seventy-five and eighty. Wherever Ellen was going, she was in a hurry.

"But it's nothing like the UCI case," said Kelner pacing up and down the room. "That guy—what was his name?"

"Asch. *Dr.* Asch."

"He actually stole the material and sold it to third parties. He ran off to Mexico City for Christ's sake."

"That may be," said Thomsen, "but as far as the business is concerned, there might as well be no difference. There is such a thing as a duty of care. I'm not saying we should fold, Henry. I'm just saying if we don't handle this right we could be killed."

Kelner closed his eyes for a moment.

"But why should she want to make trouble after all this time? What's in it for her?"

"Money, probably."

Kelner nodded, a little more comfortable with a problem that could be measured in dollars.

"In other words," he said, "she might make a deal."

Golding watched Ellen turn into the car park, then rolled on down Newport Center Drive. He made a right, then another, then came back up onto the junction where Ellen had turned off. He pulled over and turned off the ignition. The Mercedes was parked diagonally across two spaces in the middle of the parking lot. He climbed over the low brick wall that separated the lot from the sidewalk just in time to see Ellen going in through the front door. He forced himself to count to twenty before following her in.

The marble lobby was chilled like a meat locker. Golding entered cautiously, then walked across to the elevators. One of them was still climbing.

"Excuse me, sir?"

He turned. A kid in a uniform was smiling at him.

"Can I help you, sir?"

Golding looked back at the elevator. It had come to a halt on the ninth floor.

"Sir?"

The kid was still smiling, but Golding could tell he was spooked by his rumpled clothes and two-day stubble.

"Yeah, I'm looking for Bernstein Beekman," he said—the first thing that came into his head.

The kid frowned.

"Bernstein, Beekman? What is that, a law firm?"

"That's right," said Golding. "Divorces mostly. Custody disputes."

The kid turned and looked at the directory, which was on a Lucite panel up over the reception desk. Golding started down the list, looking for every entry on the ninth floor.

"I'm sorry, sir. I think you must have the wrong building."

Golding walked over to the reception desk scratching his head.

"I could have sworn this was the address they gave me. How often do you update this board?"

The kid gave him a look, starting to get suspicious. Golding saw the first name on nine: CARLYLE & ROWE, ATTORNEYS AT LAW. Was that what Ellen wanted? A lawyer? It came to him that she was planning to sue Alpha Global. She was probably going to tell them about this crazy PI who wouldn't leave her alone, and here he was standing in the lobby. Then, below Carlyle, he saw another name for nine: THE HARPER CLINIC (RECEPTION).

It was like a light coming on.

"I'm afraid I don't see how I can help you, sir. Sir?"

Golding put up his hands, already backing away.

"That's okay," he said. "I guess I made a mistake." Then he stopped, bringing a hand to his forehead. "No, wait a second. On the ninth floor. Nine. That's what the guy said."

The kid went behind his desk and pulled out a ratty-looking ledger. "I'm sorry, sir. There are only two companies on nine." He looked up. "Neither of them by that name."

Golding walked back across the baking asphalt, looking up at the windows on the ninth floor, trying to guess which were Harper and which were Carlyle, trying to work out why the hell Ellen would want to go back to the place she had received treatment.

"Show her through," said Thomsen, leaning over the intercom. He shot Kelner a look and smoothed his tie. Kelner was draped over the couch, with a stupid smile on his face. The door opened and Ellen Cusak walked in. It looked like she had been crying.

"Ellen," said Thomsen, shooting out a hand, "great to see you again."

34

That afternoon in the office Golding logged onto the Internet. It took him about five minutes to find what he was looking for. The Harper Trust Fertility Center had its own Web site, containing five screenfuls of information about its procedures and staff. He started scrolling.

"Fertility problems affect ten to fifteen percent of all couples wishing to have children. The causes may be medical, surgical, or psychological. While these problems are not particularly unusual, they may be so fraught with emotions and anxiety that couples often hesitate to mention them to family, friends, or physicians."

Under the "leadership" of Dr. Richard Thomsen, the Harper Trust claimed to provide state-of-the-art treatment, calling upon gynecologists, urologists, endocrinologists, psychiatrists, psychologists, and other specialists "to consult as necessary in a two-part program of evaluation and treatment." The diagnostics stage involved a battery of potential tests, including sonograms, biopsies,

X rays, semen analysis, antibody studies, postcoital sperm/mucus interaction tests, and extensive psychological evaluation. The whole process could take several months to complete. And that was before treatment even began.

He hit PRINT and sat reading in the empty office, screwing up his eyes against the late-afternoon sun. He wondered how Ellen Cusak's psychological evaluation had turned out; wondered if Dr. Thomsen and his colleagues had reached the same conclusion the adoption agencies had, and had offered their services anyway. He flipped over a page and looked down the list of possible treatments. For the woman they included microsurgery, laser surgery, the use of hormones and drugs, as well as things Golding had never heard of: the GIFT Treatment Program, whatever that was, intracytoplasmic sperm injection, and embryo hatching. He wondered which of them Ellen had undergone, tried to imagine what it must have been like—the months of tests, examinations, drugs, surgery more than likely, of waiting and longing for positive results. He wondered what it must have been like for a shy young woman, not yet twenty-two, to surrender her body continually to the probing and testing of strangers—all of them men, judging from the list of staff—and all, apparently, without success.

Dr. Thomsen's curriculum vitae was impressive, at least it looked impressive. He'd graduated in 1977 from Jefferson Medical College in Philadelphia, and had completed a research fellowship in obstetrics and gynecology at the University of California, San Diego. He was a founding charter member of the Society of Reproductive Surgeons, and was "a principal investigator" in various clinical trials of reproductive technology, carried out with FDA approval. He had set up the fertility center in 1989. His colleague Dr. Henry Kelner was similarly qualified. The message from the Web site was loud and clear: the Harper Clinic was at the cutting edge when it came to fertility treatment. The only thing it didn't talk about was the cost of it all. Golding couldn't guess at what couples typically paid, but he was willing to bet it was at least fifty thousand dollars. That meant an up-market clientele—very likely, given the location in Orange County, the kind of people who might attract publicity, who might be anxious to avoid it. But then again, it was just a fertility clinic. It wasn't a rehab or AA. How hard could it be to get into the place if you really wanted to? He leaned back in his chair—thought about the nervous-looking kid he had encountered in the lobby. He wondered just how good their security was likely to be.

35

"Golding? Are you okay?"

Andrea Craig walked behind the reception desk.

"Sure," said Golding. "Why wouldn't I be?"

He followed her gaze down to his rumpled pants and scuffed shoes, figured he wasn't making such a good impression these days. Keeping her eye on him, Craig pressed a button on her intercom. Reynolds came through preoccupied and grouchy.

"Mr. Golding just got here, Mr. Reynolds."

"Send him straight in."

Golding checked the clock over the reception desk. It was ten-thirty. Late, but not outrageous. The job didn't work like that anyway.

Craig was still watching him from behind the barrier of the desk.

"Mr. Reynolds says—"

"To go right through. Yeah, I heard."

He walked into the open-plan area where both Denison and Ross were working the phones, jackets off, ties undone. The hive of industry. Passing his desk, he noticed a Post-It stuck to his computer screen. Someone had scribbled *Hagmaier. 9:20 a.m.* He looked along the corridor to Reynolds' office. The door was half open and Reynolds was shuffling papers on his big desk, wanting to look busy when the employee walked in.

Golding picked up the phone and punched in the number.

"Hagmaier."

"Larry? Hi, it's Pete Golding. You called me."

"No, you called me. I picked up your messages. It's been a little crazy the last couple days, which is why I didn't touch base. So what have you got for me? Something juicy on the skating coach?"

Golding tried to laugh.

"No, no, I . . . I just wanted to ask how it was going. Whether you'd had any luck with the ice-rink canvass."

"Oh, right. Your brilliant lead. No, no luck so far. We had a couple of possibles but they didn't check out."

Golding nodded, frowning, trying to decide whether this was good news or not.

"So you calling it a day?" he said.

"Not yet. Soon as we get our head from Dr. Gallo, we're gonna circulate the picture round all the rinks and skating clubs in the state, see if anyone recognizes our lady. As well as press and TV, if we can swing it."

Golding heard Reynolds clear his throat. He turned. Reynolds was looking straight at him, a sour expression on his face. Golding turned away.

"Oh yeah, the head," he said, lowering his voice. "How's that going?"

"Should be ready sometime this morning. Gallo sounds pretty excited about the results."

"Really?"

"Yeah, and she's usually pretty conservative about these things. So . . ."

"I read she has quite a track record. Something like a seventy percent success rate?"

"I don't know about that. But the way things are going, any new input would be gratefully received."

Golding saw the way it was going to be in a series of vivid flashes: the head on TV, in the press, on posters; calls from the public; positive ID in a couple of days; the victim linked to Ellen—a friend, a fan, somebody she was known to have spent time with. He got a scooped-out feeling—anxiety mixed with outright fear.

"Pete?"

The voice came from behind him. He turned, held up a finger. Reynolds was at the door of his office, hands on his hips.

"She's up at CSU, right?"

"Yeah. In the anthropology department."

"Do you think she'd mind if I took a look at what she's got?"

"Marcia? Hell no." Hagmaier covered the phone with his hand, and for a second all Golding could hear was a muffled voice. Then he was back. "Let me know if she looks familiar. The head I mean. If she rings any bells, you call me, okay?"

"Sure—sure thing, Larry."

He put down the phone. Reynolds gave a curt, about-time nod, and went back into his office, obviously expecting to be followed.

The anthropology department at CSU was housed in a seven-story redbrick block in the middle of the campus, next to an expanse of brown grass that served as a

makeshift soccer field. According to a sign opposite the
elevator, Craniofacial Identification was located on the
fifth floor, together with something called Morphology.
Golding found Dr. Marcia Gallo eating a sandwich on
one of the workbenches, a spread of autopsy photographs in front of her. She was a slight woman of about
forty, with long blond hair streaked with gray. Golding
introduced himself, told her Larry Hagmaier suggested
he come by.

"Are you the photographer?" she asked, still chewing.

"Photographer?"

"We've been expecting a crime lab photographer,"
she said. "He was supposed to be here an hour ago."

"I'm sorry, no."

Gallo wiped her fingers on a paper towel.

"Guess he had another gig, huh?" she said, glancing
at the corpses in the photographs. "What did you want
to know?"

Golding told her he was a PI and that he'd been
working with Hagmaier on "developing leads."

She stood up. "You ever seen anything like this before?"

"I saw a couple of things on A&E a few years back.
That's about it."

"Things have come a long way since then," she said.
"Here, follow me."

She led him through into a bright airy room divided
into working areas by benches and tall metal shelves.
The whir and hum of computer equipment and exhaust
fans was amplified by all the hard surfaces. On one side
of the room there was a computer with a big eighteen-
inch monitor. Gallo pressed a key and suddenly they
were looking at a three-dimensional image of a skull in

shades of white and gray. Jane Doe no. 273 was missing several of her back teeth on the right-hand side.

"We scan the skull with a laser and feed the data into the computer. Then we construct the face using known average tissue thickness measurements of various anatomical features, or landmarks," she said, punctuating her words with keystrokes, each of which added a block of flesh to a part of the skull. "The joy of this approach is that we can alter these parameters to take into account any additional data we have about the subject—age, weight, clothes size, and so on—and create a new face accordingly. We call it volume distortion. We're adding to the database on these landmarks all the time."

"So this is—what we're looking at is an *average* face, given the parameters of the skull, right?"

It didn't sound too promising.

"That's our starting point. But obviously in this case we know a lot about the woman concerned. We've adjusted the tissue thickness and shape accordingly."

Golding began to wonder when he was going to see the finished product. He had a feeling it was going to look like something from a video game, a cyberface, but then he noticed a form away to his left. It looked like a bust, covered with a white sheet. Gallo told him that her team had gone on to make a model of the head, with the help of a Professor Ridley Taylor from the School of Art and Design.

"Rid's an expert on skin textures, hair, and pigmentation. He really brings the work to life."

Gallo was still talking when the crime lab photographer, Leo Nash, showed up.

"Sorry I'm late," he said, putting down a big metal case. "So, this the head?"

Gallo turned from the screen. "Yep. I was just explaining—"

"Great. Let's go."

Without waiting for permission, Nash lifted off the sheet, and Golding was looking at the head of a woman, so real he felt her sudden presence with a jolt. Curly red-brown hair fell to what would have been her shoulders. She had brown eyes that were a little too close together for her to be beautiful, and a nose that was slightly flattened near the top, as if it might once have been broken. She stared intently, almost myopically, into the middle distance. It was the face Golding had seen reflected in the patio doors. He was sure of it. He saw her pale arms, the snowflake pattern on her sweatshirt, heard her singsong voice: *Show Momma what you can do.*

For a few moments nobody spoke. Then Nash's flashguns began firing as he moved from one side of the face to the other, then around again.

"Of course the eye color's a guess," Gallo was saying. "We'd need to analyze her DNA to be sure about that."

"Wait a minute," said Golding. "You forgot something."

"What?"

"She should be wearing her glasses."

Back at the office he was barely through the door when Andrea told him that Reynolds wanted to see him *urgently*. He knew he was in real trouble now, but somehow he couldn't make it matter to him. He just hoped it wasn't Ellen who'd complained.

Reynolds glanced up from his papers when Golding walked into his office, then carried on working.

"Sorry about just now," said Golding. "There was something . . . I had to deal with."

Reynolds just gave a nod, still looking at his papers.

"You look like you've been up all night, Pete," he said without looking up.

"It's the heat," said Golding. "It keeps me awake."

"Right. The heat. Right."

It looked like he wanted to say something but didn't know how to get into it. Finally he tossed down his pen and leaned back in his chair.

"You went to see Mrs. Sayers last week, is that right?"

It took a moment for Golding to realize what he was talking about. Then he remembered the dead dog.

"Sure."

"It seems her husband violated the restraining order we acquired."

"She thinks he ran over her dog. But she doesn't *know* he did. Could have been anyone."

"She says you were *unsympathetic* and *unhelpful*."

Golding folded his arms. He couldn't believe this was what Reynolds was really annoyed about, that this was supposed to be urgent.

"I just gave her the facts. We can't go after her husband if she can't prove he was there. Unless you're suggesting we find his car, check the tires for dog blood, and have the crime lab people analyze it. Personally, I think Mrs. Sayers is a little paranoid."

"Well"—Reynolds gave a tight little smile—"I think we should leave Frank to make that kind of presumptive diagnosis, don't you? Besides, paranoid or not, she is still our client. That's why I want you to go down there again this afternoon and talk the whole thing through with her again, security arrangements, everything."

Golding waited for more.

"Is that it?"

"No. It isn't. I talked to Neil Blackwood the other

day. He was under the impression that I suggested you call him."

This was it: the shit hitting the fan. Golding looked down at his feet.

"Then he got the wrong impression."

"He also told me you've been taking an interest in that unsolved they turned up on Ms. Cusak's property."

Golding looked up, held Reynolds' gaze for a moment.

"Yeah, I had a few theories. I thought I could be of help."

"He said you think the victim's connected with Ms. Cusak somehow."

"I never said she was connected."

"Then . . . how come the interest?"

"Because . . . Because I think it's interesting."

"Not for us, Pete. Not for us it isn't. We're not paid to dig around in our clients' backyards."

"Is that a joke?"

Reynolds had become very pale. A muscle twitched in his cheek.

"No, Pete. No it isn't." He shifted forward in his chair, planting his elbows on the desk. "Pete, have you been seeing—I mean *watching* Cusak?"

Suddenly Golding's mouth was dry. He heard himself deny the accusation, but was unsure of what exactly he'd said. He looked around the room, took in the retirement case with its ribbons and badges and gold-plated handcuffs, the framed commendations, the neat stacks of files, the minutes of conferences and seminars: a film of order stretched over chaos and despair. Reynolds' voice droned on.

"Because I've been hearing things, Pete. You understand what I'm saying?"

"What I do in my own time is my own business," said Golding, realizing he was over the line now. This was man-to-man, just short of a fight.

Reynolds stared, cold-eyed.

"No, Pete, that's *wrong*. Our clients are *our* business."

"But Ellen Cusak isn't our client anymore, is she? You arranged that."

Reynolds was shaking his head.

"Wrong again, Peter. *She* arranged that. The client arranged it. Just like Madeleine Olsen did." Reynolds nodded, getting up a head of steam now. "You know, that's just your problem, Pete. You don't seem to know the difference. You don't seem to know where you stand." He jabbed out a finger. "In fact, the truth is you don't know your goddamned job."

For a second there was complete silence in the room. It was Golding who broke it.

"So, Tom—what? You firing me?"

Reynolds pushed back from his desk.

"Hey, now I think of it—yes. Hell yes. That's exactly what I'm doing."

36

Even with the bedroom door closed, Ellen could hear Maria moving through the house with the vacuum. The clock said 11:05, but she couldn't bring herself to get up. Getting up meant taking a shower, then dressing and then dealing with breakfast. Maria would try to get her to eat something, and they would have another argument. She hadn't eaten since her visit to the clinic. She just wasn't hungry.

The meeting hadn't turned out the way she'd hoped it would. Afterwards she wondered what it was she had been expecting anyway. The doctors had been understanding, sympathetic. They had spoken to her softly and distinctly as if she were a disturbed person. Dr. Thomsen had talked of the pride they took in their work, of the extreme rigor of in-house procedure, of the impossibility of what she was suggesting. When she had shown him the data, he had pointed out that even if the test results turned out to be legitimate, they could have come from several sources. There just wasn't enough information to be able to form an opinion. He had agreed to give the matter his serious consideration and to get back to her. She had left the building with a powerful sense of having been dealt with rather than helped.

That night Sam Ritt had called wanting to change an appointment. Laura Mead had called, telling her about some guy she had invited to her lunch party. Lenny had called just to see how she was doing. Each time she had let the machine handle it. She had nothing to say to anybody.

Maria came to the bottom of the stairs and changed nozzles on the vacuum. The throaty hum became a high-pitched whine as she started up the carpeted steps.

Looking up at the ceiling, Ellen realized that things had changed for her. The house had changed. It was as if Doug had moved back in. She knew the master bedroom was empty, but somehow it didn't feel that way. And being where she was, in the smallest of the guest rooms, felt wrong. Out of nowhere she was seized by a feeling of intense anxiety.

In the bathroom she drank a glass of water and tried to control her breathing. Then she stepped on the scale. She had burned two pounds in two days, and now hovered around 116. Stepping off, she turned to face the medicine cabinet. She did not look in the mirror as she opened the door and took out the Prozac.

She walked out onto the landing. Maria was halfway up the stairs, back bent, arms vigorously sweeping the head of the vacuum. She watched her for a moment, wondering if she realized how lucky she was, how blessed.

She continued along the landing. Despite the fact that she never used the master bedroom anymore, Maria kept it clean and ready. There was fresh linen, and even a vase of flowers on the mahogany commode. Ellen sat

on the edge of the bed and looked out at the garden.
The pool house was a squat rectangle against spiky foliage. The leafy shadows were frightening again. Golding had made them frightening with his talk of buried
watchers. It was crazy. Golding was crazy. Scrabbling in
the dirt, trying to . . . God only knew what he was trying
to do. She thought about the way he had looked when
he pulled back the tarp and jumped down into the hole.
Despite her efforts to shut it out, to screen it all out, she
found herself imagining the body propped up in the
earth, staring straight at the bedroom window through
dirt-smeared glasses.

On the landing Maria switched off the vacuum. She
thought she had heard the phone, but now there was
nothing. Then she heard Ellen's voice, speaking softly.
She approached the door to her room and pushed it
open. It was empty. Then she heard the voice again,
coming from the master bedroom. It sounded like
Ellen, having an argument but trying to keep her voice
down. Maria edged closer, listening now. She was worried about Ellen, worried that something was going
wrong with her.

"Just tell me where I have to go," she heard her say.
"Yes. Yes, I'll be there, just . . . No, I'll be alone. Yes, I
promise."

Something bad was going to happen, Maria was sure
of it. She listened again. This time she could hear nothing. Gently she pushed back the door.

Ellen was sitting on the bed, the telephone in her
hand. She was shaking. It looked like she had gone
crazy.

"Is everythin'—is everythin' okay?"

Ellen just stared at her. Then she hung up the phone.

"Everything's fine," she said. "Everything's great." She stood up and went to the window, looking down at the empty swimming pool. "I'm going to a birthday party."

37

Golding pulled over at the corner of Newport Center Drive and forced himself to sit quietly for a minute, his hands on the wheel. He felt angry, euphoric, a little out of control. He remembered the last time he had seen Jackie, what she had said to him before she left: Sometime you're going to hurt somebody. But he wasn't going to hurt anybody. He had felt like hurting Reynolds, at least telling him what he thought, but he had just walked away. And here he was sitting calmly in his car, working out a way to help Ellen. The clinic was his only way forward now, he was sure of that. He had to find out what had happened there, find out why Ellen had gone there—find out how wrong he had been about her. Because he had been wrong. He was only just beginning to understand how much.

He picked up his cell phone and punched in the number.

"Harper Trust Fertility Center."

"Hi there. This is Detective Raymond Lubett. Could I speak to Melanie Jackson, please?"

He pulled out Lubett's fake badge. The photograph on the reverse didn't look anything like him, and the lacquered brass shield was noticeably smaller than the real thing. Any cop in the world would have known the difference right away.

"Hello?"

"Ms. Jackson?"

"Speaking."

"This is Detective Raymond Lubett, LAPD. Am I correct in thinking you're the office manager there?"

"Yes, that's right."

"I wonder if you could give me a few minutes of your time."

"Did you say LAPD?"

"That's right, ma'am. It's just a routine thing. I'm in the area right now and I'd like to stop by. It'll only take a few minutes."

"Stop by? Here?"

He squinted up at the building, alternate bands of whitewashed concrete and gray-tinted glass.

"I just happen to be in the vicinity. It would sure save me some time."

"Well, I guess . . . what exactly did you—?"

"It's a security matter. Like I say, it'll only take a few minutes."

"Security? Well, yes, I handle that to some extent. . . . But I think Dr. Thomsen would want to talk to you if this is anything serious."

"I don't think that'll be necessary. Why don't I explain it all when I get there."

She hesitated for a second.

"Well, okay. I guess."

*   *   *

Riding the elevator to the ninth floor, he couldn't keep still. He turned and looked at his reflection in the dimly lit mirror. His hair was a mess, and he looked as if he hadn't slept in days. For a moment he had a sickening sense of vertigo and had to close his eyes.

Melanie Jackson was an African-American woman in her mid-thirties with short braided hair. She had a narrow office overlooking the parking lot, crammed with gray filing cabinets and straggling plants. An air freshener in the corner gave off a soapy smell of artificial roses.

"I told Dr. Thomsen you'd be coming," she said, showing Golding to an upright chair. "He's in the O.R. at the moment, but he should be out shortly."

Golding nodded as if that was just what he wanted to hear. On the desk he noticed a small framed photograph of a little boy maybe three or four years old, wearing a yellow bow tie over a red-checkered shirt. Except for a furry toy bumble bee suspended from a corner of her triple-decker in tray, it was the only personal touch in the room.

"That's very kind, but I'm sure I won't have to bother him. Like I said, it's just routine."

Jackson looked around uncertainly. Golding had a feeling she wanted to ask for some ID but didn't know how to go about it.

"Can I get you anything?" she said. "Water? Coffee?"

"No thanks. How long have you been in this job?"

"I used to be Dr. Kelner's secretary," she said, sitting back down. "I got moved into this job about a year and a half ago. In all I've been here . . . must be seven years."

She gave a little shrug, as if to apologize for a lack of ambition.

"So you joined in 1992?"

"Sure, right. So . . ."—she folded her hands in front of her—"what exactly can I do for you?"

Golding gave her what he hoped was a serious-cop look.

"Ms. Jackson, you're probably aware there are certain groups—fanatical groups that disapprove of establishments like these."

"Fertility clinics?"

"Abortion clinics, fertility clinics, basically anyone who interferes with what they believe is the God-given order of things."

Jackson nodded, already looking alarmed.

"Well, we monitor these people, and recently we received intelligence that one of these groups may be planning some form of direct action in the Southern California area. So we thought it might be helpful to alert all the possible targets and make a thorough check of security arrangements."

"Oh . . . oh, right. I see."

Golding flipped open his notebook.

"I should begin by asking if you've ever had security problems in the past? Break-ins, that kind of thing."

She took a moment to respond.

"No, I don't think so. At least I don't remember anything."

"You're sure? No question of things disappearing ever? You must have a lot of valuable equipment here, plus confidential records, even embryos, right?"

"Sure. But most of the most valuable stuff's pretty bulky. Plus I'm not sure how a thief would go about selling it. I mean, it's not like these are color TVs."

"But you do have professional security?"

"At night, yes. There's always someone here."

"So, let's—let's take an example. Say I wanted to get into your storage area. Let's say I'm one of these religious fanatics and I want to shut down the system, kill the embryos. Provided I get past the security guy, what's to stop me?"

Jackson put her head on one side and thought about it for a second.

"Well, for one thing, you'd need a pass to get into the lab—that's where the living material is stored. And the only people who have a pass are the technicians that work there—that's a three-man team at the moment—plus Dr. Thomsen and Dr. Kelner, of course. Even *I'm* not allowed into the lab unaccompanied"—she smiled—"in case I screw something up. It's like that here. You go where you need to go and that's it. Partly on account of the people who we treat here. They expect privacy."

Golding looked down at the blank page of his notebook. Before he arrived he'd been so certain he knew what had happened, so certain of the answers. But either Melanie Jackson was a first-class liar or he was way off the mark. He wondered if it was possible she just didn't know, if Thomsen and his partner could have covered something up. Or maybe they hadn't found out about it either. He needed to dig a little deeper.

"I see," he said. "Well I guess that . . . that about covers that. Would it be okay if we took a look around the lab?"

She was watching him now, a doubtful look on her face.

"Well, I . . . in a way I'd rather Dr. Thomsen—"

Golding stood up.

"It'd be real quick, ma'am."

The lab was up on the tenth floor, along with the two operating rooms. Golding and Jackson were obliged to put on gloves and face masks before being buzzed in by a heavyset technician with black-rimmed spectacles and coarse gray hair. It was a lot smaller than the facilities at CSU, but seemed just as high-tech. Along one side of the room there was a series of bridged-steel cabinets with digital temperature and humidity sensors built in. Large white microscopes, centrifuges, and other expensive-looking equipment were lined up on the bench where another couple of technicians were at work.

"This is George Margolis," said Jackson. "George, this is Detective Lubett of the LAPD."

"Hi." Margolis looked down at Golding's out-stretched hand. "Oh, we don't do that in here." He laughed. "So what have you done, Melanie?"

"Nothing—yet," Jackson said. "The detective was just asking about our security. Wanted to know if the place is safe from religious fanatics."

"Apart from Wendy Nailor, I think so. She's Southern Baptist."

Golding looked around the room, trying to imagine someone breaking into it, trying to imagine them coming in through the window, in through the air vents. But he couldn't. The windows didn't open and the air vents were narrow and covered with a fine steel mesh. No one could hope to get in and out undetected.

Golding turned to Margolis, decided to take another line: "To be a technician here, you need qualifications, right?"

"Sure. You can't just walk in off the street."

"Suppose you faked the qualifications?"

Margolis shrugged.

"You'd get found out, sooner or later."

"Has that ever happened?"

"Here?" Margolis frowned. "No way. We have a pretty experienced team. Regular kind of people. Most of them have been here for years. I don't think we have any religious fanatics."

Golding wrote the word *years* in the notebook, then added a question mark.

"How many years are we talking about?"

"Oh, well, I don't think we've recruited a technician since . . . since '96."

Jackson looked puzzled. She was probably wondering what this new line of inquiry was all about. But it didn't matter. Even Golding's inside-job idea didn't seem to match the facts.

"Well, thanks," he said, starting to back away. "You've been real helpful."

They were heading for the exit.

"Say, there is one other thing," said Golding. "Are any of your people—this is gonna sound a little crazy—have any of your people been big ice-skating fans? Big followers of the sport: Michelle Kwan, Tara Lipinski, that kind of thing?"

Margolis and Jackson shook their heads.

"Not that I can remember," Jackson said. "I guess a lot of people watch it on TV, but . . . a big follower? No, I don't think so."

"Unless you count Stacey Rudnick," said Margolis.

There was a moment's silence.

"Stacey who?"

"Stacey Rudnick. Used to be a hygienist here a few

years ago. Basically she used to clean"—he glanced at Jackson as if expecting a reprimand—"although round here that means more than a little light dusting. In some work areas we need complete sterility. Anyway, she was a huge Ellen Cusak fan."

Golding felt like his heart had stopped.

"Why? You interested in her?" said Margolis.

This time Jackson was looking more than puzzled.

"I'm not following," she said. "Are you suggesting that—?"

The pager in her pocket sounded. She pulled it out and looked at the number.

"I'm sorry, I'm going to have to run," she said. "George, will you see Detective Lubett out as . . ."—she gave him an uncertain look—"I guess as soon as he's done."

Golding watched her walk away. He had a feeling Dr. Thomsen would be over any minute.

"This woman, Stacey Rudnick, what happened to her?"

"She was fired," said Margolis. "Well, to be exact, she was asked to leave. Same difference."

"When was this?"

"Oh, must be, I don't know, five, six years ago. I don't know about religious fanatic, but she certainly was seriously weird, that's for sure."

"Why exactly was she fired?"

"I don't know, she pretty much stopped doing her job the last few months she was here. Used to drift around with this stupid smile on her face like she was high on something, which she probably was. I felt sorry for her, though. She was pregnant when they canned her."

Golding reached into his jacket for the Polaroid shot Leo Nash had given him of Gallo's head.

"Is this her?"

Margolis looked at the picture. The flash was reflected in the model's glass eyes, hiding the pupils. It gave the face a strange, androidal quality.

"Jesus, she doesn't look so good," he said. "She's grown her hair, too. She used to have it kind of short and spiky."

"But it's her? This is Stacey Rudnick?"

Margolis hesitated.

"I guess. She looks kind of funny, though. When did you take this?"

"This morning. It's a reconstruction."

"A reconstruction?"

"This woman's body was discovered buried about six weeks ago in Ellen Cusak's garden. The face has been reconstructed from her skull."

Margolis swallowed, handed the picture back.

"How about that. You know, Cusak was here one time."

Suddenly he looked very uncomfortable. It had to be strictly against the rules in a place like this to divulge the identity of clients.

"That's okay," said Golding. "I'm aware that Mrs. Cusak was treated here. This would have been in 1993, right? When Stacey Rudnick was still working here."

Margolis frowned. He was sweating now.

"That's right. Now I remember, it was like the biggest thing that ever happened to her, as a matter of fact. She kept bringing flowers."

"Flowers?"

"Yeah, you know, leaving them around the place

where she thought Ellen Cusak was gonna be. All kinds
of stuff. Like I said, Stacey was . . . well, pretty weird."

"And how soon after that did she get fired?"

Margolis ran a finger along his jaw.

"I guess . . . Sometime after. A few months maybe."

"By which time she was pregnant."

"I'm sorry?"

"You said she was pregnant."

"Right, right. Yes, she was, I guess. She said she was,
anyhow."

"You didn't believe her?"

"In the end we did. Yeah, I mean, she got the bump.
It was just earlier on she . . ." Margolis sighed. "What I
mean is, there didn't seem to be a man in her life. Plus
she was always making up stuff. You never knew what
to believe. I'm telling you, half the time she was on another planet."

"So what you're saying is, no one had any idea who the
father was?" said Golding. "She never said anything?"

"Well, she *said* it was this guy in our team, this technician. They used to hang out together. But the thing
was, we all had him down for . . . We were *convinced* he
was gay. At any rate, he and Henry Kelner were *very*
friendly."

"Henry Kelner? Remind me who he is."

"He's like the number two here, a surgeon. And,
well"—Margolis shrugged—"he's gay. He doesn't make
a secret of it, least not anymore."

Golding was confused.

"And Rudnick used to hang out with him? With Dr.
Kelner?"

"No, with Dr. Kelner's friend. His name was Hewish.
Funny kind of name."

Golding made a note.

"At school the girls used to call him You-Wish. I remember Stacey saying that. I guess he wasn't that popular. We just called him Hughie."

Golding stopped writing. He'd heard the name before.

"His real name was Robert," said Margolis. "Robert Samuel Hewish."

"Bob," said Golding, getting a tingle at the back of his neck.

"That's what he liked people to call him. 'Course that meant they never did. Now I think about it, he was into ice skating too. Had all these magazines. I guess that was another reason we thought he was . . ."

Golding tuned out, his mind racing. He'd guessed that one of them had been working here, that the embryo theft had been partly an inside job. It hadn't occurred to him that they might both have been. But it made sense. They had to have met sometime before, Hewish and Rudnick, perhaps at the rink-side, perhaps at some fan club meeting. Most likely he, with the more senior job, had found an opening for her at the clinic. Either way, it must have felt like more than luck, more than chance, when Ellen Cusak had walked in through the door wanting, needing a child, yet unable to bear one. It must have felt like they had been chosen to play a part in her life—a reward for their devotion, their love. Except that somewhere down the line Hewish had decided that he wasn't going to share.

"Detective?"

Margolis was frowning, looking into his face.

"Tell me about Hewish," said Golding.

"Oh—quiet, hardworking. Kept himself to himself. I kinda liked him actually. He dropped out of med school somewhere in Illinois, worked as a paramedic. He

should have been a doctor because he had a real interest in the work here. He read everything."

"What happened to him?"

"He left. About the same time as Stacey, more or less.
A few months before maybe."

Golding stared.

"Any idea why?"

Margolis hesitated.

"This could be very important," said Golding.

"I heard . . . I heard he screwed up."

"Can you be more specific?"

"There was some problem with one of the embryo
cultures. Yeah, that was it. If you ask me, I think Hughie
was just curious. Like I said, he was really into the science of it all. Maybe he wanted a closer look, I don't
know. Maybe he was screwing around with technique.
Anyway, we lost some material, apparently, belonging
to a client."

"Material?"

"Viable embryos. Part of a culture. They had others. It
wasn't a big deal, but Richard—I mean Dr. Thomsen—
took it pretty seriously. Everybody was questioned. I
don't know what they concluded, but what I do know is
Hewish left right afterwards."

"Did you ever hear where he went?"

Margolis shook his head.

Dr. Kelner came hurrying towards the laboratory,
Melanie Jackson in tow.

"You should have told him to wait, goddamm it."

"I'm sorry, Dr. Kelner. He said it was just routine."

"Routine, my ass." He slid his card into the swipe lock
and pulled open the outer door. "Get onto LAPD right
away and check this guy out. Go!"

Kelner yanked open the second door. A couple of technicians looked up from their workbenches, surprised to see him without a mask. Detective Raymond Lubett had already left.

38

Up close the rink is a field of pure white. The girl, moving fast, her hair pulled straight by an icy wind, looks like she is about to cut a clean arc over the frosting. When the candles are lit, there will be shadows; in the dancing ring of fire the girl's face will flicker and glow. Staring at the cake, he is surprised by the memory of another face held close to the flames, of sparkling eyes behind smeary lenses—then the same eyes dead, specks of blood on the dirty sclera, small black specks like coffee grounds that he tried to remove with his fingertip but couldn't.

He blinks and stands, wondering if he was right to ask the baker for this particular cake. He doesn't want to be pulled off-center by old business. He wants to be poised, he wants to be balanced, he wants to be everything she could wish for.

The baker had been reluctant enough. He'd flipped through his catalogue—moistening a finger to turn the page—showing all the cakes he did; you could have a baseball diamond, or a football field, even a basketball

court, but no rinks. Then, when he had realized he was
going to make an extra buck, he'd perked up a little. An
old guy with a silly chef's hat. He suggested having the
figurine cut her name on the ice—trailing the name like
a plane trails skywriting, but Hewish had said no. He
wanted a figure of eight.

"So the little girl's eight years old?"

"Five."

He'd had to explain that the figure of eight had other
meanings, among which, if you turned it on its side—infinity. *Infinity.* It was also the shape an embryo made at
its first cleavage, the first step in the transformation of
embryo into person. He didn't say this, though.

He touches one of the simple white candles, making
sure it is firmly in place, and again the face looms beyond the tiny points of flame. Nat bangs on the door,
screaming for her mommy, and he jerks around, hearing
it now, but the door is open to the backyard, and there
is no Nat, because he's only remembering that night
three years ago.

He is alone in the house. Nat is not due back until
five.

He told Stacey not to light them, but she lit them anyway; well ahead of time.

"We can blow them out," she said. "Light 'em again
after. It won't make any difference."

"But the wicks will be black."

She lit them anyway.

Stacey could never wait. In the hospital they had told
him that autistic kids were like that. They couldn't wait.
There was no point trying to reason; you just had to dis-
tract them with something else. Stacey wasn't autistic,
though, she was manic-depressive like him—bipolar.
Thinking about her now, he is surprised by a feeling of

loss so acute his eyes prick with tears. He snatches up the knife and rests his finger against the blade to steady himself. He is labile—liable to rapid change. Normally he would take something for it: Xanax, Valium, Litarex, Depakote, Prozac, Zoloft, Paxil, Luvox, Wellbutrin. He favors the selective serotonin-reuptake inhibitors, but they screw with his libido, so for a month now he's been flying on an empty tank, dipping and rising, using his momentum to stay aloft. He walks along the passage to his room, opening the door with the key. Once inside, he puts the chains across. He takes three milligrams of Xanax. He lays down in the dark.

The room is lined with pictures. One of his earliest memories of childhood is of sitting alone in his room with the lights off, waiting for the steam trains on his wallpaper to bloom out of darkness. He was three years old when his father was dragged under a train in the Louisville freight yards—dragged under and cut in two, and sitting in his darkened room, he would strain to recall his father's face while the trains came out of the walls.

Directly above him, covering the hole where he ripped the lamp out, Yelena smiles down, her face full of love. The room is lined the way a uterus is lined before the arrival of the precious guest.

The house is infested. Every month or so he sprays the kitchen and the other rooms. He takes furniture out into the backyard and washes it down with detergent. But he never touches this room. Sometimes he will put one picture over another, but he would never take a picture down. The ceiling is heaven, the walls are hell. Over the door the stiff paper of glossy magazines and expensive medical books is pasted and pinned half an inch thick: pictures of women, pictures of deformity, of ulcers and injuries. Behind the paper the bugs are safe. After a couple of minutes a faint seething sound starts up, a sound like rain on a tarpaper roof.

"Endometrium," he says softly. "Endometrium." Normally the word has a calming effect, but not today. Despite the Xanax—enough to floor a normal person for twenty-four hours—his head crackles with the static of remembered voices.

"But the wicks will be black."

"So what?"

"She'll *see*."

"She won't care. She's only two years old, for Christ's sake."

"If I can see it, she can see it!"

Stacey pinched out the flames. "Christ, you'd think she was *your* fucking kid!"

So he had put her straight.

He tries to close his mouth, but it comes open again. His hands flicker and twitch.

He had put her straight. Told her what was what.

"I don't *fucking* believe you!" she shouted.

He cut himself taking the knife from her. So she was the one. She grabbed it first. She was shrieking. There was blood on her lips where she had bitten herself. And all he could think of was to shut her up, to stop the terrible noise. Nat was shrieking too, locked out for the surprise they had planned, banging on the door, shrieking for Mommy.

He tries to turn his head towards the noise, but the Xanax holds him now, pressing down like the gravity of a giant world. The bugs sound like rain on dead leaves.

He remembers the startled look in Stacey's eyes. Her hands came up. He struck again, snagged, struck—snagged on bone. The handle of the knife was slick and warm. She fell back against the table, grabbing for the edge. Her lips moved as she tried to speak, and he hit her again, punching her backwards, snapping his arm out straight in jerky, crazy jolts. She tried to grab the blade, *did* grab the blade, he ripped it back through her clutching fingers and then down into the middle of her chest—back and down, back and down.

In the stillness the walls press in.

He could hear nothing but his own gasping breaths. He forced himself to stop, to listen. Behind the door Nat was crying. The cake had slid off the table. What was left of the little rink was spattered with red. A big piece of broken frosting was caught in Stacey's matted hair. Her eyes looked bigger without the glasses. They stared unblinking, unable to believe what he had done to her breasts.

Ellen stuffed the .38 into the glove compartment as the car rolled down the driveway. Her print dress clung slightly between her shoulders where she was perspiring. She felt husk-light and hollow, but clearer too, more lucid, better than she had in a long while. At the bottom of the drive, waiting for the gate to swing back, she flipped open the glove compartment and checked the gun again. Checked it to be clear that *this* was what she was doing. The gun would go into her shoulder bag. He wouldn't see it until it was too late. But what if he searched her? She pulled out into the street, shaking her head. Why should he? He loved her. He was crazy about her. He was crazy. He would do whatever she said.

He had told her Mommy wasn't well. He had given her a pill in a glass of warm milk. She'd seen her mom screaming before, so it wasn't something she couldn't believe. She fell asleep at the kitchen table as he talked to her. After he'd put her to bed, he went back into the living room. That was the hardest moment: standing there, looking, seeing what had happened. Her legs stuck out like a puppet's when you cut the strings. Her blue dress was rucked up around her thighs. One of her heels had broken. He picked up her glasses from underneath the TV. They were a little greasy because she had spent the afternoon cooking. She was always touching them, readjusting them, so you could tell what she had been doing from looking at her glasses. But there was no blood. He stood like that for a long time holding onto the glasses, unable to think. Then he walked across the room and put them back on her nose, trying not to look at the eyes, but seeing them anyway, and seeing the specks of blood in the dead whites.

He started to clean up, talking all the time, asking her why she'd done it, asking her why she'd made him do it. And she answered. Her mouth didn't move, but she answered—told him what a selfish pig he was, what a stupid pig. He ran a bath for her, putting in lots of her favorite bubble bath. Then he took off the stiffening clothes, lowered her into the water, left her in pink bubbles while he finished in the room.

It took him seven hours. He rolled up the rug and stuffed it into a trash bag. He washed down the walls and the furniture with Mr. Clean.

When he was finished he went back into the bathroom. He asked Stacey if the water was still warm enough. But she wasn't speaking now. She just stared. He pulled out the plug and very gently lifted her out. The clean body was worse. The wounds were like little red mouths. He couldn't resist touching. He put her bathrobe on and carried her through to the living

room—sat her in front of the TV. After her bath that
was where she liked to sit. He cleaned her glasses and
put them back on. Then he switched on the TV. Images
danced in her lenses. An animal documentary. He put a
tape in the VCR, a compilation. He sat at Stacey's feet
and held her cold hand. Yelena danced for them the way
she had always danced, and Stacey wept because she
was so perfect.

The address was in Burbank. She was supposed to be
there at six. Taking the ramp up onto 134, what she was
doing started to filter through. She looked at the people
in their cars and was shocked by how normal everything
seemed. A wobble of panic had her reaching for the
phone. She punched in Doug's number. He ought to be
the first to know: this was his child too. Then she realized that what she had to say to him would come across
as so crazy he'd just think she was back to the worst
days of their breakup. She put the phone back down
and tightened her grip on the wheel. She had to take it
a step at a time, the hardest step first. If she called anybody, things would screw up. Things would screw up so
fast, and then she'd have the rest of her life to regret it.
Golding would want to kick down the door. Lenny
would just call the cops. She'd seen enough footage of
sieges to know how they ended: the bodies came out
on stretchers, and then you saw the inside of the
house—the arsenal of weapons, the shrine. Bob had said
he wouldn't hesitate. He'd kill Natalia, and then himself.
And she believed it.

Natalia had cried when he told her that Mommy had
had to go back to the hospital. He said they were going
to have to find a new home, to be nearer to her. They

moved out the next day and for the next eighteen months kept moving. He was terrified the body would be discovered, he was terrified the police would come looking. But day after day nothing happened. He got jobs stacking supermarket shelves. Then he took work as a night watchman at a warehouse in Commerce. Everywhere they went he had to find someone to look after Nat. He told people he was divorced. When the women got too nosy, they moved on. In a trailer park in Belvedere Gardens he got his neighbor, Mrs. Lopez, to look after Nat while he worked. Mrs. Lopez had three of her own and was glad of the extra cash. She didn't ask any questions, and when he was too down, or drunk, or strung out, she would keep Nat in her trailer.

When Nat was four years old, he told her the story of her real mommy. He told her how he and Ellen had met when she first came to L.A. from Kiev, and how they had fallen in love. They were in the trailer. Nat got a complicated look on her face. He thought she wasn't buying it. He showed her some of his pictures. He told her that she had her mommy's eyes. She just stared at him. Then she told him she knew.

"You know?"

She nodded, shy.

"Mommy Stacey told me," she said.

"And you know it's a secret, don't you?"

"Yes."

"It's our secret. Our special secret. Just the three of us."

Ellen left the freeway at Alameda Avenue, and then turned north on Hollywood Way. Her hands were sweaty on the wheel. She kept saying the child's name to stay focused.

*   *   *

He opens his eyes. Someone is in the house. He reaches down for the detonator switch, and then sits up on the bed. Light filters in between the boards over the window. Someone is moving around in the kitchen. He checks his watch. It's five-thirty. He stands up, listens. Quietly he unlocks the door and makes his way along the passage.

Nat is standing in the middle of the kitchen. Mrs. Chave brings her back from school but never hangs around.

"Do you like your cake?" says Hewish.

"Is that my cake?" she says, pointing.

"Do you like it?"

She nods, but doesn't look at him.

"What is it, sweetheart?"

"Is Mommy coming?"

"Yes, baby."

She bites at the knuckles of her left hand.

"She'll be here any minute," says Hewish.

"So . . ." She looks at him now with her blank green eyes. ". . . are we hiding?"

39

Crossing the parking lot, Golding broke into a run, although he didn't yet know where he was going, where he was in such a hurry to be. It was too much at once. It was twisted and diseased. And there was only one person in the world he shared it with. He saw in his mind's eye the letters, the cramped black writing, like driving rain. *The next momemt comes so quickly, and the next, and beyond all nexts, already almost now.* Page after page after page. He saw the watching corpse, the black mummified head staring up from its desert grave. He heard the voice on the tape. *You see, I see you, Ellen.* He wanted suddenly to be rid of it all, to vomit it up like bad meat. He wanted to wake from the nightmare and discover that Bob had never existed, that he had gotten it all wrong, that Robert Samuel Hewish was just a regular guy someplace living a regular life.

It was seeing Ellen return to the Harper Trust after six years that opened his eyes. He'd read about embryo theft in the papers. So he knew that an unborn child could have been stolen from her, brought to term with a surrogate without her knowledge. In his head he had reconstructed how it might have happened. But in his heart he had never believed it could be true, not until the Harper people told him that Robert Hewish, author of the Bob letters, had actually been working there at the time of Ellen's treatment. Then all at once the possibility—the only possibility that fitted *all* the facts—had hit him: Ellen Cusak was innocent.

He saw it now for the first time: he had never believed her. The things the press said about her, that her enemies cursed her for, the snide suggestions of child abandonment, of success bought with some shameful sacrifice, of dark secrets behind the facade of innocence and light—he had believed them all. Or, rather, he had *wanted* them to be true. He had wanted to know that she was flawed and soiled, that she was, in spite of her beauty and talent and grace, a human being like him: part victim and part violator, in her own way as irredeemable and incomplete as he was. He had projected his own corrupted childhood onto hers, believing in the abusive father, even once or twice imagining—it sickened him that he had even thought it—that the child might have been Stepan's. He had even believed her complicit in murder. He had wanted her to be screwed up, damaged, impossible, because that way he might begin to deserve her, and she him. There would be a bridge between them that he might one day hope to cross.

But she had been telling the truth. There were no dark secrets, no lies. His reluctance to believe her was only further proof of his unworthiness, of how far apart they really were. If there was a bridge, a connection, it was between him and Bob: they at least shared the same goal. The rest was delusion.

He picked up the phone and dialed Ellen's number. He didn't even know what he was going to say to her. He just knew he had to tell her what had happened, and what he'd learned. It was all he had.

It was Maria who answered.

"Sorry, Mrs. Cusak is not home right now."

Golding wondered if Maria had been instructed not to take any calls from him. It wouldn't be surprising.

"Can you tell her . . . ? Tell her I've learned something very important about the Harper Trust. About Bob. Did you get that?"

"Yes, yes. About Bob. Is this Mr. Golding?"

"Yes. Just—"

"From the Alpha Protection?"

She sounded anxious.

"That's right. Look, Maria, is Ellen there? I have to talk to her. It's urgent."

"I'm sorry, Mr. Golding. She is out."

"Do you know when she'll be back?"

"No. She left *mucho de prisa*. I don't . . . I don't know."

She wanted to say something but wasn't sure if she should.

"Maria, did Ellen say where she was going?"

"No. She just say she was going to a birthday party. I'll give her your message as soon as she is back."

He rang off and sat for a few moments in silence, wondering if that was the truth, if Ellen wasn't really sitting there, shaking her head, telling Maria that she didn't want to speak to him. Even if she was out, he knew it was too much to hope that she would actually call him back. She wanted nothing more to do with him. He felt something tickle the back of his hand and saw tiny black flies crawling over his skin. There were more of them on his shirt front and cuffs, still more on the windshield. He squinted up at the sky and saw the sun dissolve behind a screen of cloud. It came to him that whatever he did, there was no way for him into Ellen's life now. She and Doug had the child they had always wanted. Maybe the police and the courts would get her back, and maybe not. Maybe the existence of the child would reunite them, and maybe it wouldn't. But whatever happened, it was nothing to do with him. He had no say, no role.

He started the engine and pulled out onto Newport Center Drive. The midafternoon traffic was light, and he was soon heading north again on the 405, trying to keep his speed down, hitting eighty-five and over just the same. He thought about Ellen, seeing her more clearly now, seeing how it must have been for her. In the past it had been hard to look beyond her success, beyond the ambition and determination her achievements implied. It was hard not to see those qualities as touching, tainting, everything in her life. But there had always been deeper currents than that. He pictured her for a moment, spinning on the ice, and it seemed to him that her whole life had been a struggle to fill the void, to anchor herself somewhere: with her father's love, a husband's devotion, a home, perhaps, somewhere along the line, the adulation of a sports-crazy public—above all, with a family, with children. He could only guess at why she felt that need. Perhaps it had begun when she fled her home, perhaps it went back even further than that. The thought that he would never know, that he might never speak to her again, was too much to bear.

At Signal Hill he pulled into a gas station and bought a soda. He felt spent, ragged. He loosened his tie and leaned against the vending machine. Despite the low clouds, it felt hotter than ever. His skin itched. He drank the soda and bought gas, although the tank was still half full. He had a sense of being at a crossroads somehow. Opposite him a black guy was filling up an old white Cadillac. In the back window there was a grimy toy Snoopy, its head bobbing gently up and down. For a moment Golding had a vision of Mrs. Sayers and her flattened dog, wondered if she was still expecting someone to come see her that afternoon. The thought of Reynolds turning up there, contrite and apologetic, struck him as the funniest thing in the world. Suddenly he was laughing out loud. The black guy looked at him out of the corner of his eye: another crazy person on the streets of L.A.

Back in the car, he flipped up the roof, turned the air-conditioning up to max and kept it there until the sweat on his body had turned cold. Then he picked up the phone again. Hagmaier might be persuaded to keep the LAPD from charging him with impersonating an officer if he was in time to save them from printing all those copies of Dr. Gallo's model head. Still feeling shaky, he flipped through his wallet, looking for the number. It was still only half past four. If Hagmaier put his foot down, he could arrest Hewish while he was still on duty at Alameda Studios. It would be a lot safer that way. Who knew what kind of arsenal he kept at home?

He stopped halfway though dialing. It wasn't going to be that way. He switched the phone off. Hagmaier wasn't going to arrest Hewish, or if he did, he was going to have to let him go. Because they were going to need evidence. And where were they going to get it? Stacey Rudnick's body was at least three years old. That meant her killer had had three years to dispose of the murder weapon, three years to destroy the bloodstained clothes, three years to clean out the trunk of the car, or sell it, or both. He wouldn't even need an alibi because the chances

were the police would never be able to establish exactly
when the killing took place. They might be convinced
Hewish was guilty, but without a confession they could
never prove it. They might have better luck pinning
Grossman's killing on him, if they were prepared to reopen the investigation. But there were no witnesses to
that crime either. Unless the crime lab people got very
lucky very fast, Robert Hewish was going to be walking
free in a matter of hours. And after that, anything might
happen. He might lose his job, his home, even his child.
And it would all be Ellen's fault, because she didn't appreciate what he had done for her, the sacrifices he had
made. Because she had destroyed his life. And just like
Arthur McGinley, he might decide there was only one
way to correct that injustice, only one way to level the
score.

The guard on the barrier looked at him like he was
trouble.

"Joe Walsh? He expecting you?"

"No. Just tell him I'm here, will you? It's urgent."

The guard picked up the phone and started talking. A
couple of heavy stake-bed trucks edged past on their way
off the lot, drowning out his words.

"You see this lane here?" he said, pointing away to his
right, but Golding was already on his way.

Joe Walsh was on the phone when he arrived. The office was hot and there was the same stink of men in uniform. A stand-up fan had been installed to boost the
single air-conditioning unit lodged in the exterior wall.

"They shouldn't be in that part of the lot," Walsh was
saying. "They should've been told that. . . . Yeah, you bet.
I'll get right on it."

He hung up, pushing himself back from his desk with his thick, freckly arms.

"Hey, Pete. What brings you back here?"

"I'm fine. Do you have a guy works here—?"

"You look like shit, if you don't mind me saying so. Heat getting to you?" He got up and went over to a watercooler. "These goddam prefabs heat up like a brick oven. They keep promising to move us, but . . ."

He poured himself a cup of water and gulped it down.

"Do you have someone working here called Robert Hewish?"

Walsh sniffed and wiped his mouth with the palm of his hand.

"Hughie? Sure I do. You met him."

"You never told me his name."

"Well, his name is Hewish. So what?"

"I want to talk to him."

"Uh-huh. About what?"

"About Ellen Cusak."

Walsh raised his eyebrows in a show of surprise.

"You still on that? I thought that was . . . Oh, you want some water?"

"No thanks. Let's just say there are some loose ends."

Walsh refilled his cup and walked slowly back to his desk. Golding could feel the anger building inside, knowing the guy was making him wait just because he could.

"Loose ends, huh? But what's it got to do with my man Hughie? I mean, I thought you took care of that problem with, er . . . What was his name? Grossman, right?"

"I didn't take care of it. I think your man did, as a matter of fact."

Walsh studied him for a moment.

"How's that, Pete?"

"Hewish was the one found Grossman in the trailer, right?"

"You know he was."

"Hewish was the one who got Grossman thrown off the lot. He got you to report the guy to his union. Ellen Cusak never made a complaint. She didn't even know about it."

"The makeup lady, Hershey, she complained."

"But she *didn't* complain. You told me that too. She said she didn't have the time."

Walsh took a folded handkerchief from his pocket and dabbed at the flesh beneath his chin. He shrugged.

"So what are you saying? My guy was a little hard on Jeff Grossman? What's the matter? You getting a guilty conscience or something?"

Golding straightened up. Maybe it was the heat, or maybe Walsh was so hung up playing been-there, done-that he couldn't stand being around anyone with a tougher reputation than his.

"You ever take the trouble to check this guy out?" he said.

"He's been with us for almost two years. He's one of my best men."

"So you said. Ever check his references? His employment history?"

"He joined us from Full Circle Security. I talked to his boss myself."

"Full Circle Security?"

"Yeah, they're a good firm."

"They're a *lousy* firm. They take anyone and they pay the worst rates in the business."

"So we gave the guy a break. Anything wrong with that?"

He wondered what Hewish could have done to get so firmly into his boss's good books. Was it the same thing he'd done for Dr. Henry Kelner, the surgeon at the Harper Trust? Was Walsh gay too? It didn't seem very likely. Maybe Hewish was just good at getting around people, playing them. But then, of course he was. You only had to look at the way he'd played Ellen Cusak. All you'd have to do for Walsh was pretend to lap up all the war stories from his time on the force.

"He ever mention he used to be a lab technician?" Golding asked.

"What?"

"He ever mention the Harper Trust? I guess not. Maybe that's because they fired him. They found out he was a thief."

Walsh put his handkerchief away, making a big show of folding it neatly, then went around behind his desk and sat down.

"You know, Pete, people get fired sometimes," he said, once he had the desk between them. "And it ain't always their fault. It happens. It could happen to you. Now me, I think people are entitled to a second chance sometimes. I think if they're willing to knuckle down and work hard and play by the rules, then they deserve that. You, on the other hand, I guess that's something you just don't believe in, right? Pistol Pete. Shoot first, ask questions later. Jeff Grossman, he's sad, he's pathetic, but he steals your client's underwear, so he has to die, right? Well, I'll tell you something. I'd rather have Bob Hewish on my team than a trigger-happy executioner like you."

Golding tried to smile. He wanted to let Walsh know where he was wrong, he wanted to ram the truth down his throat. He came forward and put his hands on his desk.

"Just tell me where I can find him." His voice was thick with anger.

Walsh stared at him for a second, swallowed.

"He ain't here. It's his daughter's birthday. He's giving her a party."

Golding felt the blood drain from his face.

"He took the afternoon off," said Walsh.

"Where? Where does he live?"

Walsh laughed again, nervously this time.

"Are you crazy? That kind of information is—"

Golding reached across the desk and grabbed Walsh by the shirtfront.

"Jesus! Jesus, Hal! Get in—"

Golding yanked him up onto his feet and pushed him against the wall.

"*Shut the fuck up.* Now I want that address. *Now.* You get it for me."

"You're crazy. You're fuckin' crazy. You should be—"

"You wanna see crazy? *Huh?*" Golding reached inside his jacket for the Beretta, pushed it into Walsh's face. "This is Pistol Pete you're talking to, remember? Shoot first, ask questions later. But it's your lucky day, because I *am* asking you. Now. Where does the son of a bitch live?"

Walsh pointed a trembling finger at his Rolodex.

Golding reached over and picked it up, flipped through to H. Hewish's was the first card there.

40

He walks through to the back of the house and out into the yard. Low clouds hang like smoke in the sultry air. Despite the Xanax, he feels wired. He can't settle, can't *be* right. He has waited for this moment for so long, always visualizing it as a culmination, but, confusingly, what it feels like most is the end. He looks over the fence at the broken patio furniture next door, and for a hard, staring second considers running. But the thought of leaving everything behind—his routine, his room, his things, his relationship—is too blank, too scary for him to even formulate. He needs time. He needs things to slow down, to stop. He blinks and reminds himself that this is all happening now, that he's supposed to be hiding now—supposed to be getting ready *now*. They're hiding. They're going to give Mommy Ellen a big surprise.

Ellen took a right onto Oak Street, then pulled over. Her hands were shaking as she stared at the map, the mesh of black lines marking out the grid, the tiny street names: Cordova, Avon, Lima, California, *Ontario*. A voice inside her head said: *Turn around*. It was a voice she had heard a thousand times: the voice of fear. She knew how not to listen.

Out of nowhere, he's remembering the national championships ten years ago. The Blue Jay Ice Castle at Lake Arrowhead. Stacey and him holding hands as they moved through the jostling crowds, Stacey talking breathlessly about the competitors, the rivalries, the new routines. Nicole Bobek was her idol in those days. She told him that once she had collided with her on a rink, that Bobek had been wearing Anaïs Anaïs, and that was why she always wore Anaïs Anaïs herself. He remembers Stacey watching the contest, totally absorbed, her hand squeezing his thigh every time someone completed a double axel or a triple lutz. Most of all, he remembers Yelena. The blue tunic. The beautiful, perfect face, upturned to the light. The unbearable tension as everyone waited in silence for the music to begin. The Brahms Hungarian Rhapsody in F-sharp Minor. And then the dance that changed everything, that destroyed everything.

They talked about it all night, Stacey and him, sitting in the kitchen. They talked about what Cusak's appearance meant for the other stars. It took a while, but at four in the morning Stacey finally admitted that Yelena was the most beautiful thing she had ever seen. All the same, something had changed between them. They were irritable with each other. He took the car and disappeared for a couple of days. It was on the road that he wrote Yelena his first letter, signing it "Bob."

After he got the job at the Harper Trust, they bought a Ford van and fitted it out like a camper. On weekends they would drive hundreds of miles to see Yelena compete. On a trip to Lake Arrowhead to watch her train,

Stacey got close enough to get an autograph. Afterwards they argued bitterly over who it belonged to. Even then Yelena was slowly destroying them. Her magic had already enveloped them, made them prisoners, although they did not yet know it. They would know it only when she had taken everything and they had nothing.

When he heard from Roger Gerrard that Cusak and her husband were going to have treatment at the clinic, he was sure it was Gorman who had the problem. Stacey was sure it was Ellen, and Stacey was right. Cusak ovulated normally, but the ova did not attach to the lining of the uterus. Dr. Thomsen recommended in vitro fertilization and implanatation of the embryo. There was only a twelve percent chance of success. He stole the charts of Cusak's endometrial cycle and put them on his bedroom wall. The first attempt at implantation was a failure, and the second ended in miscarriage after three days. But by then Stacey had already seen what had to be done: she would carry Cusak's child for her.

He was against it at first. They argued about it endlessly. Stacey wrote a letter to Cusak, offering herself as a surrogate. He destroyed it, told her if she tried to contact Yelena again he would kill her. He wrote to Yelena himself, followed her, watched her. He saw the people that surrounded her. He saw that her struggle to have a child was a desperate bid for something real. He explained in his letters that she was not alone, that he loved her just as, given the chance, she would love him.

Yelena never answered the letters. She didn't need to.

Ellen cruised down Ontario counting the white numbers stenciled on the curbstones, then pulled over and parked in the shadow of a big fir tree. It was a quiet, tree-lined street. A couple of houses farther up, a sprinkler was working. She took a couple of deep breaths and adjusted her rearview mirror until she could see number 348. It looked out of place between the neat middle-class bungalows. A ratty-looking box of a house with board walls, it had gray plastic awnings over the front windows, one of which was boarded up, as if the glass had been broken. A heavy-duty chain-link fence choked with ragweed and vines seemed designed to shut out the world. Now that she was here, Ellen wasn't sure she could take the next step. She didn't think she could threaten somebody with a gun, and she knew she couldn't pull the trigger. She flipped open the glove compartment and looked at the .38. She sat like that for a long time, then put the gun in her bag.

When they were still living in the two-story house in San Gabriel, Stacey would walk Nat through the house looking for Daddy. It was one of their games. At almost two years old, Nat was already grown-up—watchful and quiet—and she would go through the house, holding Stacey's hand, watching as Mommy opened cupboards, or yanked back drapes, and he would wait, hiding in a closet, or under a bed, the blood beating thickly in his throat. Stacey knew all the hiding places, and she would go through them one by one, pointing silently sometimes so that Nat could open a door herself. It took forever for them to come to him. Then, finally, Nat's little shoes would appear going past the bed, and he'd hear her breathing through her open mouth. Later, when Stacey was gone, there were no games for a long time.

The house is silent.

Lying in the musty dark, looking up through a gap in the boards that run the length of the hallway, he is overwhelmed by a sense of how crazy this all is. Everything is going too fast. He starts to cry. Hot tears stream down his face, and he has to press his nails into his palms to get a grip. This is not the way it is supposed to be. He squeezes the tears out of his eyes and blinks up at the bare bulb in the hallway. He is not even wearing the right clothes. He should be in his tan suit, but the suit, still in cellophane from the dry cleaners, is on the bed in his room. He pictures it draped across the bed and in the same picture sees that the door is not locked. For a second he has a sensation of falling backwards. He works his head around to get a look at the steel hasp below the doorknob, but he can't see it. All he can see is the top of the door. It looks closed. Then he feels the lump of the padlock in his pocket. His mind starts to jump and snag, making it impossible to think. Ellen mustn't see his room. In the welter of impressions, this comes through as clear as neon. She must not go in there. It's too soon— too soon for her to understand that side of him. He puts his watch up against the hole: five-thirty. She's due any-time, will appear at any time, but despite the risk of fucking up, he can't stay where he is. She'll come in through the front door, and the first thing she'll do is walk into his room. He knows it. He is shuffling towards the back of the house, worming along on his elbows and knees, moving fast, scattering roaches, when he hears the doorbell.

Ellen rang again, and stepped back from the door. The window to the right was boarded up tight, but through the other window, through the half-closed drapes, she could see a single bed. There was some kind of Muppet toy on the pillow. A child's room. A car went past. She turned to watch it go down the street. Then rapped on the door. It moved under her knuckles, wasn't locked.

Like the doors in nightmares, it wasn't even properly closed.

The hallway floods with daylight. He clutches the .38 against his heaving chest. He took it from the canvas knapsack—took the .45, then put it back, preferring the .38. But it's all wrong. This is *all* wrong. He doesn't want to scare her. He drops the gun and for a second can't think at all. He looks at the wires running up into his room. The switch is up there, taped to the leg of the bed, but he can cut the wires. He can close the circuit down here, get the juice into the detonator, solve everything. Is that what he wants? He doesn't know. But what he does know is that he can't do it without talking to her, without looking into her beautiful face and telling her the truth. He presses his eye against the crack in the boards, straining to see her as she comes into his house. A shadow moves on the ceiling.

"Hello?"

Her voice. Like a silk scarf being drawn across him. He strains, the muscles in his powerful neck bulging, trying to get a look at her.

A passageway going through to the back of the house. An odd smell like disinfectant and engine oil. A bare bulb on a flex. No rug, no pictures. A door to her right leading to the room with the boarded windows. The door to the left half open: the child's room.

Ellen brushed hair back from her damp forehead, hesitating.

"Hello?"

She listened at the closed door for a moment. There was a hasp under the doorknob but no padlock. She thought of storage, she thought of secrets. She knocked again. Behind her something stirred. She came around, reaching into her bag for the gun, her fingers closing on the cold metal. She made sure the safety was off, pointed it at the open door of the child's room.

"Is there someone there?"

Quiet now. She took a step forward, saw posters on the wall, pictures of her aged eighteen, pictures of her jumping. The Muppet animal was a pajama case. She reached into the mouth and pulled out a little stretch cotton jacket.

"Nat?" she said softly.

She pressed her face into cotton. On the far wall, next to the head of the bed, there was a wardrobe. The scuffling sound. Someone was inside. Suddenly she knew it. She checked back in the passageway, listened. Something had moved. And now, now that she was really listening, she could hear breathing—very faint, but distinct. She held her own breath, trying to identify the source of the sound. Her heartbeat pulsed in the tips of her damp hair.

"Is there someone there?"

She looked back at the wardrobe. Still holding the gun out in front of her, she took a step forward. She reached for the doorknob.

Walsh signaled for Hal Levey to shut the fuck up. He rubbed his throat as he talked down the phone.

"Yeah, that's what I said: assault with a deadly weapon. He pushed a gun in my face . . . Peter Golding."

Levey was nodding eagerly, lapping it up. The police officer logged the complaint—not nearly quick enough for Walsh's liking.

"You'll find him at 348 Ontario Street, Burbank," he snapped. "And you'd better get over there real quick. I think this asshole's gonna hurt somebody."

*   *   *

A little girl's clothes. Dresses. Neat little Lycra slacks—plaid and paisley. Blouses. None of it really clean. In the bottom of the wardrobe—sandals, sneakers.

Ellen walked out of the bedroom and went along the passage to the back of the house.

A living room. Two armchairs and a couch. A coffee table. On the table a cake. A sensation in her chest like a knot being drawn tight. She pointed the gun into corners—irrational, the fear starting to confuse her. The place didn't look lived in. There were no magazines, no plants, no kiddie things. The smell of disinfectant was strong here. She looked at the cake. Saw the tiny skater, saw the figure of eight, saw the five candles, saw the knife. A noise from the kitchen brought her up straight. She pointed the gun—moved into the doorway.

But the kitchen was empty. Standing at the sink, she looked through the window into a little yard. Someone or something had moved across the window, she was sure of it. It could have been a cat, a bird. She twisted around, stabbing out the gun, starting to lose it now, her face streaming with sweat. Her legs were shaking. She opened the door and went out into the yard. A roll of hose. A board pulled away from underneath the kitchen window. She squatted down, peered into the darkness, saw bugs, saw guns. The voice in her head said: *GO*.

She went back into the house, telling herself that it was empty, that Bob had decided to run. Back through the house to the street door. It was the quickest way out.

Back along the bare passageway. The front door was open. She couldn't remember closing it, couldn't be sure. She listened and listened, but there was nothing now: no breathing, no movement. She was alone. She let the gun come down, relaxing her shoulders.

There was only one room she hadn't checked.

Golding cut straight across oncoming traffic on Burbank and thumped into the speed dip at the entry to Ontario. Leaning out the window, looking for house numbers, he clipped a trash can and sent it spinning over the sidewalk. Then he saw Ellen's Mercedes parked in a driveway. He slewed to a halt and jumped out of the car. Carrying the Beretta tight against his thigh, he crouch-ran across the lawn, his eyes on the windows of the house.

Then stopped dead.

A woman was staring out at him, a cookie held to her lips, eyes wide with fear. Then he saw the rustic numbers on the door reading 443, a car that wasn't Ellen's at all, wasn't even the right color. He'd cut across from Buena Vista too high up.

A room lined with paper, with pages. Light from the hallway picks up edges, torn corners. A musty smell of bugs and paper. A room so thickly lined that at first she thinks of scales on a fish. But as her eyes adjust she sees pictures: genital injuries and fistulae; injuries to the vulva; injuries to the vagina; cysts and syphilis; lesions and tumors. To Ellen just horror: burst fruit, split pods, rotting meat. And faces, eyes—the blank, bemused stares of bewildered sickness. She takes a step forward, her breath held, and a board moves under her foot. Two boards have been pulled up, then put back without being nailed down. She sees wires coming up through a gap. Wires. It means something, but already she is looking at the pictures again, unable to take her eyes away.

Above the single bed: a woman lifting an embroidered nightdress to show the camera what happened to her body. The homely garment, so familiar somehow, so banal, pulled tight over the hard, distended abdomen—massive, vein-streaked, sleekly taut. Too horrified to think, too horrified to move, Ellen looks up at the ceiling, sees herself smiling down.

"Yelena."

Him.

She turns—slowly, not wanting to see, not wanting to hear. The blood is pounding in her head.

He is standing in the doorway, his hands held loosely at his sides. A pleasant-looking, slightly heavy man with short dark hair and deep-set, unblinking eyes.

"Yelena."

She aims the gun, sighting the Warner Brothers logo in the middle of his T-shirt.

"I didn't want you to see this."

It takes a moment for his eyes to adjust. Then he sees the gun. He points.

"What's this?"

"What does it look like?"

He nods, manages a flickering, uneasy smile.

"Yelena."

"Where is she, you sick son of a bitch? Where's my child?"

"Your child? No, no, Yelena. No." His voice is suddenly soft, patient. Then he is showing her his open palms. *"Our* child. Yours and mine, Yelena. It would have to be, don't you see?"

"Have to be? What are you talking about? Tell me where—?"

"Oh Yelena, Ye-lena"—the voice wheedling now, edged with impatience—"you don't think I'd do all this for *him* . . . do you? For Doug." He shakes his head, his shoulders swaying. "Doug Doug Doug Doug . . . he was never, Yelena, *never* . . ."

It feels like her legs are going to give.

"What . . ." She has to swallow hard to speak. ". . . What are you saying? What did you do?"

"I'm saying Doug's . . ." He shudders, mouth twisted in disgust. "Doug's *muck* went into the trash."

"Muck?"

"That's right, Yelena. I thought you knew. Didn't you get my little card? When Stacey knew she was pregnant, I wrote you. I told you: *We are one.*"

She clutches her forehead, can't think straight, can't make sense of his words.

His eyes dance, sucking in her distress, her fear.

"For Stacey it was the easiest thing in the world," he says, laughing. "She blew up like a balloon."

It hits her then. Like a physical blow: *Muck.* He is talking about Doug's sperm. He took Doug's sperm and substituted his own. *His* sperm. *Her* egg.

Revulsion twists her stomach.

"You see," he says softly. "You see now? After all we've shared, can you still be angry?"

He takes a step towards her.

Ellen jabs the gun out straight.

"Don't make me do it," she snaps.

Something in her voice gets through to him. He hesitates, looking down at the gun.

"I'll do it," she says, though even now she's not sure she can. "I'll kill you."

They are four feet apart. Ellen gets a two-handed grip to stop the gun from shaking.

Then he turns his back and walks away.

Ellen is so astonished, all she can do is stare at the

empty doorway. By the time she gets into the passageway, he has disappeared.

A movement to her left brings her around, finger tight against the trigger.

A little girl is standing in the middle of the bedroom, the pajama jacket in her hands.

The guns are all under the house. He can't believe he dropped the .38, can't believe he was frightened of scaring her. She wanted to kill him. She threatened his life. He sees her face again in the moment she said the words *I'll kill you*. His rage sears like burning circuits. Get the gun. He's opening the back door when he hears the voice. He freezes. A man. In his house. He hears the urgent, breathless voice. He steps away from the door.

The first thing Golding saw was Ellen and the little girl, Ellen kneeling, weeping, clutching the kid tight in her arms.

Her head snapped up as he came into the doorway. She looked at him without seeing.

"Where is he?"

A siren whooped in the street. Ellen looked through the window as a squad car thumped up onto the sidewalk.

"Ellen, where is he?"

She looked back at Golding, his face beginning to register. She pointed a trembling finger.

"In back," she said. "Just walked away."

He turned, the Beretta in his hand, and then he was gone. Beyond the child's sweet-smelling hair, through the doorway into the other room, Ellen saw the wires again. This time she understood.

"Pete."

Golding tried to screen out the sirens as he walked

along the passage, the gun out in front of him. He was seeing everything at once. The room, the table, the cake.

"Pete?"

Ellen. In the passage behind him. He started to turn.

"Pete, the house is—"

The knife went into his neck so fast, so easily, it was like a magic trick. Then Hewish was there, up close, crazy, ripping the blade back out and stabbing again, deep into the shoulder this time, deep into the lung, grunting with the effort. Golding tried to shout, sprayed blood, fired into the floor. Hewish yanked at the knife, but the heel of the long blade snagged under the clavicle. He pulled again, bringing Golding over against him hard. They kicked and skidded in blood. Golding was trying to turn, but Hewish was against him, struggling to free the knife. Golding's gun roared, filling the air with smoke and splinters. Then, suddenly, he was free. Hewish staggered backwards. Golding fired again as Ellen came along the passageway, firing *her* gun. She kept firing until the hammer was striking empty chambers.

The room was thick with smoke.

In the street, sirens and the sound of police radios.

Someone was trying to draw breath. Ellen looked down at where Pete was convulsing on the floor, the handle of the knife sticking out of his shoulder. She threw down the gun and grabbed the lapels of his blood-spattered jacket. Then she pulled.

V

Real
Friends

41

Tuesday, October 26

The explosion at 348 Ontario Street took out all four exterior walls and blasted a crater five feet deep. Houses on either side were extensively damaged both as a result of the blast and the fire that subsequently engulfed the building. A police patrolman died of his injuries. By the time firefighters brought the blaze under control, nothing of number 348 remained standing. Forensics teams began sifting through the site the following morning.

Pete Golding stabilized nine hours after being admitted to the trauma unit at L.A. County USC Medical Center. The knife had missed his subclavian and carotid arteries, but left him with a partially severed bronchus, a punctured lung, and vertebral nerve damage that threatened for a time to leave him paralyzed.

In and out of the operating room, he saw everything through waves of anesthetic and painkillers. He had visitors after the first operation, but for a while wasn't sure who they were. Frank Romero was one, Tom Reynolds another. He remembered seeing Jackie, although that might have been a dream because he saw Maddy Olsen too, and that couldn't have been real.

The cops never stopped coming: first a Detective Lerner from the Burbank police, wanting to go over the events leading up to the incident, including the alleged assault on Joe Walsh. Then Detective Wolpert of the Pacific Division, asking all kinds of stuff about the Jeff Grossman case. Finally, Larry Hagmaier and Matt Kronin. It was slow death by a thousand questions. He couldn't always remember what had really happened and what had only happened in his head. Sometimes it got so mixed up that all he was left with was a picture of Ellen bending over him, her hands in his lapels, screaming at him to get up. Sometimes, as he drifted out of consciousness, her head would become the clay head, her eyes glass eyes, staring out at the world from Dr. Gallo's workbench, and he would wake up in panic, thinking Ellen had died in the house, and that it was her body that lay black and shrunken in the grounds of the Brentwood house.

It was from one of those dreams that he woke to find Ellen sitting beside his bed. When she smiled at him, he knew he must be dreaming, but then she touched his arm, was really there, had visited before, it turned out, but had never found him conscious. She was the one who gave him the fullest picture. She told him how she half carried, half dragged him out of the front of the house, and how one of the patrolmen had seen her and come to help. They had just got him down behind the patrol car when the explosion happened.

The Burbank police seemed satisfied with her account of the preceding minutes. A fire department investigation left no doubt as to the cause of the blast, or that a large quantity of homemade explosives had been in place beneath the house. Robert Hewish had dreamed of spending the rest of his life with Ellen and Nat, but at the same time had been planning the next best thing: to send them all to eternity with a two-hundred-pound fertilizer bomb. Unable to reach the detonator switch in his bedroom, he had crawled under the house to bridge the circuit manually—that was the police take on events, anyway. It explained why the human remains recovered from the scene were so widely scattered. A positive ID would take some time to establish, but preliminary examination of pelvis fragments indicated a male of Hewish's approximate age and build.

As Ellen talked, Golding saw that she had changed. She was still the private person Doug Gorman had described, was still inside herself, but somehow the inner darkness, the darkness Golding had always found so attractive, had been displaced, pushed aside by a new radiance. It was clear that becoming a mother, however disastrous the circumstances, meant everything to her. In a bizarre way Hewish had made her whole.

Natalia, the child she had found at the house, had been made a ward of the court in Burbank and was staying in a foster home. Ellen talked about how she visited her there every day, how they got on wonderfully, how Nat had been brought up believing that she, Ellen, was her real mother, and that it would only be a matter of time before she turned up to claim her little girl. She remembered Mommy Stacey very well, but only as one of the many caregivers employed by her father over the years. It was Ellen, perceived through the magic window of the TV screen, who had been the constant point of reference. For Nat at least, the nightmare of August 27 contained elements of a fairy tale.

Ellen's attorney believed that it was only a matter of

time before she was granted custody, provided, of course, that her claim to be the child's biological mother could be substantiated. However, it was likely, given the unusual circumstances under which the child had been raised, to say nothing of her father's death, that the court would want her to undergo protracted psychological evaluation. If it was decided that Nat had special needs, there was an outside chance the court would decide that Ellen was unsuitable to act as parent or guardian.

The hearing had been scheduled originally for early December, but Ellen's attorney was able to have it moved forward to October, given the potential for press intrusion in the case. The city authorities raised no objection. Golding asked how Doug Gorman had taken the news that she had a child. Ellen said that she wasn't going to be the one to tell him.

The next day she came back, and Golding was able to sit up and talk more, although mainly he listened. She told him she knew he'd been right about Hewish, but that she had been frightened for the child. She had been afraid that if anyone had tried to pressure him or threaten him, he would simply have killed her. She'd hoped that maybe what Lenny had said at the beginning had been true, that a man who had taken his fantasy so far, to such insane lengths, would simply *be* insane, disorganized; that face-to-face he would simply crumble and do what she asked. And if that didn't work, there was always money. She had been prepared to give him everything in return for the child.

Her third visit was the day before the hearing, and she had cut her hair short. She was nervous. Golding had stayed off the painkillers that morning so that he could be more alert for her. She told him she had already sold the house in Brentwood. Despite the rush, it had brought in more than she'd expected. As soon as she could, she was going to take Nat to live in the mountains. Apparently, Detective Hagmaier had done his best to keep the child out of the press's coverage of the story, getting them to focus on the murders of Stacey Rudnick and Jeff Grossman, but she was worried that as soon as they got wind of the custody hearing, everything would come out and the feeding frenzy would begin. She didn't want Nat to be around when it did. Golding realized then that she was saying good-bye.

She thanked him for saving her life. She thanked him for being there in spite of the way she had acted. He told her, truthfully, that he couldn't have helped himself. It was a difficult moment, shadowed by uneasy recollection. But then she took his hand and told him that she understood, and her words went through him like a healing wave. It was a long time before he saw her again.

Tom Reynolds asked him to come back into the office when his health allowed it, and they came to a wary accord that involved forgetting their last encounter. But despite the fact that the Cusak case had been good for Alpha, it became clear that there was no trust between them anymore. After a couple of weeks of skirting around the subject, they both agreed that it would be better if Golding left the firm. Reynolds said he'd do anything he could to help, and insisted on paying him three months' salary to keep things amicable.

He was free then—free for a time to consider his future. But, going about his daily life, going to the hospital for physiotherapy, or to the local gym to get back in shape, he found he could never quite let go of Ellen, or of Robert Hewish. They were on his mind, more or less constantly.

Finally, one quiet Sunday afternoon, he took down the pictures of Ellen from the walls of the living room and put them in a carton, together with the old newspaper reports and skating magazines. He couldn't bring himself to throw them out, but didn't want to catch himself looking at them anymore. He told himself they were part of an illusion, a half-truth that he had come close to mistaking for the real thing.

Late in November Larry Hagmaier called to see how he was doing. He said the Hewish case was being wound up and asked if he wanted to see the report, said he thought he'd earned the right. Golding read it in Hagmaier's kitchen—a fat file of statements, police reports, forensic evidence. They talked late into the night, Hagmaier relating how the case had taken him as far afield as Kentucky and Illinois.

It was in Louisville that Robert Hewish had been born in the summer of 1961. His father had been a freight yard worker, but he'd been killed at work when his son was only three years old. Hewish later told psychiatrists that his mother had taken to casual prostitution, although this was impossible to verify. In 1977 she died from an overdose of barbiturates, and her son was sent to the St. Francis Orphanage in Jefferson County.

By that time Robert Hewish had been through four different Louisville high schools. His grades were poor and his reports spoke repeatedly of disruptive behavior. In 1978, shortly after his mother died, he was arrested for holding a knife on a fourteen-year-old girl while a friend had sex with her. The case was dismissed for lack of evidence. It wasn't until he reached community college in 1979 that he began to show a different side to his character. A biology professor wrote that with better self-discipline and organization, Hewish might even make it to med school. A year later he transferred to Quincy University, from which he graduated with a near perfect 3.89 grade-point average. He entered the Southern Illinois University College of Medicine, in Carbondale, in the fall of 1984.

It was in med school that things began to go wrong again. His work was often sloppy—perhaps because of his part-time work as a paramedic—and some of his classmates suspected him of cheating during exams. After he failed a required course in obstetrics and gynecology in his third year, his student-faculty committee met to review his status. One resident told the committee that Hewish had written a report on an elderly patient he had not actually seen. Gaps in the patient's charts appeared to confirm this, and Hewish was dismissed just three months before graduation. He turned to fulltime paramedic work for the Adams County Ambulance Service, but left six months later after crashing a vehicle and being found in possession of controlled substances.

In November 1988 his name showed up again, this time in Los Angeles at Our Lady Queen of Angels Hospital on Hill Street, where he had been working as an orderly for several months. Central Division police officers were called to the apartment of a man called Joseph Leahy, a technician in the hospital's cytology department. They encountered Hewish on the way out of the building and noticed blood on his shirt. Leahy had been so badly beaten he needed reconstructive surgery on his face. Hewish was arrested. Neighbors said they had heard shouting and screaming coming from the apartment, but Leahy later claimed he had been

mugged by a stranger on his way in. The officers at the
scene were convinced Hewish was responsible, but
Leahy refused to press charges. On searching Hewish,
they found capsules of Litarex, a lithium carbonate
compound used to prevent episodes of manic-depressive psychosis. When questioned about the drug,
Hewish claimed that he was "bipolar," a term he clearly
preferred to that of manic depressive. He also claimed
that Leahy had made sexual advances towards him, although he denied that this had provoked him into violence.

The stalking began the following year. Hewish's first
victim was a thirty-five-year-old woman called Claire
Macaffrey, an administrator at the Matrix Center in
Santa Monica, where Hewish had succeeded in getting
a job as an assistant technician. According to the complaint, Hewish started following Macaffrey home, waiting outside her house in his car. Her seven-year-old son
thought he saw Hewish in the yard one evening. At
work he watched her constantly. Attached to the complaint was an anonymous letter that Macaffrey believed
had come from Hewish. Golding recognized Bob's style
immediately. The letter said she was too good for her
husband and her children; that they did not appreciate
her or realize how lucky they were to have an "Angel in
the house."

Macaffrey did not report the matter to the police
straightaway, but went instead to her employer, Dr.
Ralph Simmons. Simmons confronted Hewish with the
letter, and threatened him with action if the harassment
continued. A week later Hewish assaulted Macaffrey in
the company parking lot. Macaffrey was not hurt, but
Simmons fired Hewish anyway. When Hewish approached Macaffrey's house again, she obtained a re-

straining order. Hewish immediately breached it and was arrested for contempt. On the advice of doctors, the presiding judge imposed a suspended sentence of six months, conditional on Hewish agreeing to treatment at a state psychiatric facility. Treatment took place at the L.A. County USC Medical Center under the direction of Dr. Nathan Young.

Hagmaier gave him the essentials of the medical report. During analysis Hewish had talked at great length about medical matters, especially obstetrics and gynecology, impressing Young with the depth of his knowledge. It was clear he had studied the subjects to an obsessive degree. Young suspected that there was a misogynistic element to this fascination, especially when Hewish revealed feelings of contempt towards his mother. He talked of his earliest memories—of sitting alone in his darkened room at the age of three, straining to remember his father's face until it bloomed out of the darkness. By the same exercise of will and imagination, he'd found he could erase his mother as she went about the house or lay passed out on the sofa. When Young asked if he ever saw his father, or heard his voice, or talked to him, Hewish had become evasive. There was no mention in the interviews either of skating or of Yelena Cusak. Dr. Young diagnosed Hewish as suffering from a schizoaffective disorder—the first time Hewish's potential for delusion was recognized. Young prescribed Prozac, but no treatment program was pursued.

Sometime during the next two years Hewish met Stacey Rudnick, though Hagmaier had no idea where or when. Most of this time Rudnick was working on a packing line in the city of Commerce. Her coworkers remembered her as a quiet girl, and a keen amateur skater. They recalled her elation the day her tickets came through for the national championships at Lake Arrowhead. That was the year Yelena Cusak grabbed the world's attention by winning silver. They were surprised when Rudnick returned from the event tired and sullen, having "had words" with her boyfriend, presumably Hewish. No one could recall the subject of the disagreement. A newspaper report in Hagmaier's press file went further into Rudnick's background, and discovered that she had been taken into care for eighteen months during her childhood, following reports of parental abuse. They also came up with claims that Rudnick had been a compulsive liar.

Rudnick and Hewish were still together when, in 1991, he faked a résumé and applied for a job at the Harper Trust Fertility Center. By this time, according to LAPD research, Hewish had already begun accumulating weapons, including two handguns and a hunting rifle.

Golding set off for Milwaukee by car three days after reading the report, hoping that a long drive would help him to decompress. His mom was better now, Jackie had told him. She'd wanted to come down to see him when he was in the hospital, but hadn't wanted to upset him. Pete told her about his leaving Alpha, and she asked what he was going to do next. He said he had no idea. Jackie said it would mean a lot to her if he came home for a while. He'd agreed. He'd told himself it was something he needed to do.

Hagmaier let him take photocopies from the report. He read and reread them on the trip, in motel rooms and roadside diners. He wanted to define Hewish more completely. He wanted to see every manifestation of his madness in bright colors. He wanted every difference between them underlined. He thought about sending the report to Ellen for the same reason, but in the end decided against it.

He read the report again at a Sizzler twenty miles from his mom's house. This time just to keep from thinking about the reunion that was about to take place, and what he was going to say to his mother after all the years of silence.

Los Angeles, December 2, 1999

It had rained all day, but looking out past his reflection in the kitchen window, Pete Golding could see a break in the clouds over in the direction of Topanga Canyon, and decided that tomorrow was going to be better. There were even stars up there—two stars, in fact, side by side like headlights on a dark road. Pete scratched at two-day stubble, and gave his glass a swirl. He had been planning on an early night. He had been planning on going to bed sober. But here he was, wide awake at half past ten, watching the ice melt in his fourth glass of bourbon. Tomorrow morning's early start loomed like one of the cold fronts they had described on the evening news.

He had to be up early for a job interview. It was Tom Reynolds who had set it up, introducing him to a private security firm based in Santa Monica that did bodyguard and general advisory work. They were looking to raise their profile, and liked the idea of having him on the payroll. After thinking about it for a week or two, he had decided to accept their invitation to come in and talk about how he might fit in. The truth was, he hadn't come up with any better ideas. He was getting a little old to start a new career from scratch. If things worked out, maybe he could sell the place in Van Nuys and move closer to the ocean. He thought about that as he sipped—thought about running on the beach every morning, watching the seabirds.

Of course, if he took the job, Jackie was going to be disappointed. She had assumed he'd be getting out of security work after the stabbing incident. He had nearly died, after all. Jackie wanted him to move to Wisconsin. Having decided that she wasn't going to be coming back to L.A. herself, she kept trying to sell him the idea of a "fresh start" in the Midwest. Maybe she thought their family reunion had gone better than he did. Perhaps she really thought the old scars would heal.

They hadn't talked about the past much during his visit. Dad hadn't even been mentioned, except once, in the kitchen, when his mom thought he was out of earshot. It was clear to Pete that she for one considered the whole episode closed, or if not closed, then at least too painful to reopen. That was fine as far as it went. They could sit at the table and act like everything was normal. They could look and behave like a family in recognition of the fact that they *were* family, for Jackie's sake, perhaps even for their own sakes, but that didn't change the past or reconcile them to it. There were some wounds that never healed, some feelings that never changed. He knew that now.

He finished his drink and was emptying the ice into the sink when the phone rang. He walked through to the sitting room and picked up.

"Pete?"

It was Lenny Mayot. Pete hadn't seen him since he'd

come into the hospital one afternoon to tell him what a hero he was.

"Yeah, Lenny. How you doing?"

"No. How are *you* doing? How's the shoulder?"

Pete took him through the details: the therapy, the healing, the rehabilitation. Lenny told him he was a hero again, and said if there was ever anything he could do, any favor, any advice. . . . Then he cracked wise about nurses he had known, about the last time he'd had his prostate examined. Behind the jokes Pete sensed a problem.

"So, Lenny . . . ?"

"I wanted to talk to you about Hewish," said Lenny, suddenly serious.

Pete closed his eyes. It was still hard to think about Hewish without reliving that moment in the house, the moment the knife went into his neck. He had hoped to put it all behind him with the reading of the report, but he was beginning to see that, like the ugly scars on his neck and shoulder, it was always going to be there.

"What's to talk about?" he said.

"Well, I've been trying to get some sense out of LAPD, but you know what they're like."

"What kind of sense?"

"About Hewish. I read something about how they recovered bits of the guy. Bits of someone who they thought was the guy."

"That's right."

"So he's dead, right? There's no doubt about that? Because when I called LAPD, this guy . . . Hagmaier?"

"That's right. Larry Hagmaier."

"He told me it was ongoing, and that he couldn't talk to me about the details."

"Hewish died under the house, Lenny. I spoke to Larry Hagmaier a couple of days ago. The coroner put some fragments together, some of the guy's lower jaw, and was able to get a match with dental records. It was Hewish."

"So how come—?"

"Hagmaier's probably waiting on the coroner's report before making it official. When they're ready to talk, they'll talk to the press. That's all this is: procedure. I'm telling you, he's dead."

"Thank Christ," said Lenny, sounding genuinely relieved. "I mean, I didn't really have any doubts, but Ellen . . ."

"What about her?"

"She just won't let it go. Talking all kinds of crazy stuff about how the guy could've had a remote control to set off the bomb, that the body under the house could've been someone else. You know, horror movie stuff. And this weekend—I was just up at her place in the mountains—this weekend she gets a letter, one of these sicko letters."

Pete frowned, thinking of Ellen opening the envelope, pulling out the letter, knowing that she still wasn't free.

"I thought you screened those," he said.

"I do. We do. Anything that comes to my office we look at very carefully. But this went to the old Brentwood address and it looked kind of official. She has an arrangement with the post office. Stuff goes there, it gets rerouted to my office. This thing was in a brown envelope. It had 'Private and Confidential' typed on it. I figured it was something from her accountant. Anyway, there's a picture of Ellen skating, and this spooky picture of Hewish next to it. You know all those pictures of him that came out in the press after the explosion?"

"Sure."

"One of those. And the guy—whoever it is—wrote 'We are one' under the pictures. We are one. Then there was all this obscene shit about how he's going to find her. It freaked her out."

"Understandably."

Pete massaged his eyes for a moment.

"Well, whoever it came from, it wasn't from Hewish," he said.

Lenny let out a long sigh.

"Maybe you should call her," he said.

Pete looked at the poster on the wall, and nodded.

"Because she won't listen to me," said Lenny. "I told her Hewish is dead. I told her that as long as she's famous, she's gonna have these sick fuckers chasing after her, but that Hewish can't hurt her anymore. Her or Nat. I tell her all this, but I can tell she's not really listening. If you spoke to her, told her what Hagmaier told you, maybe it would get through."

Pete shrugged.

"Well, listen, Lenny, I don't mind . . . I mean, if you think it's going to help, but hey, I don't think I even have her number."

Lenny made a little choking sound.

"What?"

"I said—"

"I *heard* what you said, but I just can't believe it. I just assumed, when she came to the hospital to see you that . . . I mean you saved her *life,* for Chrissake!"

"And she saved mine," said Pete.

Lenny was almost shouting now.

"Honest to God, Pete—this kid. Sometimes I think she doesn't know who her real friends are."

There was some rustling of papers. It sounded like Lenny was leafing through his phone book.

"Okay, listen," he said. "Pete? You still there?"

"Yeah, I'm here."

"You got a pen?"

Just after one a.m. he was back in the kitchen. It was impossible to sleep now. He had left a message on her answering machine, telling her he had good news about Hewish. She'd probably get right back to him, and in a short while they would meet up to talk.

He wondered where exactly her place was. He knew she went to Lake Arrowhead from time to time. They talked about it in the press. It was almost a three-hour drive to the mountains. He might end up staying the whole weekend. He might get to see her teaching Nat to skate. And they might talk about things: about Robert Hewish and the case, about Doug and Lenny and her whole life story. He knew more about it now than anyone. She might want to talk to him.

He got up and walked to the window. He heard Ellen's recorded message in his head: *I'll get right back to you.*

He looked at the face reflected in the glass.

The face smiled.